To Kat.
I hope yo...

VILLAINS

NEVER

DIE

By

Nick DeWolf

Also By Nick DeWolf

Novels:

Frightfully Ever After

Pulling Strings

Short Stories:

Rusty's Run

Find More At:

www.facebook.com/NickDeWolfAuthor
www.twitter.com/Nick_DeWolf

For

All the Heroes who are a little bad

All the Villains who have a touch of good

And Everyone in between

CHAPTER ONE
THE BEGINNING

You know, I never planned on being a supervillain. That gawky, unassuming, bright young man from fifty years ago would never have even considered standing atop Mount Fuji, laughing maniacally as giant robotic moles armed with thermonuclear warheads burrowed their way toward a seismic fault line in an attempt to take all of Japan hostage. But somehow, that was me.

You see, most supervillains are outcasts, rebels, freaks. They are shunned by society because of their beliefs, their appearance, their raw and frightening power. They are abused as children. They are abandoned and have to learn to fight to survive. They find it easier to hate the world than to accept it. They sneer and snarl and focus on anger, greed, resent, all the negative emotions. Hell, one villain called Blackheart emitted them as hypnotic waves. Once, he drove an entire stadium of people into a murderous rage. Absolutely ruined the World Cup that year. Worst part? It wasn't even on purpose. His favorite team was eliminated, and he just couldn't help himself.

Did I mention that most villains are selfish too?

Selfish, reclusive, secretive; they mumble to themselves a lot. They don't have significant others, or at least ones that stick. And if you asked them, after they came out of the spandex closet, if they ever knew what they were going to be, most of them would say, "Yes. I always knew."

I... did not. I wasn't reclusive, just shy. I wasn't secretive, just uninteresting to most people. I was a big brain in a world of medium-sized minds. My family didn't get me. Working class parents raising a bunch of kids they absolutely loved but never planned for. I was the shining star in some ways, according to everyone in our lower west side apartment building; Danny Endwright, he's so smart. Danny Endwright, he's got potential. Danny Endwright, he's going places.

And go places I did.

First black kid to win every scientific competition within fifty miles, I got bumped up the ladder of educational institutions until I landed at a posh private school. There, I astounded the white teachers... and enraged many parents and students... by graduating at the top of my high school class, and two years early. When I went into college at sixteen, I was tall, thin, nerdy, not unattractive, and completely driven to advance my own intellect. A full ride carried me through the three years it took to get my undergraduate. I had a Masters and a PhD four years after that.

I got a postdoc position and worked in a lab where I was allowed side projects.

I went to parties.

I grew an afro.

I drank some beer.

I even kissed a few girls.

Fifty years ago I didn't want to rule the world. I only wanted one thing -- to break down the mysteries of gravity. Maybe it was some metaphorical symbolism for defying everything that held me down... but probably not. I despised philosophy. Things were what they were and nothing else, and gravity was something to be conquered. It was one of the great natural forces, something which man simply had to abide by.

I disagreed.

And so I devoted myself. I followed the track toward professorship. I was looking forward to a little lab, or maybe a big one, filled with eager graduate students. There'd be inept undergrads failing my classes, coming to me in tears, and me not doing anything to help them other than suggest they try harder next time. I was going to spend my days writing grant proposal after grant proposal. Life would be fulfilling. Routine.

Delightfully bland.

Thursday would be spaghetti night.

But none of that happened. Instead, I used graviton engines to lift Manhattan into the sky. I bounded across the surface of the moon in an enhanced exoskeleton, looking for the perfect rocks for my lunar trebuchet. I rode in the eye of a three-mile wide tornado moving entirely under my own control.

Thursday was still spaghetti night. I find some routine to be comforting.

But fifty years ago? Nothing about me said I would become one of the most feared men on the planet, that my name would be synonymous with terror. Everything was pointing toward boring old Dr. Daniel Endwright.

Nothing predicted the development of the terrible and deadly Doctor Dendrite.

CHAPTER TWO
THE WAYWARD GIRL

Oh crap. Oh crap, oh crap, oh crap. What the hell? How... what... I...

Breathe. Breathe damn it. Calm down. Get the keys, unlock the door, get inside. But I can't. My hands are shaking. I'm drenched in sweat from running like a lunatic. But my feet are cold. Why are -- oh yeah. I'm in stockings, and it's winter. Where are my shoes? I'm holding them. Wait. There's only one. Where's the other one? Crap, where did -- I must have dropped it when I took them off. Goddammit, my feet hurt. They hurt, and they're cold.

What the hell? Stop thinking about your stupid feet and get inside, Candace!

The keys clatter. It sounds like someone dragging a chain over a metal pipe. It's 3:00 a.m., and I'm alone on my front stoop, twitching and panting. If anybody's watching, maybe they'll just think I'm some stupid drunk girl having trouble getting inside. Most of these houses are college students, too. Wouldn't be the first time. I mean, it's not like they're going to automatically assume I just ran miles (in high heels, no less) through the city to get away from an exploding warehouse where two guys were killed by a bunch of people in spandex after a job went wrong.

That would probably not be their first thought.

When I finally get inside, I spin around and slam the door.

Dammit! Stupid, stupid, stupid! Samantha's room is right over the door. She knows when people come in and out. I probably just woke her up. And though I party hard sometimes, I usually don't come home looking like this.

And that's when I notice it. My jacket is covered in blood.

Someone else's blood.

Okay, woozy. Very woozy now. No, no, no. No fainting. Deep breaths. Wait -- fast breaths? What keeps you from passing out again? Oh god, everything's going sideways. I spread my feet, reach out for the wall. Please don't leave a big, red hand print. Please. I don't -- I can't clean that up right now. I...

Oh god.

They're... they're dead.

Charlie and Parker. They're dead. They got killed and I saw it and there was so much, so much blood and...

I wait while the world spins around me. When a wave of cold sweat rushes out to replace the hot sweat that's covering me, I manage to raise my head.

It's quiet. There might have been a bump from upstairs when I was just about ready to hit the floor, I'm not sure. Either way, Samantha doesn't seem to be awake. For a second, I could swear I almost hear her breathing.

Okay, now would be a good time for me to haul my ass upstairs.

My heart is a bass drum in my chest. I scamper up the first few steps, but it's no good. My legs are half-cooked noodles. The adrenaline rush is over and I'm shredded. I stand on the stairs for a second, a minute -- an hour, for all I know. I close my eyes and grip my hands into fists. I ask them to stop shaking just long enough for me to get up the stairs and into my room. Something comes back to me, something from the warehouse. It was after everything went crazy, after all the fighting started. It was after -- no -- it was before the explosion. It was my hands. My hands were shaking like they are now and they felt so strange and I tried to close them and then...

My bones aren't broken. Why aren't my bones broken? That explosion was huge. The windows exploded. The walls cracked. Everyone went flying. How am I okay?

I check myself. Maybe I have internal bleeding. I poke and prod and squeeze. Nothing hurts. Well, everything hurts, but not like I'm-broken hurts. Like, I've-just-lived-through-a-damn-war hurts. The check wakes up my legs, gets the blood moving again. I look back at my hands. They're not shaking (as much), and whatever memory was trying to rise up kind of falls when I hear another little bump from upstairs. Probably someone rolling over, dropping their phone or something. Whatever. But it's enough that I keep moving.

Thank goodness none of my housemates have super early classes. It isn't unheard of for students to be waking up around now, getting early morning lectures. I haven't even thought about my classes for the day. Because, seriously? Least of my problems.

Every step I take is an elephant sneaking down the hall. The click when I turn my doorknob is a firecracker going off. It's like I suddenly have super hearing.

Oh my God, what if I do?

No. Stop it. The door always clicks. The house is just quiet. I'm still on edge, still in panic mode, and I still haven't gotten into my room and figured out what the hell I am going to do.

A few minutes later, the buzz from the electric radiator is keeping me distracted while I work at getting my shit together. I'm down to my tank top and undies. There were stains on my shirt and leggings, as well. Everything is spread out on a towel on my bed. They look like props from a horror movie. I wish they were.

I search the piles on my floor for something to wear, but I don't even know how. I just watched people die. I just ran for my life. Why am I looking at pajamas? This is all new to me, and my brain is overflowing with thoughts; none of them good.

I think about taking off, disappearing. I think about calling the cops and telling them what I saw. I think about how I can play this whole thing off, like nothing happened, just keep going to classes and...

Classes where Parker should be sitting. Classes he'll never finish. Will I get to finish them? If I go to jail, can I still get my degree through correspondence courses?

And then I think about my mom. Oh crap. I... I wanna call her so bad right now. I just, like, I want her voice.

Yeah, right. Because what would I say? Hey, hi, I've gone and screwed up bigger than I've ever screwed up and it'd be really great if you could wire me, maybe, a billion dollars (which I know, for serious, she probably has sitting around) so I can run off to some private island and escape international law forever and ever?

And then I think about how disappointed she'll be. How maybe this is the one, you know? I've finally pushed it so goddamn far, now she'll have to at least talk to me, right?

Jesus Christ, what a mess. All of this stuff is running through my head, but honestly, it's really just a distraction. Because there's something else that I really, really don't want to think about.

Those eyes. Those black eyes; inches away from my face, he stared at me, into me, through me. I don't know. He was hanging upside down. He'd just knocked some mobster twenty feet through the air, into a stack of crates, and then swung back and saw me. I thought... I knew I was going to die. Right then. He came in closer and I could see his body -- no, I could see what was covering his body.

Spiders.

He was covered in spiders.

I'd heard the stories. He was... I mean, hell, he was supposed to be dead. Or gone. Vanished. Something. No one had seen him or anything in, like, twenty years. He was so scary they didn't even like talking about him on the news. They never showed pictures. He was evil. Wherever he went, death followed. And I came face-to-face with him, with one of the Triad of Evil.

Araknis.

I stop moving, stop breathing. I close my eyes and push it all back, all down. I sigh, big and long, and let the tears fall. But then that's it. I don't have time right now.

The down comforter poofs as I drop onto the bed. The noodley feeling is back in my legs. Even with the radiator, I'm cold. When I reach for the edge of the blanket, I stop. The jacket is there, shimmering and stained. My unsteady hand can't hold it, and it slips to the floor. I just leave it there. It doesn't feel like mine anymore, anyway.

The blanket wraps around me, a thick hug. I roll onto my side. My eyelids are really heavy. I should be getting a plan together, making preparations. What do I need? An alibi, a getaway bag, to get rid of these clothes, as much cash as I can find... What else?

I imagine I'm a character in a movie, some clever con artist or master cat burglar who has gotten in over their head. I've just pulled a job. I'm trying to sell the loot when suddenly the cops come barging in and break everything up. The buyers, some sleazy gangsters, think they've been set up. The cops wanna take everyone down. Things get crazy. Shots are fired. I make a break for it and manage to sneak out, but now I'm on the run and everyone is looking for me.

I try to think that way, but I can't. I'm not a clever con artist, I'm a nineteen-year-old kid at MIT. The buyers weren't gangsters, they were two dudes in spandex with superpowers. And the cops weren't the cops, it was the freaking Justice Brigade.

Goddamn, Candace, what have you gotten yourself into?

One of my housemates gallops down the stairs and I end up with my ass on the floor. For one second, I'm sure my bed is on fire, and the police are outside in full riot gear. Then I realize I fell asleep. I had things to do and I fell asleep and now it's 8:34. My housemates are up, so now I'm screwed out of pulling a vanishing act. My bedroom is over the kitchen, so they probably heard my butt-first dismount. They know I'm here, but do they know anything else?

Oh yeah, sure they do. They've just decided to have bacon and eggs before calling in the national guard to take me down.

Dumbass.

I grab the first thing that looks almost clean, and the thought of bacon and eggs makes me acutely aware of just how hungry I am. It's amazing what absolute terror does for your appetite. So instead of planning my getaway, I shove the blood-stained clothes under my bed, take a deep breath, and head downstairs.

"Lookin' sharp, Candi."

Ugh. I'm not even down from the last step and Samantha is already making comments about the fact that I'm wearing...

6

Oh, yeah. Yikes. These patterns don't match at all. I'll give her that one.

But she's still an unbearable princess, smirking in her silken, fleece-lined winter robe. It's not even 9:00 a.m. and she's already got lipstick on and her perfect blonde hair is just so...perfect. It must be exhausting, trying to look better than she is and acting like she's somehow in charge.

Usually I would retort with something stinging and visceral (because seriously, who died and made her queen?) but I decide to take the high road and don't even respond. Okay, that's a lie. I can't think of anything to say. But whatever. I'm tired, I'm goddamn hungry, and right now Samantha is the least of my problems. So I just push past her and head for the kitchen. That's when I notice it.

The hallway is usually a game of bumper cars around now. I don't see anyone frantically charging at me, a book bag in one hand and a pop-tart in the other.

Something's not right.

I hear the TV in the kitchen. Samantha follows me in, but she's pretending to be casual. Annie and Brit are there, staring at the screen.

"Wha --" I clear my throat and try again. "What'cha watchin'?" Why am I talking like that?

Brit shushes us.

Annie says, "There was a --" but stops when she glances my way. Her big doe eyes, hidden just beneath her cute little bangs, dart up and down over me. "That's a..." a little smile creeps up on the side of her mouth, "... cool new look." She says in the most sober way she can manage.

Samantha looks at a well-manicured nail and says, "Candi, you don't need to try so hard to make us laugh at you. We do that anyway."

"I hate you too, Samantha." I reply. Well, that felt better.

Brit shushes loudly. They're watching the news, and I don't like what I'm seeing.

MIT.

Police cars.

The building Parker and I broke into last night.

More police cars.

The warehouse, with a veritable shit-ton of police cars.

"What's, uh... goin' on?" Yeah, that sounded natural.

Annie apparently didn't notice. "Didn't you hear?"

"No, I..." was busy hiding evidence. "... just got up. Slept in."

"Wait, don't you have lab in like, twenty minutes?"

Oh shit. "Oh, well..."

"Doesn't matter." Brit cuts in, with the enthusiasm of someone going in for a root canal. "Everything is cancelled."

What? I expected a class or two, maybe the lab being shut down. "You mean, like, for the morning, yeah?"

"No," Brit says flatly, "everything. Classes, labs, they're practically shutting down the school."

Oh. Crap.

Samantha sighs and turns up the volume. The announcer on the news is using his 'Exciting Action News!' voice.

"Local police, who have been relieved from the area by federal agents and the Enhanced Superhuman Operations Agency, have released limited information regarding last night's dramatic and tragic battle. Two of the civilians who were killed during the melee have been identified as Charles Bruntley and Parker Stapleton."

They spin up pictures of both guys. Parker's photo is from his school badge. He thought he looked cool and original. Really, he was a white kid who stole his style from a manufactured K-Pop boy band.

Charlie's photo looks like a mug shot. Probably because it is a mug shot.

"Stapleton," the announcer continues, "was a student at MIT and is believed to be involved with the stealing and selling of university property, which kick-started the events of last night. Bruntley has previously been indicted on assault, robbery, grand theft auto, possession of a concealed weapon, and battery charges. He served six years in federal prison and since his release, was believed to be heavily involved in organized crime in the greater Boston area."

For all of the drama from the announcer's face-hole, I can't help but notice how none of this sounds sympathetic. They're dead. Charlie screamed when the spiders covered him like black paint. Parker's head was obliterated when tights guy hit him with hands of steel, just to move him aside.

But the news doesn't know those details. The ESOA is already starting to cover it up. They've taken over the crime scene, and deep in the lowest levels of my gut, I have a sinking feeling as to why.

The announcer stops shuffling papers. He leans in toward the camera. His voice goes into 'and now for the bad news' tone. "At this time, the extent of Charlie Bruntley and Parker Stapleton's connection to the supervillains known as Bearserker and Brass Knuckles is undetermined. It is known that they were present during the superhuman altercation which has left both Lux and Ironsides, members of the Justice Brigade and two of the world's greatest heroes, in critical condition."

I think I'm going to throw up.

Annie is knocking gently on my door, her timid little voice drifting through like smoke through a sheet.

"Candace? Are you okay? I mean... do you, uh... we kinda thought that, um, you know..."

You kinda thought it was a little weird how your housemate ran from the kitchen, fumbled upstairs to the bathroom, dry heaved for five minutes, then cried for a bit before locking herself in her bedroom, screaming obscenities, and knocked several large objects to the floor before finally going quiet?

That's what she means to say. What she actually says is, "Do you wanna talk about it?"

She's such a sweetheart. For a moment I think about opening the door. Then, I hear the soft murmur from Samantha.

"I knew it. She's on drugs."

Annie shushes her and turns back to the door. "Candace, could I come in?"

My eyes are closed. With one hand I'm pinching the little bit of nose between them. The other is holding my phone up to my face. The screen is lit, and at the top of the text thread is a single word.

Mom.

The last text was from four days ago. She told me she was going to Japan for business and we should have lunch when she got back.

I never wrote back. God, I'm so freaking stubborn and stupid.

Annie and Samantha are still out in the hallway, murmuring to each other. I just want some silence for a minute, but because I'm lying on the floor, their voices roll across the hardwood from the hallway like they're standing next to me.

"I bet Parker was her dealer or something." Samantha whispers.

"You know he wasn't." Annie says.

"Or worse," whispers Samantha, "her boyfriend."

Ugh. She's so clueless. Parker was my business partner, my tutor in the world of organized crime. Not that he was a gangster or anything, Parker was a classic misinterpreted genius: skinny, weird, misunderstood; he was too bright to be one of the punks, but too angry at the world to be part of academia.

Annie exhales sharply. "Samantha."

"Hmm?"

"Go away."

There's a pause, then I hear Samantha's slippered feet shuffling away.

If I'd wanted that kind of fun, I'd have gone with Charlie. Goddamn. God. Damn. Skin like warm sand, kept his hair trimmed, hazel eyes, and ripped like you gotta roll the 'R' when you're saying it. R-r-r-r-r-r-ripped. Generally, guys are dickheads. I'm not saying that Charlie wasn't, but he was the kind of fine that keeps me swinging both ways.

As a note, I never did anything with him; we just flirted a lot. I knew better than to get in with someone like him -- neck tats are sexy as shit, but also a clear indication of people who like things a bit painful. Parker was an outcast rebel, but Charlie was a straight up criminal, and I know my limits.

The relationship between the three of us was simple: Charlie worked for the local mafia. Technically, they're not mafia because they're white-white but not Italian white. Doesn't matter, they did all the same stuff. I researched everyone he worked with, pulled records, made sure none of them were homicidal lunatics (I'm a thrill seeker, not an idiot). He was our buyer. He told Parker what his clients wanted. With a school like MIT, there's enough groundbreaking equipment that you're getting into some seriously high level sales -- I'm talking corporate espionage shit and experimental gear funded by the military. We weren't stealing TVs. We were stealing untested tech that could make or break a company overnight.

Parker would take the order. Unfortunately, just because you're a student at MIT doesn't necessarily mean you're given a golden ticket to any lab on campus. The big projects are only worked on by a select few.

That's where I came in.

I don't have access to the restricted labs, but I do have a good background in not letting locked doors stop me from getting what I want. See, my mom has this 'don't let anyone tell you no' attitude about life. She doesn't believe in giving up. It's what helped her build a goddamn global empire doing... well, I actually have no idea what she does. She doesn't talk about it and never has. She never talks about anything from before I was born, and nothing about what all her extended business trips are for. I stopped asking personal questions pretty early. All she ever said was, "I do whatever is needed to make the world better for you."

Thanks, mom. I guess it should mean a lot.

But whatever. She's goddamn respected and so from her, I got a lovely, don't-take-shit-from-anyone-instead-take-what-you-want attitude. Then, my Uncle Danny helped me to reinforce that with some technical knowhow.

Clarification: he's not my actual uncle. I don't know anything about my family, because mom won't talk about it. I know she's Puerto Rican. That's it. Uncle Danny is her coworker or partner or something. He's just as freaking secretive as she is. Anyway, he's a super-genius (not actual, giant head throbbing with veins super-genius, just crazy smart) and taught me all about computers, coding, hacking, all that crap. He showed me how to get around firewalls and break down security systems. He came with us on a lot of the trips where I would get stuck with whatever nanny of the month I had while they went off to do... I dunno, Business Things. Then we'd all go to the beach for a couple days and we'd build these intricate sandcastles. Or maybe we'd go skiing, and he'd complain that they were designed poorly and would teach me about fluid dynamics and shit. I'd listen, but I just wanted to ski. He was funny, and playful sometimes. He's cool. Distant too, but I think more because he's scared of my mom.

Everyone's scared of her.

What all this leads to is me feeling like the rules don't apply, and by breaking them, maybe I am somehow closer to my mom. So, I teamed up with Parker, which makes me wonder now, if I had just behaved myself instead of acting out like a stupid child, would Parker still be alive? Would Charlie? Parker was, well, he was smart and all, but he needed me. I copied keycards, reproduced IDs, wrote code to override security systems, all the bad-ass stuff. We'd go in together, take what we wanted, and head to the handoff with Charlie.

The sad part? I wasn't even doing it for the money. Mom's loaded. I've never done it for the money. I just...

"Candace?" Annie's voice slides under the door like a secret lover's note. "Samantha is gone... not for good, unfortunately."

I want to smile at that, but can't right now. The little line where the words I'm supposed to type to my mom is blinking. My thumbs don't move.

"Candace?"

"He wasn't my boyfriend." I'm not really saying it to Annie, but I hope she hears me.

There's a shuffling sound in the hallway and I hear a gentle thump. "I know." Annie's voice is louder. She's kneeling by the door, I can tell. That's when I realize the bloody clothes are under my bed, but poorly hidden.

"Candace? Are you okay?"

"Yeah!" I'm scrambling like a startled cat on a linoleum floor. "Yeah, I'm -- just hang on a second, okay? I'm just... I'm getting dressed." Yanking open a drawer, I cram the clothes in and slam it shut. I look around, making sure there's nothing I missed before opening the door.

Annie is on me like a hug ninja. I never even saw it coming, and yet here we are, standing in my doorway with her wrapped around me, saying, "I'm so sorry," over and over again. She even shushes a couple of times, the way you would a kid whose ice cream just fell on the floor.

I sigh and reiterate strongly, "He wasn't my boyfriend."

"I know." She says softly.

"I barely knew him."

"I know."

"And that's not... that's not why I got so upset, alright?"

"Of course."

"So let's just drop it, okay?"

"Okay."

"Great." I wait. "You can let go now."

She does, but she stays real close, just in case I may need another hug. Which I don't, but I kind of totally do. God, she's such a good person. It's so much easier when I can just hate everyone. Part of me wanted her in here before, wanted to talk to someone about what's going on. Now I just want to be alone. I need to sit down and figure this out. Instead, I turn around and start moving stuff around my room, trying to think of my next steps.

"So, Candace?" Annie asks as though she's not sure if she's allowed to speak.

"Yeah?"

"Why did you get so upset?"

I'm on autopilot in the kitchen. I don't even know what kind of cereal I just poured into my bowl. I've got a one-in-three chance -- Samantha's organic whey wheat soy protein blend, Brit's flavorless Cornflakes, or (and here's what I'm really hoping for) Annie's Frankenberries.

I never answered Annie's question. I just kind of mumbled something and told her I needed to do some work or whatever and got her out of the room. It got me thinking, though: nothing had happened. What was up with that? It'd been hours since the warehouse, and the military hadn't broken down our door yet. Seriously, important people were hurt last night. We're not talking your garden-variety vigilante here. This isn't The Daring Dynamo or Dark Avenger; Lux and Ironsides are Justice Brigade. These guys are old school, iconic figures. They've been busting bad guy heads for, like, forty years! You'd think there'd be a goddamn mob outside my house right now, pitchforks and torches a blazin'.

Then it occurs to me -- I don't have a record, you know? Also, I had a hat on and a scarf covering some of my face. So, even if they had a video from the warehouse, they may not be able to link it up with anything. Social media isn't my thing, and whatever accounts I do have, I put up avatars. There was an explosion, but I didn't get hurt. Even if they had some DNA from a hair or something, my stuff isn't in CODIS (the Combined DNA Index System the Justice Department uses. Damn, I watch too much TV. Or maybe not enough.) If they knew I was involved already, they would have found me.

Either they don't know yet, or they aren't going to find out at all.

I have time. No one knew I was there.

The news is just playing the same report over and over. They bring up the pictures of Parker and Charlie. My stomach twists less this time. They show images of the warehouse. They show the school, the campus, the lab we broke into.

But they don't show my house. They don't show a silhouette of a person with a big question mark in the middle. In fact, they don't show any sign whatsoever that there was another person involved. For all anyone knows, my roommates included, I was home all night, asleep in bed.

And suddenly the muscles in the back of my neck ease up a little.

I lean back in my chair and take a bite of wonderfully delicious sugary cereal. Oh Annie, don't ever grow up.

There is a distinct possibility I may be able to walk away from this. For the next few days, I just have to play it cool, be as surprised as everyone else, be shocked and horrified (check and check), and then get on with my life. Don't give anyone a reason to suspect, and they won't.

Candace, you are one lucky little girl.

Brit walks in just as I stand up. "Leave it on," she says flatly. "I wanna see if they're opening access to the high level labs."

Brit is a rock star on campus. She's brilliant, hard-working, and had her pick of new tech projects. She'll come out of MIT with more job offers than she can count. Even with all that, she leads her entire life in a constant state of 'whatever'.

I take my bowl and head for my room. I should still prep a just-in-case bag. Also, I need to figure out what I'm going to do with those clothes; I can't just toss them into the garbage and I don't want to use the laundry here at the house. Maybe I'll pack them away until the next three-day weekend, take them to my mom's apartment in Boston and try to get the stains out there.

As I walk through the hallway, I don't even notice Samantha, despite her best attempts. Finally, she says, "Hey there night-owl," with a sly grin and a little wrinkled nose. I freeze, then turn. She's putting on makeup in the hallway mirror, but her eyes aren't looking at the fire-engine red going onto her lips. They're on me.

Princess can even grin with her eyes.

This is the part where any normal, innocent person would say 'I'm sorry?' or 'Come again?' Instead, I just stand there, my chest going up and down faster and faster and my mouth open like an idiot.

"You must have been having a good time last night, Miss Candi."

The spoon in the bowl begins to tinkle. I tell my hands to stop shaking.

"I'm not sure exactly when you got back, but it must have been around, what? 3:00? 3:30?"

I ask my hands to stop.

"Whatever you were doing must have been pretty exciting though. You sounded like you'd just run a marathon."

I beg them. Plead with them. Offer them a cash bribe.

"I assumed you were out with Parker. Not like you have any other friends around here. I thought you two were pretty cute together, in that odd, punk-rock kind of way." She presses her lips together and puts the lipstick in her Gucci bag. "Anyway," she digs around, her eyes down, "I guess I was wrong. If you'd been with Parker, you'd have seen what happened at that warehouse, right?" Her eyes flash up in the mirror, locking with the reflection of mine.

I'm a deer in headlights. Frozen. Caught. There's no way she's letting this go; it's what she's always wanted, a chance to put herself on top. She hates me. I can tell by the way she's staring, waiting for me to do something, anything. She's watching every little muscle twitch and now all those feelings of fear and dread and panic I'd been letting go of are falling on me like a hard rain.

And then, it happens. I feel... something. It's there, in my hands. Like, not what I'm holding, but inside my hands. In the bones, the veins, the muscles. What the hell? It's like they're swelling or expanding or stretching or, or, or something. Oh god, what's happening? They're shaking. I can't stop them from shaking and Samantha's staring and I'm staring back and my heart is racing and now there's this crazy roaring in the back of my ears and it's getting louder and louder and my hands are aching, aching so bad they feel like they're going to explode and I can't, I can't, I can't --

"Hey!" Brit shouts from the kitchen. Samantha breaks eye contact with me and instantly the roaring and the feeling, they're gone. I squeeze the cereal bowl and move my totally normal not-almost-exploding fingers.

What... the hell... was that?

"Hey!" Brit shouts again.

Samantha turn to the mirror again. She's trying to catch my eye. I let her. That feeling doesn't come back, and so I just glare at her like I normally would.

Nothing to see here, sorry.

Brit says with a nonchalance that borders on brain death, "They're doing a press conference or something."

Frustrated, Samantha turns and shouts, "Who?"

Brit sighs, audibly. "Captain Turbo, bitch, that's who!"

CHAPTER THREE
THE NEW HERO

No way.

Captain Turbo. The. Captain. Turbo. Is less... than twenty feet away from me.

No. Way.

Okay. Okay. I, Antonella Garcia, will keep it together. I am highly trained special military personnel. I am the newest wave in the fight against supervillains. I have powers, and know how to use them. I have been in combat situations against people who can shoot fire from their hands and lift cars over their heads. And I kicked their butts. I will not, I repeat, not go full-on fangirl here. Not with all those cameras and reporters watching. Be cool.

Be. Cool.

... Ay Dios mío!

He's standing at the podium in front of me, talking into the mics. I've seen this, like, how many times on TV? Dozens? Hundreds? But this different. I can feel his voice now. I can practically reach out and touch him. I'm used to seeing his face (what's visible through the mask anyway) and a bit of his upper body. Right now, I've got a view that's mostly cape, but being this close, I'm seeing things I've never noticed before.

Like, for a dude that's in his seventies, his butt looks great. Suddenly, I'm not a fan of these black military cargo pants I'm required to wear. Maybe I can talk the leadership into just a little bit of spandex.

Speaking of which, I can't tell what his outfit is made of. It's not spandex, elastic, rubber, leather, or Kevlar. There's a plastic kind of sheen to it, but it definitely isn't a solid synthetic layer. Where the colors meet -- red and white verticals against a navy blue background, good ol' American flag colors -- you can see the grain of tiny mechanical knit work. Whatever made that outfit made it to last. And I don't mean the regular wear and tear of a busy day. This is Captain Turbo; the guy makes it a habit to fly into burning buildings.

He turns his head and says into the mics, "Local police were removed from the crime scene in order to maintain even the most minute traces of evidence. As always, the Justice Brigade and the Enhanced and Superhuman Operations Agency thank the local law enforcement officers who put their lives on the line every day."

His perfectly combed hair -- more salt than pepper now -- bobs up and down as he speaks. Every time his head moves, it's to emphasize something he's saying. It's like watching a polished politician speak.

I mean, he should sound good. He's had a lot of practice. They formed the Justice Brigade thirty years ago, and he's been the spokesperson for them the entire time. The face of justice, the greatest hero on Earth.

Captain. Freaking. Turbo.

Wow.

"As you all know," his voice is like the mid-range notes on a cello, "the policy of the ESOA is to alert the Justice Brigade of any situation where super powered criminals are involved."

This is all standard rhetoric, basic press conference fodder. How many times has he given this speech? Does he have it memorized? There are teleprompters, so I guess he could be reading. But it's all coming too easily, too rehearsed.

How will the next part sound? The part where he says something unrehearsed?

There's a loud gulping sound next to me. Lucien, his Adam's apple bobbing up and down in his long, skinny neck, breathes through his nose, high and nasal, between each massive swallow of milk. When he finishes, I lean over and whisper, "Moustache."

Honestly, he's lucky mi abuela isn't here. Doesn't matter that we're on international television, she would just lean over with a napkin and start rubbing his face.

Wait a minute, I wonder if they're watching this. Uh, yeah, of course they are. They always watch stuff like this. I know exactly what's going on, everyone who was home is packed into one room, all the grownups staring at the TV, my cousins watching on their phones. Did they cheer when they saw me? Were they as excited as we used to get when Tío Pedro would be on TV? It's been forever since that happened. It's been over a year since I've even seen them. Since I've heard their voices. Since I gave all that up to be a hero...

No. No, no. Not now. Get it together, Antonella. You're on TV. You can't be that woman sitting in the back, crying.

I give myself a massive mental slap across the face and push all that stuff down.

Lucien uses a napkin to dab at the edges of his mouth. He leans toward me as he puts the empty glass down. "Thanks," he whispers with the kind of voice they put in haunted house movies. "Don't know what I'd do without you." The sarcasm isn't dripping... it's pouring. He's baiting me, like he always does. And just like always, I open my mouth to respond. Before I can, a different voice grabs me by the back of the neck.

"Both of you, shut up." Sosuke is on my other side. His posture is perfect, one hand folded over the other in his lap. It's the sitting version of 'at ease'.

"Agent Corvis," he says without looking at Lucien, "clean your face. Agent Garcia," his eyes never come close to looking at mine, "pay attention."

Lucien sighs. He's always looking to start trouble, preferably the kind that ends with a fist fight, but he listens to Sosuke. Thank god for that; Lucien is dangerous, but Sosuke?

Captain Turbo says, "We were aware that both Bearserker and Brass Knuckles were involved in the transaction of stolen merchandise. It was believed that at least one, if not several, more superhumans were involved."

I've read the report. I know exactly who was there.

"The battle which ensued was extremely violent. Unfortunately, several civilians were caught in the crossfire between the Justice Brigade and the supervillains."

'The supervillains'. Not Araknis. Captain Turbo's been instructed not to say it. I'm not surprised. No one has heard from them since the Japan incident over two decades ago. A lot of people think they all died when Mt. Fuji erupted, or when tidal waves came in. We've lasted over twenty years without an attempt at global domination, without hundred-foot tall robots or laser-shooting gemstones or three-mile wide tornadoes. Nothing. Everything I know of them, it's from word of mouth -- old news reports, videos caught during their attacks on humanity. I never had to live through the fear that they induced, how entire governments would panic when one of them showed up somewhere.

There are villains out there today, but nothing like Doctor Dendrite, Wraith, and Araknis.

The Triad of Evil.

If Captain Turbo announced that even one of them was alive, had been seen last night, this press conference would get really, really rowdy. Instead, he takes a deep breath and says, "It was during the fight with these villains that the other members of the Justice Brigade, Lux and Ironsides, were..." He pauses. I can't see his face, but all the camera flashes stop. The shuffling feet, the scratching of pens, the rustling all stops.

Here it comes.

He swallows and continues, "Lux and Ironsides were gravely injured. Lux received near-fatal blows at the hands of Bearserker. Ironsides... fared even worse. Currently both are in critical condition, under the care of the military and ESOA medical staff."

I know for a fact that right now, every member of my family is frozen, shaking with fear. But I'm not really thinking about that, because something strange is happening. Well, I guess it was happening all during the speech, or maybe I was just too star-struck to notice from the beginning.

Turbo's shoulders are sagged. His head is a little drooped. He's a little hunched over, and his stomach isn't as flat as it used to be. The fabric stretching against his love handles is suddenly obvious. When his head turns, I notice the skin on his jaw isn't as tight as it should be.

"At this time," he sounds remorseful, "it is unknown if Ironsides will recover from his injuries."

The silence is thick. Reporters are shocked. Cameramen aren't looking through their lenses. Ironsides, the man who head butted his way through three feet of solid steel to save the President. Ironsides, the man who jumped from a plane and used nothing but his body and maximum velocity to slice through Admiral Anarchy's battleship.

Ironsides, the indestructible man.

Captain Turbo's baritone breaks the silence with the most professional voice he can muster. "This being the case, the ESOA and the Justice Brigade have come to a difficult decision. As of this morning, Lux, Ironsides, and myself, Captain Turbo, are officially retiring from all superhuman and hero activities. The Justice Brigade is, hereby, officially disbanded."

If this were a movie, right now there'd be jump cuts to the following scenes:

A huge crowd in Times Square, watching all of this on the enormous screens, flipping out and rioting.

Dogs howling at the sky.

A baby crying.

A bar full of supervillains all dancing an Irish reel.

An apron clad housewife standing, staring at the TV in shock as a soapy glass falls to the floor and shatters, unnoticed.

You know, I wouldn't be surprised if some of that is actually happening.

Maybe not the dog thing.

And then, out of nowhere, the room just explodes. Cameras are flashing like crazy, pop-pop-pop-pop-pop-pop-pop, and everyone is shouting. Reporters are asking questions, civilians are freaking out, several people are crying, and someone in the back looks like he's about to throw a chair. Holy crap. This is not what I expected.

Captain Turbo is still talking, trying to calm people down. Reporters are pushing forward, all trying to get to the front. They're literally climbing over each other. I see faces getting red. I see looks of panic. This is getting ugly, fast, and next to me, Lucien is on the edge of his seat. He looks thrilled, ecstatic at the chaos. If he dives into that crowd, people are going to get hurt. My head switches to combat mode. I'm checking the room for exits. I'm making plans. How much distance can I put between me and the crowd?

How much do I need? Where are the points of defense and attack? What's the main objective? Who do I --

"That's enough!" Captain Turbo's voice rips through the room like thunder. Everyone freezes.

Me included.

For one moment, it's the Captain of old. His chest and shoulders rise up and down as he breathes heavily. I'm suddenly glad that I'm sitting behind him. His mask exposes his eyes and I can only imagine the look he's giving those reporters right now.

"That's enough." he says again. This time, though, it's not for the reporters.

It's for himself.

His shoulders go down again. His head falls.

He looks... tired.

"I know," he says, just loud enough for the mics to pick up. "You have questions, and you deserve answers. But I... I ask that you give me a moment."

Oh god, his voice. It's grandpa telling little Billy why he has to move away to the nursing home.

"I would like to think that thirty, twenty, maybe even ten years ago, in a face-off with a criminal like Brass Knuckles, I would have defeated him easily." He looks sideways and I see a small smile eek its way up across his face. "Aw hell, I would've beaten him silly." His eyes go up. He's seeing it in his mind. A huge right hook across the villain's jaw. A knockout of evil, another victory for justice. His hands squeeze the podium and, for just one second, everyone in the room thinks he's going to take it back. He's going to throw his chin into the air and hit us with that perfect smile and say he'll go on fighting, fighting for justice and peace and all things good in the world. Then a wink, a pose, and he's off!

But his chin doesn't go up.

His smile gets smaller before fading away.

His eyes roll down.

No wink.

No pose.

Just the years and years of hard work weighing him down.

"Last night," he says, "was an unfortunate reminder that the heroes of yesterday have reached the end of their era. We can no longer protect the world we love so dearly, the people we cherish, and the peace we sought to achieve. We have had our triumphs, and we have... made our mistakes. But we always tried our hardest to do what is right. And now, unfortunately, it is time for us to rest.

"I was lucky. I fought Brass Knuckles to a standstill, and came out unscathed. I wasn't carted off in an ambulance as my companions... my brothers-in-arms... Lux and Ironsides were. I see this as a blessing, maybe even a small reward for my good deeds. And so, I will take this opportunity to walk away, to take off my mask and live the rest of my life knowing I did everything I could to make this world a better place. To live my last years in what I hope will be peace."

Oh man, it's taking everything I've got to not make this an ugly cry. Anyone with a dry eye in the room should be thrown in jail.

"But who will protect us?" someone shouts in the most unprofessional of ways. It wasn't even a reporter, but before Captain Turbo can even look in their general direction, someone jabs a recorder in his direction.

"What about Bearserker and Brass Knuckles?"

"Do you not intend to avenge Lux and Ironsides?"

"Is Ironsides aware of this decision?"

They should have clapped. They should have stood and clapped, cheered and saluted him as he proudly left the stage. They should have let him make his exit with some dignity before opening their mouths.

"Did Lux give his consent to this announcement?"

"Are you quitting because you're afraid of being hurt too?"

Captain Turbo raises his hand and tries to get control of the situation.

"Will this be a repeat of your previous retirement announcement after the Japan incident?"

The air around him burns like a strobe light from all the flashes.

"How do you think your corporate sponsors will react to this?"

He tries to answer, but the questions are coming and coming.

"Will you discontinue your toy line?"

"I --"

"Have you selected a replacement?"

"Well --"

"Will there be a new Justice Brigade?"

"The ESOA--"

"Who else is equipped to handle Brass Knuckles?"

"I'm sure that --"

"Will you come out of retirement if any major villains do?"

"Please, I --"

"Can anyone stop these villains?"

"I'm not --"

"Why have you deserted the people when they need you most?"

"Please!" And right when it looks like Captain Turbo is going to rip the podium from the stage and hurtle it into the crowd like Tarzan throwing a boulder into a pack of hyenas, a woman's voice cuts through the room.

"Ladies and gentlemen." Her microphone is dialed up so loud there's a little squeal of feedback. Everyone goes quiet. "That's enough."

At the edge of the stage, Lieutenant Colonel Tamika McTier climbs the stage and begins walking toward the podium. Her muscular legs move back and forth, stretching her military issue knee length skirt to its absolute maximum. Her heels clip-clop a little as she holds the mic up and says, "I believe Captain Turbo deserves a bit more respect than that."

She walks right up to Turbo and salutes. He's clearly in shock at the sight of a woman who barely comes up to his armpits strutting across the stage in full military regalia and saluting him. But she holds the salute until he returns it, then drops her hand for a shake. Her tiny fingers are promptly enveloped by Captain Turbo's massive mitt. There are snapshots galore. They both look out and smile -- him with teeth, her without -- and she uses the handshake to ease herself in behind the podium.

"Considering the announcement Captain Turbo just made, I believe a round of applause is in order." Her perfectly manicured hands come up and begin clapping. The reporters don't catch on right away, but when they do, it goes from clapping, to cheering, to a standing ovation.

I have to fight the urge to stand up, to scream and wave my arms in the air, to run over and hug Turbo and tell him he's the best. It helps that right next to me, Sosuke is sitting still as a stone. I wish he was showing some kind of emotion, joy or anger or anything. But he's not. He's just... intense. It's weird, and it's been getting stronger throughout the whole press conference. I'm going to be totally honest, I don't like the way he's looking at Captain Turbo.

But McTier turns and gives us a little nod. Sosuke doesn't hesitate, not for a second. He's up and clapping.

But not like he means it.

I choose to refrain from the whole hugging thing. But I do let out a little, "Woo!" When I do, Sosuke's intensity increases one tick.

Even if the applause was forced, Captain Turbo brightens at the sound. He's raised his arms to the cheering of entire stadiums. When Molnar the Malevolent showed up at the summer Olympics and tried to kidnap all the political heads of state, Captain Turbo KO'd him on live television and stood listening as the entire world gushed.

God, that was amazing.

"Thank you," McTier says into the mic and the applause starts to die down.

Next to me, Sosuke is the first person to stop clapping and sit. Something has his ire up. His eyes -- weirdly electric blue -- are staring hard. I think they're going to burn a hole in space-time.

And if anyone could do that, it'd be Sosuke.

McTier speaks before any of the reporters can begin haranguing her. "Thank you for the generous showing to the amazing Captain Turbo. He has been a hero and an inspiration to us all over the decades. On behalf of the United States Government, I thank and salute you, sir."

There's a smattering of applause. Captain Turbo just beams. He's puffed out his chest for the pictures and put his fists on his hips. I can't help but smile a little.

"As you heard earlier," McTier continues, "with Captain Turbo and his compatriots leaving the world of crime fighting, the Justice Brigade is officially retired. But since, as many of you have pointed out, the threat of superhuman criminals remains, the Enhanced and Superhuman Operations Agency, in conjunction with the United States Military Forces, has put a plan in motion to deal with the so-called 'supervillain problem'."

A murmur runs through the crowd. This is news to everyone and, from the tiny expression of shock in his eyes, Captain Turbo is no different.

"As of this morning," McTier continues, "we have activated a specialized team, trained and prepared to deal with any and all superhuman types. Unlike the Justice Brigade, which acted independently from the ESOA." She gives a slight head tilt, but doesn't look directly at Captain Turbo. It's not mocking, not insulting. It's just that they have finally been able to correct a previous mistake. "This unit will be under the ESOA umbrella, with full access to all government and military resources. Their orders will come directly through government channels, and they will act as a task force similar to the National Guard."

McTier shifts her face from one side of the room to the other, typically at the end of each sentence. She has an attractive, round look; round eyes, round cheekbones, hair pulled back so tight you can see the curvature of her head. It should make her seem soft, but instead it reminds me of a tiger's eye stone; beautiful and dark, but hard.

"Like the Justice Brigade, this joint ESOA/Military unit will consist of three super powered agents. These agents have gone through rigorous training and are more than capable of responding to any superhuman threat." She flashes a smile. It's so well-rehearsed, I'm sure that everyone watching her on TV falls for it. "At this time, I would like to introduce you to the team leader, Special Agent Sugiyama Sosuke."

22

Lucien cackles as we walk down the hallway. "I think my favorite part was when you said 'there will be no spandex'." He grins like a zorro, long and thin. Predatory. "And that, no, you wouldn't explain all of our powers for the world, including our enemies, to hear. Really man, why didn't you just come out and call them all idiots?"

Part of my power is that I can feel things through my feet. Well, through my whole body, really, but especially my feet. It's kind of like sonar. Because of that, my shoes are specially designed to help me connect to the ground. It makes me super aware of things, and right now I'm picking up that Lucien's walking is as erratic as the tone of his voice. He needs a glass of milk to bring him down. Sosuke's steps are rhythmic and clean. Up ahead, McTier's heels sound like a broken clock. I don't have to assume that she's not pleased with how things went at the press conference.

"Agent Corvis has a point," she snaps.

Oh yeah, definitely not pleased.

"At the next press conference, you may want to employ a little more... tact."

"I'm a soldier, ma'am." Sosuke's voice isn't loud or soft, harsh or gentle, taut or loose. It just is. His words come out like solid things that travel through the air and hit their targets precisely.

"You're also the leader of this team and its public face. So, I'm going to say it again." She stops and we stop behind her. She doesn't bother to turn to look at him. "The next time you are on camera, I'd better see... something else."

As we head into a conference room, Lucien says, "You know, if you're looking for someone the people can relate to, why don't you put The Bleeding Heart out front?" He sneers at me. His teeth are too small for his head. "That's your code name, isn't it?" His sunken eyes dart back and forth between mine. Twitches in the tiny muscles throughout his face tell me that he's getting worked up, waiting for a reaction from me. Wanting one.

He's just dying for a fight right now.

"Stow it, Corvis." Sosuke says as he walks by us, taking a chair. Lucien doesn't move. I sigh and look away from him, hoping that'll end it.

"That was quite a show out there, young man," says a deep, deep voice.

My heart skips a bit as I spin, along with everyone else in the room. What the hell? Captain Turbo is in the doorway, one arm on his hip, like he's been waiting on us for hours. He must have been right behind us, but I didn't feel a thing. Not a step.

Damn, he is good.

23

Without even looking, I know that Sosuke is standing, the chair he was in a second ago spinning behind him.

Things may have just gotten a little more dangerous in here.

Turbo continues as if nothing is wrong. "If supervillains are half as scared of you as those reporters were, well, you'll do fairly well at your new job."

Wow, condescending much? With one hand on his hip, the other arm dangling casually, who is he trying to impress here? I'd think that after his retirement speech, he'd want to slip out of costume and disappear into the crowd. Yet, here he is, swaggering into the room like a tough guy cowboy.

"Colonel McTier is right, you know. A little bit of charm goes a long way with those folks. You may want to consider softening the image just a little bit."

He walks within inches of me. I smell shaving cream and hair gel. The amount of space he displaces is amazing. There's something about his body, I can't tell if it's the way he moves or what, but it's like his muscles not only need their own space, but about three inches of air around them to be cleared at all times. He's older, he's retired, but I still get the feeling bumping into him would be the same as bumping into a concrete wall.

And as Captain Turbo meanders around the room to no destination in particular, Sosuke follows with only his eyes.

"I'm just saying," he gestures into the air, "I don't see much potential for marketing. I mean, the diversity is great, and having a girl on the team," he looks at me, "good for you, young lady."

I shoot him an are-you-kidding-me-with-this-bullcrap look, but he totally doesn't read it -- older white guys never do -- so I fire a can-you-believe-this-bullcrap look to McTier. She doesn't even glance at me. Totally stone faced. She's older too, hard to tell how much, but I bet it's enough that she's learned when to just shut up and let that stuff roll off.

But I'm a different generation, and don't give a crap who he is, fangirl or not. That sexist garbage doesn't work for me. Still, the room is already tense enough, so I'll be bringing this up later.

Turbo's still talking. "The military look only takes you so far, but I don't know how well the --"

"We're not here to sell toys." Sosuke throws the words like a dart. Turbo stops and gives him the once over. He gives a 'good for you, kiddo' kind of smile that tells me he doesn't consider anyone in this room a threat.

That is a very poor state of mind to be in right now.

"Well," he says with a tiny shrug, "I'm sure the ESOA is smart enough to start you small and let you work your way up. And remember, if you ever need help, I'm just a call away." He makes a little click with his cheek and

24

winks, as if to say 'Got it?' before he heads for the door.

And right then, I think it's over.

"We don't need your help."

Damn it, Sosuke...

Captain Turbo glances over his shoulder. Sosuke's voice is a pinpoint shot, but Captain Turbo's is like a subwoofer. "Excuse me?"

Sosuke stares. "Our first mission is to clean up your mess from last night. Brass Knuckles and Bearserker are to be taken into custody and questioned."

I check McTier. She's not doing anything to stop this. Lucien's hands are twitching. With my power, I can feel his heartbeat through my feet. He's a dog getting ready for a chase.

Turbo raises an eyebrow. "Just the three of you?"

Sosuke's face doesn't change, but his muscles are tightening and loosening, preparing. "The three of us are more than capable," he says. "I plan on apprehending Brass Knuckles, personally."

Come on, McTier, do something already.

"And when I do," Sosuke says, "there isn't going to be any 'standstill'."

Captain Turbo's chest bounces as he chuckles. "Is that so? Well, when you do, make sure you tell the reporters you did it all by yourself."

Sosuke's heartbeat picks up. "I don't plan on plastering my face all over the television like a clown."

Oh. Shit.

It happens in an instant. Captain Turbo is across the room so fast my eyes can barely follow. He's almost hovering, I can barely feel him with my feet. But before he moved, there was this weird humming, a vibration from his body. What the hell was that?

No time to think about it. Turbo's up in Sosuke's face, growling, "What did you say?" with a tone you wouldn't expect from the world's greatest superhero. Sosuke opens his fists. The hairs on my head, the tiny ones on my arms, all stand up like they would when a thunderstorm is right overhead.

My own hands open up. We're not on the bottom level of the building, but the floor beneath me is concrete. I can work with that. If I'm quick enough, maybe I can separate them. If not, I really don't know what the outcome is going to be. Captain Turbo is one of the most prolific crime fighters on the planet. He has super strength and speed and agility and can fly. He's the guy who fought the twelve members of the Sinister Shaolin Squad in hand-to-hand combat and beat every one of them.

But Sosuke...

"Stand down, Agent Sugiyama." Lieutenant Colonel McTier says.

Sosuke and Captain Turbo are still staring each other down.

25

"Stand down," she says again. "That's an order."

Holy hell, that was intense. Now I know what people mean when they say they need a drink. Not that I do. I'm clean. And it's against the rules, anyway. But I know something that's not against the rules.

Jumbo Honey buns.

Well, okay, yeah, they kind of are. I'm on this super strict diet and those definitely do not fall under either the protein, vegetable, or unrefined grains categories, but damn if I don't need something good right now. I want my mom's sopapillas or pastel de tres leches. If I were home now, she'd take one look at me and whip it up, with a little tiny sprinkle of cinnamon on top. And no, it's not traditional, but that's how I like it, and that's how she'd make it. Really, I'd kill for anything from my family's kitchen, or my dad's grill. As I walk through the deserted hallways of the ESOA building, I try to keep myself from thinking about how it smells when we have a carne asada at home.

How much I want to be there right now.

How much I don't want to be alone.

Is this it? Is this the life of a hero? It's not... it's not what I thought. When I was a kid, I watched them on TV -- flying around, saving people, doing good. I never really considered what down time was like for them. How absolutely isolated they were. I knew better than most kids, what the heroes... the big ones... had to give up. But it just never clicked.

Until I had to give it up too.

Hijo de puta, ¿dónde están las máquinas expendedoras?

I'm glad to be out of that conference room. After McTier stepped in, we had the room cleared in a minute. Neither Sosuke or Captain Turbo said anything after that, which is probably for the best. We have an hour before our briefing, which will be en route to Boston. We're flying in by supersonic jet -- which, okay, that's pretty cool -- and we're going after Brass Knuckles and Bearserker. I just hope they're the only two we find.

There doesn't seem to be anything or anyone on this entire floor. Peeking into rooms, I see lots of expensive equipment, mostly medical, and some beds. This is the second floor I've found like this -- our tax dollars hard at work -- and in a moment of frustration, I decide to do this my way. Closing my eyes, I focus all my attention on my feet.

And that's when I feel it. Something mechanical moving, down the hall, all the way at the end. Something... breathing.

As I get closer, I hear a mechanical hiss and a beep from a heart monitor, as well as a television with the volume down. The hissing is rhythmic, high and forced, then low and whining. The heart monitor coincides with the hisses, moving at a similar pace.

A respirator.

After few steps, I peek in. Curtains are drawn around a bed. Through the gaps, I see old man feet, a bunch of equipment, and tubes. Lots of tubes. Going in, coming out, from and where to, I don't know.

Hiss high. Hiss low. Beep. Beep.

I approach slowly, quietly, but there's no point. I'm not going to wake him up. Nothing is. The curtains pull back. His hair is still dark, but with gray streaks running through, mostly above his temples. It's tousled, unkempt. They can't really comb it because of the breathing apparatus that's strapped on, covering everything from his nose down to his chin. Some of those tubes go into his nose, and a big one is going down his throat. His eyes are closed and caked with sleep.

Ironsides, the indestructible man.

Hiss high. Hiss low. Beep. Beep.

My god, his hands are big. To say his fingers are like sausages... and not those fancy organic chicken breast sausages that are skinny and flavorless. I'm talking the Italian sausages, the kind that come five to a pack and feed a family of six. But it's funny, because Ironsides isn't that big of a guy. His feet don't even reach the end of the bed.

Hiss high. Hiss low. Beep. Beep.

The tips of his fingers are yellowed. They look dirty, but I know it's from cigarettes. There are calluses across his fingers, old and permanent. They're strong hands, mechanic's hands. Before he became Ironsides, he put in time on Navy vessels. That's how he got his powers; he was exposed to radiation during the atomic bomb tests. Everyone else on got cancer. He got lucky. Something about being in a room with metal alloys that somehow fused with his body, making him the toughest thing on the planet.

On the outside, anyway.

Hiss high. Hiss low. Beep. Beep.

As I walk around the bed, his face disappears behind his enormous beer belly. I was in Thailand a year ago on a training mission and I saw a billboard of him. It was a terrible picture, too much hair gel, too much make up. They'd tried to put concealer on all the smoker's wrinkles. In his hand was a bottle of some brand name alcohol. Whiskey, bourbon maybe. He endorsed several of them, along with unfiltered cigarettes.

The picture on the billboard was from the chest up, the bottle practically held higher than his head. They had to shoot that high. No one wants to see a guy shaped like an Anjou pear wearing spandex.

Hiss high. Hiss low. Beep. Beep.

At the other side of the bed, I look at all the readouts on his heart monitor. I don't know why. I don't know what ninety-five percent of them mean. I just feel like, maybe if I look long enough, I'll see something... anything. Maybe I'll see there's an irregularity to his theta brainwaves. I'll mention it to the nurse. He'll tell the doctor. The doctor will call in her team and they'll all come rushing in and turn on some crazy device that reactivates his conscious mind and at the end of the day, good old Ironsides will open his eyes and turn to me, uttering a low, 'Thanks kid,' with a smile.

Hiss high. Hiss low. Beep. Beep.

Yeah, sure.

His lungs were already a mess. Even the indestructible man couldn't spend his whole life chain smoking without any effect. I read his medical file. No cancer, but a severe case of emphysema. The indestructible man had a weak spot, and that happens to be exactly where the bad guys struck.

Let's say that I'm more than a little suspicious about that.

Hiss high. Hiss low. Beep. Beep.

I slip my fingers into his hand. His palm is unusually warm. I feel the roughness of his skin against my own. I wish I had some kind of psychic power. I wish that I could reach him, let him know that he's not alone. Sighing and smiling, I give his hand a squeeze.

Hiss high. Hiss low. Beep beep.

Beep.

Beepbeep. Beep-beep-be-be-beep --

Oh shit. His fingers twitch.

Oh shit!

The muscles in his face spasm.

What did I do? Oh no, oh no, oh no.

He grunts through the tube and jerks. His hand clamps down on mine. ¡Qué carajo! It feels like all my knuckles are being smashed together. The respirator seems to stop, then jumps up and down wildly. He lets go of my hand, but now his arms, his legs, everything is shaking. I hold my aching hand between nervous fingers and look at the head of the bed, searching for the call button but there's so much damn equipment, I can't find it.

"Oh come on," I say to myself. There's always a call button! "¿Donde esta?" I push tubes aside, but they just slip back into place. I shove the monitor and dig through the cables. I can hear more grunts coming from his throat.

¿A donde? ¿A donde?

Be-beep beep-beep. Be-beep beep. Beep beep. Beep. Beep. Beep.

28

I'm still digging, searching as his tremors slow. His limbs relax again and the grunting stops. His face is red and flushed, the veins on his neck are standing out, blue highways beneath his skin.

Hiss high. Hiss low. Beep. Beep.

My own breathing starts to slow down. My heart comes down from its breakneck pace.

"Hello there," says a voice from the curtain behind me.

I'm not going to say I let out a little squeal. But I'm not going to say I don't.

I spin around. I was so focused on Ironsides, I forgot to check for other people. I figured they would have given one of the world's greatest heroes his own room.

But there, sitting in the other bed, is the most famous Mexican in the world. The Lord of Light, the shining star of the Justice Brigade.

Lux.

His face is long, his chin is strong, his moustache is well trimmed, mostly white. He still has a good head of hair. And his eyes? They're focused on me, unblinking, not cold, not hot, but ready to become either at any second.

He's holding a metal cane up, pointed slightly at me. He must have used it to pull back the curtain during the chaos a minute ago. He doesn't say anything, just stares. How strange this must look to him; one minute he's sitting, quietly watching TV, listening to the constant rise and fall of Ironsides' respirator. The next, everything is going to hell and there's some Chicana shouting like an idiot.

And then, when he says something to get her attention, she stands there, staring at him, gape-jawed and silent. I mean, if he knew, he wouldn't blame me. And it's not just because he's famous. It's not just because he happens to be the one person in this world that I hold above all others.

I suspect he's waiting for me to say something, to explain what I was doing to his partner. Or maybe he wants to know if I can stand there with a cartoonish look of surprise on my face all day.

My brain fires electrical impulses to every part of my body, telling it to actually do something. Unfortunately, there seems to be a traffic jam directly above my mouth. All I can do is hope I'm not drooling.

He still hasn't put the end of the cane down. His eyes don't dart around. Instead, they just look me up and down, taking note of everything. His breathing is slow and steady, barely noticeable. What is noticeable are the bruises. A large purple and black splatter covers half his jaw, and the cheek on the other side is a swollen mound with a bandage. I can't even imagine what the rest of him looks like at this point.

He hasn't called for security, so he either thinks I'm not a threat, or he's waiting for me to make the first move. Maybe he's so whacked out on painkillers that he has no idea what's going on. But I doubt it.

The cane hovers.

"It is the poison," he says softly, informatively. His voice moves like his eyes do, smooth. Excellent enunciation. Slow, but not dragging. Instantly, I feel like I'm speaking with mi abuelo again. "There is no cure for it. All they can do is stabilize him. The tremors, they happen now and again. But they always stop. I wonder, each time, if he will make it. It seems, this time, he did." His eyes -- and the cane -- hover on me. He's made his move, shown me his position in the situation. Now it's my turn. I manage to close my mouth long enough to swallow. A good start.

"Hola," My voice suddenly seems high and frail compared to his. Come on girl, you've taken out an entire team of Covert Black Ops during a training simulation. Is this really that much harder?

Ay Dios mío, yes.

He smiles a little, the kind of smile someone gives to a particularly cute child when they do something predictably adorable. "Hola," he says. The cane drops a few inches.

I start to relax a little, but still speak formally. "¿Cómo se siente?"

"Bien, gracias."

"Escuchélo que sucedió. Soy parte del epuipo que --"

"I know." He raises his hand to cut me off. "I saw you on the TV, at the press conference." The news is playing recaps. Captain Turbo is finishing his speech. There, behind him, I'm practically blubbering.

Ugh. The Bleeding Heart...

"And don't bother with Spanish," he says as he waves his hand and looks away. My chest tightens for a second.

Oh no. Please, no. Don't be a jerk.

"The higher-ups hate having to bring in a translator." His eyes come back to me again, and there's a little twinkle in them. "Trust me. I did it to them all the time." He smiles and winks playfully.

Just like mi abuelo.

CHAPTER FOUR
TO BE OR NOT TO BE

Over the years, many villains told me it was fate -- destiny -- that I should become Doctor Dendrite. I don't believe in such things. Really, it was happenstance. I didn't want to break the law, I just wanted what was mine. I put so many hours into my work, only to have the University turn around and try to sell it for a profit.

Profit? How pedestrian. I was changing humanity. I was going to bend the laws of physics! And all they could see was a dollar sign. I should have known better, but I was young and stupid.

An assistant professor at the time, I taught classes and ran another professor's lab. Being the brightest prospect there, I assumed that when Professor Jayaramen told me I could develop my own experiments, whatever I discovered would be mine. The gravity bands were my personal project. Two bands, one around each wrist -- well, forearm really, there were a lot of components -- which could manipulate gravitational fields.

My theories were simple, but elusive. I wrestled with them day and night. If Newton had my mind, he would have spent the rest of his life under that tree, trying to get the apple to go back up again. I was tenacious.

You see, gravity is a slippery thing. Whenever you think you've got it figured out, it misbehaves. You think it's going to zig, it zags. One minute it's predictable, the next, your work table is shooting towards the ceiling at an incredible velocity.

It comes into our dimension from another. Did you know that? It comes from a dimension of all gravity. Everything there is gravity. The membranes of our universes are right next to each other. It slips through the cracks, sand through the tiniest of points in an hourglass. Then, once in our dimension, it runs loose like a drunken college freshman.

I used to give the occasional lecture to Professor Jayaramen's students on days he couldn't make it.

"Most people tend to think of gravity as something rather commonplace, simple," I would tell them. "What goes up, must come down. Right? Not quite, my friends. Because, you see, what is going up isn't really going up. It's going out. It's always going out, and then it's coming back in. When you toss a ball into the air, what you're doing is moving it further away from the center of the Earth. Then, when it comes back down at you, it does so because gravity is pulling it toward the center of the Earth. You just happen to be in the way.

"So then, all gravity must pull everything toward the center of the Earth, yes? Well I'm sure you already know the answer to that. And if you don't, you don't really deserve to be here. The Earth's gravitational pull is only strong enough to keep the objects which are currently here, here. It's also strong enough to keep the moon in orbit around the planet. And yet, the moon never seems to come crashing into the planet. It has gone up, but not come down. Also, the Moon has its own gravitational field. Odd.

"Now, how is it that both the moon and the Earth could have gravitational fields of their own, but not come crashing into one another? Are gravitational fields like magnetic polarity? Two positives repel each other, so why not? Stop nodding, they're not. If they were, the moon and the Earth would be constantly flying off in opposite directions.

"The truth of the matter is that gravity is not simply up/down. It's flexible. It's a wave. It's an invisible intangible gelatinous coating which surrounds everything. Every object which carries mass has its own gravity field. I have one. You have one. This table has one. That man sleeping in the back who will fail this class has one.

"And since that is the case, we should be able to bend and manipulate our own gravitational field without damaging the fields of other objects. Imagine being able to lift a boulder with one hand. Imagine jumping up five stories instead of taking the stairs. Imagine a world where the rule states, what goes up does not necessarily come down until we tell it to. This world is just outside of our grasp and soon, I will make it a reality."

Like I said, tenacious.

After several of these lectures, the department chair asked me, in a not-so-polite fashion, to stop lecturing about gravity. It was a slap in the face. As I left his office, defeated and deflated, I realized that it wasn't my passion for the subject which had turned them against me.

They didn't understand.

They didn't believe.

My ideas were wild daydreams to them. Even Professor Jayaramen sighed when I told him about the gravity bands, how they were getting closer to operational every day. I just needed more time for fine tuning.

They told me I was a waste of time.

I was a joke.

Had I been genetically programmed toward supervillainy, this would have been the moment, the catalyst needed for me to build a torrent of rage. I would have seethed and festered and vowed my revenge. I would have cried havoc and set their world ablaze.

Instead, I went to my studio apartment and sulked. I drank cheap beer and ate tater tots and looked over my notes, searching for an answer. When I couldn't find one, I began to feel the fool they believed me to be.

Part of me wondered if maybe they were right. Was it possible I had gone awry somewhere along the way? Had I been wrong? Overlooked something? Miscalculated?

No.

No, I never miscalculated. I was right. I was close. I wasn't a fool, what I was trying to accomplish was new and different and though they couldn't understand it, I could show them. I could show them and then everything would be better. I would regain their respect. I truly believed that all they needed was to see and my honor would be restored.

Hope seeped back into me. I picked myself up from my beanbag chair and headed for campus. Climbing the staircase inside the lab building, the soles of my loafers popped against the concrete and echoed, warning shots fired by fate. I jogged through the hallways, and as I came close to the T-section where a left led to the lab, my palms were sweating. I dug into my pocket furiously, desperate to get the keys out. The ring slipped from my hand and tucked themselves up against a water fountain. I dropped to my knees.

Around the corner, hinges whined. A door slammed.

"This is some impressive equipment, Professor." The voice was stronger, more commanding than any of the professors in the department. There was a Southern drawl to it, the type which I typically avoided whenever possible. "I've never seen anything like it."

"Of course not." Professor Jayaramen's voice rolled across the linoleum to me. "Everything you see has been built from scratch."

"So, you designed all of this?"

"Oh yes, of course, Colonel," said Jayaramen, trying so hard to be convincing, he was anything but. "I have been teaching the theories for decades."

"Uh-huh."

Quickly, I darted out, pressed myself against the wall and worked down towards the corner. Their backs were to me. Jayaramen I knew. The man next to him was the apex of physical conditioning. At least, he was as much as I could tell through his formal military outfit. He had the kinds of shoulders that have to go through a doorway at a bit of an angle.

And a great head of chestnut brown hair.

"Now," Jayaramen said, "this is still very, very much in the, uh, testing phase. There are many things which must be adjusted and fine-tuned before they're ready for military use."

"But when they're ready, they'll do what you said?"

My heart hammered. I wanted to jump out, to demand to know what was happening, but I couldn't bring myself to do it.

"Oh yes, oh yes. Of course, Colonel."

As long as I didn't see the bands, I could convince myself that they were talking about something else. Anything else.

"Incredible," there was a wisp of reverence in the colonel's voice. "Gravity, controlled by these things."

"Just imagine," Jayaramen cried, "what you could do with them."

"Yeah," the colonel grunted. I could practically hear the gears turning in his head. "Just... imagine."

Jayaramen's laugh was an icicle, jammed into my chest and freezing my will to fight back. Had I taken a stand then, things could have been entirely different. Instead, I slunk away and waited until the colonel left before confronting Jayaramen.

It... didn't go well.

I accused him of stealing my work. He said everything created within his lab was his research. I let slip I overheard him and the Colonel. He accused me of spying and paranoia. I told him that people of color were supposed to stick together. He said science is a business. I used some derogatory words relating to his morals and intelligence. He demanded my immediate resignation. I told him to place that idea where sunlight was unable to reach.

That... also did not go well.

Security took my key to the lab and pitched me out the building's front door like a drunk when the last bar closes. I told them I just wanted my notebooks back, they were personal items and I had every right to them. The guards laughed in my face and threatened me with a severe beating if I 'tried anything'.

At that point, the smart thing to do was play dumb, apologize for causing so much trouble, and leave peacefully. After that, I could have returned in the night, found the building empty, used my spare key, and taken what was mine.

That... is not what I did.

"This isn't over!" I screamed, my fist in the air. "Do you hear me? I'm getting my things one way or another!"

... One way or another? Good lord...

Anyway, people overheard. News of a deranged scientist swearing revenge upon the university and any security guards who protected it spread like wildfire. A reputation was already being formed, one which, honestly, I didn't deserve. I'm amazed I wasn't caught just trying to get back into the building. I wasn't stealthy, I was clumsy. The tower of trashcans and wooden pallets I used to reach the unlocked bathroom window collapsed twice before a pack of inebriated engineering students came over and offered to help. They shored up the hasty construction, cheered when I made it through the window, then ran when I fell through and crashed to the hard, tile floor.

After checking myself for a concussion, I made my way upstairs. The hallway was beautifully empty. I puffed, having run the whole way, and pulled my keys out slowly this time. They jingled and jangled as I slid the key into the knob, and the latch slid back with a satisfying 'tick'. I smiled and pushed.

There was a dull 'thump' and my breath caught.

Someone had locked the deadbolt... which I had a key for.

I laughed at myself for the sudden burst of fear. It wasn't normal practice to bolt the door. I took it as a good sign. It meant that the gravity bands were still inside. I was halfway through throwing the bolt when I heard it.

"Hold it right there."

There was a man at the end of the hall. He was tall and incredibly fit. I could tell, because he wasn't wearing a security uniform... as his order to me had suggested... but something much more form fitting. He didn't hold a badge or a gun or even a flashlight. His upper body was trapped in shadows, but in the sharp cut of moonlight coming through a high window, his legs were clearly visible. He was wearing jackboots.

And tights.

My only thought was, 'huh.'

I stood there, an inert mass, watching as he stepped into the moonlight streaming through the window. He had on a t-shirt crudely dyed with vertical red and white stripes, leather gloves, and had a coif of perfectly sculpted hair to match his perfectly sculpted jaw line.

And he was wearing a wide cloth with eye holes cut in it, tied in the back, Zorro style.

A mask.

Something inside me knew.

When his next foot came down, I did the only sensible thing; I left the keys dangling in the lock and dashed down the hallway. At least, the ten feet I was able to cover before he snatched the back of my shirt.

It was impossible. He'd been twenty, maybe even thirty feet away. No one could cover that amount of distance so quickly, not to mention the fact he dragged me to a complete halt before sending me flying backwards.

I ended up on my hands and knees, facing away from the stranger. I was right near the lab door. The keys dangled from the lock. As much as I wanted to run, I knew that without them, I wouldn't be able to get back in.

This was my last chance.

The man in tights snatched me again, hoisted me like a sack of potatoes, and threw me against the far wall. My feet caught the ground but my legs went to jelly. I crumbled to the side as a tremendous thud resounded on the wall where my head had been. There was a cracking noise and the tights man yelled, "Son of a --"

He wrung his fist as bits of concrete crumbled to the ground from the dent he had made. He was standing between me and the lab door, distracted. This was my chance. A spark lit up inside me. Sucking in air, I used all every muscle in my body to push away from the wall and through him.

At least, that's what I planned.

Instead, I used all the muscles in my body to push away from the wall and bounced off him like a pinball off a bumper.

He didn't move an inch.

I fell, watching pinwheels dance behind my eyes as he stomped over to me.

"Alright," he grumbled, bent down, and lifted me up, into the air with one hand.

No. He couldn't be that strong. No human could be.

He didn't even grunt.

"I've had just about enough of you," said his perfect voice. Baritone.

In response, I tried putting words together. "P-please... my wo... my work... I just..."

I rambled on long enough that he gave an annoyed sigh and dropped me. "Alright, alright, alright."

I landed against a fire extinguisher and grabbed at it for balance. It gave a squeak of metal on metal as it twisted sideways in the c-clamps holding it. "Please," I said, my eyes drifting away from the man and to the lab door just across the hall, "I just want my work."

He shook his head. My fingers tightened around the release on the extinguisher. My finger slipped through the safety pin. He reached for me, saying, "The only thing you're getting is a night in the slammer, my friend."

I yanked the pin and squeezed. A tremendous cloud of carbon dioxide and water blasted him in the chest, then spread and enveloped us both. I'd held my breath, but he began coughing wildly. I ran straight for the door. Snatching my keys, I jetted down the hallway as fast as I could. Behind me, his raspy voice bellowed, "Stop," and, "halt," and, "thief."

Thief. How ironic.

CHAPTER FIVE
AMATEUR HOUR

"Candace?" Annie's voice is a sad puppy paw, scratching weakly against my bedroom door.

My voice, on the other hand, is a pit-bull who just got punched in the balls. "Really not a good time," I bark as I pull another desk drawer out and dump it on the floor.

"I just... we're all kinda worried, you know? You just dropped your cereal and ran out and, and..." She sighs. "And Samantha wants to know when you plan on cleaning up."

I want to tell her that Princess is the least of my problems. Usually, I think of Samantha as my arch-nemesis. Unfortunately, my new arch-nemesis is the goddamn United States government.

I think the scales are just slightly in their favor.

Annie whimpers. "Candace?"

I kept my shit together through Captain Turbo's retirement speech. I mean, the guy is, like, seventy or something. He's still in awesome shape -- little softer around the middle, but who am I to talk? I could use some cardio, too -- but it was kind of expected, right? Truth is, the Justice Brigade hasn't had a lot to do since the whole Japan thing. The Triad of Evil basically just vanished afterward. Whatever. There weren't many villains left who took a whole team to take them down. And all that shit happened before I was born. Captain Turbo's been hitting softballs since then.

So, he announces The Justice Brigade is retiring. No biggie. They're old, it was bound to happen. Then, he says that Ironsides may not make it and I'm a bit nervous. But hey, I keep cool. No one knew I was involved in the warehouse thing, so I'm good. Then Agent Sugiyama got up and started talking.

And that's when my ass started to pucker.

The first thing, the first freaking thing out of his mouth?

"We believe this crime was connected to a much larger superhuman criminal organization."

And I did not like that.

"This equipment was most likely being purchased in order to further a more global purpose."

No. No, no, no.

"And because of this, we plan on finding out exactly how the equipment came to be at the warehouse in the first place."

But that's not when I dropped the cereal. That happened when he said,

"Right now, the ESOA has a special investigative and paramilitary unit en route to the Massachusetts area. Their assignment is to find anyone involved in the theft."

Shitballs.

Annie says my name again in the hallway, dragging out the vowels like she's auditioning for Les Mis. Good God, that girl is persistent! I shake my head and try to tune her out.

I'm systematically going through everything I own. I need to find every record of the passwords I lifted, barcodes I copied, and pin numbers I stole. Every time I do, I shove it in the trash along with all the fake key cards and IDs that I've made.

Jesus, I am the worst kind of thief. I left this stuff lying around because, really, I never thought it would get me in trouble. I mean, I knew it could, but not the kind of trouble my mom's money couldn't get me out of.

I cram another handful in the trash. Damn it! I don't... there's more shit to get rid of, I've still got the bloody clothes under my bed, I haven't made a getaway plan, I don't know what I'm doing or where I'm going, I'm surrounded by IDs and barcodes and... and...

Wait. Wait a minute.

Fake IDs.

Barcodes.

Scanning of barcodes on fake IDs.

Into computer systems.

Which record them.

Record the person who came in and out of...

Oh. Oh shit.

Last night. I have to think about last night. Stop, think, rewind. I see everything in my head, like a movie playing backwards.

Me, running. Massive explosion. The warehouse. Fighting. Spiders, spiders coming out of that guy's skin. Blood, so much blood from Parker's head being caved in. The Justice Brigade. The deal with the supervillains in tights. Charlie, meeting with Charlie.

What was before that?

Driving to the warehouse. Leaving the lab.

I start to slow down the movie.

The fake keycard I used to get us into the lab. Sneaking through the secured access hallways. Hacking the elevator system to get there. Before that, there was the regular floors, the ones we already had access to.

Slow down a little more.

Walking through the hallways, through the lobby like everything was normal. The building. The front door.

And now I play it in real time.

That moment. That funny little moment with Parker where we both went to open the front door at the same time. Where he smiled, and I smiled.

Where I used my real keycard to open the door.

Oh... damn... it.

I didn't even... I go into that building all the time! It was just habit. I wasn't thinking when I, I...

This is bad. This is beyond bad. The ESOA is sending a team, but they're out of D.C., so it'll probably be another hour before they're at the building. Going through the files in the system and stuff, maybe another half an hour. We weren't the only people there, but it was, like, 11:00 at night and neither Parker nor I actually went to the labs where we work. They're going to review the log-ins and see. I've got two hours, if I'm lucky.

How much booze can I drink in two hours? How far could I get if I just jump in my car, right now? Could I get to an airport? Take my passport, buy the first international ticket, and fly to wherever, call my mom when I get there and tell her she needs to hire some crazy good extradition lawyers? Or maybe they've already locked down the airport. Hell, maybe they've locked down the whole town.

I'm hyperventilating or something, super-fast short breaths and my heart is pounding but my whole body is weak. I feel like I'm falling. No, wait, I am. I'm falling. I'm down, folded up like a wet towel after a shower. It probably hurts. I may have some bruises. Don't really notice. I can't, I can't feel anything. The panic from now is mixing with the exhaustion from last night and I just can't.

I'm going to prison... if I'm lucky.

Shit-sticks... what if they waterboard me?

The world is all out of focus, but I hear something besides the screaming in my own head. It's Annie. She's out in the hallway, but she's not whimpering anymore. "Candace?" she says. "Are you -- what was that noise?"

That was the sound of my life coming to a screeching halt, girl.

"Candace? I'm coming in."

The door to my room clicks.

"Oh my God!" She says it as one solid word; Ohmigawd! The floor thumps against my face as she runs over. Her arms go around me and she starts pulling me up. I'd swear that each arm makes at least a full rotation around my torso, she's holding me so tight.

Annie's not big by any means. She's got a tight little body. She's built like those one-minute hourglass timers you get with board games, you know,

Pictionary or something -- thin in the middle, girl even has a little six pack -- but not too voluptuous outside of that. Still, she manages to haul me up to where I'm sitting. She's yammering the whole time, ohmigawd, ohmigawd, ohmigawd, right in my ear. Maybe it's the noise, maybe it's her hot breath condensing on my skin, there's even, like, a tiny chance I feel guilty about having her lift me up, because I finally reactivate some muscles and keep myself from falling back down.

"Candace? Candace can you hear me?"

Oh my god, yes. Yes, I can hear you. I raise a sarcastic eyebrow. Clearly, it is not enough, because she says, loud and long and slow, "Can you hear me?"

I sigh. "Yeah."

"Okay!" she says, suddenly bright and chipper. But then serious, "Okay. Good. That's good." She's nodding furiously and licking her lips a lot.

"Yeah," I say, less than bright and with a severe lack of chipper.

"What... what is going on with you? Are you sick?"

"No." The words come out by reflex.

"Are you --"

I look away. "It's... Annie, I can't..."

She doesn't get it. How could she? But I'm screwed. I'm totally screwed. And she's in my room, touching my stuff, and now I'm thinking about how her fingerprints are getting on things and I'm going to have to explain that to the government investigators and along with everything else going on in my brain, I'm going to have to try and protect her now and, and, and...

I look at her and it's not that I'm crying, it's just that my eyes have too much water in them. "I'm in trouble, okay?"

She nods. "What happened?"

"I can't tell you."

"Why not?"

"Because..." I pause.

"Candace," her big eyes staring hard into mine, "what happened?" she says, and goddamn if just having her there doesn't make me feel like maybe, maybe everything isn't going to go to absolute shit in the next two hours. Because if nothing else, I've got her.

So I tell her. I kind of start at the beginning, then jump to the end, then go backwards, then start over again. I leave out some of the gorier details. I don't talk so much about the explosion, because I'm not sure about it, where it came from, if... if I was somehow involved.

If it came from me.

But everything else. She gets the whole shebang. Now, she's looking at the floor, processing.

40

"So," she says, "you've been stealing."

"Yeah."

"From the school?"

"Yup."

"Since we were freshmen?"

"I --" Technically, I've been stealing from places since before I knew her, but that's not important. "Yes."

She nods, that kind of nod a parent does when a kid admits that they totally screwed up on a school project they were supposed to be entirely responsible for. And it works. Jesus, I should have just called my mom. At least I'm used to her being disappointed in me... but then always hugging me after and saying she's not. But I can tell she is... but... oh to hell with that. Telling Annie was supposed to make me feel better, not wracked with guilt. Ugh, this girl.

She says, "The investigators are going to, to assume that you were a part of it. The supervillain thing, not the stealing thing. Because, you know, you were a part of that."

My jaw clenches a little. I say, "Yes, I was."

"But not the supervillain thing?"

"No."

"And not, like, the fighting or anything?"

I only hesitate for a second. "No. Of course not."

"Okay." She takes a deep breath, and lets it out slowly. "Oooookay. So you've got, like, maybe two hours."

"Yup."

Her eyes meet mine. "What are you going to do?"

"I'm..." I shake my head. "They're gonna figure it out, right? Everything is in that computer. They're not going to stop."

"I know," she says softly. "That agent guy sounded serious."

"Japanese," I say quickly.

"What?"

"He's Japanese. At least, his name is."

Her eyebrows come together. "So?"

"You said Asian."

She stares, blankly.

"'That Asian guy sounded serious'. That's what you --"

"Agent," she says.

"What?"

"I said agent guy," she over-enunciates, "not Asian guy."

"Oh."

41

She nods her head and gives a breathy little laugh. It doesn't really lighten the mood.

I smush my fingers into my face and move everything around for a second. Standing up, I start milling around the room, looking for things I can pack up.

Annie watches as I head to the closet. "What --" She hesitates. "What about your mom? She can probably --"

"No." I stuff some jeans into a backpack.

"But she --"

"No." I say again.

Annie pauses. "You haven't told her."

I really wish that had been a question.

"Candace, she's --"

"On a goddamn business trip, just like she always is."

"You know she'll help you if --"

"Annie, this... this isn't -- those guys from the Justice Brigade got killed."

"They're not dead."

"Yet."

Annie opens her mouth to respond, but ends up closing it instead. She turns her head and gazes into space.

I keep stuffing things into my backpack. "It doesn't matter how many lawyers my mom hires. I'm going to be locked up in a tiny little room for a really long time." A tiny little room where I'll never see her again.

"And they'll find you because?"

"Because I'm a dumb-shit and left a huge freakin' calling card." Never sit across from her at dinner.

"And hacked the elevator security," she says, half to herself.

"Yup." Never lean against her while we're watching a movie in our pajamas.

"And used a fake ID to get into the lab."

"Yup." After a while, I won't remember how soft her skin is when she holds me in those few moments where our walls fall down.

"Which you made, after breaking into the system and stealing the access codes, right?"

"Yes, Annie. Yes. I did all of that. I'm a total disappointment. Even with everything I've been given, I still turned into a criminal, okay? I'm never going to be anything great, and I'm never going to be as important as... whatever. Just take me away and lock me up so I can't waste all that stuff that's been done for me anymore. Happy?"

She's quiet, but not feeling-bad-about-the-fact-I-was-just-a-total-bitch-to-her kind of quiet. She's sitting there, looking at the floor like there's a differential equation she's one step away from finishing.

"Candace?" she asks softly.

I don't snap. "What?"

"Can't you just erase the fact that you ever went into the building?"

Annie, I love you, girl.

CHAPTER SIX
FAMILY TIES

Lux asks me where I come from. The answer, New Mexico, makes him laugh. He starts to cough a little at the end and his hand goes to his bandaged side. I pretend not to notice, but I do. He pretends not to notice that I'm pretending that I don't notice.

"You are American, ¿verdad?" he asks. His voice is a little scratchy, so I reach for the water nearby. He takes it with a thankful nod.

I tell him a brief history of me. Born in New Mexico to immigrant parents. My dad came over the border when he was a boy. My mom was the last born into a big family, but first born in the US.

"And you, ah, grew up here?" he asks, casual as can be. So we talk about family life. Well, really, I talk about family life and he listens, saying, "Sí, sí," whenever I pause. I tell him about New Mexico, about how we tried to keep as many traditions as we could.

It doesn't occur to me at the time how funny it is; I'm some random girl sitting in a room talking to one of the greatest superheroes who has ever lived, and he's asking me about my quinceañera, about who made the best carnitas -- mi abuela, of course -- and about how many times my tíos offered me beer. He laughs, big and from the belly, when I talk about how every tía would bring rice to every big dinner because they never talked about it beforehand... but then there never seemed to be enough rice for everyone. It's like we're two people waiting in a bus station for a long ride to somewhere we both need to be, but have no rush to get to. I should be asking him about his past, for tips on crime fighting, about his time with the Justice Brigade, but every time he asks something and I answer, he smiles. I can't say no to that.

"My family?" he says, grinning, "very much the same. We stuck together. Very close."

I pinch my lips together to keep them from breaking into a big, toothy, schoolgirl smile. Yeah, I know all about your family, Lux. More than you know, actually.

He asks, "Are you the youngest? The oldest?"

"Three of four."

"Ah!" He opens his palms to me. "I am the oldest of four. Oop, no. Five."

I gave him a 'You're in trouble mister!' look. "It's been that long?"

He shakes his head. "No, no, no. The youngest, she was, ah, born after I left. On this side of the border, the only one of us who did not have to cross."

I nod slowly. Down in my lap where Lux can't see, my hands wring together. Do I say something? Is now the time? Does he know? Can he tell?

But he keeps going. "By the time she was anything more than a little baby, I was busy catching criminals. Fighting supervillains."

"Was that before or after you teamed up with Wraith?" Oh no. What -- why did I say that? It just slipped out. And of course, I regret it immediately. Lux's face doesn't move, doesn't twitch, but his eyes do. They were so warm, so happy. Now? It's like there's an interrogation table between us.

¡Rayos! Stupid, stupid, stupid.

Before I can apologize, he says, "Wraith came only a little bit later."

"I... I'm sorry. I shouldn't have --"

"No," he says as he turns away. In the silence, I wonder if that no was the last thing I'll ever hear from him. But then he says it again, softly. "No, no, no," and he turns back. "She was a part of my life. I would never have come as far as I did without her. And I have accepted what I did back then." He pauses. "The choices that I made."

All the talk of family, of brothers and sisters and tradition and homemade tortillas, it had made him seem so young. But now his wrinkles are chasms carved by time and filled with the decisions he'd made. He sighs and adjusts his blanket. The bandages across his chest are speckled with fresh red dots.

Deep in my gut, an anger that surprises me churns.

My eyes come back up and Lux is staring at me. He's curious. No, he's thinking.

No, suspicious.

I lean my head back a bit. All of a sudden I realize that I'm on the other side of that interrogation table.

"What do you know?" he asks, coolly. "About me and Wraith."

He already knows what I know about the two of them. The government tried to cover up their connections after she joined the Triad of Evil, but there was too much info out there. This was before the internet. Newspapers and photographs don't just vanish, and somebody is always finding an old article about the two of them buried in a stack in the corner of their grandparents' house and uploading it.

I tell him that I've seen the photos from back then, the two of them standing proud as the police hauled away some criminals or bandits or even the occasional supervillain; him, lean and muscular, chiseled jaw, his costume mostly white with padding like a football player's on his chest, shoulders, shins and forearms. In each pad was a bulb that glowed, lenses he had constructed that helped him focus the light he could generate into different forms. And there, next to him, was Wraith; thin, elegant, her complexion a deep umber with cool undertones. Her costume was a constant, swirling catch of smoky grays dancing like fat leaves of seaweed caught in a gentle current.

I mean, I don't say it in those exact words. I just say I've seen them.

"And so what story have you heard about us?"

I've heard more than the public. I know they were a team, they were probably lovers. I know they worked better than any other duo. Him, the Lord of Light. Her, the dancing darkness. I know what the files said about her abilities, that she showed incredible potential. That she was probably stronger than he was, but his ability was one of the only things that could cancel hers out. I know that Captain Turbo made an offer to Lux to join the Justice Brigade, but didn't make one to Wraith. I know Lux took it, and it didn't go over well. Wraith got insanely jealous and soon after that, she turned. And not just a little. Not just a hero gone sour kind of turned. She went all in, didn't hold back, didn't seem to keep a shred of her morals from their crime fighting days.

I know she killed.

I know she was there in Japan when things went wrong. When the Triad of Evil killed millions. And I know, after that, she disappeared, just like Araknis and Doctor Dendrite.

But I don't tell Lux that I know any of that. Instead, I think about his question.

'... what story have you heard about us?'

So I ask, "What story would you tell me?"

He pauses, then sinks back into his bed. Head cocked, a little smile creeps across his face, then come back for a long rest. And I can't help but think it again:

Just like mi abuelo.

"I will never forget the first time I saw her," Lux says. "Well, I didn't really see her as much as I felt her. When she punched me. In the face."

I grin and snort like an idiot. He smiles. This is going to be good, I can tell.

"I would like to note, it was a cheap shot. But a damn good cheap shot. Never saw it coming. That was her, ¿cómo se dice? M.O. Modus... operandi. She'd sneak up, silent as a wisp... and knock you on your ass." He slaps a fist into a palm and barks out a laugh. He's there, in his mind, living it all over again.

And he's loving it.

And so am I.

"It was, of course, a misunderstanding. Well, not the punching me part.

46

She meant to do that. But the why, that was not clear. You see, I had been staking out a gang of bank robbers for days. Do remember, mijita, this was before all the monies in the world were just numbers in a computer.

"They had finally made their move, and I had managed to stop the crime. It was very daring, I assure you. I leapt in, shouted, 'drop those bags', and when they tried to take me down, I started throwing my fists and... ah, well, that's not the part of the story you want to hear, is it?"

Well, no, it isn't. But I would be totally fine with hearing that one, too. Of course, he doesn't give me a chance to say so. He just keeps going and I drop my chin into the palms of my hands, my fingers curled up next to my face, elbows on knees, and listen with wide ears and wider eyes.

"Anyway, there were quite a few men to fight, and I did a very good job, but I was all alone and two of them managed to get away. Of course, I was not about to let them escape. So, I pursued them, through the alleys, up the fire escapes, across the rooftops. I chased them for blocks and blocks. Behind and below, the police struggled to keep up.

"Now, at this time I was not a well-established hero. But this... this was going to be my big moment. All I had to do was stop these last two thieves, and I would have my face all over the papers. Captain Turbo, he was working on the other side of the country. He had paved the way for us masked crime fighters, and I was ready.

"So, when I jumped down from one rooftop to another, tucked and rolled, then stood up, I was ready to make my final leap and claim my fame.

"And that's when Wraith came swooping in. She..." he draws out the word, a scolding index finger bouncing in the air. Even after all these years, he's still frustrated with her for it. But he's forgiven her, too. Probably a hundred times over. "She saw the police chasing after me while I was chasing after the criminals and she thought --"

I gasp. "That you were one of them?"

"That I was one of them!" Lux says with a shake of his arms. "She comes out of nowhere, punches me," he puts a fist to the side of his face, "and the next thing I know, I am on my butt, looking at the stars while my prey are getting away. And when I get up to chase them? A whirling cloud of smoke and fog spins around me, cutting me off from the thieves. Instantly, I realize that it is another one, a person like me; with powers. And because they stopped me from the chase, I assume --"

"No,"

"-- that they --"

"Oh no,"

"Oh yes."

I slap my legs. "You also think --"

"She's with the thieves."

The laugh takes up my whole mouth. I cover it with my hands, but it still gets out.

"I hold up my hand," he does, sticking it straight out, slightly behind him, "and shout to the police, 'Stay back'! Which, from my perspective is me telling them to keep their distance in order to stay safe. But Wraith, she thinks I'm telling them to stay back..."

I roll my eyes and say for him, "Or else."

He nods, once, slowly. "So now we both think that we are the hero and the other is the villain. I shot a beam of light a thousand degrees hot into the mist and for a second, I see the flash of an arm. Then, poof... gone. I fire again, and again, and again. But now the mist, it swirls and spins like sand caught in the waves. It comes close, and I get hit. Pow!" He shakes his head and grins. "She had one hell of a punch, mijita."

My grin says it, 'I bet she did.'

"Now, the police are drawing close. If I don't do something, they're going to think that both of us are the bad guys. So, I raise my hands," he does, out to the sides, "concentrate," in his palms, light starts to appear, climbing up his arms like a pale golden aura, "and boom!"

It's a hundred camera flashes going at once. I close my eyes but still see fireworks.

And that's him, injured, tired, and without the lenses that help him focus. I can only imagine what he was like in his prime.

When I open my eyes, the room seems dark. Lux is just a shadow in his bed. My pupils slowly dilate back out. He's sitting back again, staring out the window with a wry smile. I lean forward. "And?"

When he turns, that warmth in his face from when we'd talked about family, about home... about the things we love... is back. "The mist spins together and makes... her." He pauses. His breathing is deep and slow. "Arms up, guarding herself. She lowered them down, and looked straight into my eyes."

¡Dios mío! This is it. He's going to say it. All the rumors, about how they were more than partners, how they were actually in love, people have been talking about it for decades but Lux would never... and now, here, with me, he's going to admit it. I'm holding my breath. I'm gripping the chair beneath me. My shoulders are ratcheted up to my ears.

Come on, just say it. It's fine. I'm safe. He doesn't know it, but I'm closer to him than anybody he's met in years. I promise. I am. Just, just say it...

His voice gets soft and low. "In that moment, she was..."

"Beautiful?" I chirp.

His eyes flip to mine. He pauses. "Terrifying."

... ¿Qué?

He grins.

My jaw drops. My shoulders drop. My butt, which I hadn't even realized had been hovering over the seat, drops. Ouch. I let out a huge sigh and don't just roll my eyes, I roll my whole head. After a few seconds of being frustrated, the sound of him chuckling to himself gets to me. I let a smile spread across my face before raising my chin and giving him an, 'okay, you got me' kind of look. But he's not even paying attention to me. He's fussing with his sheets, adjusting the wires attached to his chest, all the while beaming like a little schoolboy staring across the room at his crush.

"So," I ask, "did you run?"

"Run? Me? Never. Not in my life." His chin slinks down into his chest a bit. "Not that I could have if I'd wanted to."

All I do is nod.

"Anyway, we stood there, face to face, and were about to get back to the fight when the police intervened."

"Lucky you."

"Mijita, it is rude to interrupt your elders."

"Lo siento. So sorry. Please, go on."

"I will."

"Gracias."

"No, thank you."

We grin. I haven't had this kind of verbal play since I joined the team, and every syllable is pure joy. How must it feel for him? I'm a year without my family. For him, it's been decades.

He takes a deep breath and makes little time passing circles in the air with his hand. "Though we both thought that we were the good guys, the police? They felt a little bit different. They surrounded us. I was sure that I would have to save them from this mad, mad woman. But, before I could even take a step, she put her hands into the air. I stood there, confused. We were taken away, then. I explained to the police that I had been the one to capture the other bank robbers, and that I had called them in the first place.

"It was nearly morning when they finally let me go. Outside, the world was just waking up. I remember the sky was pink and blue between the buildings, it seemed closer than ever to me.

"It was only an hour or so later that she was released. I had waited. When she came out, there was no mist, no twirl of smoke. Just her. And let me tell you, even without all of that, she was just as scary. There is a kind of beautiful that is so strong, so clean and sharp, it makes you wonder if the person isn't a trick, an illusion. Something that will lead you into evil. That was her.

"Which was ironic, in the end." He pauses. "She never led anyone to evil, mijita. But was herself swallowed up by it." The muscles around his eyes grow tight.

I don't know what to say right now. So the best I can do is lean in and put my hand on his. He brings his eyes to mine, and forces a smile for me. I force one back.

"I remember," he says, his voice not so steady as a moment ago, "I called to her back, 'Why did you surrender? You could have gotten away easily.' She didn't look at me, but turned her face just enough for me to see. And do you know what she said?"

I don't. Because no one in the world knows this, except for Lux and Wraith.

"'Good guys never run away.'"

Now, the smiles on our faces are real. He shakes his head and lowers his chin.

"She," he sighs, "she was a better hero than I ever was. A fighter. And not just the..." he throws a couple of punches in the air, making little 'uh, uh, uh!' sounds with them. "For others, for the weak, for anyone who could not fight for themselves, she would stand tall and never give up."

"But, she did." I can't help saying it. "She... she turned."

He glares. Behind his eyes I see an anger and a frustration building up.

"I'm sorry," I say, "but whatever happened before, it doesn't excuse what she became."

His gaze is piercing. Around his jaw, the muscles bulge and relax as he chews on whatever words he's preparing. "She did not become." Nostrils flaring from the long, slow, angry breaths. He leans forward, so close I can feel the heat from his skin. "She was made."

I go to pull back a bit, but his hand squeezes mine.

"By me."

I thought the story of Lux and Wraith would be some kind of bittersweet fairytale. Right now, it feels a bit more like a psychological thriller.

And we're at the part where everything starts crashing down.

Lux's hand isn't just warm, it's hot. Like, I want to not be touching him kind of hot. He's not glowing, not activating his power externally, but there's a weird sheen to his skin. It's sweat, but there's something else there. It's like the truth is boiling up inside of him, through him, out his pores and into the world.

And it's ugly.

"I could have stopped her," he says. And for a second, I think he means that he could have stopped Wraith after she had become a villain. But then I get it. "I should have..." His hand, wringing mine, shakes. His thin neck turns into a bunch of vertical lines as he strains to get out what it is he needs to say. With a wordless bark, he lets go of me and flops back against his bed. Under his breath, he's cursing in Spanish at a thousand miles an hour. Not the little curses, either. These are the, 'you need to go to church and talk to the priest' kind of curses.

His hand makes a claw in the air, like he's trying to rake the thoughts from his mind, get them in line so he can actually convey them. Off to the side, his heart monitor is beeping fast, really fast. If he doesn't calm down, a nurse is going to come in here and find us. Best case after that? I get a serious talking to. Worst case? I have to debrief the higher ups.

And they're nothing if not thorough.

I scoot my stool up closer to the head of the bed and lean in. "Lux, whatever you did, it couldn't have -- she made her own choices."

He says, "No," with a sigh that collapses his entire body. The energy he was putting out a moment ago begins to fade. "No," he says again, softer, with his eyes down. "It was my choice to make."

"Lux,"

"Times were different, mijita. Not better, just different. They told me it was okay that I was Mexican. That the world was ready for a hero like me. But a woman?"

It's the way he says it, a different tone, different speech pattern, imitating the voice and the contempt that it had been said to him all those years ago. It makes a nasty taste in the back of my throat.

He leans in and says with the voice, "A black woman as a superhero? People aren't ready for that, Lux." His head shakes with shame and he growls. "They didn't even know she was Puerto Rican."

The frustration fades from his voice, leaving a shallow sadness. "She wasn't angry, when I told her. I thought it would be... I don't know. A fight? Tears and yelling and all that. But instead, nothing. Just, my words and her silence. She was so strong. She was Wraith, the woman of smoke and shadows." He sniffs and swallows. "I thought she was untouchable."

I'm sure there's a box of tissues somewhere, but it would be insulting if I grabbed one for him. That's not how it works. Instead, I sit back in my chair, my lips puckered, my eyes moving to the other side of the room. I take a breath in, hold it, and say, "I thought it was strange."

He turns to me, not sure of where this is going.

"The file they gave me didn't have much in it. Some pictures, some videos. They're not sure how her power works. They know she can turn into smoke, but not how she does it. I mean, they didn't even have her real name." I catch his eyes. My eyebrows bounce up a tiny bit. "It's like someone kept all that information from them."

Pressing his lips together, his chest heaves and the letter M rolls around inside his throat. A smile, a real one, peeks through the pain on his face. "When we became the Justice Brigade, I agreed to no longer see my family. I agreed to hide my real name for their sake. I told them everything they wanted to know about me. But..." His lips twitch for a moment, finding the right way to say it. "With everything good I have done, I can never forget that back then, I made the wrong choice. I saved hundreds, thousands of lives, maybe more." He takes a breath to hold back the sob, but a tear still slips through. "But to do it, I broke a heart." His lips pull down, not in anger, but in commitment. "And so, when they came and demanded I tell them everything about her... I chose her."

Not a breath, not a twitch, nothing. He waits for me, for my judgment. His story is done, told for the first time, and it's up to me, some girl he's never met before in his life, to tell him if he's a hero or a traitor.

My lips open, slowly.

And then they close. My cheeks bunch up as the smile spreads across my face, as my eyes well up with the tears that he's fighting back. I nod once, or twice, or maybe a thousand times. My nose is running. Mierda, I'm a mess. But that's okay, because he's a mess, too. And now we're doing that thing where we cry but kind of laugh at the same time. And he reaches out and takes my hand, or maybe I reach out and take his. Who knows? Who cares? What matters is that he's letting me see him cry. He's part of that machismo world where men don't let anyone see them cry, so to do it now, in front of a stranger?

When we're all done with our blubbering and he's had some terrible hospital orange juice out of one of those crappy little boxes -- I had to help him open it, his hands are still shaky. Maybe it's because he's older. Maybe it's from the blood loss. I don't care, it breaks my heart to see it -- I ask him what happened at the warehouse.

"Why?" is all he asks.

I don't tell him that there's something needling at me, at the back of my mind. I don't even really know what it is. I just...

I tell him the truth; there's not enough info. Like, I work as a 'Special Agent' for the U.S. military and federal government.

Technically.

It's totally honorific. I know it. I got in because of my abilities. Because I kicked ass on the battlefield and showed aptitude as a soldier and (I would like to think) a potential leader. True, I'm not the team lead, but no one else is going to get that position when someone like Sosuke is around.

No -- no one else is going to get that position when Sosuke is around. There's no one else like him. He's more than just a good soldier and a dangerous fighter.

Sosuke is downright terrifying.

Don't get me wrong, Lucien isn't a pretty little copo de nieve. He's frightening, but in the way a hungry, angry, junkyard dog is frightening. I wouldn't want to go one-on-one with him, but if it happened, I could probably hold my own.

Frankly, I don't know if there's anyone out there that could beat Sosuke.

But Sosuke's a soldier; as long as what's going on suits him, he's going to follow orders and take down anyone in his way. I'm not saying he's not a big picture kind of guy, he may be, but his picture isn't the same as mine. I got the title, I'm a Special Agent, and dammit, I'm going to act like one.

The file they gave us had, really, nothing. Kind of a breakdown of events, but basic info. We know who was there, what the results were. That's not good enough. They've had access to Lux and Captain Turbo. I should have a manila folder three and a half inches thick with readouts, graphs, photos, terrible hand drawn images, and maybe even a bit of damaged cloth. Like, something I could smell or whatever and then be all, 'hey, I know this scent! It's... A-B-C!' And that would lead us to something or other and this whole thing would go down without another big fight.

The manila folder I got had, no joke, three pages' worth of info. I wrote papers in eighth grade with more sources and stats.

Lux doesn't look shocked. In fact, he looks not-shocked and shakes his head, mumbling something about those idiotas estúpidos in charge. Then, he turns to me. "Have you ever fought one?"

My eyebrows come together.

"A villain."

I give the mother of all overly-confident-so-clearly-not-confident shoulder shrugs and tell him, "Oh yeah. Yeah, I... of course."

He stares.

"We've, you know, like, as a team."

Still staring.

"We've taken down at... at least... um, well, you know. Several."

His eyes get a tiny bit narrow.

I feel like I'm going to pee my pants.

"Who?" The word comes out, an easy-peasy soft pitch. But, my swing is way off.

"B-B -- Baron Bludgeon."

Strike one!

His head tilts back a bit. "Baron Bludgeon lost his legs in a terrible accident."

"Which he replaced with cyborg legs that fire rockets."

"He is also in his sixties, if not his seventies, by now."

I inform him that sixty is the new fifty. He does not seem convinced.

"Who else?" It's a curveball this time, and I am not ready for it.

"SkyFyre."

Strike two!

"SkyFyre," he says, "quit being a villain after his wife left him and took the kids." His eyes drop, his head shakes. "Oh. He was never quite the same after that."

"Well apparently he got over it."

Lux nods slowly. Leaning forward he lets loose with a slider. "Anyone else, mijita?"

I choke. "The... it..." Maldita sea. "Martian Man."

Strike. Three.

If he'd had water in his mouth, it would be coming out his nose right now. He can't even look at me, he's laughing so hard. And frankly, I can't bring myself to look at him.

"I once saw my friend Ironsides defeat Martian Man while being so drunk that he could not even get his costume over his head. He fought in his underwear and a pair of knee high socks." His laughter dies down, fast. The sudden somberness brings my eyes up. "And now, you are supposed to go and fight the beast that did this to me?" His hand makes a rolling sweep, starting at his bruised face, and floating down across his bloody, beaten, bandaged body.

I take a quick breath. "Yes." The seething anger behind my voice matches his own. He hears it, recognizes it. I'm sure, because he doesn't look away. He doesn't say, no. He just stares at me, his eyes asking the question.

Are you really going to do this?

I lean forward. "I'm taking him down, but I..." I can't say it, can't let on that there's suspicion growing in my mind. He's still Lux, the Lord of Light, member of the Justice Brigade (retired). I have to be careful, even with him. "I feel like there's something I'm missing. I need to know more."

He nods. "I understand." Running a hand across his face, he exhales long and slow. "It was strange. From the beginning, things were not right, you know?"

My chin goes up. Oh yeah, I know that feeling.

"It wasn't getting the call in the middle of the night, you get used to that. Fight supervillains long enough, mijita, and you won't sleep much at all. Goodness," he says with a roll of his eyes, and his chin, and his whole face, "even doctors get a night off once in a while!"

I give him a little smile. Quickly, he gets back on track.

"By the time I felt the carpet between my toes, the chopper was waiting on the roof. And when I went out in my robe to yell at them, I find all of my gear, my uniform, ready to go. They tell me I should get ready on the chopper. The last time they were in this much of a rush was the... the..."

"The Japan call?"

His head rocks up and down slowly. "You must understand, it had been years since something like this. I thought it must be them, the Triad, so I jumped in. But then, when I begin pressing them for answers?" It's the look on his face. Or maybe the tone of his voice. Or his body language. I don't know. But I do. I do know.

I'm not crazy. Something, something isn't right. He knows it. He knew it then, and it nearly cost him his life. And now, he's guessing that I may be as smart as him (or at least close enough) and I'm seeing it, too.

"I called the ESOA," he says, "I spoke with the pilots, checked my Justice Brigade communicator. Nothing. So as they're flying me hundreds of miles to some place that I don't know about, I reach out..." His hands spread, and suddenly there's light coming off them, wiggling little tapers, glowing, flat ribbons moving in a breeze that I can't feel. They're semi-transparent, but thick enough that I have to look real hard to see him through them.

And I do look real hard.

¡Aya madre! I feel like I'm at a concert, in the front row, for a band that I've been listening to my entire life. I want to scream and giggle. Lux, the great and amazing Lux is using his powers right in front of me. Not just a flash or a pop, but semi-solidified light particles.

Right. In. Front. Of. Me.

This is the best day of my life. Forget when Tyrell Owens (hottest, classiest, nicest, and notably most mature guy just out of my league) walked right up to me at my locker and asked me to prom. Forget the day I discovered I had powers, actual powers that were unbelievably cool, and I finally understood why I'd always felt so different from everyone else. Forget the day Lieutenant Colonel McTier pulled me into a room and told me that I was on the team.

This is it. My role model is using his powers right in front of me as though it's nothing.

It's a miracle I keep it together. Maybe I don't. Maybe Lux is just too distracted with his own story to notice me having a complete and utter freak out. Whatever.

I'm so happy right now.

The little light waves bend around, reaching out for things that I can't see or hear or feel. Lux says, "I scan all of the police radios I can find, looking for anything."

There are a lot of people with powers. Most of them never really get the hang of what they can do. Or, what they can do is so simple: lift a heavy thing. Jump high. Run fast. They use these powers (or they don't) for what they are. Fine, that's cool.

But that's weak. Because powers are... they're like... some people are talented, you know? Naturally talented. They paint or they make music or whatever. And their talent is really obvious from the outset, and so they do the thing, and they're good at the thing, and maybe people say, 'hey, they do the thing real good' and that's enough. But others, they know. They can feel it. Everything, there's more to it than just what it is. Every talent is just the beginning. And if they work hard at it, train it, push it, develop it, try to reach further than their natural talent can carry them, they discover something:

Their thing, it changes.

It wakes up.

It becomes something even bigger and better than they ever dreamed.

Most people with powers, they never reach that point. Lux did. You don't get the title Lord of Light unless you really, really are.

So, it turns out radio waves and light waves are surprisingly similar. Lux can manipulate both. One of the ribbons extending from his fingers vibrates and for a moment I hear the faint sound of music.

Then it disappears. Lux drops his hands.

"Nothing," I say for him. He doesn't even nod.

"No information being sent anywhere. No briefing from the ESOA. Names, powers, details. None of it."

I think. "Had that ever happened before?"

"Never once, mijita." His gaze drifts past me, to the other bed. "Ironsides was already there."

For a while, I'd tuned out the sounds from that side of the room, the beeping and booping, the continuous shush-shush of the breathing device. Now, those sounds creep up over my shoulders like ants marching.

"I knew. His bloodshot eyes, the smell... like a bar. Like the cigarettes and cheap whiskey he only drank when it was bad. When his pain was..." He

56

pauses. It's one thing to know of another person's pain, inside pain, the tormenting kind that drives one of the world's greatest heroes to drink himself into oblivion.

It's another to speak it aloud.

"It was his father's death," he says, pulling back that invisible curtain. "He never got over it. There were times, on our longer missions, where I would hear him. He would call for his father in his sleep. He felt so..." he shakes his head. "He was the invulnerable man."

Hiss high. Hiss low. Beep beep.

As much as Lux deserves this moment of silence to mourn his friend, I'm on a time crunch here. My bet is that McTier is going to call us in any second. So, gently as I can, I nudge him to keep going. He nods and continues.

"So there the two of us are, outside the warehouse, waiting with ESOA. Finally, Turbo arrives, flying in on his own. I am assuming that he's coming with the information we need."

"But he's in the dark, too?"

Lux nods. "Turbo asks some questions, I ask more. No one says anything good. I do not like it. I let them know I do not like it. Turbo seems game, but even he is put out by this. There is not even a senior agent around. Just the soldiers. Finally, Ironsides decides if there is not going to be any action, he wants another drink. The soldiers, they ask him to stay, tell him that this is a very, very important mission. I tell them there are too many reasons not to go into that warehouse. What if there are civilians? What if there are undercover police?

"They tell us it's not a big deal. We can handle it. Some low level superhumans, a couple of nobodies. It's the equipment that's so important. That's all. Break it up, knock 'em down, get our pictures in the paper, go home knowing that the citizens of the world can sleep better. That's all."

I wait. "And so?"

I wonder if last night he waited as long as he waits now. "We went in." His upper lip pulls toward his nostrils, as though some horrible stench had just drifted by. "It was chaos. We hit the ground and everything was wrong, wrong, wrong. Too many people, all of them with guns. And there, in the middle of the room, Brass Knuckles and --" and now that lip of his pulls up until his teeth show, "-- Bearserker."

Beneath the sheets, his hands are fists. Beneath the bed, in my lap, mine are too.

"These two," he says through a clenched jaw, "are not nobodies."

He's right. Maybe when the Justice Brigade was still in full swing, Brass

Knuckles and Bearserker were super powered thugs for hire, mostly just muscle that went out to the highest bidder. But in the last 20 years, they'd gone from C class to cream of the crop. Both were incredibly dangerous, well-trained, well-seasoned, veteran supervillains. They had their own names and their own reps. They were their own bosses.

But they weren't in the buying and selling of merch game. That wasn't their thing. Which means that someone else had sent them there, someone with enough clout or money or whatever to hold those two under their thumb.

Now I know why this thing smelled rotten; ESOA would have known that those two were there. They would have told the Justice Brigade.

Unless they were instructed not to.

I've got a crap poker face. One glance, and Lux can tell I'm stewing on something. He cuts straight to it.

"The people inside the warehouse, they didn't know we were coming. The surprise was very real."

So it wasn't a trap, but it was close enough.

"Even with surprise on our side, the criminals knew what to do. Guns came out. Brass Knuckles turned his hands to steel and charged in for Turbo. Bearserker came for me. I tried to blast him, but..." He holds out his hands, fingers spread wide, and stares with nostalgia in his eyes. "I am not so young anymore, mijita. I missed, and the beast struck me. Hard. I fell and would have been dead if not for Ironsides. He pushed back Bearserker, but was sloppy, unbalanced. Bearserker tore at him, ripped through his costume with teeth and claws. Ironsides threw some punches, but nothing came of it. His face was red. He coughed as they fought. Bearserker knocked him down and kicked him across the floor.

"By the time I was on my feet, the criminals were on me. I fought four of them at once and put them down easily. I spun and fired a beam into Bearserker. The beast stumbled. Ironsides stepped in and landed a punch. For a moment, I thought we had won. But then..."

Shadows bleed into the wrinkles in his face. "The true monster appeared."

My eyes were as big as saucers already, but they go full dinner plate when I hear that. "You must understand," he says, "we thought he was gone. Dead, killed when the volcano in Japan erupted. There was no reason why he wouldn't have died. We... we hoped. I prayed. But he was alive," said as though he had to convince me, as though he were telling some crazy ghost story. "After so many years," he says. "Araknis."

It's not a shiver that runs through me, it's a damn earthquake.

"I only saw him for an instant. He leapt down from the, the ceiling or a

58

skylight or... he landed between Ironsides and the beast. It was fast, so fast I couldn't follow at first. He moved -- mijita, he moved as though he had not aged a day. I fired a blast, as hot as the surface of the sun. It hit nothing but crates. Araknis was in the air, leaping away. Ironsides, he was confused, but the sight of Araknis woke something in him. He bellowed and gave chase.

"I was... I was too busy, distracted with Araknis, with my racing mind. Bearserker came in from the side. If he hadn't growled, I would have never..." His hands clench. "He caught me in the chest with his claws. And then again and again. Sometimes the claws, sometimes a fist or a knee. I fell. The cuts, they were deep, so deep. I wanted to cry out, but stopped when I heard his jaws snapping, smelled his breath like rotten meat as he leaned in. I raised my hand and put a flash in his eyes. He howled and moved back. I hope that hijo de puta is blind forever."

Along the wall, Lux's heart monitor beeps faster and faster. His chest pumps up and down. Across the bandages, little red spots, fresh and light in color, appear. I want to reach out and tell him to calm down, but the heat coming off him is tremendous.

"Off to the side, Ironsides chased Araknis through the warehouse, smashing everything in his way. Turbo was still fighting Brass Knuckles. There were bodies on the floor. I heard screaming, men and... and a woman. I wanted to stand, to help my friend, but there was so much blood coming from the cuts. I was tired, dizzy. I couldn't get up. I rolled over, looked for my friends. Ironsides was practically dragging himself across the floor. His face, it was red like a terrible sun burn. The veins in his neck, they stretched against his skin. He was coughing, wheezing, spit was rolling down his chin, sweat dripped from him all over. He could barely move. And that's... that's when..."

He stops. His face comes up, and I can tell that something has just occurred to him, something he's been mulling over since the warehouse.

"Do you know how spiders hunt?"

My mouth opens, but no words come out.

"When a fly gets caught in their web, they do not just run over and bite. Instead, they let the fly struggle. They let it squirm and fight, kick and move because the more it does, the more entangled it becomes. Then, when the fly has no strength left, the spider delivers its final kiss.

"When Ironsides stopped, when he fell against the crates, clutching his chest just as I was clutching mine, that is when Araknis moved in. He swung down and crawled on top as Ironsides gasped for breath. Bending down, Araknis opened his mouth over Ironsides' gaping maw. And with that terrible kiss, he filled my friend's lungs... with spiders."

59

Behind me, I hear the bed creak as a tiny tremor runs through Ironsides' body. Goosebumps prickle my skin. I can't help but think it: What if the spiders are still in there?

I could look. With my ability, I could scan for any movement inside his body. I could feel for vibrations.

I make a conscious effort not to.

Instead, I take a steadying breath and ask, "After that?"

Lux grunts. "It was... I don't remember much. I screamed when I saw the spiders. Turbo was still fighting. I began firing blasts, trying to drive Araknis away. But with the injuries, I couldn't control them. I don't know what I hit but, but at some point there was..."

"What?"

His head cocks, as though he's listening to something faint and far away. "It was a sound, like a rumble of thunder that would not end, but also high like a kettle ready to be poured. It came very fast. I don't... I thought it was in my own head, that I was passing out due to the blood loss. But even now, my ears are ringing with it."

I sit back, a tiny frown on my face.

"And it grew, from nothing to huge, to --"

"The explosion?"

He nods.

Another person with powers? If so, why didn't they join in right away? Why did they wait until all those people died? That didn't make sense. Maybe it was some kind of weapon? Maybe it was -- I still hesitate to even think the name -- maybe it was Araknis.

But that's not his style.

One more weird thing on a pile of strangeness.

The communicator attached to my belt begins to buzz and chime. I don't need to answer it, I know what's happening. It's time for me to move out, with more information than I had before, and twice as many unanswered questions.

I stand slowly. I feel wiped out. Running the gamut of all possible human emotions will do that to you, I guess. I have to tighten up my lower back and my hamstrings for a minute. My knees kind of burn, but in that good way.

Lux asks, "What is it, exactly, you are expected to do?"

To pick up where the Justice Brigade left off, I tell him as I stretch my arms, flex my shoulders. Find Brass Knuckles and Bearserker, take them into custody.

"Is that all?"

I tilt my head slightly.

His eyes jump to Ironsides. "You are not going after him? Araknis?"

I lick my lips. I tell him that's not the plan, not right now anyway. Bearserker and Brass Knuckles may lead us there, but we're not counting on it.

"And if they do lead you there, what then?"

I stop. Partly because I don't want to say. Partly because... well, there's something about this. He's not just asking casually. He's... probing.

I tell him we have our orders.

"To apprehend him?"

I stare at him. He thinks I know an answer that I don't. Wait, what am I missing here?

"Are you prepared to face the likes of him?"

I tell him that we, the new team, we weren't chosen at random. We all have our advantages. I got to where I was by being smart, being tactical. I spent a lot of time studying other distance fighters, I tell him with a smile and a wink.

It brings a grin to his face.

I tell him we were picked because of what we could do, because of how we fought. We were chosen because there was always a chance.

"That the Triad would return," he says, his lips pulled tight.

I nod. And if they did, there would be someone who could handle them. Someone who was trained specifically to deal with them.

His face shifts. I hate seeing distrust from him. "Araknis," he asks, "is he yours?"

I don't want to say, because when I do, the next question will be even harder. "No. Araknis isn't mine."

The words press so hard against the inside of his mouth, his jaw sticks out. "Which one is?"

I try to reply, but nothing comes out.

He says, "I see," and looks away.

I'm feet away from him, but feel like there's a canyon between us. All we have to listen to is the hiss and beep of Ironsides's breathing. My boots squeak. As I round the foot of Ironsides's bed, I stare. He's there, in his bed, alone. If I hadn't walked in, Lux would be the same way; no one coming to visit, no one wishing him well, no one holding his hand. They gave all that away. They left behind their lives and their families. They'd lived as though they were alone in the world.

But in truth, they weren't.

"Lo siento," I say, "por lo que pasó. We're going to find him and we're going to stop him, lo prometto."

Lux doesn't respond.

"I was feeling lost before, unsure. But what you shared with me means a lot. So much. Gracias por todo que has hecho y dicho por mí... Tío Pedro."

Two steps from when I hit the door, he roars, "Señorita," in the same voice that mi abuelo, Lux's papá, would use when I ran out of the house to cause mischief, "you get back here right now!"

I can't help but smile.

I hate the phrase 'we have a problem.'

It's usually the last thing you hear before some jerk comes bursting through the wall of your underground lair, while wearing a cape. Or a winged helmet. Or a jet pack.

Lord, I hate jet packs. They're such a desperate cry for attention. If you're going to fly, do it without something that threatens to set your butt on fire.

... We have a problem...

It means your big plan... remote control cyborg killer whales taking the U.S. Navy hostage; miniature black hole slowly drawing the Earth out of orbit; army of parasitic microbes which drive people to believe that they're actually Labrador retrievers... has begun the inevitable spiral of failure. It is a phrase I tried in all my years of villainy to never utter. When I stood at the balcony of a floating castle, firing bolts from my lightning glove at Manhattan Island while Justice Brigade jet rocketed toward me, I still kept those words from passing over my lips.

Ugh. How embarrassing was that? It took me a year to even think about dominating the world after that defeat. Lightning glove. How gauche.

It's usually a henchman monitoring the security cameras. They see the hero jetting through the hallways, unharmed by the acid sprays and electro-nets, and they turn and say those four words which no supervillain can stand.

We have a problem.

I heard Chaos King actually took to killing anyone who dared to say that phrase. His henchmen had to constantly come up with different ways of saying it. He wasn't very good at the whole villain thing. Great costume, though.

I was fortunate. I never heard it because I worked alone. My vision was too single-minded. An army of henchmen never appealed to me. In order to be effective, henchmen must be properly motivated. In order to be motivated, they have to believe in your cause. And my cause... well...

It was complicated.

After my encounter with the masked man at the university, I worried that the bands may be moved from the university. But Jayaramen would not be so foolish. The instruments, tools, and machines I had used to create the bands were custom built. In fact, I had to invent whole new technologies just to invent the bands. Everything in that room was valuable, and Jayaramen didn't have a clue as to what they were or how they worked. He wouldn't risk breaking anything, at least not for a short period. I had time, but it was limited.

My timeline grew infinitely shorter when I saw the headline on the local paper in the morning.

DARING MIDNIGHT ROBBERY FOILED BY MASKED MAN!

... We have a problem...

I was too scared to leave my apartment that day. I sat there, waiting for the police to arrive. I packed a suitcase in case they did come. It was stupid. The police don't let you take a suitcase. Clearly, I was still in a state of shock.

When my door wasn't broken down and no one dragged me away in handcuffs, I dared venture outside. I crept to the university campus and claimed a park bench. With the local paper held in front of me, I listened. The students and professors were abuzz. A masked man. A cat burglar. The facts were, well, muddled. Some had the masked man as the hero, others thought him the villain. In one version, the burglar was after nothing more than money. In another, they were after plutonium to build a nuclear weapon. With each re-telling I would hold my breath, waiting to hear someone, anyone, say the one thing which would mean the end for me.

My name.

And yet, no one did.

Hope landed on my soul, light as a snowflake. If no one knew it was me, I could go back and try again. I could slip in and out. There was no chance that costumed rhino would be there a second time.

Heading across campus, my sight became narrowed, as though I were wearing blinders. Passing by the science buildings, I noted they had increased security. The two inept mongrels who had turned me away the day before were now in charge of two more guards. Students were being stopped before entering. Bags were being checked. I couldn't go in to confirm it, but I had to assume the locks had all been changed.

Things had gotten difficult. But that was okay, I liked difficult. I excelled at difficult. This was simply another puzzle, and I was the best at puzzles. My mind buzzed. I ran over the events from the night before, the mistakes I'd made, the factors I hadn't accounted for. Every one of them could easily be overcome with a little ingenuity. Even that costumed lummox could be stopped. When a force is met with an equal force, the two cancel each other out.

As I walked into the hardware shop just outside of campus, a smile spread across my face. Looking at the raw materials from which I could create anything, I felt a little thrill inside.

I would show them all -- Jayaramen, the professors, the students...

Even the hero.
Mind over matter.

The second break-in went considerably smoother. No teetering stacks of trashcans and crates, no drunken underclassmen. The compressed-air grappling gun fired without a problem. The aim was a little off and it took me three tries, but the hook... made from quickly welded iron pot hangers... eventually caught. The climbing-assistance device I'd devised worked wonderfully, taking the majority of my weight, cinching the rope as I climbed, and allowing me to basically walk up the side of the building to a window I knew would be unlocked. The guards, all gathered in the front of the building, had no idea I was even there. Everything was going perfectly.

Until I made it in.

The lab, my chapel, temple, sacred room that was an extension of my deepest urges and desires, was in disarray. The gauges and machines I had built were pulled away from the walls, panels popped open, wiring exposed. Parts and pieces were scattered everywhere. My blackboard of equations and calculations had been wiped clean. But all these things were inconsequential. None of them were what I needed.

Across the room, the cabinet where the gravity bands and all my notebooks were kept sat, undisturbed. I made a mad dash toward it, but unfortunately forgot that I was still connected to the rope hanging outside the window. It wasn't a complete face plant, but it was as close as anyone would want to come.

Grunting and growling and swearing under my breath... and a little bit over my breath... I rolled onto my back and wrestled viciously with the climbing device. My hands were sweating as I snatched at the rope release trigger and squeezed down as hard as I could. My entire body tightened. My eyes pinched shut in anger and frustration. Suddenly, there was a loud thump.

But it should have been a click.

And then another thump, on the other side of my head.

I opened my eyes and turned. There, glistening like black ice in the moonlight, was a jackboot.

"Oh hell," I said.

Gloved hands jerked me up with a force that was beyond human. My toes touched down and we were face to face. Or really...

Face to masked face.

"Well, well, well," he said with a big, toothy grin, "look what we have he -- "

I assume he meant to say 'here', but the word was cut short as he tried to spin me around and throw me against the wall, only to have the rope attached to my waist jerk us both to a stop. I winched and gasped as the entire climbing apparatus both tightened against my back, and dug into my crotch.

The masked man looked down at the rope. He let it go slack for a moment, then jerked me toward the wall again. I barked at the pain. He frowned, said, "Um," and gave it another try. I practically howled.

"Could you -- " My teeth clenched. "Do you mind?"

His cold, blue eyes came back to me. Without a word, he let go with one hand, snatched at the buckle, and tore it off as easily as if it were a Band-Aid. The immediate release of pressure around my groin brought a relieved sigh through my lips.

"Oh, that's so much better."

Tossing the rope back out the window, he cleared his throat and turned back to me. "Well, well. What have we --"

My knee caught him squarely in the crotch. It wasn't a light tap, either. I really swung as hard as I could. It barely phased him, but it must have caught him off guard because he took a step back. Taking advantage of him being off balance, I kicked him in the chest as hard as I could. It sent him stumbling back and I broke free, which meant I ended up crashing to the floor again, but at least this time I was expecting it.

I rolled, scampered around, and managed to get a table between us. I came up in a crouch. Between my panting breaths, I heard his deep throated chuckle.

"You just don't give up, do you?"

I didn't reply, mostly because I hadn't had any experience with repartee yet. Also, my mind was too busy coming up with a plan. The cabinet was across the room. The masked man stood between me and it. Well, really, the masked man, several tables, some chairs, and all the pieces of equipment atop them. The door was closer to the cabinet, the window was closer to me.

I began moving puzzle pieces in my mind.

Standing up straight, he asked, "What are you doing here?"

"I..." my eyes jumped over his shoulder, to the cabinet. "I came for what's mine."

He glanced where I had, then to me. "Those don't belong to you." His voice was deep, serious. His body shifted, building up to burst forward. My hands, shaking more than a little bit, moved to the small of my back. "And you're not getting them."

My fingers slipped into the small leather pouch I'd attached to my belt.

"Try and stop me."

It was a blink, a flap of my eyelids and he was across the table, vaulting through the air. I pulled back. His hand clamp down on my left arm. I swung with my right. The homemade smoke bomb burst, sending a cloud of four kinds of pepper into his eyes, nose, and mouth. He let me go, and I darted. Inside my head, the map I had created of the room spun like the needle on a compass. My hip whizzed, inches from a desk. My hand caught the side of a table and pushed off, driving me towards the cabinet. My last obstacle, a rolling chair, collided with my leg but spun away. The cabinet was there and I reached out for it. I was victorious.

Until the bastard threw a table at me.

It missed, narrowly, and smashed the tile floor before crashing into a wall. I screamed and threw myself up against a closet. The table, or what was left of its heavy metal frame and thick wooden top, collapsed to the floor. I stared at it a moment, and then back to the man who had just thrown it like a plastic lawn chair.

His mask was wet with tears. There was a river of snot coming from his nose. Every breath he took resulted in a cough or gag. His eyes, red and watery, were open, but I knew his vision was blurry. Honestly, I wasn't positive if he'd missed me on purpose or not.

"Hey!" Cough, cough, snot bubble. "I told -- " Gag, cough. Spit. "I told you." A deep breath. Back muscles straightening. An arm went up and wiped his face. "You're not... getting them."

As he glared at me, I looked around. The cabinet with was less than ten paces away. The masked man was a little further, and to the right. To my left, along the wall, the door to the hallway. I considered the possibilities, weighed the options, tried to figure it out.

Solve the puzzle.

Run.

It was the best option. He was still having trouble breathing. I could make it to the door. Even if he got his hands on me, I could wiggle away. Get out. Get away. Run. Never come back. Escape and... and...

And it hit me. A heat. A flame, deep inside that had been burning for so long. It snapped and popped and roared to life, fueled with rage that I would even consider giving up.

No. There was only one choice. The things I needed to complete myself, to be fulfilled, to quell the soaring flames lighting up my mind and being were in that cabinet, and I was leaving with them.

The masked man saw the change in me and, in that moment, he took the tiniest step back. Unzipping my jacket, I yanked it off, exposing the crisscrossed straps over my torso and the multiple pouches attached to my belt. I dropped the jacket and fell into a stance that could be clearly read by anyone.

Let's go.

His reaction was instant. The table and chair which I had dodged moments ago careened off his body as he charged. They weren't able to stop him, but they slowed him enough that I figured out what he was planning. The haymaker punch he threw missed by inches when I leaned. He threw the other hand and I ducked. His knuckles tore through the closet door behind me. I tried to slip under his arm, put some distance between us, but he must have sensed my movement. His hand came down, not in a strike, thankfully, but grabbed the back of my shirt and tossed me into the broken closet door. It knocked most of the air from my lungs, and before I could refill them, his arms were against my chest.

He pushed me straight through the closet door. The tiny space confined me. I felt his breath on my face, smelled the pepper and sweat and tears.

"Alright," he snarled, "that's enough of -- "

My hands smacked two buttons on my belt. The air thundered as a thousand volts of electricity poured into the straps on my body. Thanks to the rubber wetsuit I was wearing beneath my clothes, the electricity had only one place to go.

With a tremendous crack, the masked man rocketed back through the room, shattering a chair along the way. My eyes spun from the flash and I was surrounded by the scent of ozone. Steam erupted from the straps and smoke from the remnants of my shirt. Hands shaking, I pulled myself free of the closet. My head was spinning. At first, I thought the ringing in my ears was from the electrical crack, but it was the building's fire alarm. I tried to take a deep breath and made it one step toward the cabinet. Across the room, I heard a groan. The masked man was under a countertop, which he had left a masked-man-sized hole in. He was starting to roll around. I had to hurry.

I managed two more steps.

There was noise out in the hallway. Flashlights whipped around. People. People were coming.

Three more steps. Four more. Almost there.

The lights outside grew brighter. I clenched my fists and threw myself against the cabinet. I smiled from ear to ear. Leaning back, I grabbed the handles and pulled the doors open.

Nothing.

There was nothing inside.

A shelf, some random papers, bits and pieces of wiring.

"What?" the word was barely a whisper. "How..."

The room's door burst open.

I turned just long enough to see a white lab coat. Student, post-doc, professor, it didn't matter; if it was anyone that could recognize me, I would be ruined. Spinning, I threw a smoke bomb and ran for the window. I could hear them coughing, calling something that I couldn't make out over the alarm.

The world flew beneath me as I jumped out the window. For one moment, I thought I would forget to grab the rope and plummet down. Fortunately, survival instinct is a powerful stimulant. I clung wildly, swinging back and forth. The rope sliced at my hands as I thrashed, trying to get my feet around it as I had been taught in gym class so many years ago.

When I finally got some control, I checked back into the lab. The person inside was running toward me. Squeezing the rope with one hand, I grabbed and threw another smoke bomb through the window.

As I slid down the rope, my singed shirt reeking of burnt cotton, my muscles screaming in agony from the spent adrenaline, my heart feeling oddly cold and lifeless, I heard one of the voices of one of the dozens of simpletons I had lectured calling out from the window above me.

"Doc --" he sputtered and shouted through his coughs. "Doc -- Endwright -- Doc... D-D-D-Endwright..."

CHAPTER EIGHT
THE LAST JOB

It's a bad idea for Annie to come along, but I don't really have a choice in the matter. She just sort of met me in the hall and jumped in my car. It's stupid, it's putting her in danger, and it's a selfish, dick move.

But I really need a friend right now. So, sorry. Yeah. I suck. I know.

We're tearing ass through Boston in my BMW Z4 M Roadster. Annie just rocks and sways with the car. Most people hate the way I drive. They grip the inside of the door, the edge of their seat. They take sharp little breaths when I snap around corners. And no, I don't drive like a douche. Hell to that. I don't tailgate or flash my highs or cut other people off and then give them the finger. Dude-bros do that.

When I got my license, my Uncle Danny got me professional driving lessons. He said it was important that I be in total control of my vehicle. Once I started driving, I totally got it. I focus on knowing exactly how big my car is, how it moves, how can it accelerate and how well the brakes work. It's common goddamn decency, being aware of yourself in space. Ass-hat guys don't get that. It's the same thing that makes me a solid hacker: take up as little room as possible, move through passageways without disturbing the things around you, get where you need to be without disturbing the flow of the world and no one will even remember you being there.

So it surprises me that Annie is so calm. I'm talking as I drive, going over the plan. She's taking it all in. Weird, I've never really seen her like this. I mean, we've had classes together. She's studious as shit, model student and all that. Takes notes, focuses, blah, blah. But there's something different now. She's in commando mode or something. I worry that she's starting to freak out a little. Maybe this is too much for her.

I tell her that I need access to everything. The computer that manages the security system is in a room off the main hallway. I've seen it, poked in, snatched a few things out of there. Campus security is kind of a joke. I mean, usually the worst they have to deal with is students smoking pot in the bathrooms. I heard that fifty years ago, some guy lost his mind and started screaming about how he would get his revenge or something. Not much since then.

Anyway, the computer room's not the room I want. I want access to the little closet of a room next door. That's where the memory banks are jammed in. I'm going to hack straight into the security system, but I'm not erasing myself from the night before. Wouldn't do me any good. They'd see me walking around on the video cameras, and if I delete that footage, then they're really going to get suspicious. Instead, I'm going to create a fake series of entries. It'll look like I walked in, went to my lab, walked around the building a bit, went home.

At the same time, I'm going to make it so that Parker was the one who went into the lab and robbed the place. Since I stayed away and played lookout, they'll only have one person wearing a hoodie skulking through the halls on any security footage.

So Annie's job will be to keep watch, distract anyone who comes down the hall, give me the all clear when I'm done, and that's it.

Easy. Peasey.

She nods, says, "Okay," and stays in her super tense mode. I'm really starting to think this is a bad idea, and when we go to pull into the parking lot, I officially know it's a bad idea.

"Balls," I whisper.

There's big-ass black trucks all over the place. We have to park way further out than normal. In one sweep of the courtyard I see ESOA and ARMY stamped on a dozen bulletproof vests worn by people with very short haircuts and very big guns.

This is so beyond stupid. I was hoping there'd be some extra security, maybe local police or something. ESOA must have a field station near Boston or something. Shit-sticks! There's no way we can get through this.

I'm busy leaning forward over the wheel, gaping like an idiot, and don't notice Annie staring at me. When I do, I pull back a little.

She's not scared. Or nervous. Like, at all.

"Are you ready?" she asks.

Damn girl, when did you get guts of steel?

"I --" Outside the car, I hear walkie-talkies chirping, radio voices speaking. But they're not close by. I feel like I shouldn't be hearing that. "We can't," I say. "There's no way they'll let us in."

Annie looks around quickly. So do I. A few of the soldiers or agents or officers or whatever they are have noticed we're sitting here. If we don't do something soon, they're going to come over.

Bringing her gaze back to me, Annie says, "It's this, or go on the run. You know that's not gonna work. They're not gonna stop." She leans forward. "The worst that happens is you get caught. The best is you get away with it."

"No," I say, the thought of waterboarding coming back to mind, "the worst that happens is you get caught."

She smiles at that, a big, stupid, goofy smile like she just got asked to the prom by her secret crush. "We're worrying about you right now. I can take care of myself."

"Annie," I say, but I don't get to tell her how we're turning around and heading back, because she opens the door and steps out before I can. I call her name, hiss it through clenched teeth, but she's gone, around the back of the car, headed towards the building like she doesn't have a care in the world.

Shit.

Shit, shit, shit.

Scrambling, I grab the bag with my computer and cables and other gear in it and jog through the parking lot to catch up with her. There are people freaking everywhere. My heart is pounding just walking. I can't stop looking at them, and they're totally noticing. Jesus, stop. Stop! Just, just look forward or down or, or --

I feel Annie's hand brush mine. Just a little, our knuckles bouncing against each other, sliding like the teeth of human gears trying to lock in. I look at her, her little bouncing bangs, her cheeks rosy from the cold air. She's just walking, nothing else.

Come on. I've been in tense situations before. I've broken into places. I'm supposed to be the criminal mastermind here, the seasoned goddamn professional. It's the shock, and the exhaustion, and the everything building up. I can't get my head straight. But I have to, because if I don't, Annie's in trouble too.

I take a deep breath and put on my game face.

And when we get to the front door, I'm almost kind of slightly ready. There's two of them, big dudes, big guns, no smiles. They see us coming and I just about fall to shit. I don't know what to do or say. My hands clutch my bag. I try to breathe, but my lungs are just not having any of that and we are totally, totally screwed.

Except, Annie's there. Like, old Annie, bubbly and smiley Annie.

"Hi," she says, all big and bright. The guys nod, and something about that exchange seems so natural, I just kind of start talking.

"Hey!" I say way, way, way too enthusiastic. The guys... do not nod. "Is there, um, something going on?"

From the corner of my eye, I see Annie turn a shade of green golf course grass would be jealous of.

The guys adjust their guns. "Can we help you?" one says in a tone that says he's really not going to help us.

"I just, I mean, we, we just need to, you know, get inside so we can --"

"Building is off limits," says the other guy. Or maybe it was still the first guy. I dunno. I'm so damn shaky right now, nothing's really registering.

"Oh, but, you see, I really, really need to get in there."

"Sorry," says one of them, who is, in reality, totally not sorry.

Annie huffs through her nose. She's got that weird tense look about her. Crap crapitty-crap, I knew bringing her was a bad idea. But we're here and this is going down and if I don't do something fast, Annie may go all kickboxing class on these guys and we'll both end up in jail.

A breath shoots into my lungs and, when it comes out, it's somehow changed into the best imitation of my mom's voice it can be. "Listen, guys, I know you've been told not to let anybody in, okay? But here's the deal, I'm covering for a very important project --"

"Ma'am --"

"-- in one of the military funded facilities." The word military catches their attention. It's also a total lie. There aren't any labs like that. "We're working on something that's... well, I don't wanna say it's dangerous, but you know bad tear gas hurts?"

They both nod.

"Imagine that... in your balls."

Their legs both get a little closer together.

"Yeah, right? So, there's a two hundred pound tank of that stuff slowly pressurizing in the lab, and if I don't get in there to recalibrate the regulator on it, it's gonna start to leak out. Fast. And this stuff, no smell, no color, it's super-duper secret. And the effect?"

They're hanging on every word.

"Lasts for days. Now, the way I see it, that leak happens, I spend the next three days standing next to you in a hospital bed asking where the pain is on a scale of one to oh-god-please-kill-me. Or, you let us in real quick, I stop it from happening, and the Department of Defense doesn't want to know who screwed up their multi-million dollar weapons development program." I shrug. "Up to you."

A minute later, we're inside, taking the elevator upstairs. I'm running on a crazy adrenaline high from the encounter, but not enough to ignore the fact that this is the same elevator Parker and I took last night.

Stop it. Focus. Cry later.

We go to the lab where Annie works (to make sure things look legit) and then head for the staircase. As we creep down to the lower floors, I ask her, "You Cool?"

"10-4," she replies, with a voice I can only assume was meant to sound tough.

"What?" I try and stifle my laugh.

"Oh, I thought we were doing spy stuff now, after that performance out there."

I grin. "Nah, that was nothing."

"Seemed pretty real."

"What does that mean?"

"Nothing."

"Okay," I say, way too sharp. "Well clearly it means something."

"You just... you lied really easily out there."

"I kind of had to."

"I know," she says, but not nasty. "Sometimes we have to."

"Like you ever lie."

She doesn't say anything at first. We reach other landing and as we creep by the door, she whispers, "Candace, I haven't been completely --"

A walkie-talkie beeps. She throws herself against the wall and slaps her arm against me, like you do when you stop a car short and don't want the passenger to go flying.

Her hand accidentally lands on my breast.

The sound of booted feet comes from under the door, then fades slowly. We stand completely still until it's silent.

"Um," I whisper, licking my lips, "Annie?"

She keeps looking at the door. "Yeah?"

"Your hand?" I wait for her to look at me. It takes her a second, and a slight downward nod of my head for her to figure it out.

And I thought her eyes were wide before.

We manage to make it to the main floor without any more incidents of nearly being caught or accidental groping. We walk the halls, playing it cool, acting like we're supposed to be there. The security closet is just one more turn away, and everything is going perfectly.

Until I hear the laughter.

Dudely laughter, coming from around the corner.

I don't get a good look before I jump back, but there had to be at least four, maybe five. Not that it really matters. One would be one too many.

Shit-sticks.

We plaster ourselves against the wall. That was close, really super close. Too close. My heart is slamming against my ribs.

Annie's hand touches my shoulder. I don't look at her. She leans in and whispers, "How many?"

Shit-crap-piss-balls! We did this, made it this far, and now we're all jammed up. There's no way we can clear this hall without something like a fire alarm, which is just going to bring in more people. Goddamn it! I knew it. I knew I shouldn't have... oh man. Annie. She's a part of this, now. What was I thinking?

"Hey," Annie jabs me in the ribs. "How many?"

"I..."

We should go. We should sneak back up to her lab, take the elevator down and walk out. We'll go out to lunch. I'll buy. Burgers maybe. No, wait, what can't you get in prison? Something French. Or sushi. Fresh sushi. That'll do. Then we'll go back to the house, put on some terrible, over the top, totally inappropriate comedy, stuff ourselves with popcorn and beer, and laugh our asses off. If they're not busting down the front door by morning, I'll jump on a plane to wherever I can get, Annie will keep her mouth shut, and everything will be okay.

For her, anyway.

"Hey," she says forcefully.

"I don't know." My eyes are closed. I lean my head back against the wall. Up until now, I'd been running on adrenaline, riding the rush I get when I'm in full-on illegal activities mode. But now that we've stopped, now that there's something like this ahead of me, shit, I'm just tired. Exhausted, you know? I want to lie down and go to sleep and just pretend that none of the crap that's happened in the last twelve hours is real.

Next to me, Annie gives an exasperated huff. She slips around me and gets right up against the edge of the corner. I start to reach out, to pull her away before she gets seen, but she shrugs me off and pulls out her cellphone. She turns on her front facing camera and leans the lens just around the corner.

Five. Three dudes, two women.

Annie puts the phone away. Her lips are pursed and pressed up against the bottom of her nose. Her giant eyes are darting around as she thinks. I'm about to tell her about my plan involving going to jail when she looks at me. "How much time do you need?"

What is this, Mission Impossible? I shake my head. She just stares. I wait, she waits, we wait. Someone down the hall chuckles and we hear movement. Annie never stops looking.

"Fine," I say, giving up a fight I wasn't going to win anyway. "First, I gotta pick the lock. Then --"

"Door's already open. How long for --"

"How do you know?"

"I saw it, on the phone."

I don't remember seeing that.

"There were two doors, close together. "She says it like it was obvious. "I could see light coming through the frames of both."

That's more than just observant, that's... I start to wonder how well I know this girl.

"So," she says, almost a little impatient. "How long?"

What's she going to do, run in there and kung-fu fight all five of them? I've seen this girl get upset over a squirrel run over in the road. But the look on her face. She's...intense.

I decide to call her bluff. "Five minutes."

"Five?"

"From when I plug my computer into the servers to when everything is back in my bag."

She nods, puts her back against the wall, and thinks. Just when I'm sure she's going to say, to hell with it, she takes a sharp breathe. "Follow my lead," she says.

Then she screams.

Full-on horror movie, running-from-the-guy-with-a-chainsaw-wearing-the-skin-of-your-boyfriend-like-a-mask, kind of scream.

Now, I would like to note that my scream is actually genuine... because what the shit? She scared the hell outta me! Why is she screaming? And then, then she's off and running around the corner -- still screaming -- and so then I'm running around the corner.

Still screaming.

Annie races down the hall, waving her arms like a lunatic and screaming. Frankly, if one of the soldiers popped her right now, I think they'd be justified. Thankfully, they've just got their guns at the ready and have decided, for now, to not turn us into Swiss cheese.

"Ohmigawd!" Annie shouts. "Ohmigawd! Ohmigawd!"

The soldiers all start heading for us. The guy at the front of the pack says, "What's wrong?"

"There --" Annie gasps, and pants, and shakes her hands like a soap opera star. "There was, there was..."

"Calm down," the leader dude says. "What happened?"

It's amazing. They're not even asking why we're in this hallway. Props to Annie. "A -- a man." Annie says. "He's wearing...umm...you know...like...spandex and..."

On the word 'spandex', the soldiers go from concerned to worried. Hands grip guns, trigger fingers get twitchy, heads snap in every direction. The lead guy, Mr. Alpha Male, gives Annie a 'go on' nod.

"We -- we were up -- upstairs getting my -- my laptop and when -- when we went into the, the, the..." Annie takes a huge breath and waves her hands in circles. "When we went into the hall, there was this guy, you know?"

"The guy in spandex?"

"Yeah." Annie says. "It was all blue, but it had a lightning bolt or

76

something on it." She looks at me, clearly wanting something.

Oh shit.

What do I do? Is this -- do I say something? Do I agree? Do I disagree? Do I add something? He had, um... crap, what do supervillains have? Wings? No, that's... that's stupid. Why would he have a lightning bolt and wings? A jet pack. He had a, a, a sword? A flaming, lightning sword and... I...

Oh screw it. She's got this one covered. I'm just going to nod a lot. I drop in a, "Yeah!" for good measure. That seems like enough, because Alpha Male looks at his team and they all get that furrowed brow, we're-dealing-with-something-serious, look.

Annie continues. "So when we saw him, he looked at us and then he pulled out some kinda weird thing that kinda looked like a gun, you know? But it was all lighty and blinky and it made this weird noise and I think it was a laser blaster and so we just turned and we ran as fast as we could and I'm pretty sure he chased us down the hallway but we got to the stairs and --"

How the hell is she not taking a breath?

"Okay," Alpha Male says. But Annie just keeps going. And now she's starting to tear up. Actual tears. Maybe it's because she's completely run out of oxygen at this point.

"-- I heard him chasing us but then he stopped and --"

"Okay,"

"-- I think he must have gone back upstairs or back to the lab or something because we made it down here and I really thought we were going to die, you know? It was, it was, it was --"

"Okay!" Alpha Male doesn't bark it at her, but instead puts a hand on her arm, a strong, comforting hand. "You're okay." He says. Aww. That's actually kind of nice. But I want him to stop touching her. "You're safe. I promise. No one is going to hurt you."

Annie sniffles and wipes her cheek and looks up at him and nods and oh my god she is totally milking this and it's amaze-a-balls to watch.

"Now," Alpha Male says slowly, "what floor? Where did you see him?"

"Ninth." Annie says with a little gasp. "Ninth floor, near the one of the labs in the east wing."

Smart. We're on the west side of the building.

"Which one?" Alpha asks.

"I don't..." she shakes her head. "I don't remember. It all happened so fast. I..." She turns to me really quick and gives me a look that says, 'here we go'. "We can show you," she's suddenly a little more resolved. "We can take you up there and show you."

Alpha Male isn't buying it. He pulls back, looks at his team. They're hesitant. Annie sees it, too. She steps in, weirdly determined.

"The ninth floor has a dozen labs. I know which one I just... I just need to get up there and we can show you." She stares up into his eyes.

Come on. Come on! Just buy in. Don't break, Annie. Don't look away. You got him. He's so close, so close. He just needs...

"You have to!" The words just jump out of my mouth. Everyone -- Alpha, the team, Annie -- they all swing their heads over and stare at me. I freeze for one second. Annie looks like she's ready to punch me in the face. Okay. Okay, just, just... "This guy, he's, he's..." oh crap what am I doing, what do I say, he's what? "He's dangerous. I, I know it. He had, like, like, a laser gun and, and he... he was totally going to kill us but we got away and he's going to hurt people and you," I point at Alpha, "you're the only one who can stop him."

Everything just hangs there. Silence. A big, huge silence comes smashing down and I am nine hundred percent sure that I just totally blew up Annie's game. Oh shit-sticks, why did I open my stupid --

"Okay," Alpha says, nodding at me. Then at Annie. "Okay, you two lead us."

Yes! Inside, I do a cheerleader jump and wave my arms. It's gotta be inside, because that would totally tip these guys off that we're faking it. Also, I would never do that on the outside. Screw pep.

The team hikes up their guns and starts getting shit ready. Alpha turns to them. "We're heading up! I want one person on every other floor as we go. Call in, shut down the elevators." He turns back to Annie and me. "You stay with us. No wandering. When we get to the ninth floor, you figure out where he went, and then you're getting escorted back down. Got it?"

Annie says, "Sure," about six times in one and a half seconds. She's nodding and making her face all serious. But when she turns to me, she flashes a, 'yay!' kinda grin. I try not to smile back.

The whole unit, with Annie leading the way, starts down the hallway. I follow along for about ten steps, but make sure to slip behind them all. Alpha Male calls into his walkie-talkie, letting ninth floor know there's been a sighting and they're on their way up. As they head around the corner, I just calmly change direction.

This shit could not get any better. Annie was right about the doors being open, both the main security room and the server room. On top of that, there was an extra walkie-talkie on the desk. A quick scan of the channels and I'm tuned into everything that's happening.

My laptop is connected directly into the server units and is auto-hacking through the firewalls. It's a program I designed, so I don't feel too bad about not having to do any of the actual work. This is how I got in the first time, and the second, and every time after that. Uncle Danny helped me design it. Dude is lit when it comes to this stuff. He'd show me something, then have me repeat, then ask me to make it better. When I did, he'd lean in and bump his head against mine, then say something about how giving me everything he had. We'd laugh and keep working.

I kind of wish he was here right now. There is some crazy security in here. Like, a shit-ton of IDS (Intrusion Detection System) and IPS (Intrusion Prevention System) gateways I have to get through. Not to mention just about everything in here is encrypted. If I really want to cover all my bases, I'm going to have to dig down to the damn binary and rewrite it.

And I've only got four minutes left.

Alpha Male's voice comes over the walkie. "Alpha unit to all units,"

I snicker. Alpha unit. Of course.

"Ninth floor lab, east wing is clear. No sign of disturbance. Continuing search for suspect. Seventh floor, what's your status?"

I'm almost down to the basic programming. I've got to be careful, move with the system. If I do anything too hack-and-slashy, it's going to be easy to find.

A woman's voice comes over through the speaker. "Seventh floor, clear."

"Eighth floor, what is your status?"

"Eighth floor, no unusual activity here."

"Alpha unit to fifth floor. Have you had any sign of intruder or intruders?"

"Negative, Alpha unit." Fifth floor's a real southern gal. "The only noise I heard was y'all running up those stairs."

Judas Priest, this system is stubborn! I mean, sure, it should be. It's a security system. But come on! I've hacked banks faster than this. My program isn't going to do it, so I pick up the laptop and start working manually. It's not going to be as clean, but it's going to be faster.

"Alpha unit to all floors, continue searching but hold to your assigned area. Civilian has informed me we may be in the wrong section of the ninth floor."

It begins to dawn on me, the reason this door was open is that someone probably came in and added extra security.

Shit. Three and a half minutes.

My pits start to sweat.

"We're going to start a sweep of the west wing and -- hey."

My fingers stop.

"Where..." His voice goes all distant, like he's leaning away from the mic. "Where's your friend?"

Uh-oh.

I hear Annie, even further from the mic. "What?"

"Where's your friend?" Alpha doesn't sound happy.

"She's right... Sarah?"

Who the hell is -- oh, yeah, fake name. Damn, Annie is good. A little too good. In the back of my head, I ask that question again. How well do I really know her?

Alpha says, "Did anyone see where she went?"

"She was right here," Annie says, in the best fake hysteria I've ever heard. "Sarah?"

Alpha says, "Ma'am," but Annie starts screaming.

"Sarah! Sarah, where are you?"

"Stay calm, ma'am,"

"Sarah, answer me!"

Alpha swears through tight lips, but I still manage to hear him. A second later, he's back at the mic with his big dog voice. "All units! All units! We have a missing civilian, last seen en route to the ninth floor."

In the background I hear Annie screaming Sarah's name. Wow, that Sarah chick is lucky to have such a good friend. I smile a little to myself and go back to the computer. Just a few more layers to go.

"Alpha unit is staying with second civilian on ninth floor. All units, disperse to surrounding floors. Eighth floor, send three agents up to ninth floor and begin searching the labs here. Missing Civilian may be lost, but may have been taken hostage by intruder. Proceed with caution. Civilian goes by Sarah."

Annie's a freaking genius. They're going to be busy hitting up every room they can get into. Things are looking good.

"First floor," Alpha Male says, "check the hallway near the security closet. It's possible the missing civilian went back there."

Things are not looking good. Because why would they? Really? Can I ever just catch a goddamn break? Just one? Ugh...

My eyes race over the screen. I'm not done, not even close. But I'm also too far down in the program to just stop. If I pull the cable, there's going to be a mile-wide blazing trail that someone was here. I'm stuck, hitched into the system and there's no way I can get out before the soldiers get here.

My fingers twitch over the keyboard, but never actually touch it. I want to do something, I have to do something. But what? Ditch the computer? No, they'll hack it and figure out who I am. Play dumb? Not going to work. Do I, do I...

The hard drive. I have to fry the security hard drive. If I do that, they won't have anything to track me. I burn out the whole server, and there's no evidence, right? But then they know that someone was here so... so I just... I dunno. I lay down in the hallway, pretend to be unconscious. Maybe I smack my head on the floor for good measure. I say the guy in the tights surprised me, knocked me out, and I don't remember anything after that. It's risky, super sketchy, but it's all I've got.

Jumping up, I start searching the room. I need an exposed wire, or wire cutters. I need a socket. I need something, but there's no time! How close is the soldier on this floor? Gotta hurry, gotta hurry! But there's nothing here, nothing exposed.

So make something exposed, you idiot.

My knees hit the floor. I reach behind the server units and immediately find a massive conduit to wrap my fingers around. It's covered in rubber, which means it's carrying electricity. With a grunt, I pull.

Nothing. Doesn't budge.

Shit-sticks.

Out in the hall, I hear something. It sounds like boots.

My teeth grind and I pull again. I put my feet up against the server frames and get both hands on the conduit. The footsteps are closer, just down the hall.

Break...

The muscles in my back strain.

... You...

My face twists, the veins stick out on my temples, my arms shake I'm pulling so hard, my legs are pushing so much my butt is literally off the floor.

... Bastard!

POW!

I exhale sharply. Was that the conduit or the seam in my jeans?

The walkie-talkie jumps to life. "Shots fired! Shots fired!"

My butt falls to the floor as the muscles in my arms and legs finally give out. I don't think my complete break of concentration helped either.

What the hell? Shots fired?

"Alpha unit," says a woman's voice, "we are in the west wing of ninth floor and we have a man down. Repeat, we have a man down."

Alpha comes on, all kinds of pissed off. "What's your position?"

"I am at the stair -- oh shit!" There's a moment of scuffling, then silence.

"Please repeat," says Alpha. Nobody answers. "Do you copy?" Still nothing. And then...

81

Bang! Bang, bang, bang! They're not through the radio, they're upstairs. I can hear them, just barely. It must be right over my head.

What is happening?

Alpha Male comes on, barking orders. " Floors seven through ten, move in on ninth floor! Locate and apprehend hostile! Floors one through six, head to stairwells and begin moving upward. Do I have anyone on ninth floor with me now?" Quiet. "Someone tell me what's happening!"

"Seventh floor," says a guy. "I'm moving in on -- hey, what's --" and it goes dead.

"Seventh floor, repeat. Seventh floor, do you copy?"

I can feel it, everyone in the building is still, waiting for the answer.

Alpha says, softly, "Seventh floor?"

The mic kicks on, but it's not a word.

It's a scream.

More shots erupt overhead. Like, a ton of them. The walkie-talkie speaker bursts to life and I can hear the gunshots like baseball sized hail on a tin roof. Someone shouts, "Under attack! We're under attack!"

The gunshots keep going. I haven't moved since I fell. I don't -- is there actually someone here?

"Intruder is superhuman! I repeat, intruder is --" there's a dull thunk and nothing else. Oh god. Oh no. Is it them? Is it the guys from last night, the ones at the warehouse? Did they find me?

Jesus... what if it's him? The one with the spiders.

Araknis...

Next to me, my laptop makes a loud 'ding'. I blink a few times and look over at the screen. The program has worked its way down to the primary coding system for the whole security network.

Alpha Male comes back on. He's clearly running. "All units, all units,"

I pull myself away from the walkie. It doesn't matter. I don't know what's going on. Maybe there is a superhuman. That's not my problem. I need to do what I came here for.

"Intruder is on sixth floor! We need back up, now!"

Hey, maybe Annie has convinced Alpha Male's teammates to pull the world's worst practical joke on him.

"No! Get away! Get away from me!"

Or, maybe not.

My fingers fly. I try not to think about what's going on out there. About Annie.

"Fifth floor under attack!"

I try to believe that, at any second, Annie will come running up and we'll get the hell out of here together. But I need to finish erasing the data first.

"We need back up!"

Almost there.

"Oh god, they're on four, they're on four!"

One last thing...

"Help me!"

I slam the laptop shut, yank the cable, grab my shit, and jump up so I can go find my friend.

"Freeze!" says a live voice.

Shit-sticks.

The barrel of the ESOA guy's gun is shaking. Somehow, that makes it even worse.

"Freeze!" he says again, which is really unnecessary, since I haven't so much as blinked since he said it the first time. I don't think that I'm even breathing at this point. The walkie-talkie on the floor has gone quiet.

I've never had a gun pointed at me. Then again, I've also never been in an exploding warehouse, seen the Justice Brigade in person, watched spiders crawl out of someone's skin, or had my friend's head smashed to a pulp in front of me.

The last twenty-four hours have been full of new experiences.

I think I like this one the least.

His gun keeps shaking. I'm having a hard time not staring at it. "Listen --"

"Shut it!" He snaps. I do. Dude sounds scared. I don't like that. Scared dude with a gun is not what I want to be dealing with right now. Especially considering I've got a missing friend and, apparently, there's some kind of super-freak loose in the building.

"Bag down," he says. His eyes are crazy twitchy right now. "Hands up, behind your head."

I follow instructions. Like, super slow and to the letter. I can hear him breathing. He sounds like he just finished a run, but he's not cooling down. I wanna say something, like, 'chill man, we're friends here,' but I know better. I may be mega-rich, but I'm still a black girl in America.

He takes a step toward me and jerks the barrel a tiny bit. "Move."

I'd love to, but where, you dumb-shit?

"Now!" he says, and this time he gives a big swing of the barrel.

Okay, okay. Got it. Away from the door. Very clear now. Sorry, didn't mean to piss you off.

Jesus.

Apparently I look somewhere at something he doesn't like, because he says, "Eyes straight ahead."

Fine with me. If I keep looking at that gun, I'm gonna freak out. It's screwed up. I'm scared right now, really, really scared, but I can't seem to get the parts of me that need to know to recognize it. Like, if I could start crying, or do Annie's screaming, shaking hands thing, I could probably get out of this. But instead, I'm wild-rabbit-sitting-completely-still-because-there's-a-fox-nearby kind of scared.

Twitchy McGee walks behind me and knocks my bag over. I wince. My laptop is probably worth more than his annual salary.

I hear a plastic snap and the beep of a walkie-talkie before Twitchy says, "Alpha unit this is --"

His voice comes out of my bag with just a tiny bit of lag.

Oh crap.

I was in such a rush, I... goddamn it, I must have shoved the extra walkie into my bag.

"What the hell?" he says behind me.

My heart is pounding. My skin is cold. And it's back, that feeling in my hands. That weird pressure building up inside of them.

"Where did you..."

Like when Samantha was staring at me.

"You were listening?"

Like at the warehouse last night.

"Are you in on this?"

Right before that huge explosion.

"Answer me you little bitch!"

From down the hall, a voice shouts, "Hey!" But not just any voice. Annie's walking toward us, real slow. Her hands are up, floating by her shoulders. Each step is so smooth and careful that it looks like she's gliding.

Something's wrong.

Her hair's a mess, loose strands everywhere. Her clothes are wrinkled, and she's got a sheen on her face of sweat, like she's been at the gym for a couple of hours. And her face...

Twitchy raises his gun up and shouts, "Freeze!"

Annie doesn't even flinch. "It's okay," she says with this crazy calm voice.

"Don't move!" Twitchy barks. "Hands behind your head."

"Hey, listen," she says, totally chill. Like she doesn't even have a gun pointed at her. "You've gotta go help your friends." No, like she does have a gun pointed at her... but she's used to it.

Twitchy makes a tiny advancement on her, moving away from me. "I said don't move."

I'm out of his peripheral. Slowly, I slide my leg, getting ready to make a break for it. Annie shoots me a look that screams, 'stop'. I do, and watch as she just keeps sauntering over toward the guy with the gun.

She says, nice and easy, "We're not the bad guys, okay?"

Twitchy readjusts his gun. "Keep quiet."

"The bad guy is upstairs and --"

"Quiet!"

Annie closes her mouth. She pauses a second, then takes another step.

"Stop," Twitchy says. Annie doesn't.

Oh my god, Annie, please, girl, I love you and you've done great up until now but Twitchy is being really serious and you need to just freaking stop.

His fingers tighten around the gun. "I'm not going to say it again," he leans forward. The barrel is just inches from her. "Stop."

Annie does, but in that way a cat pauses right before it pounces. She opens her mouth. "Make me."

Okay. Annie has officially lost her damn mind.

Twitchy makes a sound and swings the butt of his gun right at her head. I open my mouth to scream. Annie leans back. The rifle misses her face by less than an inch. Twitchy carries through with his elbow, aiming for where her face is now. Annie leans back more.

And more.

And more.

And. More.

She folds... literally folds her body in half to the point where her back touches the backs of her legs.

What?

Her hands hit the floor. Twitchy is still swinging, and he's looking as lost as I am. Annie's foot comes off the ground and her leg bends, but in the wrong place. Not at her knee, but halfway down her thigh. It just comes up, and then the rest of the leg follows like a damn ribbon that those gymnasts in the Olympics dance with. Her foot comes up in the tiny space between her and Twitchy and her heel slams his chin so hard I hear a crack. Twitchy's head snaps back and he's scrambling backwards. Annie's other leg flips up and over, just as fluid as the first, and then she's putting them down and holding in a sprinter's crouch.

She leaps up, fired like a compressed spring being released, and spins her upper body so far she could check to see if those pants make her butt look big. Her leg goes slack and her foot swings out like a tetherball on a line. It's the world's most effective spin-kick, and the only reason it doesn't connect is because Twitchy is still staggering.

Annie lands and the momentum of the kick causes her body to spin. She

85

looks like a barber pole going too fast. Twitchy finds his footing. He sees her, she sees him. He brings his gun up. She charges in. There's a flash from his muzzle and a sound so loud I can feel it in my bladder. Where the flare was, right at the side of Annie's torso, there's an empty space. It's not her body, torn to shreds. It's where her body was, but isn't, because somehow, she's crunched it up, pulled the part of her that should be ribs and organs into herself, caved it in to avoid the bullets.

Her arm comes down like she's karate chopping the gun with her armpit.

And then shit gets weirder.

Her arm goes around and around, a pink, fleshy python grabbing onto Twitchy's gun and arm. She squeezes so tight he screams. There's smacks and thuds and crunches as she knees him, punches him, and head butts him like six times each. Then, because she clearly hasn't beaten the shit out of him enough, she pulls hard with the arm that's wrapped around his gun and sends him into the air, spinning and spinning before hitting the ground. His gun clatters, and Annie stands there, watching as Twitchy gives one last little jerk before he goes completely limp.

When she looks at me, she's doe-eyed Annie. "So, you good?"

CHAPTER NINE
REASON TO DOUBT

Gossamer threads of liquid swirl through the air, bending and arcing like albino solar flares whipping out into the space around Bearserker's fanged snout. With a nasty, wet sploosh, his saliva splatters across the restraints holding him. It's less of a cage, more of a series of tightly-knit stone spikes, long and thin, but stronger than concrete. They came up from the ground beneath the wooden floor, at different angles, pinching every part of his body. It's lopsided and a little sloppy looking, but it'll hold him as long as I want it to.

And it'll be as tight as I feel like making it.

He roars and snaps his jaws at me. Which, yeah, still scary. His teeth are huge. But right now, I'm not feeling too nervous.

I've got this hijo de puta and I'm not letting him go.

My fingers dig into the ground. The spikes all grow a tiny bit, lifting Bearserker up and squeezing him tighter. The twisting of his head stops. His weirdly long tongue flops from his mouth as he pants. I don't worry; his windpipe isn't completely cut off.

Yet.

But ay, the smell coming off him is awful. It's worse than, well, worse than burning hair. Because burning hair is bad, right? But melting hair? Ten times worse.

I shoot Lucien a nasty look. The acid that comes out of his skin got everywhere during the fight, and so the smell of slowly melting hair, skin, wood, glass, and everything else it touched is going to last for hours.

As much as the smell is bothering me, the way Lucien looks is worse. His eyes are jaundiced yellow, not a bit of white left in them. Sickly would be the best way to describe his skin. His hands are twitching a bit, and there's a sheen across his arms. It looks like sweat, but when it drops, the floor sizzles.

He doesn't sigh, or pout, or roll his eyes; he curls his already skinny upper lip in against his teeth and hisses. "This sucks," he says. When his power is on, well really, when he isn't holding it back, his voice gets higher. Strained. "I thought this guy was supposed to be tough." He's at a quarter, maybe a third of full release. At half, his voice becomes unnerving. At three quarters, he sounds like the evil clown that hides in your closet and waits to eat you. He laughs and cackles. He turns psychotic.

I've never heard him at full release.

So, you know, maybe it's a good thing I've got Bearserker in a cage.

And not just for him (not that I give a rat's ass about what happens to that hairy bastard). If the fight had gone on any longer, I'm pretty sure this building would be coming down around us. It's called the Hid n' Run. Stupid name. Whatever. It's in a crap neighborhood just outside of Boston, sandwiched between a chop-shop and a pawnshop called Jacks where people sell crap illegally. When we came in, the place was seedy, greasy, filled with criminal types. You know, dudes wearing costumes and carrying scepters and canes and stuff.

It was also not destroyed.

Now? Yeah, total devastation. The bar is in pieces, the lights are all blown out, a few of them are hanging from the ceiling, there's a pipe sticking out of a wall with water gushing out, and bits of tables and chairs are scattered everywhere. The booths (which were totally gross to begin with) are crackling and smoldering, and in a few places they're still burning. I see a pair of civilian legs sticking out from one. I hope there's a torso on the other end.

The juke box looks like a Dali clock painting. On the far wall, some guy got thrown head first into the wall. Okay, not into the wall like he hit it and bounced off. In. To. The. Wall. But only his head made it through the wood. The rest of him is hanging down, limp. Around his neck, the outer ring of a dartboard is dangling.

I smirk.

Bull's eye.

For the record, if any of these pendejos are dead, I didn't kill them. But there's a lot of broken bones, and a lot of blood on the walls.

Speaking of walls, the one between the bar and the chop-shop has a huge hole in it. Through it, hot blue light flashes and I hear the sounds of fighting.

Sosuke.

I don't know who got thrown through the wall to make the hole, but it doesn't matter. Sosuke and Brass Knuckles are still at it in there. There's a growl -- Brass Knuckles; Sosuke isn't the growling type; it's unprofessional -- a flash (probably Sosuke), an electric crackle and the smell of burnt ozone (okay, definitely Sosuke), a yell that's almost a scream (Brass Knuckles), and a crack of glass, a metallic bang, and a thud big enough that I feel the vibrations through my fingers on the ground.

Lucien stops and stares at the hole in the wall. The muscles beneath his eye twitch a little.

Crap.

Stepping over some unconscious thug, he starts heading toward the chop-shop.

"Where are you going?" I look at Bearserker as I say it, but Lucien knows it's for him. I say, as calmly as possibly, "We have our orders."

Lucien turns, his head tilted slightly. The sleeves of his shirt are completely dissolved. Soon, it'll barely resemble a tank top. His hair, so thin and blonde it looks more like straw, sticks to his skin. He doesn't say anything, he just stares with his yellow eyes.

I don't want to instigate right now, but I can't let him get any further. If he goes into the chop-shop, gets involved with Sosuke and Brass Knuckles, he'll move closer to full release. Things will get way more dangerous at that point. I glance around at the bar. Maybe there's some milk in a fridge back there? Probably not. This doesn't look like the kind of place that serves milk.

I say, "Our job is to secure Bearserker."

"Yeah," he practically whispers, "I'd say Paddington isn't going anywhere."

I shift my body a bit, put my shoulder toward him. I don't want to face him. Not because I'm afraid, but because I don't want to give him a bigger target. "Sosuke's handling Brass Knuckles, and his orders were to stay here."

My words take a few seconds to reach Lucien's brain. With a frustrated sigh, his eyes roll up, looking for his brain. His chin follows, and as his head drops back, he spins around, his arms swinging out lazily. A few drops fly from his fingers and sizzle like bacon hitting the pan when they land. With a wild kick, he sends a chunk of wood bouncing off the wall and begins his aimless wandering again.

I let out a long, slow breath. "Why don't you look for some milk?"

"Yeah, yeah, yeah."

There's a snarl, a weak, pointless one, and I focus back on Bearserker. His snout is getting shorter. Really, his whole body is smaller. I can hear his bones and joints popping as they reduce and realign. When he's transformed, he's almost eight feet tall. Normally, he's a little over six. Right now, he's about halfway human. With a quick twitch of my fingers, I adjust the stone spikes holding him. There's the chance he's transforming on purpose, using that to get free and have more leverage to attack the cage. But probably not. Lucien and I really beat the crap out of him. The hair on his body is falling out. Beneath it, he's got massive bruises, long gashes, and burn marks everywhere.

As I check him for life threatening injuries (orders were to secure, not terminate) my eyes stop on his hands. They're still mostly transformed and his nails are massive, curved talons. They're chipped and yellow with a stain like cooked beets.

He's called Bearserker, but they're not really bear paws. Bear paws are almost round with big pads on them. His hands, they're claws, Wolfman or monster hands. Staring at them, I think about the bandages on Lux's chest

89

and face. My fingers clench. The spikes around his neck grow tighter and he gasps a little bit.

That's right, imbécil, you stay right where you are.

The sounds from the chop-shop have stopped. Not sure how long ago, maybe a minute or two? It was right after that big thud. I assume Sosuke won. So why hasn't he come back in here? I'm about to stand up and go investigate when there's a bang behind me.

Well, not really a bang, more of a rattle and thunk. And some squeaky hinges and, well, a lot of sounds of things that aren't working the way they're supposed to.

There's no reason for McTier to actually open the front door. It's just a frame with a knob now. The door part, the part that keeps people out, is scattered in a thousand pieces throughout the bar. It would be easier to simply walk through the hole. But here she is, trying to open it anyway. It's like a Charlie Chaplin routine, Looney Tunes. I act like I don't see her jaw clenching a little as she shakes the handle. Just behind her, several ESOA agents stand, watching, not sure what they're supposed to do. As she tries pulling, one of the agents literally steps past her and through the frame.

There's no way I'm not grinning right now.

Moving back, McTier takes a deep breath, then kicks the shit out of the door frame. It swings in, bangs against the wall, and completely falls to pieces. She pauses, straightens her military uniform, and strides in, victorious. My hand goes up in salute and she gives me a casual one back. At ease.

"Bearserker." She steps right up to his head. If he could transform back into beast mode in a flash, she'd be dead. Instead, he's all flushed in the face while hanging by his neck, limp and mostly unconscious.

"Agent Garcia?" She doesn't look at me. "Don't you think these restraints are a bit... tight?" Every move, even her turn toward me, is calculated. It says volumes.

She knows. Maybe not everything, maybe not that I spoke with Lux, but she knows something is up.

Maldición.

"You didn't see him in his transformed state, ma'am." It's not a good cover up, but it's the best I can do right now. I'm trying to ignore his hands. They're pink and human and calloused now, but I'm still thinking about bandages with little red spots. "He was extremely aggressive. Vicious."

McTier raises her chin a little. I'm not sure if she's going to buy it, but then she says, "The special ops team can handle it from here," and turns away from me. I feel the muscles in my back ease up a little as I watch her wander the room, taking long, balanced steps over the debris.

And the bodies.

ESOA agents are moving in now, setting up standing lights, putting out fires, taking out the innocent bystanders.

I say that, because most of these people were in the wrong place at the wrong time. They really shouldn't have jumped in as fast as they did, especially once Sosuke started throwing lightning bolts around. But a lot of them just got used as human shield.

Or in the case of the guy with his head stuck in the wall, human projectiles.

McTier stops when she reaches him. An eyebrow gets raised in my general direction.

"Brass Knuckles, ma'am." I say. "Threw him like a spear. I ducked just in time."

I have no idea if she likes that answer or not. She keeps moving, checking everything, corner to corner. "I believe your orders were to apprehend the suspects as discreetly as possible."

"This..." Lucien's voice spikes and dips like he's had one too many. He's behind the remnants of the bar, rummaging around. There's a carton of milk in his hand, but no little white moustache on his face. "...is discreet, Lieutenant." He smirks. "For us anyway."

McTier looks at him. The corners of her mouth come up with the tiniest of movements and give the fakest of smiles. "I would suggest you drink that milk, Agent Corvis." She turns and heads past the bar for the chop-shop.

"It expired a week ago," he calls as she walks by.

"That's an order." And she disappears into the other room.

Lucien looks at the milk and scowls. I decide it's better to follow McTier than let Lucien see me grinning.

The chop-shop fared better than the bar. Most of the lights are burnt out. That tends to happen when Sosuke discharges that much electricity. It's hard to see, but there's no rubble, and most of the structures look untouched. Sosuke's a clean fighter. He doesn't waste energy or movement. He doesn't strike unless it's going to hit, and if it misses, he turns it into something else. Like Lucien, the area directly around Sosuke is dangerous to be in during a fight. He's an up-close-and-personal kind of fighter. Most are. Sure, someone with super strength can lift a car and throw it, but to have someone whose powers are designed for long range attacks? That's rare.

It's also me.

Lux was the long range fighter for the Justice Brigade. Captain Turbo had incredible speed that allowed him to cover ground, but even that has its limits. Lux could focus light beams that cut through concrete from yards away. With enough time, he could cut through steel from across a football field.

I can cover that distance in three point nine seconds.

But Brass Knuckles could not.

In the shadows, he looks like a scarecrow; a really muscular scarecrow that someone dressed in metallic blue spandex and threw on the hood of a busted up car. Behind him, the windshield is completely shattered. The dent he's lying in is weirdly Brass Knuckle-shaped. His hands are big... too big for his body. They're not brass-colored, exactly, but close enough that the name makes sense.

He's not moving. Like, at all. He's breathing, and through my feet I can use my echolocation to check his heart rate. It's there, but slow and soft. He's not just unconscious, there's something else...

"Agent Sugiyama?" McTier is standing in front of Brass Knuckles. I don't like the look on her face. It's not angry, not scared, not worried, but something in between.

"He'll live, Lieutenant." Sosuke says. He's standing at full attention, even though he doesn't have to. His uniform is barely scratched. There's a weird feeling in the room right now, and I'm not talking emotional temperature. There's a charge in the air. Maybe it's leftover from Sosuke's ability, but I dunno. It feels like... he's still humming. The battery is still putting out juice or something.

Moving in a wide arc behind McTier and Sosuke, my feet start telling me a more interesting story than my eyes can. McTier's heart rate is up. Sosuke's is coming down, but I'm right about the humming thing. His electrical ability is still active. But why? What's he doing?

Behind me there's a lot of noise, and even more footsteps. It's not just ESOA agents. From the shouts and calls, the flashing of cameras, I know that the press has arrived. Agents are working to hold them back, keep them out of the Hid n' Run, or at least whatever's left of it. This was supposed to be a stealth mission, but you're going to draw attention when civilians start getting thrown through windows.

Cameras and phones are being confiscated. Agents are setting up a perimeter. No one is being allowed to report on this.

Which is weird.

When the Justice Brigade faced off against some big bads, reporters were practically shuttled along with them. Photographers snapped pictures of haymaker punches, Ironsides tearing through doors and walls, Captain Turbo standing over his fallen foes.

So why the change? I know they're not selling toys or making a cartoon show out of us, but at least let the public know that we're capable. This is the first game for the rookie team. The whole world should be watching.

McTier sniffs loudly. "All right, good work."

A bunch of ESOA Special Ops are moving around us in flanking positions, guns ready, just in case Brass Knuckles is playing possum.

But he's not. He hasn't moved a muscle, not even a twitch.

McTier turns to the closest one. "I want the suspect checked for life threatening injuries. After that, secure him. I want him ready to be questioned within the hour."

"He can go straight to the detention center," Sosuke says, professionally. McTier whips around. The agents all freeze. Sosuke's expression doesn't change a bit. "I have everything we need."

And for once, that mask of vagueness that McTier hides behind drops. Her eyes go big, and her mouth opens a little. Her hand flies out and snatches the LED flashlight from the top of an agent's gun. The circle of white washes over Brass Knuckles's body. There are dozens of marks on his suit, spots where the spandex is burnt to a crisp. Other places, there's seared and blistered skin. His head is flopped down, away from me.

McTier marches over, and even in that tight green skirt and army sanctioned heels, climbs up onto the hood effortlessly. She doesn't even hesitate.

Because she knows now, as well as I did when I felt it. Brass Knuckles isn't getting back up again.

Aiming the light with one hand, she uses the other to bring his face up. She grabs his mask and pulls it away.

¡Santo Dios! Sosuke, you didn't...

Unconsciously, I reach up and touch my temple.

His eyes... I wish I hadn't looked into his eyes. Open and flat, they're the eyes of the dead in a still living body. He's not unconscious. He's not even in a coma.

He's been fried.

McTier traces her fingers across his forehead, over his temples. On each one, there's a dark spot the size of a fingertip. On his forehead are three more.

For as fast as McTier grabbed that flashlight, she's off the car and storming over to Sosuke even faster. "You," she snarls as she gets close, but not all up in his face. There's a distance, an invisible barrier around Sosuke. Just feet away, Brass Knuckles is an example of what happens when you get too close, and McTier knows it. "You are not authorized to use that technique without proper supervision. And even then, only under specific circumstances."

Sosuke doesn't even blink. "I believe our orders were 'by any means necessary', ma'am."

Her knuckles, the ones around the flashlight, go pale. "And I am the one who decides what is necessary."

"I saw an opportunity to gather information on our targets, ma'am." He says flatly. "He's an acceptable loss."

"I make that call, Agent Sugiyama, not you, not the other agents. Me."

If that's where she stopped, it would just be a superior chewing out a subordinate. But she doesn't. The invisible barrier bends as she steps in close. Right up to him. Close enough that he could fry her without moving.

But he won't.

Because she's in charge. Her eyes, lower than his, demand that he break attention and look at her. For a few seconds, he doesn't.

But then he does.

The barrier shivers like a soap bubble.

"Understood?"

And pops.

"Ma'am," Sosuke says, softly, "yes, ma'am."

McTier waits just long enough that everyone in the room knows this thing is settled. Then, she's walking away and saying over her shoulder, "As soon as you've processed the information, I want a full debrief, Agent Sugiyama."

"Yes, Lieutenant."

I glance back to Brass Knuckles.

The human brain is an incredible thing. But really, it's made up of two main components, squishy grey matter and electrical impulses. Sosuke has the ability to control and manipulate electricity.

He can also absorb it.

I don't know the details of how it works. I don't know if all he got was Brass Knuckles's memories from the last twenty-four hours, or if he's going to see, hear, and smell everything the guy has ever experienced. And really, I don't care.

Because the ends don't justify the means.

As McTier passes me, she says, "Good work, Garcia." I catch the tiniest whiff of sweat through her perfume.

Sosuke stands at attention. Once McTier leaves, he brings his eyes to mine. He doesn't say anything. He doesn't smile or frown or even raise his thin black eyebrows. He just stares. And I get the message, loud and clear.

Behind me, reporters are shouting. Around me, ESOA agents are cleaning up the mess Lucien and I made. In front of me is Sosuke, alone in the ring, victorious and vicious, willing to do anything to complete the mission. And as much as I want to throw something at him with my eyes, show him that we may be teammates, but we're sure as hell not on the same team anymore, I can't. My mind has already moved onto something else. I don't have time for some stupid feelings, because the situation around me is big... bigger than it was made out to be. But I'm good at big. That's what I do. I pull back. I look and strike from a distance. And right now, I've got something that needs some serious attention.

Sosuke said 'gather information on our targets'.

If Bearserker and Brass Knuckles weren't our real targets, then who are?

CHAPTER TEN
DIVING IN

Over the four months after my second failed attempt at retrieving the gravity bands, I completely exhausted my savings, emptied every bank account, sold everything which wasn't necessary. I only owned one outfit. It had been weeks since I had used toothpaste. All of my meals came out of cans which were heated by placing them atop my machinery.

And it still wasn't enough.

The raw materials I needed to re-create the gravity bands came to tens of thousands of dollars. I had barely made it through the casings and groundwork for the wiring. Most of my funds had gone into the materials to build the machines which would allow me to build the bands. I needed readouts and data which had to be checked constantly in order to make the minute adjustments to the electrical boards.

The utility bills alone were killing me.

Working out of a disheveled auto garage fifty miles outside the city in a neighborhood which reeked of violence and prostitution, I had an electrical bill which would have made Times Square jealous.

I needed to replace equipment and had absolutely no means to do so. Vendors wouldn't even take my calls... at least, not the reputable ones. There were no avenues left for me. I had no friends, no acquaintances to lend me money. I couldn't turn to a new university. My insane departure from the last one, coupled with the break-ins and followed by my immediate disappearance did not help my reputation. In truth, I was even afraid to show my face in public.

Thanks to him.

Captain Turbo.

His ridiculous name was plastered on the newspaper covers for weeks. He was all anybody was talking about. After his bumbled attempt at apprehending me, he had come forward to the public. Amazingly, he used his own failure to thrust himself into the limelight. He made both of us famous in the same stroke. Upon his word, they branded me a villain. His description of our fight, of my insidious technology, how I had evaded justice and retreated in hopes of completing my nefarious plans; he spilled these one-sided facts to the world. He gave them a reason to fear me and a reason to trust him.

And he did so without ever using my real name.

Instead, he gave me a new one.

"Though his identity may remain a secret," he spoke each word into the bank of microphones as though he had rehearsed them for hours, "all people should fear the likes of Doctor Dendrite."

I was as relieved that he had gotten it wrong as I was insulted.

"And Doctor, if you're listening, I have a message for you." That's when he turned to the camera, that little smirk moving up on one side of his face. "See you soon, Doc."

There was nothing left for me except my work. The bands had brought so much attention before, a part of me believed that if I were to complete them, I could return to a normal life. It didn't matter who had taken the prototypes, they were incomplete. I was the only person who could finish them.

But, when my last transistor tube exploded in my face, I, too, blew up. In the decrepit stink of that warehouse, I thrashed out, swinging my arms wildly across the tables and walls. I roared and bellowed until my voice, which only moments before had so gently tried to coax the small glass tube to not exceed its designated wattage, was raw and hoarse.

When I was done, I found myself sitting on the floor, my back pressed against the wall. I could feel days of sweat running down my skin. I couldn't remember the last time I had showered. My stomach ached, but my mouth had grown tired of canned stew. Everything around me, everything within me, reeked of defeat. I closed my eyes and was more than ready to let tears fall when something fell off the counter next to me.

The utility belt from my return to the campus laboratory.

It was shoddy work, rushed and unprofessional. The wiring was terrible, it was a miracle the electrical system hadn't completely melted down. With a little more time I could have done so much more. Picking it up, I moved it through my hands.

Unprofessional, but not uninspired. A few minor adjustments and I could have increased the ohms, extended the output duration. Laying it out on the table, my fingers went to work, opening the casing, breaking out the soldering iron.

A twist of wire here...

I began to think about how, if I'd made these adjustments before, that night would have gone differently.

... a new fuse there...

How Captain Turbo wouldn't have stood a chance.

... replace the diode, up the frequency...

How I could have stopped him.

... rerun the cabling to the exterior, speed up the conduits and electrical transfer...

I could have forced him to listen.

... increase the powder density to the smoke bombs. Make it more potent, possibly flammable...

I could have taken Captain Turbo down and then found whoever had stolen my bands and taken them back. Hell, with these modifications, I could have taken whatever... I... wanted...

And there, it happened. I saw it, in my mind's eye. A precipice sat before me. In my hands were weights to drag me down into a sea which held no bottom, weights my own flesh had created. I was haunted by the idea my mind had led me, yet comforted as well. It had been natural. These things which I held had come from my own thoughts. They had been borne by me. Over that edge, there were enough funds to finish my bands, to restore my name, to show the world that I was right, and they were wrong.

All I had to do was jump.

When I hit the ground, I squawked. My ankle bent to one side, shooting pain through my leg. I knew I should have gotten some new sneakers before the heist. Of course, I was robbing the armored truck because I didn't have the money for new sneakers, so yes, that was kind of a moot point.

Anyway, who knew money could be that heavy?

I dropped the bag on my weakened side. It would have been easier if I'd carried one bag at a time, but the armed guards weren't going to spend forever rolling around, gasping and wheezing from the new improved smoke bombs. It's really amazing what adding a pinch of cayenne can do.

When my ankle went from hot stinging to a low throb, I hoisted the bag. My getaway car was just around the corner. Everything was going according to plan. The alleyway was free of other cars and pedestrians, so no onlookers. I'd studied the truck's route and knew this was the best place to hit it. The drivers used it as a short cut to avoid busy intersections. I used it as a trap.

When the flash bombs went off, the driver had swerved but because it was an alley, they didn't have anywhere to go. A couple bounces off the wall, and the truck stopped. They didn't have room to turn, so the passenger had gotten out to guide. That's when I struck. Smoke bombs first, high power portable cutting torch second, and I had two sacks of money to take home.

The headlights of my car peeked from the corner. My heart hammered from the exertion and excitement. I had enough money to support me for months. Laying low for a week or so would be necessary, but then I could buy parts and get back to work. I could make so much progress, maybe even finish the bands! And if I did, I would finally be able to escape the fear which hung over me. I could free myself of the name --

"Doctor Dendrite!"

I went to look, but was immediately met by a set of knuckles. I felt air as I spun, then asphalt on my back as I landed. Every part of my body seemed to want to go in a different direction. When I finally settled, I heard it.

The sound of boots.

"Oh, motherfu -- "

He jerked me up by the leather straps which ran across my chest and said, "After all this time," softly but perfectly.

My mask -- a modified welder's mask cut small to be lightweight and equipped with an air filter to counter the smoke bombs -- had gone askew. It didn't matter, though, I could hear the smug look on his face. When I began squirming, I noticed a strange feeling throughout my body. It was as though someone had taken out half my blood and replaced it with air. I chalked it up to Captain Turbo knocking my brain around my skull like the bead in a baby's rattle.

"I was starting to wonder if you would ever make another appearance," he chuckled lightly. "By the way, love the goggles."

As I looked through the cracked lens, I saw my feet dangling a few inches above the ground. That feeling of lightness wasn't going away.

My feet had never dangled before...

"I have to say, Doc, here I thought I'd scared you straight." His fingers twisted and tightened around the straps.

"And here," I said, my voice twisting and tightening around the words, "I thought you would have learned from your mistakes."

My hands hit the release gates. Electricity, almost double what it was last time, coursed into his hands. The sparks were as bright as my flash bombs and the crack was deafening. Turbo shot off as though he'd been pulled by a speeding car. I flew back and skidded to a stop. That odd sensation vanished as my shaky legs took my full weight.

Turbo collided with a dumpster. Clouds of smoke encased his hands. He wasn't moving, but I didn't think he was dead.

Not that I really cared.

The pain in my ankle had spread to most of my leg, but I limped over to the nearest bag of money. At the dumpster, Turbo was moving his arms and legs, trying to regain some control. The fact that he could even live through that amount of voltage was amazing.

With the weight of the bag and the pain in my leg, my car seemed twice as far away. People were crowding around the end of the alley, pointing, talking. Most of them backed away as I headed towards them.

"Hold it, Doc." There was no smile in his voice, no smug grin. He was standing now, but clearly shaken. With every labored breath, his muscles seemed to grow more chiseled, more pronounced. He took a tentative step, and then another. One more, and he straightened to his full height.

I ground my teeth.

No. Not this time. I was a man of logic, of science. Emotions have no place in problem solving. I pressed down my fear. Things became crisper, sharper. I looked at the alley the way a grandmaster looks at a chessboard. I took in everything at once, and when I was done, my next step was obvious.

For a moment, Captain Turbo halted. The muscles around his eyes contracted. He wobbled a bit. The electrical shock and impact against the dumpster seemed to have delayed his nervous system from resetting fully.

But a real scientist tests their theories.

I dropped the bag in an overly dramatic fashion. A feint. The moron fell for it. He didn't notice the small Frisbee sized disk coming at him until it was halfway there.

It flew wide, a little over his head. There was a bang as it struck the armored truck behind him.

His reactions were slow.

I threw a pepper bomb straight at his face. He smacked it, releasing a burst of smoke. Two more and he was engulfed in a thick, red cloud. But with a grunt, he dove forward and started charging. It had been only seconds, and yet he'd completely recovered. As he closed the distance between us, I backed myself up against another dumpster. My hands leapt to the releases on my belt. Turbo saw. One hand closed around my arm like a bear trap while the other tried to introduce my ribs to my spine. I gasped.

"You know," he said. "I think you're running out of tricks."

"Don't..." I struggled to breathe.

"What?" he tilted his head slightly, leaning his ear toward me. "Don't arrest you? Don't throw you in jail? Don't lock you away in the nut house where you belong?"

"Don't... look down."

The idiot actually did.

The flash grenade hit the ground. The heat from it was enough to singe my legs through my pants. Turbo shouted, no words, just a cry. Blinded, he stumbled back, one arm across his eyes, the other flailing about wildly.

"Damn you, Dendrite!" he bellowed. It was very professional, a hero shout, but I could hear frustration and anger in it.

And that brought me a modicum of satisfaction.

I had hurt him, made him helpless and vulnerable. Unfortunately, I was in no condition to cash in on that fact. Breathing hurt -- later I would discover he broke three of my ribs -- and I was running out of adrenaline. Gasping and coughing, I stumbled toward the closest money bag.

"What's the matter, Doc?" Turbo's arm wasn't waving. His eyes were open, but weren't focused on me. His vision hadn't returned yet, I was sure. "You not gonna take a shot at me?"

I didn't move, didn't speak. Slowly, my hand slid to my back and I removed something from my belt.

"Guess you learned that hitting me isn't such a good idea, huh?"

A smile crept across his lips. A snarl crawled over mine. My hand moved out, in it a second disk, identical to the first one I'd thrown, the one that veered wide and hit the armored truck.

The truck that was directly behind Captain Turbo now.

"That was a good trick, setting off that little firework between us."

There was a gentle thump as I attached the disk to the dumpster.

"But it seems to me --"

My fingers gingerly slipped around the perimeter of it, spiraling toward the center.

"-- that was a last ditch effort. So unless you plan on throwing another Frisbee at me," he opened his eyes and locked them, clearly, on mine, "I'd have to say that you're out of ideas."

Twisting counter clockwise, I released the safety. "How's this for an idea?"

With a push, the disk activated. Inside, the powerful electromagnet began cranking out a tremendous amount of positive ions. Behind Turbo, its twin automatically fired up, generating an equal amount of negative ions. The dumpster lurched forward, rusty castors squealing, and raced across alley toward the truck.

With Turbo in the way.

The dumpster swept him up. There was a wrenching of steel smashing against steel and the truck lurched. Glass shattered, metal bent. On the ground, gasoline splashed. I paused a moment.

One flash grenade. One flash grenade would set the whole mess ablaze. I would never have to worry about that costumed buffoon again.

I blinked the thought away, grabbed a money bag, and began hobbling.

There was a screech. The dumpster began inching left and right. It was pointless, the magnets were too powerful. As it rocked, sparks shot out. I stopped and raised my hand.

"Hey," I said.

It kept rocking.

"Stop!"

The first flame was tiny, but within seconds the air was filled with the vacuous whomp of fire ripping through the twisted metal as one huge ball, rolling up into the sky, turning in on itself over and over again as it rose out of the alley.

The dumpster's movement stopped. I waited, unsure of what to do. Turbo was either unconscious or dead. Either way, there was nothing I could do to help him. In the distance, police sirens were wailing. Nearby, all I heard was the pop and crackle of burning trash.

I picked up the money bag up with shaky hands. My mind in a daze, unsure of my feelings about what had just happened, I bobbed and dipped and limped away. My body... and part of my soul... felt strung together, held by bad knots and cheap twine. I had the money, but at what cost? I could start working again, but was it worth it? Would finishing the gravity bands ever make up for what I had done? I paused.

And that's when a flaming dumpster flew over my head.

People screamed and ran as it came crashing down just feet away.

I didn't even flinch.

Not that I wasn't scared, but what I was seeing, it was... it was impossible. Beyond reason and logic. No one was that strong. That dumpster must have weighed at least two thousand pounds on its own. It had trash inside of it, adding to that.

And it flew.

Out in the street, the crowd had scattered. A voice inside me shouted to move. I had the money, Turbo was alive, there was no reason to stay. No crowds meant an easy escape. I just had to go.

But I couldn't.

How the hell did he do it? The question burned hotter than the flames lapping at the huge metal box in front of me.

Back at the truck, Turbo was pushing his way out of the twisted metal. His costume was mangled. The cloth from his shirt had curled away and his chest was a mix of sweat and blood and rippling muscle. His mask had tumbled, exposing most of his face.

The Colonel. The one Jayaramen had shown the bands to. I'd only caught a glimpse, but it was him, I was sure of it.

The fire rushed up. With a roar, he yanked his arm back. The last bits of sleeve and glove fell away, fluttering up into the rising waves of hot air, dancing like burnt paper. In the light, in that beautiful orange light which turned his blood to black and the steel to white, I saw it.

A flash of truth.

The casing had been modified, cleaned and polished, but the shape was the same.

A gravity band.

My gravity band.

It was him. He'd been there from the beginning. He knew where the bands were, and had stopped me from...

No.

He'd come to steal them. He'd worn the costume so no one recognized him. Or maybe he had some grand plan of becoming something greater. It didn't matter. He'd been there that first night and, and the second night... he'd said it. He said then.

'They don't belong to you anymore.'

This was his fault. Every pain and frustration and drop of anger over the past four months could be traced back to him. But all that was nothing. My suffering, his selfishness, that was secondary. Beyond those things, he had done something to bring on more than my hate, more than loathing.

He'd made them work.

Even through the people shouting in the street and the police sirens blazing, through the screaming metal that bent beneath Turbo's powerful arms, I could hear them.

They hummed.

So sweet, so faint.

So beautiful.

I screamed. Split flew from my trembling lips. Flash grenades and smoke bombs flew from my fingers. None struck him directly, but the smoke bomb powder being highly flammable, the air around him turned into a white blaze. Tears boiled out of me, covered my eyes, and I could not see if the flames had any effect. I threw and threw and threw until the movement became so wild that I twisted and staggered, toppling to the ground.

On hands and knees I sat there, gasping and panting and snarling like a rabid beast. My body flushed with adrenaline, I reached for the closest blunt object I could find. When my fingers locked around a mangled piece of steel that had fallen from the dumpster, I drove the tip down and pushed myself up. Wavering, I stood and looked at the one man in the world that I thought deserved to die.

He was kneeling, forearms crossed over his face. His entire costume was tattered and burnt. But when he moved, broke his arms apart and looked out at me, I saw that he was afraid.

Of me.

Of what I had become.

Of what he had made me into.

And that... that was better than his death.

So when the police sirens came so close that they stopped, when I heard the shouting and the stomping of feet, I made a decision.

Turbo had to live. That was the only way I would be able to find out how he made them sing.

The metal dropped from my hand, clattered to the street, and I smiled.

"See you soon," I said softly, "Captain."

THE TRUTH HURTS

Annie's driving. I can't. I'm... damn, I don't know what I am. In shock? Like, it's... I'm here, but I'm totally out of it. I don't even remember leaving the building, getting into the car. Everything is hazy. It's just... Jesus, it's too much. Everything that's happened, everything that's happening, everything that's...

Sensory overload, that's a thing, right? Too much crap coming in, not enough processing power to handle it. Sure, whatever. We'll call it a thing. That's what's happening.

I know I'm rocking back and forth. Annie's whipping us through traffic. She's driving like I do, moving the car in and out of spaces where it seems like it shouldn't fit. Like it's become flexible.

Malleable.

Bendy.

Like Annie.

"So?" she says next to me. "How ya doing?"

I turn to look at her. The world was all just a bunch of noise a second ago, but now it's coming back into focus. She's got both hands on the wheel. Her hair is still a bunch of flyaways that have been pasted down with sweat. She turns the wheel a little bit to the left.

"I mean, I just... um..."

And when I look close, I notice that her elbow isn't an elbow.

"Are, are you okay?"

It's just a curvy, fleshy tube.

"Candace?"

My eyes jump to hers.

And I scream.

So, naturally, she also screams.

And here we are now, driving a bazillion miles per hour through Boston traffic, both of us screaming. I'm probably cursing a bit too, but to hell if I know what I'm saying. All the shit I've been dealing with just comes to a head and there's nothing left for me to do but scream like a newborn baby. Yeah, that's a perfect way of putting it. A baby. Because I've been ripped away from everything I've ever known, and my life has just been changed immeasurably and permanently and when that happens, the only thing you can do is open your goddamn mouth and scream.

When Annie gets control of the car, when my lungs are completely out of breath, when we've both been panting wildly for a second, Annie shouts,

"Jesus Christ, Candace! What the hell?"

"You're a, you've, you, you, you..." I am really struggling right now. "You're a jelly person with arms!"

Okay, that is totally not how I planned on broaching the subject. There were, like, at least ten different steps in my head that Annie is completely unaware of.

"I -- what?"

"Rubber!" That's a little closer. Still not really clear. Need to break this down. "You." Good start. "Are made." Getting there. "Of..." Come on, I can do this, complete thoughts. "Rubber!" Oh, that felt good.

Annie opens her mouth and gives that, I'm-just-going-to-ignore-that kind of sigh people give when someone makes a slightly racist remark and they don't feel like starting shit in public.

I never give that look. I always start shit.

She shifts in her seat. It's weird. She totally moves normally, like anyone else, but in my head she's all wiggly-wormy or something. "I can explain," she says softly.

"Oh yeah?" I think I say it sarcastically. But I'm not really sure, so I try it six more times. "Oh, oh yeah? Yeah? Oh yeah. I... yeah. You, you can, oh... oh you just, you just do... do that, Annie. Annie the, the, the rubber person."

"Okay," she says, pulling her lips back against her teeth a little tighter, "I get it. This is... it's very shocking, and you don't --"

"Shocking?"

"-- really mean what you're saying, and so I --"

"Shocking? That's the nicest --"

"-- am going to just ignore that you're calling me that."

"-- way I would put it, Annie. The nicest --"

"Okay."

"-- possible way you could... could --"

"Okay!"

My head jerks around a little for a second as too many thoughts all try to force their way to my lips and then I just blurt out, "So what the... what... what the hell... when, when, when were you going to tell me? Huh? When was that --"

"Tell you?"

"Yes, Annie! Tell me, with words out of your mouth that, that you are a rubber person."

The car's engine somehow manages to rev up even more as Annie's lips pretty much disappear against her teeth. When she talks, she says each word like it's its own little sentence. "I am not made of rubber, okay? I'm just --"

"Are you a superhero?"

"No --"

I gasp. "Are you a villain?"

"No --"

I double gasp. "Do you have a costume?"

"I -- it's not like that."

"Are you, are you going out at night... without me?"

Her lips get all puckery.

My head jerks back. "What?"

She shakes her head. "Nothing."

"No," I say, "no, no, no. Bitch, you don't get to 'nothing' me. Not now. You got something to say, then --"

"I think if anyone needs to apologize for going out at night," she looks at me, hard, "it's you."

"Oh no." I say, sticking a finger up between us. "Oh hell no. Hell no. You don't get to, to --"

But she just keeps looking at me.

"I, I, I," I stammer, that's what I do. "That is, that is completely, there is no, no comparison for you and me and this and, and, and would you please, please stop just giving me that look? For just a goddamn second so I can, can -- shit!" I smack the dashboard with my hand. She finally turns away and the car slows down. There's quiet and I take some deep breaths. Eventually, I drop my face into my hands. I don't scream again, but I groan as loudly as I can. When I'm done, I put my head back against the headrest, stare at the ceiling, and say, "I'm sorry I called you a jelly person with arms."

I think I hear a smile on her lips. I hope I do. "It's okay."

"I know you're not made of rubber."

"Thank you."

I roll my head and stare at her. "So..."

She tenses a moment, then thinks, then works up the courage or gets past the barrier or whatever it is that she needs to do to talk about it. "My... I'm not that different. I mean, I am, but not, I'm not, like, an alien or anything. My body's similar to yours, to everyone else's. But instead of bones, I have extra muscles and tendons. They imitate bones really well, and they're stronger, way stronger, some of them. But I'm human, you know?"

"I do," I say. "And maybe, I dunno, maybe that's why it..."

"What?"

"You could have just told me, Annie."

She gives a little laugh that's not the ha-ha kind and rolls her eyes. "Right."

"Seriously. You... it wouldn't have changed how I feel about --"

"Sure." It's short and hard and crisp. "That would have gone just, you know, great."

"Annie,"

"What, freshman year? When we met? Hi, I'm Annie. I don't have any bones. What do you do for fun?"

I turn away.

"Or in class, maybe? Oh, you're having trouble with dimensional wave theory? That's rough. It took me six years to learn to walk upright."

My eyes fall to the carpet between my sneakers. "Okay, okay, okay," I sigh out the last one. "You're right. It... it must have -- I'm sorry you've had to hide it for, you know, ever."

She swings the car off the highway and into part of the city. Reaching down, she grabs the stick to downshift. I glance at her hand. It looks so normal. I think about all the times she's put that hand on my arm, around my waist while I was stumbling home, drunk, on my shoulder while we laughed hysterically at something. It's never seemed weird to me before. And now, I... I don't want it to feel weird.

My palm comes down on top of her hand. She's warm. I squeeze. She gazes into my eyes. Her cheeks turn red. "And," I say with more hesitation than she had, "you're... you're not that different. You know?"

"Thank you," she says, "but I know what I --"

"No," I say, not hard, but enough to stop her. "You don't... something is, is happening. To me."

Beneath my hand, I feel the muscles, all the muscles, in her hand go tense. "What are you talking about?"

"I... I don't know. But something happened at the warehouse, right? Something that didn't hurt me but shook the place down to the foundation."

"Okay,"

"And, and I've been getting this, this feeling like... like there's something inside of me."

"Okay," she says slower and lower.

"Like there's a, a..."

"A power?" she asks.

I give a breathy smile. "Yeah."

"Are you telling me you think you have powers?"

I nod.

Annie doesn't grin. She doesn't giggle or say, 'oh my gosh' or anything that I kind of expected. Instead, she just licks her lips, sets her face to a super serious look, and shifts the car into a lower gear.

With a jerk of the wheel, we swing around and start heading in a different direction.

"What," I look out the window. "What's wrong?"

"We need to get home."

I say her name and squeeze her hand again, but it doesn't feel so inviting anymore. "I don't think that's a good idea."

She doesn't say anything.

"I need to get out of town. Now. We both do."

She still doesn't say anything.

"Annie, we just... you just beat the snot out of a bunch of ESOA storm troopers. They're totally looking for us now."

"I know."

"Then why the hell --"

"I'm sorry," she says. "We need to get back to the house."

"No," I pull my hand off of hers. "We cannot do that. We need to be heading to an airport or a train station or --"

"We're going home." She practically barks it. "We have to."

I don't like that. There's something weird here. "Why?"

"It's... " and that barrier she climbed over earlier is suddenly back. "There's things going on that you don't understand and I have to take you back."

"Yeah?" I say. Under my skin I feel a hot prickling. "Well, maybe I don't wanna go back."

Annie clams up.

"Are you telling me I have to?"

She stays quiet. My anger ebbs toward worry.

"Are you going to make me?"

Nothing. The worry inches to fear.

"What... why are you doing this?"

"I'm sorry," she says, real soft. She reaches down to shift the gears again.

"Why are you acting like..." My eyes go wide. "Is this... am I an assignment?"

"Really," she says. Her hand is out of my view. "I'm sorry."

She jerks and I see knuckles.

CHAPTER TWELVE
LOOSE THREADS

Cheers. Screams. Camera flashes. Adoration. Love. Clapping, so much clapping.

I'm a superstar, and all I did was walk outside. Everyone is going nuts. The barricades on either end of the street are pulsating. The idol worship washes over me. They call out with, 'I Love You!' and 'You're the Greatest!' and 'You're My Hero!' and for the first few seconds I'm completely overwhelmed. I just stand there in the doorway and look at all of the screaming masses.

Screw regulations, I'm getting a costume. Maybe one that shows some skin.

I should pose. I should throw my head back and let my hair down. I should slam my hands to the ground and give these people a show.

At the very least, I should be waving.

So I reach up, raise my hand to my adoring fans and let them know that, without them, I wouldn't be anything. I turn to the right, a fat cheesy grin welling up through my cheeks. Then I turn to the left.

And there's Captain Turbo.

Carajo...

My stomach drops two feet in one second.

Turbo's turning in a slow circle, waving to all the people.

Wait, waving?

My arm drops just in time. I don't think he saw. Maybe he saw. No, he totally didn't. Because he's not even looking at me. I mean, why should he, right? He's got throngs of adoring fans to look at. He looks one way and waves, and they all go crazy. Then he turns to the other side so they can go nuts. Then he turns back.

Come on, man. Stop milking it.

Finally, when he's sucked up enough, he spins (just enough that his stupid cape does that big, dramatic, awesome looking floaty thing. Dammit. Now I want a cape.) and heads toward the bar.

Dios Santo, I don't even want to think about how many people saw me just now. I don't care about the crowds or the cops. I don't really even care about Captain Turbo (okay, maybe I do, just a little bit. Or a lot a bit.) It's the ESOA agents, the Special Ops people, Lucien. Sosuke.

McTier.

My skin feels cold and too tight and my stomach hurts and my face feels like it's on fire and I just, I just wanna get to the van. So ignoring all the people still cheering (would it have killed them to say, Captain Turbo, I love you?) I storm off away from The Hid n' Run toward the popup base camp we have nearby. As I go, I look at the asphalt the entire way.

At least that still loves me.

"Agent Garcia," says McTier, who is definitely close enough that she saw me wave at the crowd. "With me."

Ugh.

And she walks back to the bar.

Double ugh.

Right up to Captain Turbo.

Uuuggghhh.

She doesn't ask him for a word. She doesn't politely invite him to join us. She doesn't really say anything as we head for the door. She just shoots him a glance and keeps moving. He stops and waits for us to go in, but doesn't make eye contact with me.

Wow. Nice.

Not like I'm his replacement or anything. Not like I was specially chosen for this job. Not like I just helped take down Bearserker, a known and dangerous supervillain. Not like I would appreciate even the slightest acknowledgement. A smile. A nod. A hello?

Thinking back, when he and Sosuke were getting all pissy at each other in the conference room and McTier broke it up, did he even look at me? He didn't, did he? He just stared at Sosuke and then, I dunno, left or something. But definitely without looking at me.

I'm not sure if I actually growl, but I sure feel like I do.

By the time Turbo makes it through the door frame, I'm all kinds of pissed off. I try not to show it, but I don't try very hard.

Turbo looks around, sticks his fists on his hips (yeah, because that's not a clichéd way to stand) and whistles loudly. "You kids need to learn to pick up your toys after you make a mess."

That's it. I officially hate the most beloved superhero in the world.

"What you are doing here?" McTier's looking up at him, her face the same as it was with Sosuke.

"I thought I should swing by," he says casually, "make sure the junior team wasn't having any trouble."

McTier doesn't play that game. "The situation is under control."

"So I see."

As wonderfully interesting as this conversation is, I get easily distracted when, through my feet, I sense someone coming up behind me. No, wait.

Two somebodies.

111

Sosuke's just on the other side of the hole in the wall, Lucien right behind him. He asks slowly, "Is there a problem, Lieutenant?"

Sosuke's the king of keeping cool. Well, actually, he's the king of being so emotionally distant that robots would find him cold and unrelatable. The one time I saw him get even the tiniest bit worked up was in that conference room. He's got a better handle on it now, but it's still there. I can feel it. His heart just picked up. His toes are squirmy in his boots.

He really, really wants McTier to say, 'yes'.

But she just stares at Turbo. Sosuke stares at Turbo. Lucien stares at Turbo. And Turbo gives everyone an indignant eye.

Except me.

McTier takes a quick breath through her nose. "We're moving out." She starts around Turbo's considerable shoulders. "Go home, Captain."

He starts in with his big, gruff voice and says with a charming half smile, "I don't think --"

McTier snaps her head. "If you show up at another secured location, I will have the Enhanced and Superhuman Operations Agency take you into custody on the spot."

That smile of his doesn't break, but it's not trying to be charming anymore. "It's still a free country."

"You're retired, Captain," she says, heading for the door. "Go home." She doesn't even look at him.

And neither do I.

Okay, yes I do. But only as we're leaving. And only out of the corner of my eye. And only for a second.

And he's looking at me. But it's not a smile, or a fake smile, or anything like that. He's... I dunno... it's a look like I'm the only other sane person in a room full of crazies. I wonder if this is how he used to look to my uncle, the brains of the Justice Brigade. It's weird, and not what I'm expecting, and it throws me. I half walk, half stumble behind McTier. Sosuke and Lucien are following, skirting by Turbo, testing the boundaries of their stupid machismo, 'I'm going to mess you up one day, man' attitudes. I don't think Turbo even really notices. He just watches us go.

My instincts tell me to go back, to ask more questions, but the crowd around us swells. It's not the loving masses from before, but reporters hollering questions at us, snapping pictures, taking videos. It's a total opposite from before. And yes, I know all that stuff was for Captain Fancy-Cape and not me. I get it. But these reporters shoving their mics and phones in my face makes me want to put a wall of spikes sharp enough to cut their overly reachy arms off.

"What happened in there?" one asks.

We kicked ass, that's what happened.

"Was Captain Turbo involved?" someone hollers.

Only in ruining the mood.

"Why don't you wear makeup?"

I... Excuse me?

McTier turns her head halfway around. "Keep up, Garcia."

The reporters keep shouting. By the time we reach the temporary base camp and are securely tucked behind several layers of ESOA trucks and vans, I'm done being famous.

But apparently, I'm not done working.

"Gather 'round," Someone hands McTier a stack of manila folders. "We've got new orders. I want both the ops team and the Special Agents ready to roll out in ten. Medics, check the Agents. Ops, gear up. Move with a purpose, people."

And they do. Everyone is buzzing, going to this van and that. They're grabbing ammo, putting on bulletproof vests. Medics run in and check Sosuke. A crew wearing special tear away clothing goes to help Lucien out of his acid soaked shirt.

"Lieutenant," I say, almost casually. McTier doesn't looked up when she answers. "Medics, check Agent Garcia," she says as she starts walking away.

A woman comes over with a med kit and goes to take my arm, but I take off after McTier. "Lieutenant --"

"You need to be getting ready, Garcia."

"For what?" I snap. McTier doesn't like that. She stops and looks at me.

"Like I said, we have --"

"New orders, yeah." I don't take my eyes off hers. She may have just stared down Captain Turbo (pretty badass, I'm going to admit) and she even got up in Sosuke's face (a little more crazy than badass, but still, props, chica), but they're not me.

And they don't know what I know.

I put on a bit more of a professional tone. "Our targets are in custody, ma'am. Mission's over. Siesta time."

She blinks, just once, real fast. "Your mission is over when I say it's over, Agent." She spins on her heel. My foot slides an inch to the side. From it, a split the width of a human hair speeds along the concrete parking lot. When it reaches the spot an inch in front of where McTier's first step is about to fall, there's an audible crack as it widens, leaving a black, hollow lightning bolt of my displeasure for her to look at.

She freezes.

113

And now that I have her attention, "I'm not going blindly into any warehouses today, Lieutenant."

I gotta say this for McTier, she has one hell of a poker face. There's a solid six seconds where she just glares at me. I don't know what's running through her head, but my bet? I just gave up something vital -- now she knows I've talked to either Lux or Captain Turbo alone -- and she's gotta figure out which is more important, keeping me on mission or keeping me in the dark.

Because now she knows that I know.

There's a secret mission.

It was in the DC medical wing of the ESOA, right after I called Lux by the name I'd known him my entire life:

Tío Pedro.

Oh, it felt so good to call him that! I'd been waiting, holding onto that for so long. Honestly, I wasn't sure if I would ever get to meet him. I thought maybe, maybe after I was an established agent, maybe I could ask the ESOA to arrange something. Not just for me, but for him. He deserved it. He'd done so much.

I'd known who he was my whole life. When the Justice Brigade would charge out into battle before the cameras, my whole family would pray. When he came back victorious, mi abuelo, his papá, would let out tears of pride. He was the shining beacon of our family.

But also, somehow, an open wound.

An empty seat at la cena de Navidad.

A quiet sob of mi abuela, late in the night.

So when he turned away from me, I knew I couldn't leave that gap between us. This was probably my only chance, and I wasn't going to waste it. Yes, it was against protocol. Yes, it was expressly forbidden by the ESOA. Yes, I broke some of the biggest rules they had and, most likely, could be thrown into a federal correctional facility for it (like they had a prison that could hold me). But hearing him bark at me like that after I did?

Absolutely, one hundred percent worth it.

Then, I was ready to turn around and tell him everything he should have been hearing about his sisters, his nieces and nephews, his parents for the last forty years. But I didn't get to, because the look on his face sent chills through my skin. His eyes were dark and hard, filed down like obsidian daggers. I went to him quickly, and before I even sat down, he was firing things off in Spanish so fast I could barely follow.

"I don't know how you ended up here or what has happened to you, but everything you have been told about what it is you are doing... is a lie."

"Tío -- "

He just raised a hand and kept going, speaking in hurried Spanish, knowing that if we were overheard, it could be dangerous for both of us. "I didn't say anything before. I didn't know who you were or who you were working for. But now that I know..." He reached out, gripping my forearm tightly. His skin was hot. "Mijita, you must listen to me."

That's when I started to feel a little scared.

"When I said things were strange the night of the warehouse, I was trying to hint. There is more, much, much more. You have fallen into something deep, something sinister. The fight at the warehouse, the superhumans there, the lack of information, the fact that Araknis showed up out of nowhere? None of this is coincidence. Twenty years. Twenty years, mijita! He has been gone and then, out of nowhere, just shows up? No. No! It was not his way. He was sent there. For what, I do not know. But ever since that day, the day in Japan where everything went wrong, things have been different."

"Different?"

"They vanished, yes. But I knew they were not gone."

"The Triad?"

"Yes. They were too smart, too strong to fall there. People reported they had survived. The government hid this. They wanted people to feel safe. And so, I went along. We waited for them to rise again. When they didn't, everyone else just wrote them off, but not me. I kept looking, mijita. I saw things changed."

"How?"

"In the world, everything. Crime, it changed. The Triad was gone from the public, but I could still feel them, could sense their presence. They were not going to show their faces but that didn't mean they were not working, stretching their fingers across the world in different ways."

My eyebrows crunched together. "I don't understand."

He'd leaned forward, spoke softly but urgently. "I faced Doctor Dendrite. I looked into his eyes. He is not a man that would ever, ever stop. By the time Japan happened, they were so strong, the most powerful in the world. No one with that much power doesn't use it to amass more. And what happens when one person gains too much power?"

My eyes went wide. "Everyone else starts to want it."

He nodded, seeing I understood.

After that, I stood up. I thanked him, in polite and professional English, for his time and his advice before making my way out of the room, my brain firing on all cylinders.

It should have been obvious. The ESOA and the military hadn't ever really worked together before, not so closely. Ties like that don't happen overnight. By the time I'd come on, McTier was in place and running a well-oiled machine. Then, they brought me on, and the others. Not when the warehouse happened, though. We'd been training together for months, almost a year. The try-outs had been way before that. They'd fed us the line that we were just being prepared in case of an event.

We'd been prepared because they were planning an event.

The military and ESOA have a secret operation. Apparently, I'm a part of it. We all are. Our entire unit was been created to support it, and I had no way of knowing who was pulling the strings.

Until now.

McTier doesn't sigh. Her shoulders drop a little bit. Cat's out of the bag, and now she has to deal with it. "Sugiyama, Corvis. Over here." She gives a little flick of her fingers.

I had always suspected her. Before Lux, even before the press conference. How could I not? She's too calm, too calculated. I get that she's some kind of super soldier, a military prodigy and pedigree, but seriously... no one holds their cards that close to their chest.

"There's been another incident," McTier starts. She pauses just long enough to give me a are-you-happy-now look.

And for the record, no, I'm not. But I'm willing to play along, so I give a tiny nod.

"The MIT building which was broken into previously was, as of this morning, placed under hold by the ESOA. We had forensic tech teams working on the security system and a basic Special Ops team handling the building. Frankly, we didn't really expect anything to come of it, and it was pretty low on our list of priorities. That is, until two individuals entered the facility. Together, they caused a scene and led the agents on a wild goose chase. During that time, one of them completely erased all of the data from the security system -- video, keycard punches, everything was wiped out."

"And," my eyes get a little squinty, "what did the other one do?"

"She wiped out the team."

My chest tightens a little. "Like --"

"Zero fatalities," McTier says, flipping through the sheets in the top folder. I'm relieved. She almost sounds annoyed. Like, if the ops team was going to get their asses kicked, they shouldn't get to live to tell about it or something. I dunno. Maybe now those soldiers are more loose strings she'll have to snip. "By the time backup arrived, the individuals were gone. We were able to get descriptions and an account of what happened. Some factors varied, but one thing was entirely clear." She brings her eyes up. "The individual who took down the team had powers."

Wait a minute... McTier said 'she'. A woman who can take down an entire team of Special Ops soldiers in minutes? A tiny shiver runs across my skin. "Lieutenant," I ask, "do they think it was --"

"No," McTier says surprisingly fast and, well, surprisingly. It's not just informative, it's... it's a genuine, caring reaction to my worry.

If Araknis showed his face, it's only a matter of time until Wraith shows hers.

But just as fast as McTier's human instincts came on, they're gone. She clears her throat. "She didn't match anyone in our database, but from her proficiency, it's clear she's been well trained." From the folder comes a big photo, black and white and grainy. "The security system inside the building was made completely inoperable, but one of the exterior cameras caught the individuals as they left."

I take the picture. Not much to go on. Two women, my age or a bit older. The smaller one -- Caucasian, skinny but clearly muscular -- looks like any other college student. The other woman...

Why is there something familiar about her?

"Which one has the powers?"

McTier points to the smaller woman. And as much as I want to stare at her, try to match her up to the bazillions of pictures they've shown us of every known associate of the Triad of Evil, I keep looking back to the other woman.

She looks like... maldita sea, it's right there, I just can't...

"The university is working on identifying them, so that's where we're heading."

"But," I say, "the, the original thief, the student, he was working alone, right?"

McTier just stares.

The muscles around my jaw go a little tighter. They've been lying from the start, just to set a trap. They knew someone else was involved, but they didn't know who. If they had released that, let the news report on it, that person would have gone into hiding. But by letting them think they're in the clear, there's a better chance they'll surface.

I try and push down the anger that's rising up in my chest. It's not at McTier or the ESOA for lying; tactically, that was a smart move. It's at myself. I didn't jump through any warehouse skylights, but I totally let myself get involved in something, and I don't know how deep it goes.

McTier reads me well enough to know that I've put it together, so she continues. "The second woman is of little concern. I want to know if the woman with powers was at the warehouse last night."

"Lieutenant?" Sosuke has been entirely silent this whole time, and weirdly still. He's right next to me, but I'd forgotten he was there. So when McTier and I snap our heads, I think we're both surprised by the look on his face.

His eyelids are partially closed, but his pupils are snapping back and forth, up and around. His mouth is a little bit open, like he's in a haze, or trying to remember something.

Or... trying to remember something that isn't his own memory...

When he speaks, it's not slurred, but a little slower than usual. He's not unsure, he's just still processing the visuals or whatever it is he absorbed from Brass Knuckles. "Bearserker, Brass Knuckles, the Justice Brigade, and Araknis were the only super powered people at the warehouse. The girl who took out the ops team wasn't there." He raises his hand and drips his index finger on the photo with a decisive thump, right into the chest of the other woman.

His eyes, clear, focused, and as hot as lightning, snap up.

"But she was."

CHAPTER THIRTEEN
KINDRED SPIRITS

After discovering the truth about Captain Turbo, about what happened to my gravity bands, I began my early foray into the life of true supervillainy; a series of schemes, plans, plots, and heists, one after another, all engineered to either draw Captain Turbo out so I could reclaim the original bands, or capture enough capital and equipment so that I could create a new pair.

Neither of those things ever happened.

Heists are easy to pull off; strike fast, grab what's needed, and get out. As long as the target is something replaceable, a fast escape in a radar-cloaked rocket usually means success. Private companies have insurance to cover their losses, and government-funded programs are so caught up in red tape, it takes them months to realize something is even missing. No harm, no foul.

But the plots to capture Captain Turbo? Far, far less lucrative.

Most of these ended with all that stolen equipment being smashed to pieces and me in an escape pod, tending to a broken nose. Because of this, my exploits had to grow larger, grander, and more complex. Soon, Captain Turbo and I captured international attention. This led to more and more people, heroes and villains, coming into the public eye. All of a sudden, the age of super-crime and super-heroics was born. Before I knew it, I wasn't just dealing with one muscle-bound idiot, but dozens of masked morons who thought they had the right to get in my way. Some of them, I showed the appropriate respect and concern; Ironsides was pure brute force, but an invincible man determined to cave in your head is still an invincible man determined to cave in your head. Also, on several occasions, I had the unfortunate luck of encountering Wraith and Lux. I barely managed to escape.

Of course, many heroes I left stripped of pride and bathed in embarrassment. At first my reactions were harmless, but after too many caped clowns declared they would be bringing me to justice, I started getting a little more... aggressive. Several ended up in the hospital, either with broken bones or entire segments of their skeletons evaporated. A few I trapped in alternate dimensions. One, a particularly pompous model of patriarchy, made the mistake of letting a racial slur slip during our fight.

I left him naked, at the highest point of the North Pole, surrounded by genetically modified saber-toothed penguins.

Which, apparently, was a step too far. Soon after, Captain Turbo decided my nefariousness overshadowed his own glory, and therefore, I was a threat without compare. It would take far more than just one or two heroes to end my reign.

It would take... the Justice Brigade.

I had to alter my strategy entirely. Those heists that generally went off without a hitch? They stopped my next three within minutes. The plots where I usually got away with nothing but a broken nose? The first time I tried one, I ended up in police custody. Thankfully, I'd invented an entire arsenal of tech for just such a thing ahead of time.

I wasn't about to try a second time.

The heroes had formed a miniature army and declared war on me, and it seemed there was nothing I could do. Villains don't really work well with... well, anyone. Team ups mostly end in backstabbing, both figurative and literal. I didn't have much hope for assistance.

Oddly enough, for as secretive, secluded, and generally untrusting as villains are, they're openly protective of the criminal community. Anyone who takes being a villain seriously has files on all the daring do-gooders they've encountered, and it's inevitable that people will want to compare notes and get up to speed when three powerhouse heroes join forces.

Or, when one gets left behind.

I'd bugged phone lines, waiting and listening for her name. It was the early days of chat rooms, so I dropped a worm into the coding that would send me a message if she was mentioned. I had drones floating through her city at night, set to detect even the faintest wisp of her abilities. I sat in my hoverjet above the moonlit skyscrapers, waiting.

Nothing.

Wraith was gone.

But then, a call. Turns out one of the best ways to get what you want is to pay for it. I'd hit up every bar where good guys gathered, Hero Hidey Holes as I liked to call them, and offered a nice tip to anyone who saw her and sent me a line. Most refused, saying they had too much integrity for something like that. They did cater to heroes, after all. So, I offered a hefty reward, and they agreed. They were still business owners, after all.

Surprisingly, the call came from the last place I expected, a Sinister Speakeasy.

The Hid n' Run.

Whispering into the receiver, the bartender asked if the reward was real. I told him yes. I also told him if he were lying to me I'd burn down his establishment, bury his house in a sinkhole, and frame him for committing both acts as insurance fraud.

Like I said, generally untrusting.

When I arrived, the front door was hanging from the hinges. The room was filled with smashed chairs, broken tables, and not a single criminal. The place was normally dim anyway, but whatever fight had driven away the bar's regulars had smashed several of the lamps. Wraith was alone at the bar, tendrils of smoke and mist wavering in and out of the shadows.

I walked in slowly. She knew I was there, but her only acknowledgement was to coalesce for a moment, snatch the shot glass in front of her, down the alcohol, drop the glass, and slip away again. With a shaking hand, the bartender refilled it. He took a tepid step away, but kept the bottle in his hand. I could see sweat stains beneath his arms and around his neck. He was trying to stand still, but failing miserably. On the other hand, the stillness of Wraith's form within and the constant rolling of the smoke gave a sense that whatever I believed I was looking at, I was mistaken.

My hands... I remember they felt unusually heavy... finally moved. There was a blaster strapped to my side, and as my fingers passed near it, Wraith's form shifted the tiniest of bits. My heart skipped a beat, but my hand kept moving up, away from the blaster and to the bottom of my mask. I removed it, gradually, purposefully, revealing to her the face no hero had ever seen.

With just as much care, I walked behind her and, as gingerly as I could, took the stool next to her. Being near her was like being near a cobra raised to strike. Resting my mask on the bar, I took a deep breath. The place smelled like stale peanuts and cigarettes burned down to the filters.

"What she's having," I said. The bartender glanced at Wraith for permission. I made sure to keep my sight trained on him. Whatever movement she made, I don't know, but he gave a quick nod, put a shot glass in front of me, and poured dark rum from a darker bottle. Most of it ended up on the bar. With a wink, I asked for the bottle. He handed it to me gladly. Pouring myself a drink with a noticeably less shaky hand... there was only a bit of tremble to it... I let out an exaggerated sigh."It's bullshit, you know?"

Wraith said nothing.

"You put in the effort, the energy... the passion. The fire."

Her mist continued to loll about, up and down, in and out.

"All that time, wasted."

She glanced at me from the corner of her eye.

"If I'm going to be honest -- and I know, I know. You can't trust a word I say, but listen, I really mean this -- you couldn't be more perfect. I mean, I can't even begin to imagine the thought process behind that decision."

Her head raised.

"Even with you being..." I gestured with my glass, pointing from tip to toes. Her eyes followed. "... you get tossed aside. Who in their right mind would do such a thing? Huh?"

She turned a bit. Her eyes, big and round and bottomlessly dark, narrowed with curiosity.

"Huge mistake," I said, bringing the glass to my lips, then away again. "Huge."

A smile crawled onto one side of her lips. As I drank my shot, slow and smooth, an elbow appeared from the maelstrom of mist and rested on the bar. Her long fingertips came together out of thin air and danced, hovering above her glass, alighting for only a moment, as delicate as a speck of floating dust.

I felt like wiggling with glee, but instead poured myself another drink. "If I may be so bold?" She nodded her consent. "Lux is a fool."

Her fingers stopped.

"For him to choose the Justice Brigade over you --"

She used a tired sigh to turn herself away from me, back to the bar.

I'd touched a nerve, so I pressed on. "Did he come to you? Tell you he was leaving you behind, or did he just slink out like an alley cat in the night?"

With a jerk, she swallowed her shot.

"Do you... did he even think about it? Did he think about saying no?"

Her glass came down, hard. "You don't know what you're talking about." The alcohol had made her voice raspy, but there was still an edge to it.

I said, "He doesn't seem like the deep thinking type."

That edge grew sharper. "You don't know anything."

"Not like you."

And sharper. "You should be quiet now."

"Three minutes. I bet he gave it three minutes."

Razor... thin... "I'm telling you --"

"Tops."

It happened faster than I could register. The smoke whipped. I went to move to react, to blink, but she was there, behind me, the mist swirling all over my body, wrapping my limbs and torso. She had her nails against my throat, soft enough that they hadn't broken the skin, hard enough that they absolutely could. Her face was next to my ear. Her hair brushed against me. I could feel the heat from her breath as she said in a calm, not-calm voice, "You don't know anything about this."

I was terrified. My heart was pounding and every fiber of my body was surging with adrenaline. I'd wanted a rise from her, and now I had it. "I know I'm not the one you should be fighting with right now."

"No?" She snapped.

"Lux isn't going to leave the --"

"This," she hissed the word. "This whole thing is because of you. Because the great and terrible Doctor Dendrite is so evil, so dangerous, it must take the best..." Her lips snapped shut. When they opened, her tongue clicked. "Some... of the best heroes in the world to stop him. But do you know what that means? That means there is an easy solution. No Dendrite, no Justice Brigade, right? So, why don't I just beat your ass silly and drop you off with the cops? That would put an end to it. That'd get him off the team, right?"

"I suppose it would."

"Don't be stupid."

"Wouldn't dream of it."

"You'd just break out, build some giant, exploding robo-moles or something --"

"That's really not my style --"

"-- and this whole thing would start all over again."

The muscles in the back of my neck were starting to cramp from keeping my chin pointed at the ceiling. "So then, what's your solution?"

She paused. Her voice went deep. "You really wanna know?"

"I --"

A whisper. "Because I don't think you're gonna like the answer."

My mouth twitched. "What can I say? Curiosity killed the cat."

"Interesting choice of words."

"Maybe. Maybe not."

She hesitated.

"Can you? Can you really do it?"

"I don't see why not."

"Doesn't it go against your code? Your ethics?"

"'Cause those got me so far." Her sarcasm was dripping, like the sweat running down my cheek.

I licked my lips. "I thought heroes always found another way."

"Maybe that's the problem, you know? We're always trying to figure something else out. This, this just seems more... how would you say it? Logical."

"Now there's something I can relate to."

The mist spun across me, pulling our bodies closer as she said through clenched teeth, "You can't relate to anything about me."

"I dunno," I said casually, "seeing this side of you makes me wonder. Maybe this, right here, it's not the best idea."

"You have another one?"

"I've got something in mind."

"Go for that blaster, Dendrite, and I swear I'll --"

"You'll what? You'll kill me? Cut me open and parade my hide all over town? Because that'll work. That'll bring him back to you."

She laughed then, but not the kind of laugh I wanted to hear. It was almost... disappointed. "For a guy who's got doctor in front of his name, you are so dumb."

"Tell me, Wraith, would you really become the thing that you hate?"

"What choice do I have?" She took a breath, the kind that comes in two parts because one isn't enough to keep the sadness down."Nobody wants what I am."

"Lux doesn't know --"

She shouted, "This isn't about Lux!" and her tendrils sent every stool around us flying.

As the room settled, I sat in the silence of my own ineptitude.

"You're right," I said, sincerely. "I'm sorry. I am... I'm incredibly stupid and insensitive, and I'm sorry. I just... I've got all these thoughts of my own and sometimes, sometimes I forget to listen."

Her nails didn't retreat from my throat, but eased.

"This isn't my first time here, at this bar. I come here sometimes to meet a friend, the Histerrorian. Yes, I know, I know, he's... not good at being a villain. His whole shtick, stealing historical artifacts and then doing nothing with them, it's not really, I mean... it's not hurting anybody. It's illegal. Not really all that terrifying, either. But what can I say? He's a pal, and even someone like him, someone like me, we just, we need... others. Right?" I peeked at her from the corner of my eye. She was listening. I continued.

"We get together, after a heist or a plan goes wrong. We usually sit in that booth. He likes the old-fashioned ornamental lighting fixture on the wall there. It was probably bought second hand at some thrift store, but hey, it makes him happy."

Bit by bit, her fingers loosened.

"We'll get a bottle, much like this one here, and we'll sit, and we'll pour, and we'll talk about how hero A avoided booby-trap B and broke machine C which led to us implementing escape plan D, but not before getting punched or kicked or zapped in body part E. And then the other will recount a similar time in their career, and back and forth and back and forth. Then, when the bottle is empty, we'll tip our glasses, surrendering ourselves to the weight of the world, put our hats on, and wander home."

Her body began moving away from mine.

"The last time was maybe a year ago. Things started out normal, I don't remember who told the story, but when the bottle ran dry, when it was time to go, he broke the silence between us with an odd question. He asked me if I knew why. Why we kept trying our ridiculous plans. Why we refused to just give up and fade away into the annals of time. I didn't tell him my reasons; he was a pal but that's... I like to keep my personal and professional life separate. But when I didn't speak, he leaned across the table and told me."

I turned, just enough to look her in the eye.

"Justice, he said. For some wrongdoing against us, some inequality we've had to face, some unfair card we've been dealt, we are all seeking our own justice. Then, he asked me if I knew what was stopping us from achieving that justice. I didn't know what to say, so he filled in the blank for me. The most treacherous of sins. Pride. For it feels righteous, and yet, it drains us of the one thing we need to find justice."

"And what's that?" she asked me, doubtful and cautious, but interested as well.

"The one thing that can cure pride," I said. "Honor."

Her eyes went big. I slid off my seat.

"The honor we deserve. The honor we earned. The honor which was taken from us in that wrongdoing."

She nodded, once, so tiny I don't know if she was even conscious of it.

"We can take back our honor, but only if we're willing to fight for it. To show the ones who took it that our justice is greater than theirs. Our honor is not for them to claim."

Her chest rose and fell. Her eyes jumped back and forth between mine. I glanced at the booth behind her. My face softened.

"When he finished, I put on my hat and said farewell. I thought it was a drunken rambling, nothing more. But that night, just like tonight, I'd only heard, not listened." A sigh, unhindered, unashamed, left me. "I reached out to him a few weeks back. When I got no response, I went looking. He died three months ago. Apparently, he'd been ill, some condition that had plagued him for most of his life. I had no idea. He never..." A weak laugh made its way out. "Personal and professional, right?"

"Yeah," she said. Maybe because she understood, maybe because she didn't know what else to say.

"I understand, now, why he was so obsessed with the past. It's because he knew he didn't have a future." Walking around Wraith, I rested my hand on the back of the booth's bench seat. "I went to his grave. It was plain and simple, the best his family could afford. They'd laid him to rest under his civilian name, Timothy or William or some such thing. His villain identity was never released to the public. Anyone passing by would think he was just another person, another footnote in the big book of the past.

"I took a bottle of Scotch with me. After a long pull for myself, I poured a drink on his grave. I played our last conversation over and over again in my head. He'd known. I'm sure he'd known then that his time was coming, and he had done me the great honor of passing on what little he had. And now..." My hand came off the seatback. I turned, my eyes fighting to hold back the pain and sadness and anger that was welling up in them. "... I've passed it onto you."

Wraith's mouth opened, words brewing behind her teeth, held by her tongue.

"I really am sorry for earlier. I only heard you before. But now, I'm listening." I began walking toward her. "I don't believe in fate, Wraith. I believe in what I know. You've been wronged. Your honor has been taken by men. Arrogant, selfish, self-absorbed men who are so scared by the power you wield, their only defense is to shame you into thinking you can't fight back." My feet stopped, my toes inches from hers. I leaned in, through the mist surrounding her body that rose up to keep us apart, and whispered into her ear. "But you can."

Without looking at her response, I spun on my heels and headed for the bar.

"You said," I called over my shoulder, "we couldn't relate." I grabbed the rum. "Through some odd coincidence, the same thing that happened to you, happened to me." My fingers snatched both of our glasses. "And I have been fighting, every day since then, to reclaim what is my given right." The rum splashed down. I dropped the bottle on the bar, picked up my mask, slipped it under my arm like a soldier, and faced her with a drink in each hand. "My pride told me that this fight was for me and me alone. But those who wronged me... who wronged us... have come together. They've amassed their forces so you and I can never beat them. Not... alone."

I raised my glass.

"I'm willing to put my pride aside, for our greater goods. I'm willing, Wraith, to do whatever it takes. I'm going to get justice, with or without you."

I swallowed the rum, smacked the empty glass on the bar, and offered her the other. She looked at it, then to me. Tentative, she took it. The moment it left my hand, I headed for the exit. "Three minutes. I'll give you three minutes." Slipping my mask on, I headed out into the dark road. The downdraft and spotlights from my hoverjet exploded around me. With a mechanical whine, the stairs lowered, crunching against the pavement. I put my foot upon the first step and looked back into the bar.

It was empty.

Two clinks, glass against something hard. She was at the top of the stairs, her smoke and costume blowing in the wind, red fingernails shining like fresh blood in the light. She didn't smile, or laugh, or cackle, or anything like that. She simply raised the glass and said, "Let's go."

Behind my mask, I grinned.

Well, shitballs.

I'm dead.

Not sure how it happened. Maybe Annie drove my car into a telephone pole. I bet she felt really guilty after, you know, punching me in the damn face.

Wait! Maybe that's what did it. Parker, poor stupid Parker, used to go on and on about how, if you hit someone's nose just right, you can push cartilage up into their brain. I would tell him he was watching too much anime. Then he'd ask me if I had another way to 'occupy his time'. Then I'd punch his arm, just hard enough that the answer was no, but just soft enough to keep him thinking that the answer may one day be yes.

God, I was such a bitch to him.

And now he's dead.

And so am I.

I am one hundred percent sure I'm dead because I can't really feel my body, and all I can see is a soft, glowing white; like a solid cloud has descended down upon me. Never really thought about that whole heaven and hell thing, but gotta admit, kinda surprised I ended up going to the good place. Or maybe this is purgatory? I mean, there aren't any demons trying to shove a pineapple up my ass, so I guess I can't complain.

Alright, time to do the whole 'go toward the light' thing.

Ow.

OW!

What the actual shit?

My head, ohh man, that... that hurts. Pain all over the place. I didn't even know I was lying down, but I am now more than acutely aware of the fact I am not, in fact, dead. Because dead people don't feel like they're waking up hung over from a two-day rave.

My teeth hurt. She hit me so hard, my damn teeth hurt. I swear to god, she better not have knocked any of them loose. I had braces for three years when I was a kid and I will kick her ass if I need any major dental work.

I mean, with words. I will kick her ass with words. Because, you know, she's got superpowers and all.

I manage to pry my eyes open long enough to see that white haze again. Only now, the pain has made my vision oh so clear and I realize it's just a white plaster ceiling and somewhere there's a standing lamp illuminating it.

Wait a minute... I know that ceiling.

Oh crap. I'm home.

This is, literally, the opposite of where I told Annie to take me. Granted, we argued and, granted, she did kinda win by knocking me unconscious. But still...

Dead would be so much easier right now. Dead would mean all this bullshit I've been putting up with would be over. Yes, Annie would be in trouble, and that sucks for her. But considering how ridiculously screwed up everything is right now, that was kind of unavoidable.

I'm not really the crying type. I'm a screaming-yelling-slamming-doors-trashing-my-room-maybe-go-kinda-catatonic-for-a-while type person. I don't like crying, and I only do it when things are way, way beyond boned.

So when I feel those cold, wet drops rolling down the sides of my face, I tell myself it's just from the physical pain.

My lungs fill themselves, and then let it all go. I close my eyes again. I try to focus on anything else around me, and before I know it, I'm listening to my own heartbeat. Really listening to it, you know? Not just feeling it or aware of it. It's like I've got a stethoscope up against it or something. It's calming and comforting, like the best white noise ever. And once I start to calm down, other sounds, all the sounds around me, start sliding in.

"And you're sure she deleted everything?"

"Yes."

In the other room, people are talking.

No, they're whispering, but I can hear them. It's... it's not good. Not terrible, not unbearable, but not pleasant. It's like they're too close. I try and tune them out, bring down the volume, but I can't.

"What the hell were you thinking?" says the bitchiest voice I know.

"She was going with or without me." Says another person, whose voice was, up until earlier today, one of my favorite things to hear. But now...

"So you went along like a good little dog."

"I was..." Annie replies. I hear the hurt in her voice. "I was just doing my job."

"Your job," says Samantha, "is to keep an eye on her and report back to me."

Maybe it's Samantha's tone, maybe it's that their voices are suddenly too loud, then too soft, maybe it's the fact that I hate her so, or maybe it's the fact that she just confirmed something I really didn't want confirmed, but her voice feels like a tetanus shot in my head.

Annie's job.

... I'm Annie's job.

This would normally be the moment when those stupid tears start up.

Instead, everything inside me just goes cold. Samantha and Annie keep talking, but thankfully whatever's going on with my hearing seems attached to my emotions. They tune out.

Against all common sense, I sit up. Well, no, I try to sit up, but that doesn't really happen. Sparking pain in my neck. Goddamn, Annie gave me whiplash or something. So I roll with a grunt and swing my legs off the couch. By the time I'm able to stand up, their voices are too close for comfort again.

"So," Annie is clearly trying to change the subject away from the fact that I'm nothing more than some kind of stupid assignment and not really her friend.

Shit, thinking that hurts worse than my face.

She says, "What's the next step?"

"Well thanks to Miss Doesn't-Give-Two-Shits-About-Anyone-But-Herself, I had to put in the call. We're meeting at the museum for extraction."

"Okay," Annie replies, her voice soft.

"If we're lucky, we get to take on whole new identities and lead the rest of our lives. If not..." she takes a deep breath, and what comes next isn't snarky.

It's scared.

"... she sees this as a colossal failure and literally, literally, skins us alive."

Wait. She? She who?

"She won't," Annie says. "Candace is safe and that --"

"Whatever," Samantha barks. I wince at the sound. "Just, just go out there and get that worthless skank off the couch and ready to go."

Oh bitch, you did not just --

"We're leaving in ten minutes," Samantha snaps. "Got it, Fido?"

"Yeah," Annie says, super soft. I hear a pair of shoes, they sound like boots, stomping away.

Annie says, "Hey, Princess?"

Ha! That's what I call Samantha!

Oh wait, this is serious. Annie's super serious right now. I should listen.

"What?" Samantha snarks back. And then it goes quiet.

Annie says, not so super soft, "If you ever call her something like that again, you won't live long enough to be skinned."

Oh.

Oh damn.

I... I don't know what...

Shit. I'm having a lot of feelings today. I'm down, and then way down, and then I'm back up. Right now, I'm still working on processing that last

130

thing, and figuring out if my heart is racing because of what Annie said, or because I hear her heading toward me. I try to take a good breath, try to think of what to do. Do I hug her? Do I high five? I mean, should I let on that I heard? Cause, let's be real, she's gonna know. Then again, I'm still pissed at her for punching me in the face and bringing me back here and hiding the fact that she's got powers but we kinda moved past that and I need to -- Okay! Game plan! Focus on the now, girl. Annie just stood up to Samantha for me, so let's go with... um... fist bump? Hell yeah? No, that's a little bro-ski and I'm not feeling that right now. I gotta... I should say... oh god. I'm going to have to say something. Anything. Thank you? No that, that's stupid. Like, a... a joke. Maybe something about the Fido thing? Yeah. No. That, that was really mean and I shouldn't --

"Candace?"

Oh crap she's here. I turn, ready to do, I dunno, something. But instead of the thirty-six things I could have done that would have been totally appropriate, I instead freeze, then say, "That... is a lot of spandex."

Apparently, this is not what Annie was expecting, because behind her black rubber mask thingy that only shows her mouth, chin, hair, and eyes, I can see shock.

And then frustration.

Because that's not all I say.

"I mean..." and here's where my eyes go big. And my voice. And my mouth. "Damn!" It's really more of a day-yum. "I mean... that," waving my arms up and down. "How do you even get into that thing?"

"Candace --"

But I'm not done. "Wait, scratch that, how do you get out?"

"Candace --"

"I have seen scuba divers with looser clothing."

"Seriously."

"I have seen seals that were less sleek."

"Seriously?"

"But look, but look, for real. For. Real. I am not messing around. You... this outfit is straight up," dramatic pause, "dope."

And it is. Annie is looking hotter than a chocolate lava cake. It's all black and sleek but it's got some gray stripes that curve around her muscles. I can't tell what it's made of, it looks like it's got a texture, but also like anything touching it will slide right off.

I shake my head, smile, and let out a breathy, "Wow."

Annie says, "Okay," in a 'we're done' voice, but in the bit of cheek that's exposed, I see the tiniest shade of red. "Look, we've got a lot to talk about."

131

"Wait," I say. "How you even use the bathroom in that thing?"

Oh girl, you wanna smile. You know you do. But you don't. Because you're being all cool and superhero and...

Wait a minute.

"Are," I start. "So, what... what are you?"

She pauses before she speaks, and then says in a slow and concerned voice, "I don't have any bones, just muscles, and --"

"I know, I know." I wave my hand. I'm not brain-damaged, girl. I'm confused. "Super bendy, I got all that. I mean, like... what are you?"

She stares.

I lean in a little. "Hero or villain?"

"I'm..." Her breath catches. "It's complicated."

And here's the part where I say something super condescending, or passive-aggressive, or some other bullshit.

But I don't.

Instead, I just nod and say, "Yeah, tell me about it." And Annie gives that 'oh, you know' kind of laugh sigh. It stops when I put my hand on her arm. "Seriously," I say, looking her right in the eye. "Tell me. I wanna know who you are."

Her chest goes up and down a few times before she manages to say anything. "I'm –"

"Twist!"

God. Damn. You. Princess. Bitch!

I didn't hear those boots thump, thumping down the hallway, but I hear them now.

"Is little Miss Can't-Do-Wrong up?"

Annie checks the floor for her composure. She turns her body just enough that her arm slips from my hand.

I was right about her outfit. Smooth has half-melted butter.

Boots thumping, Samantha's icy tone jumps down the hall and into my personal space. "We need to go, ASAP." But what's funny, it's not Samantha that comes around the corner. It's a freaking Mardi Gras float.

She looks like she took a glitter cannon at point blank range after being attacked by a mob of bedazzlers. Her face, her clothes, her everything is covered in sparkles and tiny gems. The mask on her face, it kind of sticks off in places, big swirls and twists. She looks like all of a Vegas strip show mashed into the space of one person.

"I should have known you were awake." She says. "I couldn't hear the snoring."

But when she talks, I see it. The mask isn't a mask. If it was, it would have

132

eye holes. It would come to an end and there'd be skin beneath. The tiny diamond dot thingies go right up to her eyelids. Everything moves when she talks. The weird swirls aren't swirls, they're like tiny little glitter horns.

The mask is actually on her skin.

"Okay, we're moving out." She says. "Candi, we're going to need you to get in the car, keep your head down and your mouth shut, got it?"

No.

It is her skin.

"Are you okay to travel? Not like you have a choice."

What. The. Hell?

"Candi?" Her hand comes up between us. Those little beads are all over the backs of it, running down her now snapping fingers. "Jesus, Twist, how hard did you hit her? Hello? Candi?"

My head tilts so I can keep looking at her face. "Wow."

Samantha's snapping fingers stop. "What?"

I pause, raise a finger, and point."You got a little... something... there."

Annie snorts.

"Just, you know, maybe need a washcloth, or..."

Beneath Samantha's glitter and beads, her skin changes to match her fire engine lips.

"Some cold sore cream..."

Keeping her eyes on me, she says to Annie, "Go get the car ready." It's an order. Not a bitchy, 'I'm the prettiest in the room so you better do what I want' kind of order. The real kind. Annie nods and heads out, obediently, leaving me and Samantha in a solid silence. She's putting out a vibe right now that I'm not used to. This isn't posturing and positioning and all that Queen Bee bullshit she normally does.

"So," I say casually, "nice costumes."

"Outfits," she replies, quickly enough that I know she's not just being a bitch. That's what they actually call them.

"Got it. Though, I gotta say, the cape is bit much. I mean, it's cute, but is it functional? It's long enough to cover your butt, but too short to hide behind or anything. Does it really do anything other than say, 'hey look everyone, I'm wearing a cape'?"

Oh, she wants to say something nasty so bad. I can see the muscles behind that freaky mask twitch. Yet she doesn't, which is totally out of character for her. I let a little smile grow on my lips, and wait for her to explode.

"Hey!" A voice shouts from upstairs. It's Brit. "We've got a problem."

Samantha comes back to me. "We're leaving in two minutes, get whatever

133

you need and be ready." She spins on her heel.

"Who put you in charge, Princess?"

She heads for the stairs, with me right behind her. "The same person who thinks you're worth keeping alive."

"Who's that?"

Her only answer is the pounding of her big-ass, eggshell white boots.

"Why do they want me alive?"

Nothing but her stupid off-white cape fluttering in my face as I stomp up the stairs behind her.

"What makes me so special?"

Her pace picks up. So does my blood pressure. So does the pounding in my ears.

"Either you give me a goddamn answer or I am not getting in that car!"

She doesn't even look back. Beneath my skin, that sensation of movement, that building pressure, comes back. It works into my arms, into my hands.

"Answer me!" I bark as I grab at her shoulder. She whirls around, fast as hell, and does some kind of crazy jujitsu thing with her hands, trying to get me off her while also controlling me. I jerk back. My foot slips off the step. My arms go out, that sense of inertia takes over, and I'm looking at the ceiling, my legs all bendy and useless. I go back. My muscles all tense up. The pressure inside me gets ready to explode. My mind jumps back to the pressure I felt when that ESOA guy was shoving his gun in my face; to the sound in my ears when Samantha was looking at me in the mirror, letting me know I'd been caught; the feeling I had when Parker and Charlie died in front of me; when I saw Araknis's black, black eyes; when the spiders crawled all over his skin.

When I was in the warehouse.

The moment before the explosion.

And as I go tumbling backward, I know.

It's going to happen again. The second I hit those stairs, it's going to come out. And I can't stop it.

But it doesn't, because I never hit the stairs. I don't even really fall. Well, I do, but I don't. I'm falling, but I'm being super lazy about it. Like, someone else told me to fall, and I feel like I have to, but I'm going to take my sweet time.

Umm... what?

Samantha snatches my arm and pulls. I lurch forward, almost like I'm underwater. My feet, moving all slow and sleepy, find a good spot on the steps. I steady myself and everything goes back to normal. My lungs quickly inflate. Weird, I didn't even notice I was barely breathing.

When I check Samantha's face, she doesn't seem in the least bit surprised. If anything, she looks annoyed. We're still holding onto one another while I turn back and forth, trying to figure out what the hell just happened. At the top of the stairs, Brit is standing in her doorway. Her arm is out, fingers open, palm pointed straight at me.

And she's wearing a mask.

Are. You. Serious?

Samantha gives me another yank and, making sure the only way I'm going to fall is forward, lets go. I guess she doesn't mind if I bust my nose or knock out some teeth, just as long as I don't die. She glances back at Brit and says, "Good job."

Brit drops her arm and stares in her usual apathetic way. Her mask is, well, just a mask. There's nothing special about it. In fact, her whole costume (oh, wait, outfit... sorry) seems to scream 'meh'. It's not skin-tight, it's not polished leather. No symbols, no patterns or distinct marks. Black pants that fade into kind-of brown boots. There's a section over her chest, like a chunk of flexible body armor, that's red and has a big black circle in the middle. Everything is kind of military, sort of athletic. She's got padding almost like a football player, but more compact and sewn into the outfit. The one thing I notice is all the straps and buckles and things being held against her, things with grips and handles and leather carries and sheathes.

Things that look a lot like hand-held weapons. She's decked out with this shit, including two baton thingies strapped to her thighs.

Suddenly, I'm feeling way out of my league.

How did this happen? How did I not know? I'm living with three other people, all of them have freaking outfits and superpowers, and I was completely oblivious. I mean, I get that they hid it from me, but how did I not see?

How much of my life for the past few years has been a lie? How many decisions have I actually made for myself? Is everything I have, everything I've done been... been scripted or part of some goddamn plan that I'm not even aware of? What the hell is this? Why? Why would I, of all people, be living with super powered people?

No.

Other super powered people.

I can't breathe. I can, but I can't. I'm doing it, but too fast. No, too slow. No, I... I... shit. What --

Did they know? Did they know that I was, that I might have been... oh god. What if they did this to me? What if...

135

Samantha is up in Brit's room. They're staring at the ten or twelve computer screens that are set up. They're showing video of the areas around the house. I see little bits of movement from where I am, but I'm still halfway into this existential crisis so I don't really pay much attention. I do manage to start up the stairs.

"Hey," I say. Not sure how loud. Probably not at all, since Samantha and Brit just keep looking at the monitors.

"Back exit?" asks Samantha.

"Blocked," replies Brit.

"Rooftop?"

"Camera's dead."

"Hey," I say it again, definitely louder this time.

Samantha hisses. "Garage?"

"Oh no," Brit says with enough sarcasm to kill a person. "They decided to leave that wide open. You know, for shits and giggles."

"Not the time," says Samantha.

"Well what do you want me to say? Of course they've got it covered."

My fists open and close. Nostrils flare.

Samantha sighs, "Why haven't they moved in?"

"No idea."

Every breath is faster, harder, hotter.

Brit sighs. "What do we do?"

"We do exactly what we're supposed to do. Our job."

"Hey!" I shout. Samantha turns, but doesn't have time to flinch before my fist slams into her cheek. I wanted to break her goddamn nose, smash that stupid sparkly mask of hers, but I'm so pissed off I don't aim right. Samantha doesn't drop as much as she staggers. I lurch forward, totally off balance, and try to swing again. Brit's on me in an instant. I feel an arm, then two, and she's holding me back.

"What did you do?" I scream. "Did you do this to me? Huh?" My chest heaves as I sputter out words that I don't even know are coming. "Did you make me into this? Who are you working for? Who did this? Why did... why did they... am I some.. .some kind of experiment?" I haven't really noticed, but Brit let me go. Probably because I don't sound angry anymore. In fact, I sound like I'm crying. "I wanna know!" I sob. "I wanna know! Why is this happening? Why... why did Parker and Charlie have to die? Why did everything go wrong?"

Samantha's cheek is almost as red as her lipstick. Her perfect, unsmeared lipstick. She walks up and looks me right in the eye. There's anger there, burning hot behind her pupil. But the despise, the bitchiness and snarkiness and meanness which has made up our relationship for so long is gone.

Samantha's not there. And I start to wonder if she ever really was.

"Parker died because you're a selfish little brat." She says. "And if you weren't who you are, I'd cut your throat and watch you die."

Panting, I look right back at her. "I... I don't even know who I am."

Samantha opens her mouth to say something, but from behind her, from outside through the window and in back of the house and on top of it and just about everywhere, I hear a voice, a woman's voice that I know I've heard before, speaking through what sounds like a walkie-talkie.

"Unit one, ready?"

My eyebrows come together. "Did you --"

"Unit two, ready?"

Samantha looks at me out of the corner of her eye. "What are you --"

I put my hand up. The voice says another word, which I repeat to the room. "Breach?"

The window behind Samantha shatters and a little round metal ball bounces on the floor.Brit screams, "Mine!" and leaps forward, her hands held out like she's trying to catch a yoga ball. There's this huge, I dunno, whomp of noise, tons of air being displaced at once, and I see the world in front of Brit ripple and waver, then just die down.

"What the fu --"

"Get down!" Samantha shouts and shoves me to the floor as those grenade things go off in every bedroom. The house erupts with noises that tear at my ears. It's all too much. I can't tell things apart, but I know there's activity everywhere. In the blink of an eye, it's the warehouse all over again. All around me, people are fighting and running and shooting, but I'm on my ass, scrambling backwards, trying fight back the fear that's turning into panic in my brain.

Some guy in a ski mask slams face first into the wall near me and leaves a thick, red streak as he slides down it. He's not screaming, just making this weird, wet bubbling noise. I don't think it's coming from his mouth. I think it's coming from the giant, open wound in his throat. He was one of three guys that came in through the window. More have come in since then.

And Samantha and Brit are kicking their asses.

"We need to move!" Samantha shouts (in a weirdly clear and professional tone) as she smashes her fist into some guy's face. There's a weird crunch, like glass breaking, and the guy drops, his skin torn to ribbons.

"You think?" Brit says (in her normal apathetic way) as she spins the crazy baton thing she's holding. It hums like a TV tuned to static. Whenever she hits someone with it (which she does a lot, and really, really fast) there's a

137

crackle and a spark and the smell of ozone and burnt skin. Using one arm to fight, she grabs me and pulls me into the hallway.

We're met by the other bedroom doors bursting open and black-clad soldiers pouring out like some weird, sentient, organic liquid. They surge forward, guns up, and I hear one of them in the front shout.

"Fire!"

Oh crap!

The sound of gunfire pounds my eardrums. The pain is incredible, and I scream and drop to the floor.

But I don't die.

The gunfire just goes on and on and on. And then, just as fast, it stops. When it does, I realize the only sound I'm hearing is me still screaming.

"Chill," Brit says, calm as can be.

Her hands are out again, fingers spread, palms aimed at the group of soldiers who are standing like a bunch of wide-eyed fools. Clearly, they've never seen anything like her before. All over the ground in front of her are fired bullets, tossed like confetti.

Some dude near the back of the pack pushes forward and fires a burst. Bam-bam-bam-bam-bam! My hands go back up over my ears, but I keep my eyes open. The bullets fly out, all enthusiastic, determined to pierce and puncture and kill. They make it halfway between the gun's barrel and Brit, then just give up on the whole thing. Most of them slow down and fall to the floor with the others. A few push on through, hitting Brit's shoes and legs with the destructive force of violently thrown popcorn.

There's this pause, where all of the soldiers with all of their guns come to the realization that it's not going to work. Clearly, this was something they had not prepared for. I can relate.

I was not prepared for what happens next.

From Brit's room, Samantha shouts and sends the a soldier crashing through the doorway, smashing through the banister, and tumbling down to the first floor. All those shocked soldiers in the hallway with us snap out of it. They come rushing forward. Brit jams her arm out. The first wave goes limp and drops to the floor. Samantha runs out of the bedroom and freaking jump spin-kicks some dude. Brit grabs one of her batons and moves in. Her other arm is out and anyone who runs at her goes from warrior to weary in a few steps.

"Down!" Samantha barks. I realize she's shouting at me, but I don't really react. "Downstairs!" she shouts. I kind of nod and look around, even though the stairs are right next to me. After a few seconds of staring at the top one, I start to crawl over. And then, I hear it again, that woman's voice.

"Unit two --"

Goddamn it!

"-- breach!"

The front door doesn't just swing in, it's torn from its hinges by the battering ram. More soldiers swarm in, their guns up and ready. A few head into the lower level, but a bunch of them get to the bottom of the stairs, see me at the top, and take aim.

"Brit!" I scream.

Their guns roar. Brit throws herself against whatever's left of the banister and sticks her arm out.

Ow! Son-of-a-Bitch!

The bullets don't fall asleep like the others did, but hit like stinging paintballs. I'm shrieking and flailing and scampering back to the bathroom at the top of the stairs when something that feels like a bowling ball slams my hip. I guess Brit's power couldn't hold all the bullets back. My face hits the tile, but I manage to squirm into the bathroom and kick the door shut. Bullets start tearing the outside of it to shreds.

Holy crap, holy crap, holy crap. Oh, it hurts. I can't, I can't even... the bullets are still coming. The screaming won't stop. And I don't know, I don't know if it's them or if it's me. I can't, I can't even move my leg it hurts so bad. The bathroom door swings open and someone falls through. Their face is all ripped up and they're not moving. They're dead. Oh god, what... what do I do? What do I do? I can't, I'm... I'm --

I'm feeling it. The pounding in my ears mixes with the thunder of the bullets and turns into a wall of static sounds. It's everywhere. It's inside me. I feel it in my bones, resonating. It's hot and it's cold and it's moving and it feels like pressure and pain and if it goes on any longer my bones are going to crack and explode from the inside out. I can't keep it there anymore, mostly because I don't want to. I just, I just want to let go. For one second, I want to let go of everything.

But if I do... then it really will be the warehouse. And everyone in this building will be dead.

And I can't let any more people die because of me. Even if they're trying to kill me. I can't.

Air shoots in and out of my lungs. My eyes dart back and forth between my hands. They're vibrating. Not shaking, not twitching. Vibrating. Like a guitar string during a Metallica solo.

I make a fist. I press and press, but nothing happens. It just gets bigger and louder and now I can feel it in my teeth, in my sinuses. I know that I'm making sounds, grunting and squeaking and gasping but I can't hear any of it.

139

The noise, the noise is unbearable. It's a gunshot that never ends. It's sonic feedback, high and low at the same time.

My toes are curled. I desperately have to pee. My abs are trembling and I can feel the tendons in my neck straining to the max as I try to fight this, try to keep this from happening again.

But then, through the noise, through the static, I hear something. It's small, and far away, but I hear it, at the edge of my auditory spectrum.

"Candace!"

I look up, and it's Annie. Annie, standing in the doorway, in her outfit. And behind that mask, it's really her. The Annie I know. Not the bad-ass from the lab building. Not the masked person taking orders from Samantha. Just cares-about-me Annie.

And for her, I have only two words. "Help me!"

She doesn't hesitate.

Her body twists at the waist, a full one-eighty. My hands are on fire. Annie grabs Brit and pulls her in. The feeling, the pulsing and throbbing is a millimeter away from its breaking point. Annie shouts something. I squeeze and clench and grind my teeth and tears are falling from my eyes. Brit takes one look at me and jams her hands out like she's about to be hit by car.

Which, honestly, would probably be better than what's about to happen.

Jesus, guys. I'm sorry.

I'm so sorry.

My power explodes.

Brit's ability, whatever it is, smashes against mine. They're two ocean waves, traveling in opposite directions. But my wave is bigger. All around me, walls crack. The sink and mirror shatter. Brit slides backward, but she doesn't give up. She strains -- notably, for the first time since I've known her she actually looks like she's trying -- against the force, pushes her own hands back at it. A second later, Brit's power takes over and everything in the room goes from an eleven to a two.

So when I look down at my hands, I see it. There, swirling between my palms. No color, but a shape. A rolling, quivering thing. It looks like the air above a fire. It shifts and oscillates, and as I move, the tone and pitch change.

Holy shit. That's it.

Sound. It's pure sound.

And it's beautiful.

Brit grits her teeth and pushes deeper into the room. The ball of sound dissipates like dust into the wind. I feel that same thing when I almost fell down the stairs but didn't. What little energy is left in my muscles vanishes. Everything goes limp; legs, arms, hands, even my lungs.

140

Unable to stop myself, I hit the floor face first. It should hurt like a bitch, but I weigh as much as a wadded up piece of paper. My lungs still can't do anything, even though my brain is blasting messages to them.

"Stop! Stop!" I hear Annie shouting. "You're gonna --"

"She's fine." Brit sounds like she just went for a run. An angry one. Her words are a little broken. "Goddamn, that was ridiculous."

I hear fighting going on downstairs. No, I can hear everything going on downstairs.

Every. Single. Thing.

And it's not a tangled mess in my head. It's -- I mean, look, it's a lot. Voices, footsteps, clothes rustling, boots thumping, hearts beating, triggers snapping, pins hitting the backs of bullets, bam-bam-bam, shots fired, shouting, liquid (sweat and spit and blood and I can almost tell which is which) falling, splattering, running out onto the floors. Each sound reaches out to my ears and strikes them perfectly, never too loud to hurt, but never too soft to miss.

This... this is amazing!

Annie wraps her arms around me -- literally -- and pulls me up. She looks down at me, fear and worry etched into her face. "Candace?"

"So," I say, grinning, "when do I get my mask?"

Around us, the world is chaos. But right now, we're just looking at each other and smiling like idiots.

Her nose wrinkles a little. "I'll lend you one. But first, we gotta get outta here."

I just nod. Then she spins me up and we're headed into the fray. Well, really, Annie heads into the fray. Well, really, the fray kind of heads into us. A few soldiers come rushing toward us. Annie moves in, way faster than I've ever seen her before. I can't even really tell what happens, all I see is a bunch of limbs whipping around. Her body is a windsock in a typhoon, this way, that way, totally wild; but half a second later, one of the guys is on the ground and the other is tumbling through the air towards the first floor. Soldier number three is coming up behind Annie.

My lips squeeze together. I spread my feet and pull my hand back. I feel the vibration there, growing and growing.

Okay. Okay! I can do this! It's go time, girl! Put on your best Serena Williams, tough-ass woman face and throw down some sound! You're gonna mess with my friend? This... is what... you... get!

Brit's hand snatches my wrist from behind. "Uh-uh," she says in my ear. Which she doesn't really need to, because I can hear freaking everything because I am... The Sound Master! oh no that's stupid, I don't like that at all.

141

Anyway, Brit doesn't know that yet. I'll explain it later.

"Come on," I whine.

"No," she says as though she's telling me for the fiftieth time that I can't have the candy bar in line at the grocery store. Which actually happened once. I was real stoned that night.

"I can --"

"No."

"Fine," I groan.

Brit lets go. "Follow me. Don't do anything stupid." She leans to the side. "Twist, you cover us."

With a loud crack, Annie puts soldier number three's head securely into the plaster wall and says, "Got it."

Brit starts down the stairs. I turn back. "Twist?"

Annie's breathing is heavy but controlled as she walks down the stairs sideways. "It's my... you know..."

"Codename?"

"No," Annie says. "It's... it's my name. It's who I really am."

"Should I --"

"No," she says quickly, glancing at me with a small smile. "For you, I'm Annie."

I grin.

It should probably be noted that during this entire time, stupid ass-hat soldiers have been shooting non-stop. Jesus Tap Dancing Christ! These guys are beyond persistent. I mean, live to fight another day, right? That's a thing? It'd be one thing if they even stood a chance, but this is sad. There are at least three, maybe four dozen of them down and not one of us.

Heh. Us. I'm part of a team! I mean, haven't contributed much yet. Really, hindered more than anything else. Maybe I can be the mascot?

Brit is -- wait.

I jam my thumb at Brit. "What about her?"

Annie leans in close and says, over the gunfire (seriously, you don't need to do that. It's annoying), "Languria."

"Oh, that's cool."

"Right?"

"Hey, Languria!"

She turns.

"Cool name."

She smirks. "Thanks."

So, Languria (it just rolls on the tongue, you know?) is in front of me, using that weird energy stealing power to stop all incoming fire. The bullets are just falling down. I lean in real close and shout over the sound.

"How do you do that?"

"Kinetic energy," she says. "I can cancel it out, but only when it comes close to me."

Makes sense. That's how she stopped the concussive force of my sound explosion, but left the actual tones and pitches in the air.

Over and over again, she uses the same tactic: let the troops shoot until they're out of ammo, then take them down one at a time. And though she's definitely using spin kicks and shit, but there's nothing martial arts about this. She fights like a goddamn gladiator. Yeah, she's precise, but she's brutal. I'm kind of having a hard time watching. Which is a vast improvement over just two minutes ago. Ever since the bathroom I've been... calmer? I dunno. At least, more accepting of the whole thing. Seeing the sound, feeling it in my hands, it was watching the puzzle of my own life being solved in front of me. Maybe that's not right. Whatever. All I know is things are starting to feel right.

Samantha (who joined up with us and is busy taking out the stragglers along with Annie) shoves my back. Apparently, she thinks I shouldn't be taking the time to step over the unconscious bodies.

I snark at her, "Watch it, Sammy."

"Princess." She snaps.

Wait... what?

"Wait, what?"

Come on, what else was I gonna say?

"It's my name," she says.

"It is?"

"I... you called me that earlier."

I pause. "Oh! No, no, no. That's what I call you in my head."

She stares.

"It's short. For the Bitch Princess."

Those red lips of hers roll in and the little gems all over her face crinkle and crack as she tries to hold back the anger but some real ugly wrinkles come out anyway. Someone behind her shouts, and she whips around on them. They swing one of those extendable nightsticks at her. Princess ducks and as the guy tries a backhand, drags her palm and fingers against his sleeve. Where she touches him, it looks like his arm went through a cheese shredder.

The super-fine-cut kind.

Threads of fabric laced with skin and blood fall down. He pulls back, as any normal person would, and Princess slaps an open hand across his chest. The same thing happens. He goes to cover that, and she gets his arm, his other arm, his shoulder, side, ribs, hip, thigh, knee. Each one looks like nothing more than a playful smack, but she's literally tearing the guy to pieces.

I'm glad he's wearing a helmet; I'd hate to see his expression right now.

Another guy runs in with the same idea and the same weapon Mr. Cheese-Skin had. Princess dodges his swing and claps her palms together. There's not a slap of skin on skin, but a crunch like someone smashing a beer bottle into the pavement with a thick soled boot.

Princess opens her palms like a book and blows.

This dude should have worn a helmet.

A cloud of glitter splashes across his face and neck. I only see him for an instant before his hands fly up. The cuts are tiny, almost microscopic, but there are thousands of them. Tens of thousands. It's like he fell from a speeding truck and landed face first on a strip of housing insulation.

Princess doesn't even follow up. The guy just screams through his hands and falls backward. She turns back to me.

"My name," she says slowly, "is Princess Snow."

"Huh," I say. "I would have gone with Ice Slice."

She squints. "Garage. Now."

"Or Ice Prickle."

"Move."

"Wait, wait..." I grin. "Cold Cuts."

Annie snorts.

"Now!"

We make a strong push and leave the foyer. I mean, what's left of the foyer. If I live through this, I know my mother is going to bitch me out because we lost her security deposit.

The last of the ESOA are finally retreating to the backdoor. They're all shouting stuff like, 'pull back', as we walk toward the garage. They're making a lot of noise, but there's something else going on here. Two seconds ago they were full-on charging in. Now, all of a sudden, they change it up? That's never good.

Over their actual voices, I hear other things, words spoken at normal levels.

The walkie-talkies.

Before, I had no control over what came into my ears. Now? Even with all the chaos around me, I can pick a sound wave out of the air and separate it from the rest. My ears kind of buzz when I hear the sound I want. I can feel it, feel the tiny hairs tingling with just the right pitch. And the pitch I'm looking for is that woman's voice.

"Unit two, fall back to secondary strike position."

I know that voice, dammit!

Also, that doesn't sound good. I turn to Annie. "Hey, I think they're --"

But Princess Snow is bustling us into the garage. No one can hear me over the soldiers. Or, if they can, they're not paying attention. Brit's crazy-ass, thunder-horse GT Mustang is the only car there. I say crazy-ass not because it's got flames and all that shit (it's just simple black), but because under the hood is an engine Brit modified herself, and I'm ninety percent sure that most of the crap she put in there isn't legal.

To be clear, we go to MIT. This is not an uncommon hobby. Brit just happens to be particularly good at it.

The hairs inside my ears tingle, and I know what's coming.

"Unit three," says the woman on the walkie-talkies, "prepare the blockade."

Oh shit. "Listen," I say, but Princess Snow opens the passenger door, barks, "Everyone in!" and Annie gives me a less-than-polite nudge.

"Hey!" I shout as my head gets pushed down. "Wait, listen, they're --" The GT's engine roars to life. My face hits the back of the leather seat. Annie isn't just pushing me, she's practically climbing in on top of me. "They're doing something out there!" I grab the backs of the front seats and pull myself up. "They know we're coming!"

Annie pushes me back against the seat with one arm (damn, that girl is strong!) and buckles me in with the other. "Don't worry," she says.

"But,"

"Unit three," says the woman, "get locked and loaded."

What?

Princess drops into her seat. "Are we ready?"

Languria revs the engine. "Yup."

"Unit two, prep the explosives."

What?!

Princess clips her seatbelt. "Punch it."

"No!" I shout. "Wait!"

"All units --" says the woman.

Languria grins just a bit. "Yee-haw."

"-- engage."

Oh hell.

Tires squeal. I scream, going over the edge on a two-hundred foot roller coaster kind of scream. Languria's GT lurches forward as she pulls out the clutch. It feels weird, like the car weighs too much or something. But I'm not really thinking about that.

"Door! Door! Door!" I shout, because the huge wooden garage door is still down. The car charges, and I don't even have time to close my eyes. The front bumper touches it, like, the tiniest of bits, and the entire door snaps up and out like a mousetrap going off.

What? Wait... what! First off, the door usually rolls up into the ceiling, but now it swung out like a shutter. Also, it's freaking ancient! It usually takes a solid thirty seconds to open for me and...

Okay. More secret. Cool. I mean, not cool. But whatever. Not really the thing I should be focused on now.

Instead, I'm focused on the fact that there were soldiers right outside the garage door. I know this because I see them flying up through the air. I also now get what that woman meant when she asked if they had the explosives ready. Behind us, those same grenade things are going off all over the garage door. If it had opened like normal, even faster than normal but not flipped up, those things would have gone off all over the car and we'd be dead. But we're not, and Languria drives us toward a small army of soldiers who are currently opening fire!

Since I'm already screaming, I just keep going with it. I mean, why stop when I'm already all warmed up, right? The bullets pound on the car, but after the first few don't come in and kill us, it dawns on me that the GT feels sluggish because it's been weighted down with bulletproof armor.

Languria heads straight for the barricade of soldiers and trucks. The engine has been beyond supercharged, so there's barely a loss of momentum as we send steel and glass and soldiers flying and tear through.

"Yeah!" I scream from the back.

No one else seems to share my enthusiasm. Come on, women! Team spirit!

Languria cranks the wheel and sends us drifting, trying to get on course with the road. There are other soldiers up ahead, another couple trucks, but nothing that her monster car can't handle. Her tires are just straightening out when I hear something... different. A sound that's high pitched and low pitched at the same time. Like, a snap and a crack of something big.

The street beneath us.

There's this crazy rumble, like someone unloading a dump truck's worth of bricks all at once. Languria slams the brakes. We pitch sideways, and I see the damnedest thing out the window.

Stalagmites.

Dozens of them. Huge, jagged, and taller than the car. Some, the biggest ones, are in a perfect line that cuts off the road. Others, long and thin with tips that look like stone needles, are angled just right to pierce the car windows.

As we jerk to a stop, I follow the line of them back. There, at the very beginning, crouched down with her hands on the ground, is some Latina in military fatigues.

CHAPTER FIFTEEN
DIVIDE AND CONQUER

What's the point of this? Why did McTier send in the Special Ops teams if she knew there were superhumans inside? She said we'd tracked the one from the MIT lab, the single woman who'd taken down an entire unit. And look, a lot of the ops guys are overconfident dicks, but that doesn't mean they're not trained. So sending in a bunch more than before might have been effective...

But I'm right here. Sosuke and Lucien are right here. We could have moved in and handled the situation so much better.

People died in that house. I heard it over the coms. They were getting slaughtered, and McTier just sat in the van and told us to wait. Even after more superhumans showed up, she told us to wait. So I did. I kept my ass on the bench and tried to figure this thing out.

If all McTier wanted was to question the people inside, she would have sent us in. Which means that the people, the information they, that's not the target. She wants something, or someone, else.

She doesn't want the superhumans taken down. But if they escape, they would relocate. They'd go to whomever it is they take orders from.

And that's when we're supposed to hit them.

It's a fox hunt; Sosuke, Lucien, me, we're the hounds. The soldiers that went in were just beating the bushes. They were disposable. It was clear when McTier said, calm as could be, "All units, engage."

Now? She's leaping out of the van and saying in a much less calm voice, "Agent Garcia!"

Whoever is driving that car is a pro. It swings into place, inches from my spikes, and rocks to a halt. The entire thing is riddled with welts. Considering those are fully automatic weapons, I'm going to assume it's been customized.

My fingers twist. Under the car, ten tiny peaks appear. They're miniscule now, but can be ten feet tall in a blink.

Literally. That's all it takes when they're this close to me.

I don't want to kill whomever is inside. If they try and make a break for it, I'll immobilize the car.

"Garcia!" McTier shouts. Wow, she's actually flustered. "What the hell do you think you're doing?"

"Protecting and preserving human life, ma'am."

Her entire face frowns. "Your orders were to stay in the van."

"You said all units engage, I assumed it meant us, too." I hold back my smile. "You should have been more specific."

148

McTier wants them to make a run for it. She probably has units ready to chase. That doesn't help me. If I'm going to figure out what's going on, I need to get the info as soon as possible. Stopping them, detaining them, and trying to get one away for questioning is my best bet.

"Pull down your spikes, Agent." McTier says.

Flattening my palms, I try to figure out what they're doing in the car. The engine in that thing is a beast! I can't see anything with my seismic echolocation other than a car shaped vibrating thingy.

"Agent Garcia,"

I close my eyes and focus. There's four of them. They're moving, but not much. I have to be ready for when they make a break for it. There's a weird thing with the car, it kind of jerks and something changes shape up top.

"Garcia!" There's panic in her voice. My eyes open. That something on top of the car is pointed right at me. My hands drag to the side. Spikes, thin but fast, shoot out of the ground in a wall just a foot in front of me. The whole world turns into sound and noise and pressure and pain.

¡Dios mío, no, no, no, no!

I'm hit. I'm hit. Something... where? What's going on? I can't... Jesus, help me. I'm up. I'm in the air but, but everything is hot and... and I'm rolling or falling or tumbling and I don't know which. I can't find the ground. My feet can't find the ground and my stomach churns and there's stinging all over me. My ears aren't ringing, they're screaming. It was, it was right there. It hit the wall, whatever it was. My hands touch the ground. I'm down. I'm on my side and I'm down. I have to get up, I have to move but nothing is working. What if they're coming? What if they fire another? Come on. Come on! Get up! But I can't even figure out which way is up! My head is all over the place and when I go to push with my arms I just... I just... I just...

Hands. I feel hands on me. They're pushing down, and not entirely gently. Oh crap oh crap oh crap I'm bleeding out. I'm bleeding out and they're trying to staunch the bleeding and --

"Calm down, Garcia."

... McTier...

"You're fine. Relax."

... hija de su puta madre.

I take a couple actual breaths and manage to open my eyes. McTier is over me, checking my arms and legs.

"Nothing major. Some scrapes and cuts." Her voice sounds like it's coming out of a sleeping bag in my ringing ears (which, noteworthy, I'll take ringing over screaming any day). "Does anything feel broken?"

My arms and legs move without any major pain. I'm breathing okay. I

149

shake my head.

"Can you stand?" she asks.

"I," The world isn't spinning anymore. "Yes. Yes, ma'am."

"Good." she says, and steps away from me without looking back. "You're needed. Get up."

Just in case, I sit up real slow. Nothing pops or snaps. Off to the side, the tiny nubs that were my defensive spikes are crumbling.

Santo cielo, that was close...

"On the double, Garcia!"

Worst bedside manner. Ever.

Still, hearing her snap makes my training kick in. It takes a second or two, but I'm on my feet. My ability ramps up, and I feel stabilized. Seismic echolocation turns on and already an image for what's happening is building in my head.

Maldición, there is a lot happening.

Everyone's in the street. The car is still in the same place. Either the people inside decided to abandon it, or they were forced out. Doesn't matter now. Lucien and Sosuke are fighting two of them. There's a lot of movement going on, which means that their opponents are either extremely capable at dodging close range or --

"Garcia," McTier is right next to me. "Two of them escaped down through that alley."

There's a flash of hot blue light and a crunch of stone. On one side of the car, next to the barrier I made, Sosuke swings and a woman in... wow... a ridiculous all-white outfit with a cape and way too many sparkles slips in under his arm. She slices with the edge of her hand and Sosuke dodges. She moves in, jabbing at him with the tips of her fingers. He evades, but just barely. I can feel his feet, sense how he's shifting his weight back and away.

He's retreating. She's actually pushing him back. This is bad. Sosuke never gets pushed back.

"Garcia," McTier continues, completely focused. "The two that ran, both female, one was wearing what looked like a specialized superhuman uniform --" by which she means a costume "-- the other was in civvies."

On the other side of the car, Lucien is staggering towards a woman who has her hands up. It's weird, he looks like he's drunk or, or underwater or something. I can tell from the state of his shirt that he's generating acid, but he's not doing anything with it. He's struggling just to move. When he does manage to fling his arms, the acid drops just fall to the ground.

No, they don't just fall. They go down way too easily...

McTier is still talking. "Your orders are to pursue them. Do not engage

150

unless necessary. Follow them and report in when they've stopped."

Lucien backs off and seems to gain back some strength. He comes in again and the same thing happens. The woman goes to smack him with some kind of weapon, but it smokes the second it touches him. She's scared to get close but still completely debilitates him.

"Garcia!" McTier snaps. "Do you understand?"

My legs, feeling stronger and more solid every second, bend. Crouching feels good. It gets my blood rolling again. Fingers spreading across the asphalt, the two I'm supposed to pursue appear in my head. They're moving at a good clip, but not sprinting. "Roger, Lieutenant. Pursue the suspects --"

"But do not engage," she says sharply.

I pause. "Have Lucien and Sosuke switch."

McTier's head ticks to the side.

"Trust me."

Before she can respond, the ground under my feet cracks loudly. A pillar shoots out, pushing me fifteen feet in the air. I ride it, leap off, and use the force to propel myself over the fight. A mid-air somersault, quick landing at the mouth of the alley, roll to absorb the shock, and I'm on my feet running.

My targets are a little over a hundred yards out. I should be at a good following range in under two minutes. But that's McTier's plan, not mine.

McTier said not to engage. She said it twice. They're going to meet with someone, and even if that's not the final target, it's the next person McTier wants. Once that happens, these two women are expendable. And the way things are going, McTier will be giving me the kill order.

So, since I don't kill people just because I'm ordered to, I think I'd rather bring them to a halt and find out what's so damned important that the government is willing to risk my life to get it.

No, not just my life, but my tío's life.

I run a little faster. Breathe a little harder.

CHAPTER SIXTEEN
THE THIRD WHEEL

Wraith wanted to know why we were in the middle of nowhere, Arizona. I told her that I was looking for something which could be useful to us.

"Wait," she said, turning away from the hills of red rocks and green cacti rolling up on either side of the car. "Something, or someone?"

I declined to answer.

"You're serious?"

I continued to decline to answer.

"They're stories."

"Every myth is borne from a kernel of truth."

"Why do you think we need someone else?"

"Because we want to beat them."

"We just need --"

"Nothing's worked," It was what we both knew but didn't want to say. Cresting a hill, we could see the flat valley of desert up ahead. The drop off to the right was steep. I slowed the car and shifted in my seat, unable to find a comfortable position.

She tilted her head, then said in a softer tone, "That's not true."

I stopped squirming.

"We pulled off those robberies just fine. We got all that equipment, those chemicals from the secret government base. You ran the tests, built the machines, made me a new suit. You put time in on me, made me stronger than ever. All that sure worked."

I nodded. "Yeah, I know. You're right."

"Damn right, I'm right."

I smiled.

"We can try again," she said. "A new plan, a different approach. Something."

"If... if it were just Turbo and Lux? Absolutely. But three?" I shook my head. "No matter how strong you become, Lux's ability can still negate yours to a degree. So it only makes sense that I handle Lux. Fine. You can absolutely beat Turbo. The problem --"

"Ironsides," she said, her breath thin and angry.

"An invincible man," I said with a sneer. The car pulled around a curve a little too hard. "Nothing gets to him. I've tried it all. I mean, Turbo's strong and fast --"

"And he's got those bands of yours."

I pushed the accelerator a touch. "He does. And that makes things even more difficult. But, he's not indestructible. Electricity seems particularly effective. Great. Lux's ability is powerful, you know that well enough."

Now it was her turn to be a little squirmy. But she wasn't. Because Wraith never got squirmy. I say that not out of frustration or jealously, but out of respect. Instead, all she did was let out a small, "Mm-hm."

"But he's not a close range fighter," I continued. The road, a switchback leading us down and down, wiggled back and forth. The tires chirped a bit as we went. "Physically, he's the weakest. That detriment is more than made up by Ironsides. There's no... if I handle Ironsides, you have to deal with Lux and Turbo. If you handle Ironsides, I have Lux and Turbo. If you have --"

"Okay," she said, hard. "Okay," she said, soft.

I took her cue. The car slowed. "No matter how we shift the equation, the figures don't balance." We came to the bottom of the hill. A slow, rolling curve deposited us at the entrance to the great expanse of stone and sand. It was midday, and the world around us glowed like embers stoked by a gentle breeze. Shadows were thick and dark as tar. Inside me, something stirred, some primordial sense of self-preservation. The further we drove, the more I felt like a mouse in a field, small and exposed. Maybe it was knowing that sitting next to me was a fearless predator. Or maybe it was the fact that out there, somewhere, may be something even more deadly.

"So what do you know that I don't?"

It was a fair question. "That... I'm sorry. I didn't --"

"It's fine."

"I wasn't keeping secrets."

"I know. Shut up and talk."

I do. "There's been another incident."

Her voice raised the eyebrow for her. "A house completely covered in cobwebs?"

"Yes."

"It's a natural phenomenon, happens every few years."

"The last time was four years ago. Then two before that. Then three before that."

"Fine. And each time, it shows up in the papers. Lots of pictures. Tabloids run stories about monster spiders created from nuclear weapons testing. A month later, it fades away because it's totally normal. Biologists said."

"True."

"So?"

"This time, it's not being reported."

She paused.

"Anywhere."

Turning her gaze to the landscape, to the bluffs and rises hazy in the distance. They were red, angry blurs against a cobalt blue sky. "Is there a chance?"

My hands floated over the steering wheel. The road ahead vanished like the point of a great, black needle. "Any chance is better than none."

"Okay," she said, somber. Then, with a complete tonal change, "So tell me why we're driving a Crown Vic."

"To complete the illusion."

"And why am I wearing this blazer and skirt?"

"Because you need to look the part."

"And why are you in that awful suit?"

"Because I don't have the legs for a skirt."

She chuckled at that.

Forty miles ago, we'd seen a sign that said something about no gas stations for fifty miles. It should have indicated that there wouldn't be anything for fifty miles. Not a billboard, not a mile marker, not a posted speed limit. Nothing. Eventually, we came to the first manmade object, a sign worn pale by sun and pimpled with bullet holes. It said, 'GAS', and had an arrow. We turned onto a road that was neither dirt nor paved, but something in between. At the end of it sat a structure, one story, irresolute between waves of heat. As we came closer, the building took on an odd shape, as though it had been draped in a thin, white sheet.

"Wow," it was more a sound than a word. Next to me, Wraith stayed silent, but her eyes spoke for her. Together, we leaned down, looking through the windshield.

These weren't cobwebs found between rafters in an attic, these were nets, tightly knitted, and spun from shimmering silk. Stretching across most of the building's exterior, they criss-crossed, making the faux Spanish Mission style building impossible to see in places. Off to the side, the gas pumps were untouched by the webs, as were the cars... station wagons and a few trucks... parked about the lot.

The building's front had a two-word sign. The only one I could make out was, 'Diner'. Police cruisers and other government vehicles were scattered, some in parking spaces, others pulled off into the desert terrain. I pulled our car between a small gap in the vehicle barricade meant to keep curious onlookers... and the media... out. To our sides, men in state trooper uniforms with wide brimmed hats and aviator sunglasses took notice. Several of them spoke into walkie-talkies. A few started toward our car. More than one plopped a hand on the back of their holstered guns.

154

Wraith took a slow breath. I knew she was powering up before the mist even drifted from the openings of her well-cut suit. There was a tiny sound, a hissing of her body sublimating which I had come to know well.

"Wait," I said, stones crunching under the Crown Vic's wheels as it came to a stop.

Wraith shot me an uneasy glance."Why?"

I put the car in park and grabbed a large, gaudy gold watch which had been sitting in the cup holder. "Information," I said, pushing two of the buttons on the watch. In the console of the car, something let off a tiny beep. From within both our suits, identical beeps came. I glanced at Wraith. Reluctantly, she reeled in her ability. We opened the doors and stepped out.

I was hot before I even stood up.

How do people live in places like this?

"Excuse me," said a man with a voice as big as his belly. I nodded at him, but my attention was on the diner. I'd seen the pictures from previous incidents in years past. It was different up close. The threads were incredibly long, some stretching from the ground out front all the way to the roof. The sections where the webs overlaid seemed impenetrable. It was a beautiful wash, like layered strokes of a painter's brush. Breaking that magnificence was a rough, triangular gash someone had cut in order to reach the front door.

"This area is off limits," said that man whom I already didn't like. His moustache was more salt than... well, not pepper. His hair was a tawny brown and thin around his temples. My bet was that under his hat, a failing comb-over covered a swath of scalp made pink from the sun. He had a way of walking that told me he'd been physically strong at one time, but years of riding around in a car and paperwork had worn him down. He probably got winded going up a flight of stairs, let alone the nearby hills where I suspected evidence of this event could be found. I took immediate note of what looked to be the clearest paths between the hills and the diner. Wraith was doing the same. "I'm going to need you people to get in your car and move on outta here."

Ah. You people. Not folks. What a charmer.

Several officers started moving toward us. I'd asked Wraith to wait, but that would only save these men for so long. When I reached into my suit's interior pocket, the big man's hand went to his holster. I didn't hesitate.

"Senior Special Agent Newton with the DSI, Department of Scientific Investigation." I flashed a forged badge good enough to give me access to nearly every secured building in Washington without raising red flags.

Behind his sunglasses, the big man squinted. His hand didn't move from the holster. He jerked his chin, indicating a couple of skinny men in suits who were taking serious interest in what was happening. "FBI's already here."

"Did I say FBI?"

He chewed on that for a minute, then looked past me. "And you are?"

I snapped my badge shut. "That's Senior Special Secret Agent Sombra, ESOA." That caught attention, not just big man's, but anyone in earshot. "I'm just escorting her."

"ESOA?" he said, taking the tiniest step back. "The, uh, the one that --"

"Was created to be above the FBI, CIA, DIA, DoD, and NSA, and is designed to deal specifically with enhanced superhuman activity," I rattle off. "Yes, that one. Now, you better lower that hand, officer. You're making her unhappy."

He hesitated. On the other side of the car, that distinct hissing from Wraith started. I reached for my watch.

"Sheriff," the FBI agents were stepping in. The shorter of the two gave the sheriff a nod, who in turn lowered his hand and shuffled his feet. All around us, the sheriff's men went back to what they were doing. Or at least acted like they were. "McCloskey," the agent extended a hand, but not a smile, "FBI. Did I hear correctly? ESOA?"

"That's correct," I said, taking his hand. "I'm Newton. This is Sombra."

"Newton?" The sheriff hadn't taken the hint it was time to retreat. "Sombra? You sure those are your real names?"

"Would you prefer Clay?"

Everyone, myself included, turned. Wraith wasn't just staring at the sheriff, she was cutting him to pieces with her eyes.

"Or maybe Jackson, or Jefferson?"

"I'm... uh..."

She tiled her head. "Senior Special Secret Agent." She stepped up to him. "You're not at a pay grade high enough to hear my real name." Her words pierced him, and I got the pleasure of watching him deflate into a sad little lump of a man as she stared him down. Then, she sent him off without another word.

"So," McCloskey said, long and slow, watching as the sheriff meandered away, "y'all think this is, uh, a --"

"Possibly," I said. I'd already lost interest in McCloskey. No... I never had any. I wanted to get in that diner. I began wandering the perimeter, Wraith and the agents following. We made our way around the entire building, stopping out front. We were twenty, twenty-five feet from the front door, and I could already smell it.

Death.

"We need the place cleared," I said.

McCloskey pointed toward the door, "Well, we have some people inside, trying to --"

"Now," Wraith said, not harshly. There was no need.

"Um," the agent hemmed and hawed for a second before nodding. "Okay. Sure. For how long?"

I gave him an incredulous look. "Until we're done."

There are a lot of details I could go into here, about the space itself, about the way it was set up, but none of that's important. It was a crappy little diner in the middle of nowhere which had survived because it was the only place there was to be. A counter, some tables, an opening in a wall where food was passed from a small, dirty kitchen. The norm.

Even with the electricity still running, even with the large windows which made up the entire front wall, the room was dark. The webs had obscured everything. Inside, they ran in every direction -- floor to ceiling at times, up and down at angles, in columns, sometimes blocking off entire corners of the room. More slashes, from the police who had arrived trying to make their way through, littered the first few feet of the space. There was a pair of aviator sunglasses hanging near head height from one web, and a state trooper hat from another. Deeper in, equipment left by the FBI team was in various stages of being set up. I saw med packs, battery powered lights, evidence collection kits, and a few rudimentary scientific devices. The workers hadn't been there for long. Or rather, they'd been there long enough to build up the nerve to go in and get started.

I pressed forward.

The smell was intense, but not overpowering. Honestly, I'd expected worse. Ducking under a thick web, I stopped. A stray color stood out against the pale threads. Reaching up, I plucked at it. Behind me, Wraith glided between the webs. She had an incredible sense of space and her own body within it. Nothing ever touched her, unless she wanted it to. Upon seeing my hand, her eyes narrowed.

A hair. Human. Black, long, thick, straight, and strong.

We looked at each other, then followed the web to the ceiling. There, we found a shape, bound and spackled to the ceiling with webs, limbs askew, a black waterfall of hair pouring from a hanging head.

"Santo Dios..." Wraith whispered. "What did this?"

"I don't know," I said, taking in as much as I could of the body. There was no blood coming from it, and none on the floor beneath us. "I have a few ideas, but..." It appeared to be intact, no missing chunks.

157

"But?"

I pocketed the hair, glanced back at Wraith, and moved past the FBI's equipment, into the main part of the dining area. This was the center. Whatever had happened, this is where it had started. Beneath our feet, tiny cricks and cracks of crunching things sounded. At first I thought maybe the linoleum floor had broken during some kind of scuffle. Moving my foot, I found instead black and deep brown spots between the webs on the floor. Pieces of things broken. I bent down.

Spiders. Already smashed before I was there.

They'd tried, at least, to put up a fight.

"Two more," Wraith pointed to a table across the room. The bodies, one tied to a chair like a prisoner ready to be tortured and the other on the floor, were completely cocooned in spider silk. Spots of cloth and skin were barely visible.

"And three over there," I said. "One's..."

"I see."

It was a man, easily six feet, overweight, wearing what appeared to be an apron. Probably the cook. He was completely upside down, webbed just enough to stay aloft. His skin was swollen and deep purple in places. His mouth and eyes were open, frozen in a silent scream of horror and agony.

"Necrosis," I said, pointing to the thick, navy blue lines running from spots of flesh clearly deteriorating faster than others.

"But why?"

I bent down to examine the mummified bodies near the table. "The annual rainfall of this desert is three, maybe four inches." Their skin showed no signs of flesh deteriorating toxin. "That's just enough water to keep plants blooming and attract the few larger herbivores who may live here, javelinas, rodents, so on." They were meant to be preserved... for later. "This year, though, the rainfall barely reached half that. Do you know the last time the rainfall was reduced this dramatically?"

She nodded. "Four years ago. And two years before that. And three before that."

"If food is scarce, animals tend to relocate. Those that don't, must become more... resourceful."

"And that's what you want?" Another fair question. "That's what you're hoping to find?"

I responded with only a resolute gaze.

"What makes you think you'll be able to control... it?"

Shadows moved across the sheets of web covering the windows. Voices were calling out. The sheriff seemed to be getting impatient.

158

"I... we both know what it's like, don't we? To be hungry for something? This," I gestured around the room, "this is a hunger easily filled."

She wasn't convinced, not yet, but her silence told me she was willing to go along a bit longer. I began leading us back to the front door.

"So what's the plan?" she asked. "Make camp here until whatever it is comes back?"

"That could be weeks, months even."

"How do you know?"

"There were seven cars out back."

"And six bodies," she said with a sigh.

"We should assume at least a few of these people were traveling together. Whatever came here, didn't leave empty-handed."

"The hills?"

"That's our best bet."

"That's also a lot of territory to cover."

"I know."

Shielding my eyes, I stepped through the roughly hacked hole in the webs. The FBI agents were there, waiting with their team. All around, the sheriff and his men were heading over. They'd been moving around to the back of the building, probably trying to sneak in and listen.

"Well?" McCloskey asked. "Is it a --"

"Do you have any water?" I asked. My lips were drier than the sand beneath my feet.

"Um, I -- yeah." He turned to someone and made a flapping, drinking motion with his hand. Before he could turn back, I raised my arm, slapped a blatantly fake smile on my face, and called.

"Sheriff!"

It was kind of pointless. He was bustling over anyway, hands on his belt, puffed up like a pigeon during mating season.

"Sheriff," I said, "I need to know something. Who was the first person on scene here?"

"Uh, that'd be Officer Daniels."

"Is he here?"

The sheriff turned and belted, "Jacob!" After which, a skinny, blonde who looked as though he were barely out of boyhood came running over.

"Officer Daniels," I extended my hand. He took it without hesitation, and shook it with a nod and a smile. "You were the first here? No other witnesses?"

"No, sir." He said. "I stopped in for gas and saw --"

I held up my hand. Behind me, another of the sheriff's men had wandered

159

within earshot, his hand drifting over the button to the microphone on his shoulder. The team from the FBI was nearby, most of them with their backs to us, but none of them saying a word to one another.

"Agents, sheriff, we're going to need to speak to Jacob alone."

The sheriff huffed and, somehow, managed to puff himself up a bit more. "I don't know if I'm comfortable with the two of you interrogating my man."

Wraith crossed her arms. "I bet you didn't have a problem with these fine lookin' gents from the FBI asking him questions."

The sheriff's cheeks, and whole face for that matter, flushed with anger. But before he could speak, McCloskey stepped in.

"I can't speak for the sheriff here," he said, "but I know my partner and I would definitely feel better about being in on that conversation."

I sighed. "I really don't want to have to pull rank here, Agent."

McCloskey stood up a little straighter. "Well I think that's what you're going to have to do. And if you do, I'm gonna have to get my supervisor on the horn and see what he thinks about it."

McCloskey wasn't going to back down. His partner was there, hands on hips, waiting for an answer. The sheriff and his men, the FBI team, everyone was completely focused on what was happening.

"All right," I said, reaching into my suit. "Jacob?" From my inner pocket, I retrieved the counterfeit badge and held it out. "Could you hold this for a second?"

Confused but polite, he took it from me. The sheriff and agents, equally confused, watched.

A flick of my arm and the gold watch was exposed. Pushing on the face of it, there was a click and a whir as its exterior ring segmented and expanded into various levers and buttons."I believe it's time to speed things up. Wraith, if you please?"

She nodded.

"Wait," McCloskey said, "did you just call her..."

With a hiss, her hair began moving, drifting about on a breeze that wasn't there. My fingers pinched the controls on the watch. Behind the crowd, panels on the hood, doors, and roof of our car snapped open, revealing a dozen mechanical arms with machine guns attached.

"Oh shit!"

The guns roared. Wraith transformed. People barely got the chance to run and, when they did, the guns either followed them, or Wraith did. The sheriff tried to shout something, but Wraith silenced him for good before racing to the back of the building. Five seconds after they started, the guns stopped. After that, it was just me and Officer Jacob Daniels, who was standing in a state of shock, his hands up near his face in a useless defense.

Well, not entirely useless.

"Don't drop that badge," I said, as it danced between his shaking fingers. "It's the only thing keeping those guns from shooting you."

He shivered, looked at the badge, then back to me, then to the bodies surrounding us. He may have tried to say something, but it was just quick breaths that came out. With a jerk, he reached for his gun. He didn't make it halfway there before Wraith was on him.

"Now, Jacob? Listen, I need you to... please stop squealing, she hasn't even hurt you... I need you to answer some questions."

He whimpered. Sweat ran down the side of his face. Urine ran down the front of his pants.

"When you showed up, did you see anyone or anything leaving this building?"

"Nuh -- nuh -- no. No, sir, no. I, I --"

"You're sure?"

"Y-y-yes."

"Did you see anything moving?"

"The... the sp -- the spiders."

"The spiders?"

"Y-yeah. They, they were ev-everywhere. Spin -- spinnin' the web... the webs."

"On the outside?"

"Y-yes."

"Okay. Okay. Good. That's good. And you're sure you didn't see anyone?"

"No."

"What else? Anything that seemed odd?"

"No, no I --" a tremor ran through him, accompanied by a loud, panicked cry. "The back."

I raised an eyebrow.

"The back door, the one by, by, by the dumpster, yeah? It was, it was open. And there was, there was tracks."

"Footprints?"

"No. Like, something was, um, uh --"

"Dragged," Wraith's voice came from the rolling smoke, ethereal and broken. Jacob nodded fervently.

"I, I just thought that, you know, someone had taken out the, the trash or, or something. You know?"

"The tracks," I asked, trying to hide my excitement, "where did they go?"

"Just, just, just out the... out the back."

My hand shot out, taking the fingers Jacob was using to hold the badge and squeezing them even tighter. With a rush like wind running through the trees, Wraith slipped off the man and vanished around the building. He and I stood there, still. His eyes wandered over his now free hand. To his gun.

"Don't," was all I said.

Wraith sped back from around the other side and ended up behind me. "Gone," she said. "Too many people have been back there."

A low growl rolled up through my chest. That was it, the only lead we had.

"Jacob," Wraith's voice partially solidified, as did her body, "what happened to the spiders?"

He looked at her half formed shape, confused. "The... what?"

"You said there were spiders. They're not here now. Where did they go?"

"I --" he paused. I felt his hand twitching, moving as he tried to gain control of his racing mind. "I, I saw some of 'em goin' in -- in a line. Like, like ants, you know? I thought I was, I dunno, goin' crazy or somethin'."

"Which way?"

"The --" with his free hand, he pointed. Out the back, same as the tracks. Straight into the desert and then...

"Those hills," I say, my gaze wandering over them, "do they have caves?"

"Um," he nodded a few times. "Yeah. Yes. They --" he pointed again, a bit to the west, where the hills broke away into crags and bluffs. "There. It's reservation land. Indian. They, they got a bunch of old, you know, like, places that they, before they started, you know, buildin' houses and --"

"Got it," I said, a smile spreading across my lips. "And you're sure it's that way?"

"Yes. Yes, sir."

"Thank you, Officer Daniels. You've been most helpful." I slipped the badge from between his fingers. The guns rumbled. "Let's go."

It was nearing dusk when we reached the base of the sheer rock face. I'd insisted we walk, and Wraith never made a peep about it. Along the way, we'd spotted more spiders, dead, lying on the ground. I'd gathered several to examine later, but even a cursory glance told me they were anything but normal. My first clue was that we even found them. In the desert, any little bit of biological matter that doesn't defend itself is bound to be eaten by something. Their bodies were untouched. The animals of the desert were afraid to even go near them.

They were, in fact, arachnids. Most of them had body types similar to

162

spiders found in the desert and other places, but there were inconsistencies which, during our long walk, I felt the constant need to point out.

"These ones, do you see the enlarged abdominal casing?"

"Mm-hmm," she said, for probably the hundredth time.

"There's a huge space for the organs required to create and spin the webs but... but at a cost which doesn't make sense. Their other systems are entirely compromised. And look!" The goggles I'd gotten out of the car buzzed as they zoomed in on the tiny carcasses in my hand. "The chelicerae are practically non-existent. They, they have no way to bite or feed on prey. It's as though they've evolved, sacrificing everything else, to be the most productive and efficient web spinners possible. While this one is almost nothing but mouth parts and venom glands."

"So those are the spinny spiders, and those are the bitey spiders."

"All spiders are bitey spiders. They have to eat."

"Not those ones."

"I... but that's impossible."

"You do realize you're talking to a woman who turns into smoke, right?"

And on it went, my hoverjet floating hundreds of feet above us, me using my watch to have it send helicopter drones which took the spider specimens up and brought water and food down. We followed the trail, hiked past more cacti than we could count, and watched as the rocky, red cliffs grew closer. Before we reached the base, we saw the caves. They were maybe sixty feet from ground level. In front of them, ancient structures sat, mostly gone, eroded by time. There had been a tribe living there once, long ago. I wondered if what we sought now was what drove them away.

Wraith said, "You know, in some Native American folklore, spiders are seen as good things. The Hopi have Spider Grandmother, the creator of humans. They're mythical figures. Practically gods."

I licked my lips. "I wonder what happens when a god gets hungry."

We started the steep climb.

"There's something I need to tell you."

She kept going.

My feet shuffled for purchase. "One of the cars at the diner, it was a station wagon."

"There were a couple of them. So what?"

I had to put my fingertips on the rocks to steady myself. "One of them had suitcases, duffel bags."

She waited for me to get to the point.

"I saw..." A quick grab of a branch, and I pulled myself up. "There were books in the backseat. Kids' books."

She stopped. "The bodies at the diner, they were adults."

I had to keep moving, or else I would get stuck. "Yeah."

Her chest rose and fell. "There's a limit," she said, using the same tone she used on the sheriff. "If we go up there and find a monster like that, I'm going to --"

"Slay it?" I asked. "Heroes all think the same."

"Well what the hell do you plan on doing?"

Gripping the edge of the rock above me, I called back through gritted teeth, "I'm going to put a collar on it. That way, it only hurts who I want it to." Straining, I tried to pull myself up over the lip of the edge.

I didn't even hear the hiss. She rushed, completely enveloping me for a moment. When the dusk sun hit me again, she was there, above me, crouched on the ledge, holding my wrists. With her help, I came to stand at the mouth of the cave. From that inky black came two things, the smell of death and decay, and a sound.

Breathing.

From my back pocket I pulled a pale, rubbery disc. Pinching the middle, a sealant cracked and I tossed it in. It swelled from the chemical reaction happening within and began emitting a light similar to that of bioluminescent marine life... which is where I discovered the chemical compounds... only considerably brighter. Bouncing a few times, it came to rest against something white and round.

A skull.

Bones, horns, leathery skins, and dried feathers dotted the cave floor. The walls had markings all over them, roughly smeared lines and stripes, some taking on primitive shapes of animals and stick figures. They weren't petroglyphs, per se. Their style was more... infantile.

The light ball pulsed gently. Further in, the breathing stopped. We waited, silent.

Crunch.

Crunch.

Crunch.

My eyes darted, trying to find the thing moving beyond the light. It walked... or crawled or slithered or whatever it did... slowly. Wraith saw it before I did, because next to me the smoke erupted around her body. I stole a look at her.

Fear. For the most fleeting of moments, she showed fear.

This was a bad, bad idea.

Rocking back and forth, melting out of the shadows, a figure appeared. At first, it was hard to see. But the closer it came to the light ball, the more

164

defined it became. Or, I should say...

He.

Though bare, his feet were so dirty the skin could barely be seen. Across his massive torso a tattered shirt... lord only know what its original color had been... was stretched as far as it could go. The same for the threadbare pants he'd pulled onto legs as thick as oak tree branches. Whatever part of his face wasn't covered in a bird's nest of black beard was obscured by the briar bush of equally dark hair that stuck out and down and every which way from his head. He was more than just disheveled, more than dirty. He was bordering on inhuman.

He lumbered forward, eyes on the glowing ball. I'd attached several weapons to my belt during our hike, and I felt an intense desire to grab at least five of them. But something held me back. Maybe it was how he hadn't charged in, or how he had failed to acknowledge our presence. There was something else, too.

No spiders. Not even cobwebs, not that I could see.

Where were they?

He stopped in front of the ball. Crouching down, he picked it up with fingers that were thick and powerful and dirty as a blacksmith's tongs, yet delicate as could be. He rose and stared at the light, turning it over in his hand. His eyes shone like black glass. His lips rounded, and he cooed softly.

Leaning to the side, hoping to get a bit of a better view of his face, my foot dragged against the rocks.

His eyes snapped up. Within the echoes of the cave, we heard it.

The skittering.

Hundreds of thousands of tiny legs.

Scanning the walls and the floor of the cave, there was no movement. Would they come from the carcasses? Would they pour from the hollow eye sockets of the skulls? I checked everywhere, the inside, the outside, the ground beneath our feet.

Nothing.

Wraith's breath caught in her throat. I followed her gaze.

There, on his arm.

No.

From his arm.

Holes the diameter of pencil erasers had opened up across his arm, and his neck, and his face, from which a living, thickening, crawling sheet spread across him. Their bodies covered and dimmed the light ball, making him a living shadow in the dark.

A shadow that came toward us.

165

Wraith's ability didn't hiss, it popped like a vacuum being filled. My arm shot out in front of her.

"Wait," I said, with what little voice I could muster.

The shadow moved faster.

"What?" she snapped.

With a twist, I opened my watch and cranked every button I could.

He started running.

"We have to --"

"Wait," I said again.

He dropped the light ball and bounded on all fours. The watch clicked and chirped. Above us, the hoverjet came closer.

Wraith's storm whirled. "He's --"

"Just..."

The watch beeped. The man changed trajectory, racing up the wall of the cave, crawling as fast as a sprinter could run. Wraith went full smoke. To the side, a mechanical whirring filled my ears. I stuck my arms out, one in front of Wraith, the other open and waiting. The man reached out. Something hit my hand, flexible and crinkly. I snatched and swung it forward.

"Here!" My voice rebounded again and again, down the cave.

The man stopped, his spider covered face inches from the brown, grease stained paper bag in my hand. He made no movement to take it, just hung there, upside down, staring. Across his body, the spiders writhed.

"Here," I said, softer this time. "This is for you."

Slow and fluid, he took the bag. It took every bit of control I had to not pull back as the spiders brushed my skin. Still upside down, he uncurled the bag's top and reached in. Even over the stench of rot and filth from the cave, I could smell the deep fry oil, the cheap mayonnaise and pointless amounts of salt.

Pulling the burger out, the spiders went to work, peeling back the bright orange parchment paper wrapping. He sniffed it and, for a moment, I feared he would reject it. But from the squirming mask on his face, a mouth appeared.

"Mmmm..." Even without words, I could tell that his voice was deep.

Behind my still outstretched arm, Wraith began to solidify. The man didn't seem to notice. Or, if he did, he didn't care. He was focused on the burger. The spiders spread across the top of the bag, diving inside to find what else there was. With a savory chomp, he got almost half the burger in.

His eyes, dark as obsidian glass, met mine. "Are there fries?" he asked, hopefully.

"Uh, yeah." I said, surprised. "Yes. There are."

His eyes went wide and he reached in excitedly, pulling out a handful and shoving them into his mouth. "This is good," he said. "Thank you." His voice was... odd. He spoke slowly, and a little broken, highlighting the wrong parts of the words at times.

With a big smile, I said, "There's another burger in there, too."

He stopped chewing the fries and looked at me, then at Wraith, then back to me, his eyes unblinking, waiting for an answer to a question which he didn't know he had to ask. It took me a few seconds.

"It's... it's okay. You can have it. We're fine."

He nodded. The bag rustled. The spiders, working together, dragged the burger to the top.

"We don't get stuff like this a lot," he said around a mouthful of fries.

"I can see that," I replied, looking past him at all the bones. "Is this where you live?"

"Uh-uh," chomp, slurp, "this is the food place. We live up there," he pointed up... well, down for him, as he was still hanging from the ceiling. I noticed that his feet weren't actually gripping the cave's ceiling. The spiders were holding onto it, and then creating a massive living chain which held him up.

"Oh," was all I could think to say.

"Could I see more?" Wraith asked. "Of your food place?"

His chewing slowed. His movement slowed. The spiders slowed. He stared at her, not looking her up and down, not darting all around. Just... stared into her eyes as though they were the only thing in the entire universe he cared to look at.

"I won't take anything," she said, gently. "I promise."

He did not seem convinced.

She took a small step forward. The spiders picked up in pace. "I'm... we're looking for someone. A person from the diner."

"The building you went to," I said.

"Oh," he said, long and low, "that." The spiders had pulled back from his face enough that we could see a look of shame. "We didn't mean to do it. We just... the desert is dry. No animals are here. We got so hungry."

"Of course," I said, understanding, but no less disturbed.

"We don't like to eat people. We wanted food." One of his legs detached from the ceiling. As he spoke, he stretched down, dropped from the ceiling, landed on his feet, never even coming close to dropping or tilting the bag of food. "Everyone there, they made so much noise. They scared us. Then, they got scared too. It just sort of happened."

"Did you bring any of them here?" I asked.

167

He nodded. As massive as his body was... broad shouldered, thick limbs, muscular chest and neck... he stood on bent legs and with a curved back. His posture kept his head below either of ours.

Wraith leaned in. "Was there a child?"

He tilted his head.

"A... a boy or a girl? A --"

"The little one?" he asked.

Wraith's jaw muscles tightened. She nodded.

"We..." he looked out, to the desert surrounding his cliff. "She was crying a lot. We didn't like all the noise, so we took her."

"Took her?"

He pointed. "We carried her, to the people who live way over there."

Wraith held her sigh of relief for a moment. "And she was okay?"

"Uh-huh." He said, practically shoving his face into the bag. "I think she was sad or something. I don't know."

Let free, the sigh traveled across Wraith's body, ending as a smile on her lips. "Thank you for not hurting her."

"Even we know that." His mouth couldn't fit all the fries in his hand. "Little ones are special."

She looked at me then, and gave approval. I took a step toward him. He looked up quickly, his fingers tightening around the bag. I stopped.

"What would you think," I said, "about never being hungry again?"

CHAPTER SEVENTEEN
THE CAVALRY

I am so goddamn sick of running right now. The blisters I got running from the warehouse have burst, reformed, burst again, and are currently turning into pools of screaming hot lava on my feet. At least I'm wearing sneakers this time. I think I'd rather be taken down by government super agents than do this in heels again.

Annie grabs my arm and steers me around a corner. A trashcan goes tumbling as I wing it with my hip.

"Shit!"

Annie feels me dropping and yanks me back from the edge of a full-on dirty alley face plant. My legs start working again, but they're all wiggly and my muscles are on fire. No, they've passed being on fire. They're cinders and ash at this point. Every part of me is covered in sweat. I'm hungry. I've got a stitch in my side, my lips are dry, and my head keeps doing that ridiculous pigeon bop with every other miserable step.

So when Annie says "Come on," and gives me another little tug, I just can't do it. Swatting her hand off, my whole body gives out, and the only thing that keeps me upright is the brick wall I manage to throw myself against.

Oh damn, does that feel good.

The brick is all cold and when my body hits it, I swear I hear a sizzle. Annie stands nearby, rocking back and forth, panting. I can tell she's anxious about not moving, but her eyes are anxious about the fact that I look like I'm dying. How the hell did someone like me end up with a friend like her?

Wait, that reminds me.

"Annie?" I pant the word out.

"Yeah?"

"I heard." My whole torso is throbbing along with my heartbeat.

"Heard?"

"You --" pant, pant, "-- and Princess." Gotta slow down. May barf. No? Okay. "At the house."

"Oh, yeah." Whether she's tired or embarrassed or what, I can't tell. "We have to keep moving. The museum isn't far."

"Thank you."

"For what?"

"For caring about me."

She smiles. "I --"

What she is, is cut off by the crack of stone from beneath our feet. To the side, a wall of stalagmites bursts out of the ground. Shards of concrete pelt us as we scramble back from it. When my hands drop, I see that the direction we were headed is completely cut off. The stalagmites are huge, at least ten feet, and the tips look razor sharp.

I step back and a bit and Annie falls into my peripheral. She's staring down the alley, the way we came. I follow her eyes.

The Latina.

Oh, shit.

She's squatting down like before, hands on the ground, one knee higher than the other, head up, face blank. She's close enough that I can get a good look at her this time. Right away, I notice something.

"She's... familiar..."

"From the press conference," Annie says, her voice super-duper serious. "Special Agent Garcia."

"Right," I say, but don't really agree. There's something else about her. I dunno what it is, but now's not the time. Annie's weight shifts, slowly. Garcia doesn't move a muscle. We're all staring at each other. I can't remember the last time I blinked. Even from this distance, when I focus in, I can hear her. She's breathing hard. She not only had to follow us through all those twists and turns, but had to catch up. I'm winded, but Annie's in stupid-good shape. Maybe we have an advantage here.

Garcia stands up, real slow, and plucks at something near her ear. A milky white plastic earpiece comes out, the kind Secret Service agents wear. She fastens it to her vest and flips a switch on her belt to turn it off. Before she does, I hear something come through.

"Garcia, report your location."

It's the woman who gave all the orders to the soldiers at the house. But it's not just from then. It's from before. Where? Where is it from, and why does it send shivers down my spine every time I hear it?

"Hey," Annie whispers, "you see that turn there? The one between her and us?"

I do. It's the only way out besides going over those spikes (which I bet Annie could do in an instant, but only by leaving my ass behind) or through Agent Garcia.

"You're gonna go down that street, okay?" she says real fast.

No. No, I don't like this.

"I'm gonna get in close and distract her."

Not a good idea.

"You stay back, and when you see your chance --"

We should stay together. When we're together, things are... things just...

"-- you go for it."

I feel safe, with you, Annie. Don't... I don't want...

"You remember where we're going, right?"

Please don't leave me right now.

"I promise, you'll get there just fine."

Please...

"Wait for an opening," is all she says. Then, she's gone. By the time I turn my head, she's covered half the distance to Garcia. Her body, it's...

Holy. Shit.

She doesn't move like a person, at all, in any way. Just a minute ago, all her limbs and everything were normal. Maybe a little bendier than normal but, but not like this. Without bones and a ton of extra muscles there's nothing holding her limbs back from creating perfect, fluid movements. She's a millipede or an octopus or something. There's this wild flurry of movement, and yet she moves straighter than a laser beam. And for one second, I start to think she's going to pull this off.

There's a crack and a pop as a massive stalagmite bursts out of the ground right in Annie's path. Garcia dropped fast, faster than I could follow. The spike's point misses Annie's head by inches, and that's only because she springs out of the way. Suddenly she's running up the alley wall. Another spike pops out, thinner and longer this time. Annie dodges that one, too. My eyes jump to Garcia. She's calm as hell. Her arms twitch, her hands sweep across the ground, and shit goes crazy.

Spikes burst out, one after another, boom-boom-boom, angling towards Annie as she comes down the wall and back to the street. Boom-Boom. They follow her up the opposite wall. Boom-Boom-Boom. Faster and faster. The alley starts looking like a giant meditation crystal. Spikes are everywhere.

Annie flips and glides and slips around them, over them, under them. It's incredible that she can actually see them in time to react. Some spikes smash into the alley walls, piercing them. Others collide with previous spikes, shattering them to pieces. None of them hit Annie directly, but most of them get real close.

She slithers like a snake between two and, when she pops out the other side, she's within thirty feet of Garcia. She spins into the air, dodging another, and now it's twenty feet. She wraps her leg around a spike, swings off it, and launches herself to ten feet. She ducks under a row of fat spikes and comes up. Five feet. She leaps off the newest spike's side, spinning in the air, her leg twirling around and around for a massive kick.

Holy shit girl, you got her!

Garcia's hand slaps the ground

There's a massive, shattering crack.

No...

Spikes erupt like a blooming flower. They spread around Annie, completely enveloping her. There's a ripping sound, shredding cloth and skin. I don't mean to, but I clap my hands over my open mouth.

The flower keeps growing. Within, I see movement, a black blur squirming and racing around. Some of the spikes intersect and begin breaking away. There's crashing and clattering, snapping and smashing. The movement races down toward the ground. The entire flower tips as a spike, at least three feet in diameter, smashes up through the ground. The slithering blur that is Annie goes flying through the air, back, away from the collapsing spike-flower of death.

She lands in a pile. I can't tell what's her head and what's her body. With a few quick flops, she moves back toward me and begins to take a human shape. On the ground, between where she landed and where she is now, there are streaks of blood.

She stands, but stumbles. There's a huge cut on her shoulder and the arm attached to it doesn't seem to be working so well. She's got cuts everywhere. Her heart is racing. She's bleeding, a lot.

Annie, who's fighting to protect me because she cares about me, because she's more than just my best friend, is bleeding. For me.

I will be goddamned if I'm going to let her get hurt anymore.

My fists curl up and I take a step.

Crack!

A spike shoots straight at Annie's head. She jerks to the side, and I hear her grunt as blood sprays up from her cheek. Twisting, she falls onto her ass. Another spike comes out from behind. She rolls, ducks a third spike, and tries to stand. From the side, a spike shoots out and slams into where her ribs should be. She shouts and falls. There's no blood. The spike was blunt. Another blunt one hits her from the other side. And another, and another and another and another. With each, she grunts or gasps or groans and, when the last one hits her right in the gut, she makes a sound that pulls hard on the muscles around my heart. Her back hits the wall. Her eyes roll up. She struggles to stay up.

There's a massive snap from the ground in front of her. Four bolts of earth come out, punching through the wall behind her just above and below her armpits. Crying out, she pulls against the spikes, tries to wriggle free. Two more come out, heading for the edge of her torso. She pulls it to the side to avoid them. Then two more on the other side. She has to squeeze in to not get punctured, and when she stops, she's completely pinned in place. There's

172

a little more writhing, a pull or two, but she's out of strength. Her breathing is fast and strained, but it starts to slow down. Then, it almost stops. My feet, my legs, my entire body has been absolutely useless up until now. But suddenly, I'm running, sprinting over to Annie. My hands grab at the stone bolts and I scream, holler at her to hang on.

Please hang on.

"Come on," I grunt as I pull. "Come on!" They don't budge. "Annie!" She doesn't budge, either. "You can get out!" Her head is all flopped down. "Come on, girl! Move!" She's not even twitching. "We have to go!" Her eyes are closed. "We have to go..." I hear a shuddering breath, but I can't tell if she's moving. It's hard to see.

With all the tears.

Over my own big, belly sobbing, I hear Garcia's boots grinding on the broken pavement. Panic shoots through me. I try to push through the stone bolts, get in front of Annie to protect her from whatever's coming.

But nothing does.

All through the alley, the spikes are breaking. Not the ones holding Annie, but all the rest. They're crumbling away, turning into dirt and dust. Way down, the huge flower snaps and pops, its petals drop with thuds. And there, behind it, I see her standing.

Garcia.

Untouched, unmoved, stone cold and rock-faced. She's not even breathing hard.

That bitch.

Jaw clenching, eyes locked on Garcia's, my fingers curl into fists and I step back.

Annie's hand grabs me. Not tight, but enough that I go all soft inside for a second.

"Go," she barely manages to get it out.

"Annie --"

"Museum..."

I lean in as close as I can and say, resolved, "No."

"Go."

"I won't leave you. I --"

"She..."

I freeze. Annie's head rolls up just enough that I see a tiny smile.

"She's there. She'll protect you."

She? She who? Who the hell am I supposed to meet?

But Annie's head droops. Her fingers fall away. Her breathing...

Oh god...

It's there. It's tiny, but it's there. I can hear it, but just barely.

Garcia's feet move.

My head snaps up, and whatever look there is on my face stops Garcia in her tracks. I pull back from the pillars holding Annie in place. Garcia watches me, same way she watched Annie a minute ago. We're facing off, yards apart, old-west-gun-fighter kind of shit right now. Her fingers are opening and closing. Her feet are spread. I'm dancing, shifting my weight from one foot to the other. My hands are twitchy. I'm ready, ready to go. She's just waiting. Her chin goes down, but her eyes stay up.

She's ready. She's taking this seriously.

Good. Freaking good. Because I am too. I am so ready. I am beyond pissed right now. And even though I'm new to this, I know what my power can do. I blew the hell out of that warehouse, almost blew up my own damn house. And now, I'm gonna throw everything I've got, everything that's been building up inside me right at her and those stupid goddamn spikes. I'm gonna knock her on her ass, and once she's down, I'm gonna get Annie the hell out of here. I'm done. Done. No more. No more running, no more fear, no more letting these bastards push me around. I've got the power. You hear me, Garcia? I've got a huge power, and I'm gonna use it. I'm letting the whole world know that they... cannot... mess with me and my Annie again!

I shout. She drops. My hand pulls back like a major league pitcher. Her hands hit the ground. I swing and throw and...

Nothing.

No sonic boom. No ten-thousand decibel sound wave.

Wow... I have never sucked so hard in my entire life.

The ground a few feet in front of me cracks.

Oh, no.

The ground explodes. I throw myself back, covering my face with my arms. Gravel sprays me, scratches my arms and pelts my chest. I half scramble back, half roll over as I listen for the next burst, the cracking sound that always comes before the spikes. When it doesn't come, I stop, listen, and hear something very, very different.

Breathing.

Big, deep, heavy breathing.

Slowly, I open my eyes.

Where I was standing, just a minute ago, there should be a spike. Instead, there's a stump, a stone platform, ragged and uneven at the top, that was a spike. There's rubble all around it. It's big, big enough that it would have knocked my ass to the ground, probably broken my ribs or worse. Garcia wasn't messing around, man. Wow.

But it's not the stump or the rubble that I'm looking at. It's the shape, the shadow on top of it, half buried from crashing down as the spike erupted. The shape has legs. Big, thick, muscular legs and arms to match. The torso... well, it's hard to tell what's really there, how big the shape really is. Because it's covered.

Encased in millions of spiders.

CHAPTER EIGHTEEN
WHAT YOU DON'T KNOW CAN HURT YOU

Dios mío oh Jesus oh Christ ayúdame somebody help me diosito, por favor no...

He's here. He's right in front of me and I... I don't... I can't...

Araknis.

It's Araknis.

... we're all gonna die.

Do. What do I do? What do -- run. I need to run. Get up. Move. Get up! I, I can't stop staring. He's here and I'm looking at him and the spiders, the spiders are... Jesus Christ... I can feel them. I can see them in my head.

They're inside him. They're crawling around in his body, through his muscles and bones and, and -- oh crap, I'm gonna be sick. They come out through his skin. All over. His arms, his legs, his... his face. There are holes in his face and they're coming out and swarming over him in a black blanket and all I can see through it are his eyes.

His huge, cold, dead eyes.

I'm not ready for this. They, they trained us and told us and McTier said we were ready, said we'd be prepared. But he's, he's so much worse and I can't even move so como diablos, how the hell am I supposed to fight?

I have to go. I have to move as fast as I can and get away. There's no way, no way I can beat him. He's not... I've fought supervillains and cyborgs and people who can stretch like elastic and turn into animals and shoot lasers from their eyes and fly and lift cars and summon thunderstorms and read minds and breathe poison and a hundred other things.

But they were human. No matter what they could do, they were human.

He's a monster. A nightmare brought to life.

And he's going to kill me.

He moves, and every muscle I have jerks. His head turns, slowly, away from me and to the woman on the ground. From the way she was acting, I thought she had a power, but now I realize the other three were protecting her. I had sent a spike to knock her out, disable her. I was going to question her, find out why those three were willing to put themselves in danger for her.

But now that's not going to happen, because Araknis is going to kill us both.

He turns just enough so his eyes can roll to the side and find the woman behind him. Then, he's still as a statue. It's freaky as hell. On top, the spiders move constantly, a slithering sheet across his body. But the form underneath barely moves at all.

The mask of spiders pulls back. His skin is the shade of desert clay, with an undertone that says he doesn't spend enough time in the sun. His face is as boxy as the rest of his body. Behind him, the woman I was chasing creeps backward. Her mouth is open in a silent scream... just like mine is.

Which is funny, because we look kinda similar. I noticed it when I caught up. She could totally be my cousin or something.

Mierda, what's he doing? He's just... staring at her. Totally ignoring me. The soldier part of my brain is screaming to act, strike while he's distracted. I wouldn't even have to move, I could send a spike from here and there's no way he could dodge it. I'd hit him hard enough to push him back, then I'd get the hell out of this alley, back to the van, and have McTier call in a goddamn air strike and napalm this place to the ground.

My fingers dig in. My arm stops shaking. I feel the earth beneath me and make my connection and just as I'm about to act, Araknis does something I did not expect.

In a soft, deep voice, he says, "Hello."

The woman and I freeze.

"You got so big," he says. His voice is odd, but only because it's so normal. I expected something... evil.

The woman's jaw flutters like she's trying to talk, but can't. Honestly, can't blame her. I'd have no idea what to say, either. Araknis's face is... thoughtful? Like, he's not snarling or grinning or really showing any emotion at all (which is way more unnerving than if he was). There's a thought process going on, but I have no idea what it is.

The urge to strike first fades. Something very strange is going on. Araknis showing up like this is weird enough; there's no apparent reason, none of the women in the house with powers are associated with him. He didn't save the twisty woman I pinned to the wall, so he's not the cavalry, he's not the backup.

At least, not for them.

He stopped the spike. He stepped in and saved her when all the others were taken down. Whoever she is, she's that important.

She's what McTier is after.

Something moves. I feel it. Araknis is still leaning back, but his eyes are on me now. His body hasn't moved, that's not what I'm seeing in my head. It's the spiders, the ones inside him. They're shifting and scurrying.

Preparing.

"You should go," he says, and I know he's not talking to me. The woman doesn't do anything. But when he turns from her and faces me head on, she

177

gets the message and starts moving.

My legs stop trembling.

I can't let her go. She's a major piece to the puzzle of whatever is going on. If I lose her now, I may not be able to figure this thing out. My weight shifts and --

The storm inside Araknis moves to the outside. The spiders around his neck swarm up over his face.

Oh no.

The spiders slip down, off his body, spreading over the rubble in a thin wave. He takes a step toward me, one step, and everything inside me goes cold. There's no way, no way I can beat him. I can feel them, the tiny legs, the spiders are everywhere and it doesn't matter how many spikes I put up they'll just wash around them and over me and I am going to --

"He's mine!"

By the time I turn, Lucien is flying past me. Araknis pulls back (Ironsides was the only person who wasn't afraid to charge him) and the spiders on the ground mass together, a writhing ball of legs and fangs and venom and death.

Lucien tears right through it. Instantly, there's a loud hissing sound, like water hitting a hot pan. Only, it's the spiders hitting Lucien's acid soaked skin. He bounds up the stump and throws his fist right at Araknis's squirmy, spider covered face. There's a loud smack as Lucien's punch is caught in Araknis's meaty paw. They hold there for a second. Araknis is stronger, but Lucien is grinning anyway. The spiders rush down over Lucien's arm. He shouts and pulls back. They're biting him everywhere, dumping tons of poison into his body. He grabs his arm and stumbles and starts moaning.

Oh god. They're too much. He can't --

The moan starts breaking up.

Into laughter.

All over his arm, thick smoke starts to pour out. The sizzling increases. The entire alley begins to reek like the leftovers of the processing plants on the ranches outside of where I grew up. My eyes water and the inside of my nose burns. Lucien grabs his arm and starts flexing, squeezing his muscles. The spiders start falling off in thick, liquidy globs. His laughter turns into a cackle. His clothes, specially designed to resist acid, start to smolder and melt. I hear him, breathing wildly. I feel him, shaking and trembling.

With glee.

The sound he makes is barely human. It's animalistic. It's unearthly. It's a ghostly, insane howl and when his face comes up, the acid is running down his maniacal face.

He dashes in again and swings. Araknis goes to grab him again, but there's no stop, no muscle-to-muscle standoff this time. Araknis pulls back, his hand smoking. The spiders on his arm rush to the spot. Lucien doesn't even give Araknis time to back up. He lunges again and again and again. Araknis learns quick, he dodges and ducks, but Lucien's acid is splattering now, flying off like sweat from a boxer working the speed bag. Araknis puts some room between them and swings an arm. Dozens, maybe hundreds of spiders fly off, all of them spinning silky webs as they do. It's a shimmering sheet of sticky threads. The ESOA said his spiders could spin webs ten times stronger than steel cable.

The silk hits Lucien and, for a second, he's twisting and wriggling and caught beneath it.

For a second.

One of his arms pushes through. Araknis yanks on the other end of the threads, trying to pull Lucien down. Lucien stumbles, but his other arm sears through, then his head. He's snarling with anger, but the corners of his mouth are still pulled up in a little grin. He thrashes back and forth. The webs scatter. Acid drops fly everywhere. Some of them, as well as some melting globs of spider, come flying my way. My training kicks in. I roll back to put some distance, slap my hands down, and raise a small wall of spikes. The drops hit it and start burning through.

There's another of those mad howls. I twist my hands and part of the wall comes down so I can see. They're fighting at an incredible speed. Araknis is leaping about -- for a guy who's built like a tank, he is incredibly nimble -- bounding off the walls, the remnants of my spikes, anything he can use to get the upper ground. All the while, Lucien is pursuing, chasing, stabbing, swinging, shouting.

Chasing. He's chasing Araknis.

His shirt is completely gone. His pants pretty much are, too. On the ground in front of me, melting into the concrete, is what used to be his boots. He's almost there; seventy-five, eighty percent of full release. Right now, he's still able to focus on the task at hand. Any further, and there's nothing he won't do.

Nobody he won't kill.

Araknis springs up and sticks to the alley wall. His legs kick a couple times and he's fifteen feet up. One hand, the one that blocked Lucien's punch, is curled up against his body. There aren't any spiders on it, and I can see the effects of Lucien's acid. The skin is blistered, peeling, bubbling away. The spiders must have absorbed the majority of the acid, but couldn't get it all.

One punch. One punch did that.

I'm starting to wonder who the monster really is.

Lucien half snarls, half cackles. He points his arm like the barrel of a shotgun, slaps the other hand on his shoulder, and swipes down as fast as he can. Acid that can eat through stone and steel flies at Araknis.

With his hand hurt, Araknis moves just fast enough to avoid Lucien's shot. The first one, anyway. Lucien switches arms and fires again, and again, and again. The acid coming from his pores doesn't stop like sweat would. It flows for as long as he'll allow it, and the longer it flows, the more potent it becomes.

Araknis takes a direct hit. The spiders react, rushing to the spots to absorb as much as they can, protecting their host. His legs pump and he makes a massive vertical leap before scrambling for the roof.

No mames... he's running away.

Lucien shrieks like an enraged banshee. He grabs at the wall and a putrid greenish, reddish smoke pours out from around his fingertips. Then, somehow, he's climbing, jamming his fingers and toes into the brick, burning holds that last just long enough for him to reach the next one. As he ascends, I see that the hair on his head, that fine, pale, almost white blonde hair, is starting to fall out.

Full release.

He's never gone to full release before. The trainers, the scientists, and agents on hand always stopped him. They hosed him down with chemical bases to counteract the acid. They force fed him milk and doused him with calcium. Full release wasn't an option. They didn't know if they could stop him. They weren't sure if anyone could stop him; that's why he was chosen to kill Araknis.

When Lucien screamed 'he's mine,' he wasn't just calling dibs. He's been waiting for this, dreaming of it. He finally gets to go all the way.

He finally gets to kill someone.

And he's gone, up, over the wall, after his prey. I can hear him howling. For a second, I wonder if Araknis is feeling fear for the first time in his life.

But that's not my problem. Lucien isn't my problem. Araknis isn't my target.

The woman, she ducked down the alley right as Lucien showed up. She was already winded, I doubt she's gotten far. My eyes go out of focus, and I listen with my ability.

Found her.

My feet kick off, and I'm pounding down the alley, headed for the turn.

McTier and Sosuke haven't trailed us yet. The twisty girl pinned against the wall will show them that I've been here, but they won't have any idea which way I went. McTier should see the effects of Lucien's ability and realize that he's gone to full release. That should keep her and Sosuke occupied for a while.

That woman, the warehouse, our team, our targets, McTier, even the retirement of the Justice Brigade; it's all part of some bigger plan, and I'm tired of just blindly taking part in it. I want to know who has been arranging things. I want to know what the endgame is here. And if I'm going to do what I was brought into do, I want to make sure there is a good goddamn reason for it.

It doesn't take me long to realize that whoever or whatever this woman is, she is most definitely not, in any way, a well-trained, super powered, special agent of doom and destruction.

First off, she would need to do a lot more cardio for that. Seriously, she pooped out after a couple of blocks. I mean, I don't know what the rest of her day has been like, but most villains can at least push through and keep a steady jog going. When I caught up, she was hobbling along, holding her side, cursing up a storm. Unfortunately, she was also out in public, walking through a pretty dense crowd. As much as I wanted to corner her off, it would have caused a scene. We're close enough to where everything went down the ESOA would get her before I could ask any real questions.

So instead, I'm following her into the Boston Museum of Fine Arts. And by following, I don't mean I'm doing a bunch of covert surveillance and tracking techniques. I am, literally, walking forty paces behind her.

Special agents of doom and destruction usually look over their shoulders every now and again.

I let my target head in, then pull out my badge and tell security I'm with the ESOA and they need to start moving people out of the museum. I tell them not to make a scene, and don't call the cops. They give me some seriously wary glances, but I work my military hard-ass face into place, and they roll with it.

After that, I hang back and watch as the woman who is so important Araknis will jump in to save her, wanders around aimlessly, panting, mumbling, clearly not having a clue where she is supposed to be or what she's supposed to be doing.

Keeping my fingers on the stone wall, I'm able to track her movement. She mills about, checking every room she comes to, peeking in, then moving on. Security is doing a good job of slowly emptying the place out. Pretty soon, there aren't many people here besides me and her.

Finally, all the wandering must get to her, because she picks a room and drops down on one of the viewing benches. I stay outside, leaning my back next to the doorway, palms flat against the wall. I can sense almost everything, her movement, her breathing...

Her crying.

She's not sobbing, not like she did in the alley when I pinned twisty girl, but she's crying. I can hear her whispering to herself.

"I don't," she says. "I don't know what to do. Goddamn it, Annie."

Annie, that's what she called twisty girl.

"What am I --" She stops suddenly. Why? I can't... wait. There is something, movement coming toward the room from the other side. How did she pick up on it before I did?

An image flashes in my head. Someone is coming into the room, walking slowly, oddly. I try to lean, to peek through the doorway, but I can't see whoever's walking in without the woman seeing me. What's up with that weird way of walking? It's like they've got...

It's a cane. A man, from the image in my head, it seems like he's wearing dress shoes. I think they're wingtips. But, but it's weird. I can sense him because of the vibrations of his steps, of his cane and his body, but I can't hear him. He's hobbling in dress shoes into a big, empty, stone-walled room. He should be making a racket. But he's not.

Because he's been trained not to.

He heads straight for the woman. She's standing up, slowly, tentative. She doesn't know him, I can tell from her racing heart, from her body language. My hands slide along the wall. I try and peek. I can see her. She's totally focused on him. He's just a tiny bit out of sight.

His cane comes to a stop with a metallic clank.

I know that sound. It's a hospital cane.

Wait...

"Excuse me," says a deep, rich voice, "are you all right?"

My heart slams on the brakes.

Tío Pedro... what are you doing here?

He's in a tan suit and trench coat. His hair is slicked back, but his face is pale. It's obvious that he's strained himself to get here. The woman is eyeing him, trying to figure out what she's supposed to do. He's eyeing her back, but in a very different way. He looks... shocked.

"I don't..." he says, his head shaking a little. "Who..." a little smile spreads across his face and he half laughs to himself.

Are those tears in his eyes?

"You," he says, "you don't know me, do you?"

She shakes her head. "Should I?"

"No," he replies, "I supposed not. My name is Pedro."

She doesn't reply at first, but he simply gives her the space to realize what she's supposed to do. "I'm... I'm Candace."

He practically grins ear to ear. "Candace. That's a lovely name."

"Uh... thanks."

Pedro's shaking hands shuffle his cane back and forth. "This may sound strange, Candace, but you look very much like someone I know. I believe us being here is not by chance. I was called here, and now I think I know why."

My brain has been firing on all cylinders, but none of those cylinders are hooked up to the same machine. I've been so distracted by what's going on in front of me that I didn't even notice the click-clack-clicking of women's dress shoes ricocheting off the walls like a metronome. Pedro and Candace noticed though. His entire body tenses. Candace's heart picks up. On the other side of the room, a woman walks in.

She looks just like the pictures from the file, which is amazing considering that the last photograph of her was taken almost forty years ago. Her hair is different, streaks of white and grey among the black curls. There are some wrinkles around her eyes, her mouth, but they only make her look better, more mature.

More clever and dangerous.

Even though she's wearing jeans and boots and a black leather jacket, I can tell she's in amazing shape. She moves like she's eighteen years old. When she stops, she looks at Candace and smiles.

They didn't have any photos of her smiling. It's strange to see. The world's deadliest woman isn't supposed to smile like that. A member of the Triad of Evil shouldn't look so genuinely happy at something that isn't exploding or on fire or melting or screaming.

She says, warm and loving, "Candace, sweetie."

But then she looks at mi tío, and her smile vanishes. Her eyes turn as dark and cold and she says with a voice like a steel blade. "Pedro."

Oh. Hell. No.

Before I even know it, I'm leaping into the room. When my feet hit the ground, my legs fold up, my hands go down and, without a moment's hesitation, I do what I've been trained to do.

I fight.

With Wraith.

CHAPTER NINETEEN
JAPAN

And so one became two, then two became three. Integrating Araknis was, well, a little more complicated. Acclimating him to the world outside his desert took months. I had to invent whole new technologies which would allow him a virtual experience first; three-dimensional digital renderings, motion capture, the computer architecture to simulate entire environments. The product was crude... everything was boxy and there was very little shading... but it helped. His over-reactive startle reflex to lights and sounds was treated using new therapies designed to desensitize. I built enclosures, real, living controlled environments, replicas of the Arizona desert hills where he could hunt live game, sort of a 'safe place' where he could retreat and process the things he had experienced.

The things I created for him were brilliant, innovative, and groundbreaking. And they helped.

Kind of.

It was Wraith; her patience, her quiet, her stillness. At first, she would sit with him when he became distressed. She didn't coo or coddle him, just acted as a totem of calm. He came to trust her. She had a wonderful way of intuiting his needs, and then meeting them. He could spend all day in one of my machines, exposed to stimuli based on logic and methodology which would prepare him in the most efficient way possible, but none of that meant anything if she wasn't there, waiting to pet his head and ask him how it went.

I saw in him something to be fixed, repaired...

Solved.

She saw something hidden. No... something hiding that needed to be gently uncovered. She won his trust, and through her it was extended to me. After which, we brought ourselves to the world.

The Triad of Evil was born.

With Araknis's added strength, we began working toward plans which were grander in design than ever before. They had to be. The world was caught in the illusion of the Justice Brigade being the good guys. Humanity had become complacent and accepted the lies they were fed. It was no longer enough for me to get my gravity bands back, or for the patriarchy which held Wraith down be acknowledged. Captain Turbo had to pay for what he had done to me. The powers that be had to be abolished and replaced. History was being written by the victors, and our only hope was to bring the truth to light. We had to rewrite things. We had to have control.

Of everything.

So, we waged war. It was a constant back and forth, us gaining power, the Justice Brigade stripping it away. We fought, we clashed, we retreated, we advanced. Every failure on our part raised their notoriety. Captain Turbo got a toy line. Lux started non-profits. Ironsides became a spokesman for cigarettes and cheap whisky. Turbo became especially enamored with the life of a celebrity. I became obsessed with learning as much as possible about everything which could help us win. While Turbo spoke at college graduations, I used fake identities to earn seven new PhDs. He was invited to the United Nations as a chancellor of peace, and I kidnapped military dictators and grilled them on how to create subversive movements, shadow governments, and plan a coup. He licensed a cartoon show. I hijacked every satellite signal in the atmosphere and created a network of constantly flowing information which only I could control.

He played a round of golf on TV with the president.

I was playing the long game.

And so it went, on and on, in a seemingly endless cycle until one day, when everything we had built and done came to a screeching halt.

Japan.

Japan changed everything. Not just for us, not just for the Justice Brigade. For the world.

It was...

...

... how vain of me to say this, considering the millions who died that day. It was the worst day of my life.

I need to be clear; I am not without blood on my hands. I have no illusions the lives I've taken were justified. I'm a criminal and a murderer. It wasn't something I went into lightly, and I did it with no pleasure. I could go into a diatribe here, explain how the world was unfair to me and pushed me into a corner, and had there been justice for me then I wouldn't have had to and blah, blah, blah.

That's empty. It's an argument so shallow I can only hide there just long enough to get myself to sleep at night. I am not a good person. I may have been, once, but I made the choice to leave that behind. Others chose differently. They have their reasons. I had mine.

But never, never in my entire life did I plan on something like this. Which, I get it, all right? Nobody made me steal the warheads. No one else attached them to giant burrowing robots. Other hands did not program them to dig down to the pool of active magma beneath Mount Fuji. That was me. That was all me.

And it was me who begged, who screamed at Turbo to not smash the

185

computers. It wasn't necessary. They'd won. It was over. All they needed to do was chase us to the escape pods, then sit back and let the ESOA take care of it. Yes, the warheads were armed, but they couldn't go off, not without the signal. I'd planned it that way. We'd done this dance a thousand times. It should have been different.

It shouldn't have happened.

... but it did.

We barely made it out. The warheads were miles underground, but the shockwave hit us within seconds. Less than twenty minutes later, Mount Fuji erupted. The time in between... I don't remember much. Fear, sheer terror of what was happening snaked beneath my skin, trying to push through and out of me with a force equal to the disaster which was about to happen. Maybe it was the years of narrow getaways. Maybe it was having Wraith and Araknis there. Whatever and however it happened, I kept myself together. We dragged as many people as we could with us, a handful at most, to the escape rockets. We overloaded them, crammed people in until their bones were one pound per square inch of pressure away from breaking, and hit the ignition. Later, the Justice Brigade claimed we were using them as human shields. Several were reporters, come along to watch the Triad of Evil get smacked around, to snap photos of Captain Turbo throwing a haymaker punch, knocking out the evil Doctor Dendrite. Instead, they took photos from the porthole windows as the rockets screamed away from a geyser of lava which reached four thousand meters... that's four Empire State Buildings... before raining down searing death upon the few people who lived through the initial blast.

I could feel the heat of it, even through the titanium walls of the rocket. I wasn't sure if the screaming I heard was the rocket's afterburners, or the voices of the millions below who had not died, but would within hours.

It was... it was too much. It still is. I... I'm sorry. I can't.

We went radio silent after that. Araknis retreated to his caves. Wraith vanished. I locked myself away in my hidden castle on my hidden island. My hijacked satellites fed me images of what I had wrought. I immersed myself, forced the pictures of screaming children and collapsing buildings and fires that couldn't be put out into my mind. Fuji was still erupting. The column of smoke no longer blackened the sky above the entire country, but could be seen from miles away. The lava was flowing, inching its way across the land. I watched as scientists tried to figure out not when it would stop, but if. They had no idea, though, because the radiation from the warheads had made the entire area completely inaccessible. Those there were stuck, dying slowly, in agony. I could have turned away, but didn't. Every day brought me closer to the sense that everything I had ever done was wrong, and every night was a reminder of the quiet darkness to which I could escape.

It was during one of those sleepless nights, almost four months after the incident, my communicator started buzzing. Took me nearly an hour to find the damn thing.

'It's time we meet,' was the entire message, followed by a time and coordinates. I stared at it for god knows how long, going over and over it, as though every time I could only retain one letter more than the last reading. Eventually, her words pulled me from my stupor. Wandering into one of my many kitchens, I found a pot of coffee, poured a cup, heated it with a laser, and forced it down my throat. After another two, the haze of the last few months washed from my eyes and lifted from my mind. Unfortunately, the cloud of weapons-grade body odor surrounding me became much more apparent.

I showered and shaved. The razor's edge tickled at skin which had been numb before. I hissed with each stroke along my neck. It felt like I was scratching an itch I'd been living with for so long, I'd given up on getting rid of it. I was shocked at how long my hair had grown. I hadn't let it grow out since my undergrad days, when I'd experimented with a 'fro. It wasn't quite that long, but had become gnarled and matted. On a whim, I told a robot to spin it into short dreads on top and fade the sides and back.

Checking the coordinates Wraith gave, I saw they were for a large, public space. Bypassing my modified lab coats, masks, gloves, boots, and utility belts filled with dangerous weapons, I went instead with a pair of jeans, a linen shirt, a blazer, and a hat; all of them treated to be bullet-, fire-, and knifeproof. The hat could be thrown into the air where it would explode with a smokescreen of poisonous gas to which only I was immune. The shoes were Italian leather, handcrafted, and well-padded.

If you're going to be comfortable, start with your feet.

As my hovership -- over the years, the hoverjet had grown in scale -- raced across the open waters of the Atlantic, heading for London, I felt life pouring into me for the first time in months. Upon arriving, the ship stayed at a high altitude. I surveyed the city beneath me. I checked police scanners, tapped into military radio frequencies, and even checked data signals from phones -- texting was really just becoming commonplace at the time -- for anything indicating this was some kind of setup. When nothing suspicious came back, I checked the radar for Wraith's communicator.

She was there, hundreds of feet below me, waiting.

Taking a deep breath, I descended.

The British Museum has approximately ninety-two thousand square meters of floor space and hosts somewhere in the range of sixteen to seventeen thousand visitors a day. Even with that, entire rooms somehow go unseen for days at a time. It was in one of these spaces that I found her standing, arms crossed, staring at a sculpture. Rodin, I believe, Young Mother in the Grotto. Bronze casting. Lovely piece.

I walked slowly, glancing around, taking everything in. She knew I was there, but it didn't change the way she shifted her weight from one leg to the other, then becoming still again. My hands... I remember they felt unusually light... drifted up. There was no blaster strapped to my side, but as my fingers passed my waist, I saw her eyes shift the tiniest of bits. My heart skipped a beat, but my hand moved up to the brim of my hat. I removed it as I walked toward her, around and behind and, as softly as I could, took a spot next to her. Resting my hat against my chest, I took a deep breath. The room smelled like dried cloth and filtered air, but Wraith gave it a hint of coconut oil and honey.

"I like your hair," she said, with a sidelong glance.

"Thanks. I wanted something... different."

"You've got some grays."

I pulled the lowest hanging lock out and down. My eyebrows and eyes went up as I tried to see it. "Huh," was all I said.

"Things change, don't they?" Her arms unfolded, slowly. The palms of her hand drifted across her stomach, taking their time. I think she saw how I noticed, because she slipped them into the pockets of her denim jacket. Her silver hoop earrings tinkled like tiny wind chimes as she looked away from me.

I shuffled my feet a bit. "You look..." Huh. "Radiant."

"Thank you."

"You know, considering."

An eyebrow went up. "Considering?"

"What, uh, what happened."

"Ah."

"I didn't --" My fingers pinched and twisted the hat's brim. "I wasn't sure if you would even get in touch again."

"I needed a little time."

"Of course," I said, a little too quickly. "Yeah, of course, that's... that's... I did too. I needed to... we, we all needed some. I just... I... I wouldn't have blamed you if you, you know, you hadn't wanted to see me again."

She nodded. "You could have reached out."

My eyes fell to the floor. "I didn't know what to say."

"Why?"

"Everything's changed. I wasn't sure where we stood."

"Well, right now, I'm here, standing next to you."

For the first time in four months, I took a full breath. I must have smiled then, because she smiled back. She patted my arm, sweetly. Her fingers traced the muscles of my arm down to the elbow. Her smile faded a bit.

"You seem thin."

"Uh," was all I managed to say.

"We should get something to eat."

"Are, are you hungry?"

"No, I'm feeling a little..." her hand made circles in front of her stomach, "off, you know?"

That full breath ebbed out of me."Okay."

"But in twenty minutes I'll be starving, so..."

And then it rushed back in. "Oh. Oh! Okay. That's... sure. Let's do that. Yes. Yes."

Her head bobbed, as though she were listening to some pleasant beat. She turned her attention to the sculpture. Or, at least, seemed to. "I missed you, too."

Now it was my turn to bob.

"So," she said, soft but probing, "what's the plan?"

My mouth opened before there were words to fill it. "Well, I'm sure there's a pub or a bistro nearby. I could fly us more south, maybe Italy, but that would take a while and -- oh. You weren't talking about lunch."

"No."

"You meant... the plan. The big plan."

"Yes."

"Because I'm, like, the plan guy."

"That has been your thing for a while now."

"Yeah," I said, short and crisp."Yeah."

She waited.

"I really... I have no idea. I mean, I have ideas. I always have ideas. I just..."

"Just?"

"I don't know if they're the right ideas, anymore."

Arms crossing, she dropped an ear toward her shoulder and looked at me sideways. "Tell me one."

I shook my head, but her stare continued. And continued. And continued. I felt like a kid called on in class. With a huff, I opened the floodgates of my brain. "My castle is filled with technology decades ahead of what's available

189

now, right? I have everything needed, everything. I could stop Mount Fuji, today. No more smoke, no more lava. Or, even better, tap into it as a geothermal source and generate enough electricity to power half the country. And the radiation they're struggling with? I have machines to absorb it, compress it, and do any number of things with it. The rubble and destruction could be cleared in weeks instead of years, recycled, and used to rebuild the city. I could heal this wound."

"Why don't you?"

"You know why. They would never, not in a thousand years, let me."

"Then let them do the work. Give them the tech."

"And have them use it for nothing but their own advantage? No. I will not allow them to brand and market and profit off of my genius at the expense of those it could help."

"So you'd rather hide it away where it does no good at all?"

"No," I snapped.

"No?"

"No! Well, yes. Maybe. I... I don't..." My hands shook in the air, then dropped along with my resolve.

She waited for my breathing to slow before saying, "You're right. Things have changed. But at least you're still the same." Her coming closer, her presence alone, forced my chin up. All the strength I felt I'd lost, I could see it in her eyes. She was always stronger than me. "What we want is still out there," the warm undertone of her skin blazed, "to make the world a better place."

"You make us sound like heroes."

"I've never been anything but."

Damn, that was a good line. "We'll never be the good guys, you know that, right?"

"I couldn't care less. Let them have fake heroes and false hope. We'll give them something real. We... we are going to fix this world." She paused. "Why the smile?"

"You're usually so... pragmatic. Where'd you get all this optimism?"

The snarky response I expected didn't come. "Optimism is blind faith. I need more than that. I need something I can trust in, rely on. I need hope. You need to give me hope, Daniel, because..." Her hand fluttered, just above her abdomen. "Because things have changed, and now I need enough hope for two."

My lungs held still so long, they started to ache.

CHAPTER TWENTY
TO PROTECT THE ONES WE LOVE

What?

Why is my mom here? I mean, really, why am I even here? I know, I know; Annie told me to come here, at the museum I'd be safe, and that's why I'm here. I believed her, and so I ran my ass all the way here. Well, ran and walked and stopped a couple times because I for real thought I was gonna throw up. That damn stitch in my side hurt like a mother. But I did it, I made it, and then I realized... I had no idea what to do. I figured Annie would have a contact or something, someone waiting for me. A helicopter on the roof or a secret invisible plane, or I dunno, some dude with a jet pack or... something! But then, there was nothing. Nobody here. Just a big goddamn building and no one to help me.

She. This mysterious she Annie said would protect me. But she didn't say who 'she' was! So I'm looking at every woman along the way, and they're just giving me that, oh-shit-here's-another-crazy-one-I-wonder-what-this-bitch-is-on kinda look. And after I got tired of that, I just flop my ass down and everything that happened in the last thirty minutes -- the soldiers at the house, my powers coming out, trying to get away, the fight in the alley...

Araknis...

It all just came to me at once and I was sitting there, thinking about how if Annie were there at least I wouldn't be alone, and then this old guy comes up and starts talking to me and tells me that he was called and I start thinking that maybe he's the one that's supposed to help me and then... and then my mom walks in.

My mom came for me. Like she always does. Like I always need her to but I'm too stupid and stubborn to ask.

And calls me sweetie, like she always does.

And says the old guy's name, like she knows him.

And then, a stone spike goes right through her chest.

I heard it, that damn cracking noise. And I know my eyes went big, because my mom's eyes went big, and then bam! Up, less than a blink of an eye, there's a spike going straight through my mom's heart.

Only, she doesn't scream. She doesn't bleed or flail or die. Really, she doesn't even look surprised.

She just goes 'poof'.

The spike hits her, but it doesn't.

Because she turns into smoke.

No. Way.

I don't really get what happens next. A tornado of smoke spins around me. The whole world twirls and I'm tossed, moved. My back thuds against a wall. The smoke pulls away and I feel something solid against my chest, holding me up. While I desperately try to catch my breath and not throw up, I hear a voice.

"You lied to me," says my mom. Her hand is what's holding me up. Her voice is barely a whisper, but it echoes through the room. I don't know who she's talking to, but no one gets a chance to respond. Her arm turns into something that isn't smoke and isn't mist but somehow both. Then, her whole body changes.

'Poof'.

The smoke doesn't drift or dissipate. It doesn't float up like smoke from a fire. It doesn't fall like heavy steam off of dry ice. It moves. It twists and slithers. It's alive.

It's her.

She jets at the old man, Pedro. He doesn't pull back in fear, like any normal person would do. Instead, he drops his cane and opens his hands, which light up like sparklers on the 4th of July.

Crack!

Stone smashes against stone when the spikes come up in a wall around Pedro, high enough that I lose sight of him. The smoke, my mom, bounces off the wall like a pool ball bouncing off the sides of the table. The tip of the smoke hits the ground and, when the tail catches up, there's a flurry of movement like someone wrapping a mummy at high speed. My mom solidifies. Mostly. Her hair floats like she's underwater. Her body doesn't have a definitive beginning or ending. Her inside, her middle is nice and clear. But her edges are all blurry. She stares across the room with a look more terrifying than I've ever seen on her, and I'm the one who drove her five hundred thousand dollar Lamborghini into the pool. Agent Garcia is there, crouched on the floor in the same stance from when she and Annie threw down in the alley.

But damn, there is something going on with her face. Before, she was all business. Impersonal. Contained. Now? She's on fire.

No one moves. Mom and Garcia are having the stare down to end all stare downs. Throughout the museum, people are running toward the exits. In here, it's so quiet I can hear the dust from the spikes settling.

A pebble breaks away from one and falls.

Clack.

Like a candle going out, Mom is back in smoke form and driving forward. If I had the time, or the awareness, or I wasn't holding my breath, or all of the above, I'd tell her Annie already tried it. It isn't going to work.

Spikes burst up like they're being fired by a machine gun. Bam-bam-bam-bam-bam-bam-bam-bam. Mom starts zigging, zagging, twisting, flipping, changing directions in ways that seem impossible. Garcia's hands whip back and forth, moving way more than when fighting Annie. Her eyes are intense and focused, but I don't know if she's actually using them to see. She's doing something else, following some other way. She has to be. My mom doesn't just go side to side, she goes back, around, forward; she can reverse entirely on a dime. She's fast, so goddamn fast I can barely follow what's happening. Really, I'm not even watching her, I'm watching the spikes that are following.

The spikes that can't keep up.

Mom switches from retreat to attack and suddenly she's close, super close. The spikes come up even faster than before. They're coming up in front of her now, blocking her off. When she switches directions, there's a huge boom and a massive spike pushes her off course.

She circles back, and the spikes are following again.

Distance. It's about distance. The spikes closest to Garcia are also the fastest. Damn, that's a crazy power. The more you close in, the more dangerous she becomes.

Mom changes her strategy. She drives forward at an angle, forcing Garcia to put up spikes all over the place nearby. It looks like a forest of stone, and mom dives in, disappearing. There's a blip, a second where she's gone. Garcia stops. The spikes pause.

Mom makes her move.

It happens in a flash. The smoke rushes out, then snaps together. Mom is there, flying through the air, her fist back and ready to smash Garcia's face.

Garcia's hand slaps the floor.

Oh crap!

It's the flower of death, the one that got Annie. It doesn't just bloom, but erupts all around Mom. It happens so fast, the entire room shakes from the force of it. There's that whooshing pop sound and Mom goes smoke mode. She races up, through the spikes, matching their speed, and flies out from the top.

Yeah!

Crack.

From the top of the highest spike, another one bursts out. Mom dodges. From that spike, another comes, and another from that, and another from that, chasing her up and up like a rising lightning bolt. She can't outrun them, she's slowing down. Each one gets closer and closer. She has nothing to grip, nothing to slide off of. Another spike shoots out and she slips it, only to end up floating in the air, swirling. Her momentum is gone, she's a sitting target. She might be in smoke form, but there's still weight to her, and she can't fly! With a snap and a crack, a pencil-thin spike shoots out and when it punches through the smoke, I hear something solid get pierced.

... no... Mom...

There's a snap, like a mousetrap going off in the middle of the night. A line -- no, a super thin chain -- shoots from the smoke and jams into the ceiling. There's a mechanical whirring, a winch being spun at incredible speed, and the smoke races up. Around the last spike, Mom's jacket is hanging, stabbed through. Against the ceiling, pulled into where the chain struck, Mom's smoke whirls and congeals. She's there, upside down, feet on the ceiling. On her forearms are some wild, medieval gauntlet things. From one, the chain is sticking out, holding her in place. But up above the gauntlet, on her shoulder, is something else.

A cut.

A deep one.

With a metallic clack, whatever it is at the end of the chain releases from the ceiling and whips back into the gauntlet. Mom doesn't just fall, she literally leaps toward the floor, straight at Garcia.

'Poof'.

Garcia doesn't just jump back, the ground beneath her bursts up and sends her flying, which is a real bummer because one of mom's chains cuts the air where Garcia's stupid face had been an instant before. Another mousetrap snap and the second chain shoots out. Garcia dodges that one too, but when it stabs the wall behind her, Mom goes flying in along the line. Garcia's eyes go big.

Spikes come up in a wall just in time. Mom zips over them. Another wall comes up. Mom goes around it. Garcia starts moving back, pushing herself with the ground from spot to spot. Every time she lands, Mom shoots another chain. Garcia throws up a wall, Mom finds a way through, Garcia moves back.

Garcia. Moves. Back. Because my mom is better. She's faster and now Special Agent Garcia isn't so goddamn special anymore!

A chain wings Garcia's arm. Whatever's on the tip of those things is sharp as hell, because it cuts right through her uniform and blood sprays out. The second chain comes in and Garcia manages to move, but the chain slices across her chest and I hear her gasp in pain.

No, in surprise! There's a chain on each side of her. She's trapped. Mom's gauntlet things start winding up and she flies in toward the trapped Garcia.

Yes. Yes!

Garcia's foot stomps and the ground beneath her bursts up, lifting her five, ten, fifteen feet and rising.

Dammit, so close!

When Mom hits the pillar, she climbs. Garcia doesn't jump off, and I get why. If she's airborne, she can't use her power. Instead, she squats at the top of the pillar, her fingers dug into the stone. As it rises, spikes shoot out, jabbing at the ripple of smoke that's racing up.

Mom goes around and around, the spikes right behind her. She picks up in speed. The smoke isn't a clump anymore, just a thin line. I can see flashes of arms and legs going around and around. She moves...

She moves like Annie did.

No way... Annie learned from my mom...

With a loud snap, a chain shoots from the tip of the smoke. Garcia leans back, but has nowhere to go. Mom reels in her chain and fires another at the same time. Garcia jerks back with her arms. The pillar shudders. A new spike sticks out from the top, carrying Garcia sideways and backwards. Mom reels and fires, reels and fires, reels and fires. The chains are like whips, flipping through the air. Garcia's spike pushes her away and then...

It stops.

A chain speeds at her face.

She leaps back. She's airborne.

She's helpless.

Mom's chains zip back and fire again. Garcia crosses her arms and legs over her body, full guard. The chains hit. Blood flies. I hear Garcia's flesh rip. I hear the thunk of the tiny spears striking her bones. I hear her grunt in pain.

I hear her back hit the thick, stone, wall.

Her hands slap and the entire room reverberates with one... huge... crack.

Chaos erupts. Spikes, thin and fast, explode out from the wall on both sides of Garcia, smacking into the chains and knocking them away from her. She doesn't put a spike up beneath to hold her up. Instead, she just slides down the wall, her hands dragging against it. The spikes follow. They shoot out, smashing the pillar where my mom is still floating. Mom starts racing down, still shooting her chains out at Garcia. They're falling together, Mom's chains a flurry of speedy jabs, Garcia's spikes blocking and covering. The chains smash through the spikes, sending rubble everywhere. It's insanity to watch.

They head for the floor and, right before they land, Garcia pulls her legs up to her chest. Her hands come off the wall. She raises them above her head.

She lands, slamming her palms onto the floor. The room, screw that, the entire freaking building shakes. Dust flies up into my eyes. I can't keep my footing. I scream and pull my arms up over my head. The floor moves like a trampoline with a dozen kids going crazy on it. I'm down, rolling around, bouncing, trying to keep the bits of stone from burying me. It goes on and on and on.

And then, it stops.

After a solid five or six seconds of flailing, I figure out which way is up and flip myself into a sitting position. From every wall, from the floor and the ceiling, spikes have stuck out, a circular spiderweb of rock, all converging on the spot just feet away from Garcia. There, the spikes are knit together, a cocoon of stone, a prison cell just big enough for one person.

My mom.

Nothing happens. Garcia's on the ground, panting, gasping for breath, sweat falling from her face to the dusty floor. Chunks of spikes and wall tumble down, clacking as they go. Off to the side, the old guy is walking, slowly, toward the prison.

No smoke slithers.

No chains snap.

I focus, train my ears on the little rock ball in front of Garcia.

I don't hear anything. No breathing. No heartbeat.

My hands shake. My jaw starts to tremble. Inside me, there's a feeling like everything I am is collapsing down into one little point and I'm afraid it will fall into itself and drag the rest of me with it.

No.

Oh please, no.

Through caked lips and over a dry tongue, I manage to squeeze out a whisper.

"Mom?"

The prison explodes. Stone rains as a scream, a maddening howl of maternal instinct fills the room. Mom bursts out in smoke form, tearing through the air. Garcia's eyes go wide. There's no chance. She's done, exhausted. That last attack took everything she had. She's dead.

The world burns as a wall of pure light leaps across the room.

'Poof'.

The smoke vanishes, leaving my mom in the air, horizontal, her arm pointed out like a spear, the tip of the chain at the ends of her fingers. And for one second, one brief instant, I see her face. She's looking past me, to the side, at the source of the light.

At the old guy.

But she's not angry, or vengeful, or anything like that. She's... sad.

No. It's worse. It's grief and hurt and...

She looks betrayed.

The spike pierces her stomach so fast that her expression doesn't change. As it shoots out her back, red with blood, her eyes only go from sorrow to shocked. Her arms and legs jerk as a spasm, quick and tight, runs through her. Then, everything stops. She hangs there, folded over the spike, motionless.

And the thing inside, the ball where all of my being was falling, goes off like an atomic bomb.

CHAPTER TWENTY-ONE
REVELATIONS

I thought she was caught, it was all over, I had won. That technique, I'd been working on it for months. It was incredibly hard, like trying to squat press ten times my own weight while someone throws a twenty-pound medicine ball into my gut. I'd done it during training, in smaller forms, but never like that. But that's what it took to win against her, against the most feared, most deadly woman in the world.

Against Wraith, member of the Triad of Evil.

Now, thanks to me, former member.

... No manches...

I remember her coming at me. I remember the smoke, her screaming. My muscles didn't freeze, but I was spent. I couldn't even breathe. She moved so fast. I was helpless, and right there, I really thought I was going to die.

But then came the light.

Huge and bright and hot, it struck her in midair and the smoke vanished and there she was. My hands pushed on the broken floor without me even thinking. I just moved, moved like the military had trained me to. The spike... no... my spike went up and when it connected, I felt it.

Flesh.

Muscles.

Organs.

Her spine.

Through my hands, I felt her weight push forward and jerk to a stop. Instinct, primitive instinct and fear told me to pull my hands away, to not experience this. But I didn't. I stayed, and I felt her take that last breath.

I felt her die.

They'd trained me, walked me through, run simulations, practices. But it never went all the way. I always held back at the end. They told me when the real day came, I wouldn't hold back. I would do as I'd been taught. In my head, I always thought about how they were wrong. I would still hold back. I would pull the spike at the last second. I would show mercy, and it would change things. It would change her. She would see I wasn't just some soldier. I was more. She could be more. It would end peacefully.

I wanted it to end peacefully.

But... the military was right. I did it. I did it without thinking about it. It happened so fast and I just...

I want to blame them. I want to say it wasn't my fault. I want to wipe my hands, wash them of Wraith's blood.

But I can't. Because I know. Deep down, I know. Whatever I thought, I imagined, isn't true.

I'm no hero, and they never meant for me to be one.

And because of that, I'm going to break this thing wide open.

Because I remember a few other things, too. First, I remember the noise. It wasn't a voice. It wasn't a thud or a crack of breaking stone. It wasn't the sound of things settling. It was the opposite. It was the sound of movement and energy and building and expansion and contraction at the same time and when I turned my head, I could see it pulsating in the air around her.

The target, the woman I'd been chasing, Candace she said her name was, was kneeling. All around her, a pulse that never ended rippled. It was sonic feedback, so low it could only be felt and so high it made my eyes water. It enveloped her body, and looked like it was ready to blow. But that's not what made me move.

It was her face, the look on her face as she stared at Wraith.

Because the other thing I remember is how just before Wraith came for me, just before she flew out screaming, Candace said something.

She said, "Mom?"

It all makes sense, then; who she was, why she was so important, why those other women were protecting her, why Wraith and Araknis were involved, why Lux had come to meet her, her involvement with the warehouse, and what had caused the explosion there.

And what was about to cause another one.

I remember sending up spikes around Lux, special ones, dense as tempered steel. The ones I used to cover myself? Not nearly as strong. When Candace's sound-wave-bomb thingy went off, my barrier didn't stand a chance. I blacked out. I can only guess the outer wall of the building blew out before I hit it, or else I would probably be dead. I'll never really know for sure.

"Mijita?"

I jerk awake. There's a flutter of white sheets. I feel myself going halfway up to sitting, but I don't really make it. My arms and legs stick out like a dead bug's, and I hang there just long enough to let all the pain in the world attack my every single muscle and joint.

Ohhhhhh... wow.

Mi tío is shushing and speaking softly in Spanish and I think he's telling me to relax but for real what the hell? It's awful. I feel achy and bruised everywhere. Everywhere.

My earlobes hurt. How in the hell do my earlobes hurt?

"Ay, ay, ay, tranquila," Pedro says as he pushes me back down toward the bed. "Calm, mijita. You're safe. Be calm."

I want to open my eyes, see where I am, figure out what's going on, but I just don't think that's going to happen right now. I know we're not at the museum, but are we still in Boston? Are we back in DC? How long has it been?

What do McTier and the others know?

I think I'm trying to ask all these questions, because I hear something that sounds kind of like my voice, but instead of words, I'm making guttural collections of vowels and consonants. I sound like a cavewoman trying to explain Greek philosophy, and doing a very bad job of it.

Pedro shushes again. He sounds like mi madre when I would get a cold and fuss. His hands come down on me, like mi padre when I was sore and aching after soccer games and track meets. He's the closest family I have around me now, and he's doing a great job... but it's not the same.

Los extraño. They don't even know what's happening to me, and I can't tell them but they're all I want right now. Lo siento mi tío, but you weren't there for me. You were doing great things, lo sé, lo sé. Pero...

Then, from his hands, a blanket of warmth begins to spread. Even through my closed eyes, I can see the light he's producing. His hands move down across my body, and the heat he's making helps each muscle relax along the way. Eventually, I stop twisting and squirming and just let him work. I realize it's not just his light he's using, it's the light of our family, the warmth that he knew as a child, that I knew too. He's giving it to me, as he gave it to the world for so long.

The worst of the pain is fading, but there's enough that it can be an excuse for crying. When it goes from searing agony into extreme discomfort, I manage to open my eyes.

There are so many black, blue, purple, and slightly green bruises that my skin looks like it's night camouflaged. There are bandages all over my arms and legs. I can feel thicker, heavier gauze around my torso.

"You are very lucky," Pedro says as he tenderly spreads the blanket I kicked off. "The blast, it was incredible. Thank you for protecting me."

"Thank you," I say softly. He smiles at me, but only with his lips. His eyes tell a different story. "I can't imagine how hard that was for you."

He nods a few times, says, "Sí, lo fue," and keeps fussing with my blanket. "Lo siento."

He shakes his head a few times and says, "Thank you."

"Tío Pedro," I swallow, hard. "What were you doing there?"

He stops fussing, but doesn't answer.

"You said you were called."

Slowly he sits back in his chair. His eyes wander off to the side.

I take a long, slow breath, and let it out. "Why would Wraith call you to come meet her daughter?"

For a time, he doesn't answer. I start to think that with one stupid sentence, I've just lost the uncle I've worked so hard to find.

When he takes a breath, a huge breath that fills his lungs and pushes his face up to the ceiling, he stares through the florescent lights, through the bricks and concrete, through time itself, and says in his deep voice, "Before today, the last time I heard from her was... it was just after the catastrophe in Japan. The Triad had vanished, and we were working around the clock, trying to clean up the mess. Turbo was desperate to recover his image. He knew the world would forever blame him, blame us, almost as much as they blamed the Triad." He waves his hand, then rubs his face. I sit silently and watch. He knows that I know all of this. Everyone does, even though it happened before I was born.

The darkest day in the Justice Brigade's history.

"It was, ah, a month, maybe two after this, she called me. I do not know how. I assume Dendrite's technology allowed her to find me. We hadn't spoken in so long, and when I answered..." His lips press together. His nostrils flare. "I was so cruel." He looks at me, his head shaking back and forth slightly. "I bit at her with my words. Told her she had finally done it, finally become what everyone else always thought she was. I told her I could never forgive her and if I ever saw her again, I would take her down myself." His eyes go down and his face follows. "And that, mijita, was a truly, truly stupid thing to do."

When his head rises, I see a grin like a schoolboy after a kiss on the cheek from his crush. As much as it hurts (and it hurts a lot), I slap a hand over my mouth to cover the chuckle. His teeth flash and a laugh rolls out of him, across the bed.

"Ohhhh, she was angry," he says with a huge gesture. I laugh with him and bite my bottom lip. "So angry, she didn't say anything. Instead, my phone, it goes dead. All of a sudden, every light bulb in my home begins to burst. Bang! Bang! Bang!" With each 'bang' he flicks his fingers, little flashes appear in the air. "One after another they go out until I am the only thing left making light. The next thing I know, she's swarming around me. The smoke, it is everywhere, floor to ceiling. Then, just as fast, it ends, and she is standing there, and I see the fire in her eyes, burning so hot.

"For a long time, she says nothing. We stood there, staring into each other's eyes. I am waiting for her to strike, to try and cut me down. But, instead, she raises her hands and says to me... I didn't know." He pauses, as though her words are reaching him for the first time, all over again. "She tells me it was an accident, it was never supposed to happen and... and she tells me, she's sorry. She says it with all her heart and her soul. She says she would never do such a thing. She asks... she asks me if I believe her."

I watch as he relives that moment, probably for the ten thousandth time, and tries to come to a decision.

"I did," he says. "I believed her. I believed her then, and... " His face loses its smile, but not its joy. "I believe her now."

My hand finds his and squeezes. He brings our hands up and kisses my knuckles. With a sigh, he continues.

"Valentina stayed with me that night."

Valentina. Her name was Valentina. Small enough that he doesn't notice it, I inhale to try and stop the pain in my heart.

"When the sun rose, she was gone."

The pain I feel for him.

"I never saw her again, never heard from her. Not until today."

The pain I feel for their daughter.

He rests his forehead against our hands, rocking it back and forth. "Just like her, mijita. I didn't know. I never knew."

And the pain that's turning to a poison covered knife, twisting in my belly.

"I --" I can't breathe. I can't stop my jaw from shaking. "Tío, lo -- lo siento. I --" His hands just squeeze mine as a sob forces its way up my throat. "Yomate --"

"You tried, mijita. You wanted to take her alive, and... and that..." It takes a moment for him to settle. "It was you or her."

I reach out with my free hand and run it over his head, through his hair. There's dust and bits of rock in there. He never even cleaned up before coming to see me.

"When I first saw Candace," I say softly, "I thought she looked familiar."

His eyebrows go up. I grin.

"She has your eyes."

He smiles and kisses my hand again. "Gracias," he says with a whisper.

After we sit in silence for a bit, I ask, "What are you going to do?"

"No sé," he says with a frown. "I... I should tell her, but I do not know where to begin."

"Start at the museum," I say with hope. "Someone must have seen her."

Pedro's eyes tighten, his brow coming together. "What do you mean?"

That hope begins fading. "Someone must have seen her."

He just stares.

"Which way she went." My eyes get bigger.

His head rises.

"After the explosion." My heart starts to thump.

He frowns. "She did not go anywhere after the explosion."

Oh no.

"They found her, unconscious."

I sit up, ignoring the pain. For a moment he seems startled, but the look on my face and in my eyes must be enough for him to understand.

"Where is she?" I ask.

His face tightens. "Here. They brought her here."

There's a huge bang, like a massive metal door swinging shut, and the lights blink out throughout the building. Red emergency lights flood the room. Pedro opens his palm and a glowing ball appears. When the rumble of an explosion echoes throughout the building, a siren starts blaring. Pedro leaps to his feet, I swing my legs off the bed, and we both say:

"Stay here!"

We stop and look at each other.

"What?" He says.

"What?"

"Stay here," he says, adamant.

"No, you stay here," I say, adamant-er.

"You are injured."

"So are you."

"Get back in bed!"

"You get back in bed!"

"Antonella --"

"Where's my gear?"

"No," he says low.

"I'm going to help. Either come with me or --"

"No!" he roars.

I freeze. His whole body is shaking. The knuckles on top of his cane are white.

"I will not..." he says, as soft as he can, "I cannot lose another person I care about today."

Slowly, I stand up. Through my feet, I can tell that, stories below us, a battle is raging. A battle that one side is losing very, very badly. But I also feel mi tío's heartbeat, pounding, pounding inside him. "Tío Pedro,"

"Whatever it is," he snaps, "the ESOA can handle it. I will help them and --"

"Whatever it is?" I say, shaking my head. "Your daughter is at the center of all this. We've been out there, chasing her from the beginning. We went

203

through Bearserker and Brass Knuckles to find her. We took out her bodyguards. Araknis is gone. Wraith is..." I stop when I see the pain flash across his face. "There's only one person left."

It hits him. Reaching into his coat, he pulls out a phone and begins dialing.

"What --"

"We always kept a private line, just in case."

"Who?"

He looks at me with a smile. "Who else?"

I hesitate. Even with Captain Turbo, I don't know if we can win this. It's been twenty years, twenty years of sitting back, making new weapons, developing new technologies. I saw Araknis, came face to face with him. He seemed as powerful as ever. Wraith didn't look like she'd aged a day. She was faster and stronger than the scientists told me she would be. They assumed that she would have aged, gotten weaker, but they were wrong. She was powerful, more powerful than she had ever been.

How much stronger has he become?

When Lux puts the phone to his ear, I reach out and touch his arm.

"When you're done, let me have it."

I'm sorry, Pedro, I truly am. But we don't have a choice here. After all, it's him outside, breaking through the perimeter.

The most feared man in the world.

The man synonymous with terror.

Doctor Dendrite.

CHAPTER TWENTY-TWO
THE PROMISE

"You know I don't like spicy food."

"Just eat it," she said, stuffing a shrimp the size of a child's fist into her mouth.

"It doesn't agree with me."

"It's not that spicy."

The beach was literally across the street, behind a row of palm trees, so close I could feel tiny droplets of salt water clinging to the breeze. Even with that, the fumes from the sizzling cast-iron platter made my eyes water. "I'm going to order something else."

"No."

"Why not?"

She grabbed a tiny, cracked porcelain bowl filled with rice seasoned and fried until it was as golden brown as baked bread. "Because I want some of that."

"Here, you can have it."

"I don't want all of it."

It was difficult to not sigh. "Then take some, and leave the rest."

"That's wasteful."

Really, really difficult. "I think we can afford it."

The fried plantains were still sizzling against the paper in their little plastic basket. She snatched one with bare fingers and popped it in. "Just eat it."

"I don't --"

"If you're going to travel the world doing business with every type of person, legitimate, criminal, and everything in between, you're going to have to eat what they eat. And what they eat," she shoved the plate toward me, "is spicy food."

I glared at the dish in front of me. Even the beans looked scary. "You purposefully ordered me the spiciest thing, didn't you?"

"Yes. Now eat it."

Even I knew better than to argue with a woman who was seven months pregnant, hungry, and had superpowers.

I mean, really, I'd learned better than to argue with women. It's rude, and they're usually right.

Taking a deep breath, I picked up the fork.

"Mix it with the rice, that'll help."

"You always say that, and it never does."

"Because when you're not looking, I put hot sauce on the rice."

"What did I ever do to make you hate me?"

She stacked different things; meats that were stewed and cooked over fire until they caramelized, different vegetables that were seared until they blistered, and a lot of fried things; then cut through all of them and dug in. "What's the update? How are things back home?" By which she meant our home base of operations, the United States.

I started with the beans. "Going well. You were absolutely right about... sweet mother of god, can I get some --"

She grabbed the arm of a passing woman with skin the hue of kiln-fired pottery. Wraith rambled off something in Spanish, pointed to me, and the two had a laugh before the woman nodded and walked off. "She's getting you some milk."

"Thank you," the words barely made it out over the Medalla Light I was pouring down my throat.

"So, which of my brilliant ideas were you talking about?"

"I didn't use that word."

"Shut up and talk."

Feeling like the worst was behind me, I tried the meats. "Selectively targeting smaller corporations worked. I offered them tech years ahead of their competitors. We've netted a decent profit while simultaneously maneuvering to overtake the companies as they move to the forefront of their fields. There's already interest from firms in China, Dubai, South Korea --"

"Korean food is very spicy."

"-- and several other tech-heavy economies. I predict they'll begin offering buyouts within the next ten to fourteen months."

"Which we will reject."

"Driving investors to wonder what we've got up our sleeves, then dump everything they've got into our stocks."

"Which we cash out and use to buy large chunks of our competitors."

"Then I use a different identity to sell the next invention to the failing American companies, start the process all over again, and generate a tech war which we are always at the head of."

"And the government hasn't caught on?"

"Are you kidding? Half the stuff I'm putting out there is used in satellite and computer communications, mostly by DoD contractors. The manufacturers don't know I'm slipping in spying hardware... which I have decided to call spyware. In six months, I'll know everything going into and coming out of the government."

Her fork slowed down. "And... the Justice Brigade?" She glanced at me, expectant.

I smirked. "What about them?"

Relief raised the edges of her mouth into a smile. "That's what I like to hear." Leaning across the table, she picked up an old jelly jar that was sweating from the icy drink inside.

"Are you sure you should be having a margarita? I mean, with the baby --"

"It's fine," she said with a sip and a flap of her hand. "What's going on in the supervillain world?"

Choking is unpleasant. Choking on spicy food is five times worse. I coughed into a paper towel from the roll they put in the center of the table. "Maybe you could say that a little louder? I don't think the people on the other side of the island heard."

"Hello, hello?" She leaned back in her white, plastic lawn chair. "Pardon me, everyone? You should all know --"

"Okay," I said.

"-- that we're both supervillains --"

"Point taken."

"-- who have terrorized the world for decades."

"Okay."

"Triad of Evil? Anyone? Two members, right here."

All around us, everyone kept eating, drinking, laughing, listening to the cars nearby honking in the traffic, and rolling by on sand crusted beach cruisers while wearing flip-flops and sandals. "No one cares. You're just another tourist around here." She went back to the tremendous amount of food on the paper plates and chipped dishes before us.

"Why... why are we here? Aren't there nicer places we could --"

"I grew up here."

"It's..." I made for a speedy recovery. "Very homey. So quaint and --"

"Stop that, it's trash."

"I didn't use that word."

"Es un barrio cafre," a bad neighborhood, "but the sea is close, the breeze is warm, the drinks are cheap, and they make food like mi madre did."

"Your mother rubbed everything with jalapenos?"

"You are not going to do well in Thailand."

I glanced at the people passing by. Many of the men stole glances at Wraith. Understandable, of course, pregnancy has given her an incredible glow. Still... "Are you sure we should be here? If this where you grew up --"

"It's been a long time," she said, "and I've changed a lot. Nobody here knows me anymore." Something passed beneath her skin, a touch of something old, something she'd moved past a long time ago.

Cold bubbles from my beer soothed my tongue and throat. "How old were you?"

"Fourteen."

"And you left all on your own?"

"Snuck onto a ship, stole food, landed in Florida."

"Why fourteen?"

"Because at thirteen, my gift awoke."

"You were that eager to become a hero?" I thought she would laugh at that, or at least smile. Her outside didn't change, she just kept eating, but her voice dropped two or three notes.

"People thought I was una bruja."

I stopped drinking.

"They threw things, spit on me. My family didn't do much to convince them otherwise. So, I left."

"I'm sorry, that's awful."

She shrugged. "The world was ignorant. Florida was the same thing, and a lot of other places. It took me a while, but I found my people."

She meant Lux. Or so I assumed. I didn't ask because she changed the subject.

"Speaking of which, how are things on that side going?"

"Surprisingly well. Two months ago I gathered the heads of a dozen crime families to let them know their choices."

"Sign up and take orders..."

"Or get completely crushed. I let them gripe for a few minutes, and when the first person got up to leave, I mummified him instantly, smashed his body into powder, and threatened to force feed him to anyone else who complained."

"I'm eating."

"Sorry. Anyway, we're now involved in every major deal. We get a cut from one party, have another launder it, then place it in off-shore accounts or a shell company or --"

"Okay, okay, okay. What about..."

"Our competition?"

She clicked her tongue, shook her head, and made a long 'n' that eventually would turn into a no.

"Our contemporaries?"

"I like that. Still giving us trouble?"

"It's improved. There are only a few villains with the power to cause Japan levels of destruction. The majority, I've... contained. There are a few outliers I need to deal with, The Neuropath, Baron Bludgeon, SkyFyre --"

"I took care of Baron Bludgeon," she said with a wave of her fork.

"When?"

"A few weeks ago. He was trying to get his hands on some uranium, so I paid him a visit. I told him he was welcome to rob banks and steal gold and all that, but global domination was off the list."

I leaned forward. "Bludgeon has been a thorn in my side, and all it took was you telling him to knock it off?"

"Oh no, he refused to listen. So, I cut off his legs."

I stopped leaning forward. "You... you mean you swept his feet out from under him?"

"No, I mean I cut off his legs. And then said if he didn't behave, I would come back and cut off what was between his stumps."

"Jesus,"

"You were going to feed people mummy dust."

"Fair," When the shock waned, I thought about what she'd said. "That's why you're here, isn't it?" She didn't respond. "Bludgeon was dangerous. Fighting him was too much and you needed to recover."

The plate in front of her was, for the first time since we sat down, nearly empty. The piles of food had dwindled down to mere lumps. Wraith took a cleansing breath and sat back. The plastic chair-back bent. "I'm here," she said, through a quickly oncoming food coma, "because I needed a little sun, and she," her hands landed on either side of her round abdomen, "needed to taste the food of her homeland."

I paused. "She?"

Wraith smiled. "Mm-hm."

"A girl..." It's so silly, there were only two choices. Yet the knowledge thrilled me. My eyes were glued to her beautifully curved stomach beneath the flowery sundress.

"Here," her hand found mine and pulled.

"Oh." I kind of resisted, until my palm came to rest on the top of her belly. "Oh," I said, doing nothing to stop the smile from spreading ear to ear. I felt the movement, the wiggling life inside her. I caught her gaze and asked without words. She nodded. I bent down, bringing my lips close enough that when I spoke, her cotton dress tickled them. "Hello there, little one. Your mommy and I are... making arrangements. You're going to have everything you could ever want. And if you grow up to be as strong as your mommy --"

"She will," Wraith said.

"The world will be yours," I whispered.

"You listen to your tío."

I snapped up. "Uncle?"

She put her hands on mine. "Mm-hm."

"I don't..."

"What?"

"It's an honor."

"It's more," she said. "It's a promise that rises above everything else."

I nodded, gave her a sincere look, but it wasn't enough. She held me.

"My family was afraid of me, of what I was. That's why I left this place. It took me a long time to accept what I am. And it took me even longer to find someone else who would, too. You get me, Daniel."

"Yes, I think I do."

"That wasn't a question."

"Uh," the word spread all the way across my face, like a bad smell would.

"Don't make me regret this."

I squeezed her hands. "I swear, Valentina. She comes first, now and forever."

"Before you."

"Yes."

"Before me."

"Of course."

"Before Turbo, and the bands."

I don't know if it's that her hands grew warmer, or mine colder. But I pushed through. "I promise."

"Okay," she said, a tiny tremble in her voice, "Uncle it is."

I sighed and looked up to the sky. "Uncle Dendrite..."

"I was thinking Daniel."

"Oh. I guess that's okay."

She raised what little was left in her glass. "Salud."

"Are..." I stuck a finger in the air. "I'm sorry, but are you sure you should be drinking? I just --"

"Shut up and get me another or I'll cut your arm off."

"Yes, mom."

"Damn straight."

CHAPTER TWENTY-THREE
FROM THE WRECKAGE

Listen, I gotta be straight about this, I am one hundred percent over coming out of unconsciousness in places other than where I passed out.

It was the alarm that pulled me out of it. When that started, I shot up as far as I could. Good thing the restraints held me back, I probably would have ended up ripping the I.V. lines out of my arms. It's taken me a minute to realize I'm not dreaming. Of course, I kind of wish I was.

That way, I could still wake up and get the hell out of this horror movie bullshit.

The room is just big enough for me and the machines they have connected to me. The door is, well, let's just say I didn't even need to touch it to know it would take a tank to get through it. Outside, through the tiny window of glass so thick it could stop a missile, I see two heads with Marine Corps haircuts. Whether the room is soundproof or the soldiers are instructed to ignore my frantic screaming and the extremely vulgar curses I spend the next two minutes throwing at them, I'm not sure.

When I finally calm my ass down, I close my eyes and bring up the image of an audio mixer in my head. By playing with the dials, feeling and searching, I start to figure things out. First off, I still have super hearing (cool). Second, there isn't anything happening anywhere near by (not so cool). I can't hear people walking or cars driving by or anything. The further I reach, the more stifled my head feels. I must be underground somewhere, because beyond the few rooms nearby, all I get is solid mass and --

Something. Activity from up above me. It's far enough that I can't tell exactly, but there's definitely movement and then, boom! I don't need super hearing to know that something just shook this building, hard. The lights blink out for a second, all the machines hooked up to me go black, and then red lights come on. The little window in the door still shows those crew-cut soldiers, but they're moving around a lot now. One of them is using a walkie-talkie or something, asking what's going on. I try and follow, but this crazy siren comes on so loud it makes the muscles around my bladder tighten. I pull back my hearing and realize that the siren's out in the hallway, not in my room. That's good because now it's not hurting my ears. It's bad because I can't figure out what's causing it.

And whether I should be more or less afraid of what's happening.

Gunshots -- not in the hallway, but not too far. Then some explosions. Lots and lots of feet moving. Garbled orders coming over the walkie-talkie of the guys outside my door. Damn siren, still can't catch anything. More movement. Sounds getting closer. Something serious moving this way. What the hell is it? Araknis? Is he back? Maybe it's Languria and Princess Glitter Face? ...My mom?

Annie? God, please let it be Annie.

There's a searing sound, like meat hitting a six hundred-degree skillet, and multiple people scream.

Definitely. Not. Annie.

The guards at my door have their guns up. They're moving down the hall and shouting. I don't want them to leave. I mean, I'm no fan of being taken prisoner, but at least they're keeping me safe, right?

I extend my hearing out. There's a hissing noise, a whooshing sound and the hallway fills with thick, purple smoke. It's not the same as my mom's smoke, there's something...

The guys start coughing. Then, they scream.

Then, they stop.

All I can hear is the machine monitoring my heart. It sounds like a metal detector going over a buried submarine.

Then I hear something else, from the hallway.

Footsteps.

A second later, there's an electrical crackle. The door shudders and swings open. Standing there, surrounded by plumes of rolling purple smoke, is some tall, lanky guy wearing something between a lab and trench coat that is, in all honesty, dope as shit. It's dark green and I can tell it's the same kind of material that Annie and Languria's outfits were made of. His left hand and forearm are inside of a big glove thing, and there's clearly a lot of tech worked into it. His mask is something between a welder's helmet and a gas mask from World War II. It's slim cut and has goggle lenses. I can hear his breathing because the mask is filtering the air for him.

"What --" I kind of stutter out. That purple smoke smells terrible, and it's filling the room fast. It hurts my throat. "What do you want?"

He doesn't say anything. So I ask it again, but this time with a lot of nonsensical screaming thrown in. He takes a step forward and I flip into full panic mode. I jerk and pull at the restraints. I yell at him to back off. I threaten that I have powers. Damn, that smoke is awful. It really... something is wrong. Something bad is happening in me. He's just staring and that siren is blaring and my head is pounding and I can feel the rushing of the sound power inside of me building and building and if he doesn't back the hell off then I'm gonna --

"Ow!"

The dart he shoots me with came from the glove thing. It's the kind with the little puff on the end, like they tranquilize animals with.

"The hell is that?" I snarl. It's super fierce.

"Antidote," he says.

"For what?" I ask.

"The gas."

I frown. "You could have given me a pill or something."

"Wouldn't have worked fast enough."

His voice isn't deep and terrifying. It isn't high pitched and manic. It isn't even threatening. It just, is. I feel like I'm having a conversation with someone who doesn't really want to be having the conversation in the first place.

Someone who just marched into a government facility, took out god knows how many guards, filled the hallway with toxic purple smoke, shorted out a lock on a door designed to hold back an army, and shot a dart out of his glove.

I take these factors into consideration before I open my mouth again.

"What do you want?" Totally not fierce.

His head tilts a little. "You don't know who I am, do you?"

I should say something cool like 'Why, should I?' or 'Sorry, you must not have made much of an impression on me.' But I don't. I just shake my head back and forth a little.

His mask segments into a dozen smaller pieces and folds back, disappearing behind his head.

"Uncle Danny?"

"Hello Candace."

"What... what's going on?"

"We're leaving."

"What's with the mask?"

"I'm Doctor Dendrite."

"Oh. Cool."

The emergency lights are flashing. The hallway keeps going red, white, red white. I feel like the cops are rolling up on me. At least the damn siren is off; that thing was killing me. Uncle Danny just keeps walking. I have no idea how far we've gone, where we are, or where we're going. I assume he knows where he's going. He should, right? Not that I'm in any position to argue or anything.

It's chilly as hell. I'm not in a hospital gown, but some weird, pale grey pajama thing, and my feet are bare. The floor is linoleum and cold. Oh, and it's covered in the bodies Danny has left behind.

Uncle Danny who is Doctor Dendrite.

Doctor. Freaking. Dendrite!

"It should have been obvious," he says through his mask. It muffles his voice a bit, but now that I know it's him, I totally hear it. You'd think he would have some sort of auto-tune thing going on, making his voice all deep and Darth Vader, right? Nope. Just good ol' Uncle Danny. "When you saw your mom use her powers, I figured you would put it together."

"Look," I say as I step over some dude covered in a spider web of metal cables that 'seem to be slowly tightening, "I've had kind of a full day, alright? Not a lot of room up there for deep thinking right now."

"Uh huh," he says. Some soldiers come around the corner and start firing. Normally, I'd put my arms up and scream, but this has already happened a couple times so far, and I've learned better.

Danny holds the hand with the glove out. The air ripples and the bullets drag to a stop. Then, the ripples freeze and the world in front of us looks like transparent Jell-O, only the little bits of suspended fruit are actually deadly, deadly chunks of flying lead death.

There's a hum from Danny's glove, and the ripples start back up, but going the other way. He shoves his arm forward and the bullets all go flying back from the direction they came, pelting the soldiers from top to bottom.

We keep moving.

"I've seen that..." I mutter. He hears me, I know he does, because his head turns back a bit. "That's Languria's ability."

He lets out a single chuckle. "Now your powers of observation kick in."

I bite my lip a bit. "Did you, like, give it to her? You know? Can you do that? Do you, do you give people --"

"I didn't do anything to you, Candace."

I huff, not because I'm angry. I just... I want to know.

"I helped Languria hone her ability, taught her to control it. During that time, I studied it, copied it, and improved upon it."

"Oh," is all I say. We round a corner and all the soldiers are standing, but covered in thick, crunching crystals that are growing slowly. They look a lot like Princess Snow's crystals, only on steroids. "Where are we going?" Underneath, it looks like they're screaming.

That's not really the question I want to ask. I want to ask about my mom. I want to know how all this could happen. Why did she keep all this a secret from me? Was she running out at night and wreaking havoc since I was born, or did I put a crimp in her supervillain style? Why did she hide who Uncle Danny is? Why did she hide who she really is?

214

Was.

The muscles around my mouth all twist in different directions.

Who she was.

My teeth press together so hard my gums tingle.

She's dead.

I wanna throw up.

My mom is dead.

I wanna scream or shout or cry or twist or fall or beg or see her or talk to her or run to her or run from her or smell her hair like when I was little or bite my goddamn lips off or scratch and fight or kill or tell her I'm sorry or --

"Stop crying."

I don't even need to open my eyes to know Danny is standing right in front of me. My lungs pull, my chest heaves but no air goes in or out. I can feel the pressure inside my ribs and it hurts and it's making the pounding come back to my head. Even though my hands are squeezed into fists, I can still feel the sound in my bones and pretty soon it'll get big and it's going to want out and I don't think I can stop it anymore.

"Valentina," Danny says, "would be so disappointed right now."

And everything freezes. Just for a moment. All the twitching, the gasping, the snot and tears and crunching of my molars. It stops.

"She was the most feared woman in the world. She was a warrior who crushed anyone who opposed her. I've seen entire battalions retreat from her. I've witnessed her cut down entire armies of cyborgs, robots, zombies, aliens, and inter-dimensional dinosaur riding Neanderthal invaders. There is nothing, nothing in this world or any other which she faced with even the slightest hint of fear or hesitation. She was strong."

He bends down, inches from my face. His mask pulls back, and I see eyes as red and wet as mine.

Oh, Uncle Danny...

"Your mother cried, Candace. We all do. But she knew to save the tears for later, for after the battle was won. Then," he closes his eyes and puts the crown of his forehead against mine. I can feel him trembling, "then we can grieve our losses."

He straightens up. His eyes are still red, but everything around them has gone still and stoic. "This fight is just beginning."

My lungs manage three quick gasps. He waits for a response. I smear the watery lines beneath my eyes until they're gone.

He smiles a little. "There she is," he says. "There's the strength I know so well." With a nod, the mask snaps back into place and he walks away.

"You knew," I say, following close behind. "About her. About me. About

215

--" My eyes roll around as I try to think of the million things which are new to me but old news to him. "How close were you?"

He doesn't answer. He just keeps walking.

"Were you -- clearly everything I thought isn't true so, so..."

He stops. "So what?"

I shake my head. "I dunno, let's start with, are... are you my father?"

"No." he says. "Are we done?"

"No." I snap. "I wanna know everything. I want --"

"Fine." The word is soft, but it leaps across the hall and smacks me in the face. "I'll tell you everything, I promise. But later. Right now, we move."

"Why am I so important? Why is everyone trying to protect me?"

"Candace --"

"Everyone is --" my hands start shaking, waving as I speak. I start blurting words out, but they're just the outside. Inside, I'm building. "Everything I know is a lie and nothing I've ever thought is real," swelling, "and all these people that I thought cared about me, they keep, they keep helping me," growing and growing into a cacophony, "but not because, because -- and when they do, they get hurt or, or, or --"

There's a loud beep, like a frantic kitchen timer, from down the hall. I barely hear it over the rushing sound waves inside my own body. Danny's next to me in an instant. His gloved hand catches my wrist in the air. Holding me in place, the thick forearm cover on his arm clicks and snaps, flips itself off of him and snaps around my forearm.

"What the hell?" I bark. Something cold and metallic goes into my forearm. "What the hell?" I scream. I struggle and squirm, but for such a skinny old guy, he's stupid strong. The thing on my arm adjusts and wiggles into place. It has a big screen on it, most of which is flashing red. I feel whatever it is inside of me moving around, probing. It stings and tingles and makes my muscles spasm.

"Get it off!" I shout. "Get it off, you asshole!"

"No," he says simply.

No emotion, no sympathy.

Nothing.

On top of the machine, the big red screen fades to green. Instantly, my hand stops twitching. The pain goes away. I can still feel the machine humming but there's no tingling anymore. There's no...

Sound. There's no sound.

"I can't have you blowing up a building every time you get emotional."

When I don't thrash or fight for a few seconds, he lets me go. Even without his help, I have no problem keeping my arm up. The machine barely

216

weighs anything, but it feels like it could stop a bullet.

"Until you learn to control it," he says, "this will suppress your ability."

"And if I don't learn to control it?"

"Then everything she did for you was a waste." His words push my head down. I want to say something, to ask him how he can be so cruel.

But I don't.

Because right now, this isn't Uncle Danny. This isn't the man who played with me on the beach or took me skiing. This isn't the man who used to sit with me and build computers, who showed me how to break through a firewall on my twelfth birthday.

Right now, this is Doctor Dendrite.

I suddenly understand why people are so afraid of him, why they were so afraid of her. Staring at my reflection in his pitch black goggles, I know why my mom kept me away from this as long as she could.

I get it Mom. I understand.

And I forgive you.

"Move." he says.

With a nod, I do.

CHAPTER TWENTY-FOUR
THE MARATHON'S END

One of the many benefits of being bilingual is that when I trip on the stairs and bang against the wall, I can go off with a string of curse words so bad, even mi tío openly stares in disbelief.

My entire body is one giant funny bone. The blast Candace let out did way more damage than I thought. My muscles aren't just sore, they're bruised all the way through. So between that, and the fight in the alley, seeing Araknis up close and personal, following the woman that turned out to be my cousin, then killing the supervillain who turned out to be her mother right in front of my uncle who was said supervillain's lover, I'm spent. Done. I have nothing left to give and I have earned an afternoon of cat videos and comfort food.

Yet here I am, wearing a hospital gown and some weird nurse pants, barefoot, climbing these stairs to the roof of a building because Doctor Dendrite is trying to kidnap back my cousin who we kinda kidnapped first -- the ESOA would probably argue we 'took her into custody', but that's some bureaucratic B.S. -- and in the event of explosions, infiltration, and all out warfare, it's apparently proper procedure to shut down the goddamn elevators!

"We should go back," Lux says. His breathing is heavy, but nothing like mine. This is a brisk jog for him, I'm trying to sprint the Boston Marathon.

"No," I say between breaths. "I'm fine." Puff. "I'm good." Pant. I stare at the stairs ahead of us. So, so many stairs. "Why the roof?"

"Do you know a better place to park a giant jet?"

I growl. Sort of. It's more of a groan. But it was meant to be a growl. Whatever, I'm breathing easier now. I'm learning to manage the pain. Military training isn't just physical. I close my eyes and focus. I use my ability to scan my body. Nothing's broken. Nothing's bleeding. Pain is just a sensation, and it can be ignored.

What can't be ignored is the entire building shaking. My echolocation ability goes nuts. I see nothing but static. "Let's move," I say as dust falls around us. Pushing off the wall, I'm climbing stairs again. Pedro's behind, one hand on the rail, one hand floating near my back in case I fall. I smile.

Two flights of stairs later and we hear shouting and gunfire. Three flights and we hear screams. Five flights and I detect the low level vibration of something massive above us powering up.

"Hurry," I say as loud as I can. "We have to hurry."

On the final landing before the roof, there are two soldiers down. There's no reason to stop and check them; if either of them somehow did survive whatever Doctor Dendrite did, the first thing they would ask for is us to kill them.

The door at the top of the stairs, the heavy steel one with a sign that says 'Roof Access' isn't just closed; the edges where door meets frame are smoking. It's been welded shut.

"Stand back."

My hands slap the concrete to either side. Dozens of spikes push the unusable door, ripping out the entire frame and dropping on the roof outside. A blast of air, cold from the Massachusetts winter but hot from the jet engines, crashes against us. Everything is ablaze with spotlights. We raise our arms and step onto the roof.

Santo Dios.

That's not a jet. It's a damn sky yacht. From outer space.

"Dendrite!" Pedro's voice battles against the engines' roar. I'm sure we're too late, that the jet is going to rev up and lift into the sky at any second at a speed which would seem impossible for something so big. But, slowly, the gusts of hot air ease up. It's still loud as hell, but I'm able to lower my arms. When I do, I see them standing at the bottom of the jet's extendable staircase, silhouetted.

My toes dig in.

So here we are, the four of us: Lux, one of the greatest heroes of all time. Doctor Dendrite, the greatest villain to ever live.

And two women in hospital pajamas.

"Well," I say softly, "this is awkward."

If I weren't completely shredded from the day I've had, I'd probably be more mindful of the fact that I'm currently looking at the most feared man in the world. He's right across the roof from me, round goggles glimmering in the light. It doesn't feel real. Maybe it's the adrenaline, maybe it's because mi tío, the great Lux, is with me, but he just isn't, you know, terrifying.

At least, not yet.

Pedro steps forward. "You are not taking her!"

Dendrite taps a button on his belt and the rolling thunder from his engines turns to a deep purring. "What?"

Pedro raises his chin. "I said, you are not --"

"I'm kidding," Dendrite says with a wave. "We heard you fine."

I... what? Is he... oh. He's messing with us. Because, you know, villain. Got it. Okay, so, situation is very serious, super dangerous. Of course. Still, I feel like I need to note: I just got messed with by Doctor Dendrite. Suddenly, I'm kind of feeling like a hero again.

"Hello Lux," Dendrite says, "long time." He turns to Candace. "I'd like to introduce Lux, of the now retired Justice Brigade."

"We've met." she says, glowering from across the rooftop. "He was there, at the museum."

Dendrite's head tilts.

"He helped. They did it, together."

Dendrite pauses. "I see," he says slowly, then looks at Pedro.

No, at both of us.

"We'll finish this another time." Turning, he puts a hand on Candace's shoulder. She leans in close and says something with a smile. It's too windy to hear, but my bare feet help me out.

"That was badass."

Pedro takes a step forward. "She stays."

Dendrite pauses between steps. "I don't think so."

"I do." Pedro digs in his toes and, before I can even get my arm out to grab him, he's tearing across the rooftop. His hands, pumping up and down as he sprints, start glowing with a harsh white light. My mouth and my feet both stammer as I watch him barrel across the concrete.

Mierda!

He's halfway to the jet when Dendrite looks over his shoulder. Alarms go off in my head as he raises a gloved hand and snaps his fingers. Above the jet's doorway, a panel slides back and something that looks like a howitzer with three red neon rings at the end pops out.

"No!" I scream as I drop. The air cracks as the laser fires. The spike wall makes it up just in time to absorb most of the blast, but the force still sends Pedro flying back. Sprinting to his side, my knees burn as I slide to a stop.

No. No, no, no. Por favor Dios, no.

His sleeves are burnt and ripped. There are cuts everywhere, but it's hard to see how bad they are through all the dust and dirt on him. All along one side of his head, his salt and pepper hair is turning a deep red. My hands press down on him, trying to find the worst of the wounds so I can apply pressure, but his fingers wrap around mine. I take my eyes away from the blood dripping off his skin and look to his face.

It's the look mi abuelo gave every time someone, anyone, threatened a family member. A stare that could wear down the mountains.

Okay. I hear you, Pedro.

Grunting, he uses me to roll onto his knees. Then, one foot smacks the rooftop. His face comes up with sweat and blood running down, dripping from his chin.

"Is that all?" Dendrite calls from the stairs.

Pedro doesn't say anything. He can't, all his energy is going into staying up. But it doesn't mean he's not answering. His eyes are hot and fierce and in them I see, we all see. This is a man who will never give up. Will never stop.

This is what a hero is.

Gracias, Tío Pedro.

I stand. A gust pulls at the hospital gown, rippling it against me, sending one corner snapping back and forth off my hip. My braid swings behind me as I look deeply into Dendrite's goggles without fear or hesitation.

"She stays." I say.

Dendrite pauses. "And what will you do when I say no?"

"Whatever it takes."

And Doctor Dendrite does not like that. But before he can act, Candace pushes forward, jamming her finger out at me. "Yeah?" she shouts. "You and what army?"

"How about mine?" The voice comes from behind me, from the stairwell.

Lieutenant Colonel McTier.

What the hell is she doing here?

"What the hell is she doing here?" I squeeze the words between clenched teeth. That bitch. That goddamn army bitch. I'm gonna kill her.

Danny puts his arm out and stops me from charging down the stairs. "Don't."

"You don't get it."

"I do."

"She's the one that --"

"I know."

"But she's in charge and --"

"I know."

"So I'm gonna --"

"No, you're not."

My hands cling to his coat sleeve. He doesn't even turn to look at me.

"Stay calm. Act on your emotions and you'll end up like Lux. You need to be cold, calculating." His hand squeezes me, but not in an aggressive way. "That's what your mother was. And that's why they feared her."

My breath catches in my chest. When I'm able to let it out, I stop pushing against him. "Good," he says. His arm slides away, but as his hand passes the forearm unit he put on me, I feel him touch it. The big green light on the front changes to a series of red bars and instantly, I feel it.

The sound.

It's back. But it's different. It's not pressing, straining to fill my head like rushing water filling a space. It's steady and smooth, a hum inside of me. It's controlled.

It's mine.

"Agent Garcia, Lux," says the military bitch. "Stand down immediately."

With my power back, I don't just hear her voice, I sense it. I can practically see the sound wave in the air. It's the same one from the house, the same one ordering the soldiers to break in and try to kill me and my friends.

She walks right past Lux and Garcia without even looking at them. Her eyes are glued on Danny. "Doctor Dendrite, I've come here appointed --"

"It's McTier, correct?" Danny says. "Lieutenant Colonel McTier?"

McTier, huh? Good to know.

"I've come here," she begins again. Her voice is hard, rehearsed, "appointed with the authority of the joint military council of the United

States and the Enhanced Superhuman Operations Agency. Under their command, I hereby order you to surrender yourself into my custody immediately, wherein you will be taken to an undisclosed and secure location where you will await trial before the United Nations Council for your crimes against humanity. Either you deactivate your jet's engines and surrender yourself, or I will deploy the full force of the ESOA and U.S. Military against you."

Danny sighs a little and flips his gloved hand over. "Hang on just a second," he says, reaching for a button. McTier's gun is out and on him so fast, I don't have time to flinch.

"Don't!" she shouts. That hard-ass military training can't stop her eyes from showing that she's scared as hell.

Tilting his head, Uncle Danny says, super calm, "Oh relax, if I was going to kill you I would have done it. I just need to..." he pushes a few buttons on the glove, and it makes a happy 'bing' sound. "Good news, Lieutenant Colonel." His goggled eyes settle on her. "Stocks just went up."

Behind McTier, I see Garcia make a face. She's confused. Lux is too. And as much as I hate the two of them, I have to admit that I am as well.

"I just made another hundred-million dollars."

McTier squints. "Congratulations."

"If anyone should be happy to hear it, it's you."

She doesn't respond.

"It's quite an interesting plan," Danny says. "Did you think I wouldn't figure it out?"

"If you did, it doesn't change anything."

Danny just nods. "So, why not just shoot me? Then you can seize anything you want, there'll be no one to stop you."

"Seize?" Garcia asks. Her voice is strained, but not surprised.

"My assets," Danny calls out. "Inventions, technology --"

McTier pulls back the hammer on her gun. "Doctor Dendrite --"

"-- hundreds of thousands of acres of property --"

"It's time to surrender."

"-- particle accelerators, nuclear engines, intellectual property --"

McTier barks, "Now, Doctor Dendrite."

Hearing her give orders makes my blood boil.

"That --" Lux's voice grumbles to life. His teeth are grinding. "That's what this is about? Weapons? Power? You and your military needing a bigger, better bomb?"

McTier stays silent. Danny raises his hand like a kid in class. "Oh! And don't forget the trillions of dollars in stocks, bonds, and cash they're so desperate to get their hands on."

"Money?" Garcia's voice is laced with disgust. "This is -- you trained me to kill because you wanted --"

"It's not that," McTier says. "You don't -- the Justice Brigade failed."

Wind whips everywhere. Lux's wrinkled face twists.

McTier turns back to Danny. "They didn't drop off the face of the earth. They've been building an empire like you can't imagine. They don't just have money and property. They have everything. Everything. They own the buildings, the vehicles, the banks, the... the stock market is their daily play thing. Senators, congressmen, royal families in Europe, they have control over everyone, and they exert it whenever it pleases them. They have more shell corporations and fake identities than there are real companies and people in the world." She turns and looks at Lux and Garcia. And for real, she looks like she's really sorry she has to say this. "They won. They beat you, Lux. They beat everyone. They took over the world, and nobody was there to stop them."

Her eyes come back to Danny, hard. "Until now."

Danny doesn't say anything, doesn't do anything. Then, his hands go up and he gives her a big, slow, golf clap. "That's a lovely way of putting it, Lieutenant Colonel, thank you."

She doesn't nod, just pulls back the hammer on her gun. "Now, either you --"

"But," Danny cuts in, "you neglected to mention what happens when I'm gone."

She doesn't respond.

"Just who's going to sit in my throne?"

Her cheeks twitch, holding back the smile.

"My bet?" Danny says. "It's the same person that put together a team, specialized and trained to eliminate."

Garcia tenses up.

"The one that's been sending the Justice Brigade out on these little missions for the last few years, hoping to flush us out."

Lux looks at him, surprised.

"That was willing to sacrifice anyone's life to get what they want."

"Clearly," McTier says, "there's only one person for the job." She holsters her gun and grabs the walkie-talkie from her belt. "Send him in. Over."

A cold wind snaps across the rooftop and suddenly I get a feeling in my gut, the same kind you get when you're looking down a very high ledge with nothing but rocks beneath you.

"I told you, Doctor." McTier says calmly. "If you are unwilling to surrender, I will use the maximum force at my disposal against you."

"Uncle Danny," I say, "the stairs."

The stairwell is dark, but I can hear it.

Footsteps. Slow, steady footsteps. Heavy and thick.

Boots.

Danny, motionless up until now, tenses up. I hear his heart beating in his chest like a counter rhythm to the steps. It grows and it grows."Come on," he whispers with words that no one else in the world could ever hear. "Come on, Captain."

There's a push against the darkness of the doorway and the curtain of shadows slips back as a boot comes out.

A black, military boot.

Agent Sugiyama Sosuke.

He's dressed the same as he was, military uniform and stuff, but there's something different about him. When he was on TV, he was so bland, so robotic. But now, staring straight at Danny, I see something in those weird, florescent blue eyes of his.

Hate. Pure hate.

There a flash of light, hot and blue, as electricity jumps around Sugiyama's body, leaping between his limbs and running up him like a Tesla coil.

Oh... shit.

Sugiyama doesn't say anything; no 'en garde', no 'here I come', no 'let's do this!' He just drops into a fighting stance and launches a damn lightning bolt at us. I don't even have time to throw my hands up.

Uncle Danny's gloved hand shoots out. The lightning hits and slithers all over it. The bolt leaves Sugiyama and reels into the glove. It's held there a second, then Danny flicks his wrist. The bolt goes out like a laser beam, slams Sugiyama in the chest, and sends him flying into the stairwell.

When the light fades, Danny just stands there, his glove steaming. After a long pause, I open my mouth and say the only thing I feel truly conveys what I've just seen.

"Damn."

He angles slightly, just enough to see me through his goggles. "Lightning glove."

"That is so cool."

He turns and looks at me straight on. "You think?"

I smile and let out a single laugh. "Uh, yeah. That was awesome."

"Really?"

"You just floored that guy!"

"Well, it's gone through a lot of revisions. You should have seen the first

225

version. It looked like I was wearing a fire hydrant on my --"

Another burst of light from the doorway, and Sugiyama is moving across the roof at cruise missile speed. Lightning streams out of his feet and literally shreds the concrete as he comes at us, eyes blazing and teeth bared.

Danny shoves me to the side and everything spins as I fall off the stairs. By the time I hit the rooftop, there's crazy noises above me; yelling, shouting, lots of electricity crackling, bangs and pops and then a massive kaboom of that cannon thing Danny shot at Lux with. When I roll over and look up, Sugiyama is swinging lightning fists in every direction. Danny is dodging, but things aren't looking good. Jumping up, I head for the bottom stop. My ears hear the crack of stone.

Oh hell no.

I stop right as the wall of spikes comes up and blocks me from the jet. Garcia's hands are down on the ground. I throw all the anger and hate I've got her way. She's all stoic and professional, but... what's up with her eyes? In the alley, she was totally emotionless. In the museum, she was focused and sharp. Now... her gaze is darting around a lot. There's a little crease between her eyebrows. I can't tell from here what's up, but whatever it is, she's not taking me as seriously as she freaking should.

And that shit pisses me off even more.

Down in my hands the humming responds. Fingers curling and tightening, I think of what she did to Annie in that alley, of how I faced her down even though I didn't have the slightest idea what I was doing. And then I think about how, when she and my mom were fighting, I didn't do anything. I just stood there like an idiot and watched. I didn't help. I didn't even try because I was sure that the same thing would happen. I would put out my hand and nothing would happen.

But not this time.

This time, things are gonna be different.

On the stairs, the fight gets more intense (which I really didn't think was possible, but okay). The cannon goes off again, then I'm pretty sure it explodes. I move away as fast as I can. Out of the corner of my eye, I see someone running into the jet. Whether it's Danny going in or Sugiyama going after him, I'm not sure. I want to chase them up there, to help out, but I don't want to be in Uncle Danny's way. Sugiyama clearly isn't here to screw around.

Then again, neither am I.

And I've got another fight to pick.

I turn. Garcia's eyes get bigger for a second, then they tighten down. Now that's a look I know. That's the look she should have. She's ready, which is good, because so am I.

Let's do this.

The jet's engines roar. Wind whips around us like whitewater rapids. Garcia throws up her arms, covering her face from the blast. The second she does, I take off. Behind me, the jet does too. The wind pushes on my back and I'm charging in, my heart pounding, the pulse of sound growing in my hands. It condenses and solidifies, tickles my fingertips. I'm twenty yards away and Garcia still has her arms up, crossed in front of her face. Fifteen yards out and Lux is crouched, head down. McTier's barely able stand against the wind's force. No one sees me. They're sitting ducks.

I'm gonna crush them all.

Ten.

Take down every person responsible for my Mom's death in one shot.

Five.

No mercy.

Two.

Just like she would have.

I open my mouth and bellow. My arm goes back, ready to hurl sonic death at the woman who put a spike through my mom's back.

Garcia's arms part. She's looking straight at me, her eyes saying, 'Bring it'.

So I do.

Her foot slides forward and instantly the ground in front of me erupts into a tight bundle of spikes. My arm goes out, thrusting the sound ball right into the heart of Garcia's attack. There's a noise, beautiful and wonderful like a hundred piano strings all being stretched to the breaking point at once. The spikes shatter. Rock flies everywhere. The sound wave is more concentrated than I expected. It pushes through the wall, blows it to pieces, and sends both of us flying back. I manage to not fall over, but Garcia goes skidding. She flips over real fast and is up. She's shocked.

No.

She's a little afraid.

And I love it.

CHAPTER TWENTY-SIX
THE FIRST SHOWDOWN

Not good.

Not good, not good, not good.

... I'm in trouble.

Her sound bombs are smashing my spikes to pieces. Offensive, defensive, long, short, fat, skinny, dense, thin; doesn't matter. Every time I put one up she swings her arms and my spikes are blown to bits. The only thing keeping her back is how many I can make, but things are starting to get messy.

It's the thing on her arm. Before, when we met in the alley, she tried using her power and got nothing. Then, in the museum, it only went off because of the shock. Now, it's like she's an old pro.

Sweat drips on my hands as they scrape across the rooftop. Another wall of spikes goes up just to be turned into rubble. I dig my fingers in and go for an immediate second round, try to catch her off guard while the chunks are still flying, but she jumps back just in time.

What the hell? It's like she can predict when they're coming up. How is she doing it?

Unfortunately, she doesn't give me the chance to think about it. With a big straight right punch, she throws a sound slice at me. It's visible in the air, like a bend in the world. I launch to the side, barely dodging it. When I land, another comes my way. I have to drop and roll. Behind me a wall cracks and shatters where the blasts hit it, like a blade is slicing into it.

If even one of those things hits me, I'm dead.

A big swing of my fingers against the concrete, and a wave of extra thin, extra fast spikes spear out, aiming for her. At this point, I can't afford to play nice, to pull my punches just because we're related. She's genuinely trying to kill me, and, frankly, she's got enough power to do it. I have to take this as seriously as I can.

The spikes miss her by less than an inch. Part of her outfit shreds. I grit my teeth and go to send up another round, but she beats me to the punch and launches another assault. I jump, I duck, I roll. When I right myself I have just enough time to see her finishing off a thrust.

Hijo de perra, I'm not gonna make it!

My hands dig in. A wall bursts up in front of me. Her sound slice hits it, and the stone explodes back in my face. The rock absorbed some of the energy, but there's enough to knock me off my feet.

"Yeah!" she screams.

I've got cuts and scrapes everywhere. My muscles are screaming. This is the third, maybe fourth time she's pushed me back like this and I don't know how much more I can take. Trying to push up, my arms give out and I collapse. Using my ability, I can see her coming, sense her feet pounding toward me. I'm too strained, too weak to do anything about it.

Not good.

I give it everything I have, and I'm up on hands and knees. Her fist doesn't shoot out, but comes down in front of me. The sound bomb goes off and the force is enough to push me up into the air. I land on my feet and catch my balance just long enough for her to slam a fist covered in low level sound pulses right into the side of my face. I try to get my hands up, but it's useless. She swings again and again, connecting with each one. The inside of my head rattles and the whole world goes upside down for a second. The next thing I know, my hands are out, acting out of sheer instinct, and I manage to keep my skull from cracking on the concrete as I fall.

"Come on!" she shouts from a thousand miles away. Cold air breezes across my body. On my face, which is already swelling from her punches, it feels good. Across my body, which is wracked and expended, it's like razor blades. I hear her saying other things, stuff about not being impressed. Something about fear and how much I should have. None of it really gets through. All I can think about right now is sleep. Wonderful sleep. How desperately I want to just drift away.

Everything snaps back when her foot comes down on my chest. I half cough, half groan as she pushes the air out of my lungs. One of my arms goes up to pull her away. She's standing on the other. I claw at her leg. She just glares at me.

She's not smiling. She's not sneering or smirking or anything like that. Her eyes are bright and livid and practically spinning, but that's just the adrenaline. There's no sign of sadism in her eyes, of enjoying my pain and suffering.

This is business.

This is cold revenge.

She opens her mouth, takes a deep breath before she speaks. "You killed my mother."

I open my mouth, try to breathe, try to talk, but there's just not enough room in my lungs. "I know," she says, assuming what I was going to say, "those were your orders. You were just doing your job."

I struggle to get air into my lungs. "You --" I stammer.

"You were doing your job in the alley too, with Annie."

"No," I say in a voice so small I don't know if she can even hear me. Not that she would really care. "I did -- didn't want --"

229

"And your friends were doing their job when they broke into my home."

"Please."

"When they tried to shoot me and my friends."

"I'm... your..."

"And now," she opens her fingers. A ball of sound, twisting, swirling, distorting the world, appears, "I'm gonna do my job."

"... your..."

Her arm pulls back for a thrust.

McTier shoots her from behind.

Candace jerks forward. Her foot hits my face as she staggers. I roll as much as I can with it, but I'm gasping and coughing. Somewhere nearby, she's screaming, cursing, falling down. My head is swimming with static. I can't get anything. It's taking everything I have to not just pass out.

I think Pedro shouts something. I don't know what. He's as bad off as I am. What the hell is happening? I manage to get on my belly and use an arm to push myself up.

Candace is half sitting, half lying on the ground. She's got one hand over her chest, high, near the shoulder. There's a heavy stream of blood coming through her fingers. The screams go until McTier walks right up to her.

"Is what you said true?" McTier says. "Are you Wraith's daughter?"

Candace squirms a bit. "Wh -- what?"

McTier points the barrel of her revolver right between Candace's eyes. "Are you Wraith's daughter?" she asks again.

"Isn't --" Her teeth are chattering from the shock. "Isn't that why you were after me?"

"No," McTier says. "You were at the warehouse. I thought you could provide information. When you broke into the lab with the help of Twist, I knew you were connected somehow. The other super humans went out of their way to protect you. Clearly, you were important."

"Important?" She practically spits the word. "You have soldiers bust into my house, chase me down a goddamn alley, and kill my mother because I'm important?"

"Your mother's death was inevitable. It happened sooner rather than later because you led us to her."

Candace shivers. Spit flies from her lips as the anger wells up inside her.

"And now that I know who you are, I can't allow you to live, either." She thumbs the hammer.

Candace's eyes go wide.

Pedro tries to sit up.

My hands dig into the concrete.

Something starts beeping. Like, a timer or alarm. Everyone stops moving. After a few awkward seconds, Candace looks down at the thing on her arm. The screen on it isn't red or green, it's pulsing white. The beeping gets louder, then turn into a constant whine. Against the concrete, my fingers pick up vibration. It's slight at first, then both it and the sound and the light get bigger. Within a second or two, the light is so bright I want to turn away.

"What --" Candace says, but the sound from the alarm is too loud for me to hear anything else. She's disappearing in the light and now I hear a weird static crackling and McTier has backed away but she's got one arm up to block the light and I see the look on her face.

My palm slaps down. "No!"

McTier's revolver comes up, but my spike slams into her. The shot misses the ball of light surrounding Candace by a good foot and a half. McTier stumbles away, clutching at the gash on her arm. I cover my eyes and look away and, as fast as the light appeared, it's gone, shrinking down into a single dot and vanishing, taking Candace with it.

Sighing the most tired sigh I've ever sighed, I roll onto my back and close my eyes. Exhaustion almost takes me, but I hear shuffling. For one second, I think it's McTier coming to get rid of witnesses. When I turn, Pedro is sitting up, staring at me. His smile is small, but the tears running down his face are big and thick.

"Gracias," he says.

"De nada." I say.

McTier starts shouting something about insubordination, refusal to follow orders, court martial, blah-blah-blah. It doesn't really matter. I'm not taking orders from her anymore, or anyone else. I'm sure the ESOA will want a word with me. When I make it clear I'm willing to bring McTier's whole operation to light (and I have the world famous Lux to back me up), I think they'll back off.

But that doesn't help me with my other problem.

I close my eyes.

She's out there. Whatever happened just now, wherever Doctor Dendrite took her, Candace is out there and she's with him. She's only getting one side of the story, and neither Pedro nor I have done anything to convince her otherwise. Still, he isn't going to stop looking for her, and neither am I.

The real problem is, what are we going to do when we find her?

When I open my eyes, I see that the stars are starting to come out over us. I wonder if they're coming out over my cousin, too.

"Te veré pronto," I whisper, "Candace."

CHAPTER TWENTY-SEVEN
SAYING GOODBYE

What --

-- The --

-- SHIT!?

Oh god... I'm gonna puke. Argh! No, can't puke, shoulder hurts too much. Ohh, shoulder pain making me -- oh man I just... Oh, god, stupid stomach, just make up your mind! Okay, okay, breathing, breathing, trying to -- don't move. Can't move. Just sit, sit and, and, and --

What. What in the hell was that? One second I'm on the roof, kicking Garcia's ass, the next, that army shit McTier shoots me in the back, then I'm on the ground, the thing on my arm starts beeping like crazy and vibrating, that weird light spreads all over me and the next thing I know, McTier is about to shoot me in the head, and then I'm --

Here.

Wherever the hell 'here' is.

I'm sitting on a glowing circle of light in a dark room. It's super creepy. I already hate this. The thing on my arm is totally fried. The outside is all burnt and stuff. With my good arm I touch it, and it snaps open and drops to the floor.

The floor of some dark, empty room.

Well, what the hell? Not like today can get any more messed up.

"Hello?" I call. Nothing. I turn on my super hearing. Machinery, humming electronics everywhere. "Uncle Danny?" I shout into the darkness.

Still nothing.

Okay. Okay, I can't -- if I sit here all day, eventually I'll bleed out. I have to figure out where I am and then I gotta find something, anything to help stop this. Jesus, Uncle Danny, what did you do? Why would you break me out of there to abandon me? Like, what's --

I've staggered to my feet (which hurt like a bitch, let me just say) and when I take one tiny little step outside the light into the darkness, the whole damn room goes bug-nuts. Lights pop on everywhere, machines are turning on, diodes and readouts are flaring up, and I don't know what any of it means. Things start moving around on their own. I can hear them, see their shadows behind all the equipment around me. Some of them are big. Real big.

The main room is below me. The circle of light is in the center of some kind of platform, just, like, a foot or two off the ground. There's a lot of stuff happening, so I can't really see how big the room is, but I can tell it's

232

massive.

Nearby, something loud beeps and my heart jumps and that makes me dizzy so I kind of stumble backwards. The beepy thing shoots out a bazillion spinning green lights, little LED lasers or something, and they wash over me. I guess I should run from them or something, who knows what they're doing, but before I can even think to do it, they turn off. The thing beeps again and the platform beneath me kind of rumbles a bit. The floor opens up behind me, drops back in a section and slides away, and a big-ass thing comes up, one of those arms that they use on car building assembly lines. It unfolds fast and smooth and soundlessly, with a nasty looking claw/needle/torture device attached to the end.

And it comes right for me.

"No," I say once, soft.

It totally doesn't listen. Now the claw is spinning and shit.

"No!" I shout at it. Without the regulator on my arm, my power comes out and a sonic shockwave flies out. The machine gets knocked back a bit, and I sense the sound bouncing all around the room. Up. And up. And up for almost a mile.

Where... the hell... am I?

"Hello Candace." It's Danny's voice, but it doesn't come from anywhere in particular. It comes from everywhere, from speakers all over the room. "Don't be afraid, you're safe here."

The laser making machine spins up and starts firing again, but this time the beams combine and work together. In a few seconds, there's a hazy image of Danny standing in front of me.

"Welcome to my home. You were teleported here as part of a contingency plan on my part." His image flickers for a second, like when a computer thinks on a command you give it. "The scanner indicates you've been injured. I've deployed a tissue restoration unit. Let it work."

Torture Bot 9000 comes up behind me. It reaches, but stops when I jump back and then just sits there, all patient, until I calm down. It moves in slowly, circling around to my shoulder. The needle hits my arm and I wince. A second later, the pain vanishes.

Oh damn, that's some good shit.

"I'm sure you have a lot of questions for me," the hologram says.

"You bet your ass I do!" I snap. "First of all, why did you leave me on that rooftop, huh? Where the hell did you go?"

The image flickers again, then it vanishes completely. The room goes dark for an instant before green lasers fly out everywhere and the space around me turns into something different. From nothing, the lasers build an entire hologram room in perfect detail. There's crazy complex tech all over the walls of the space, and up front there's a huge chair overlooking a bank of controls and a massive window. As the hologram room comes completely into focus, takes on colors, I can see through the window.

Boston. It's overlooking part of Boston.

My eyes squint. "This is --"

An explosion sounds and the hologram room shakes. It's weird, because I know I should be feeling it in my body (the sound recreation is so good I can feel it in my ears, and that's even more disconcerting) but it's just the image is so damn good. An alarm starts and a bunch of the screens throughout the room jump to life. I'm trying to figure out what they mean when the one door to the hologram room slides open. Danny comes running in, mask up, a big-ass scorch mark on his jacket, his lightning glove smoking and burnt like an overcooked potato skin. He slaps a button on the wall and the door slams shut. Then another door comes down. Then another.

"Evacuation route zeta," he says, not quite a shout, but not calmly either, as he yanks off the lightning glove and throws it to the floor. "Activate defense systems, initiate lockdown, and turn off the alarm."

The engines roar. Right now, outside the jet, I'm charging in on Garcia, getting ready to kick her ass. I glance out the window, hoping to see myself being tough as hell, but within a couple of seconds, the view has shifted and they're leaving the city. From inside the ship somewhere, there's a massive electrical crack and an explosion. Everything rocks to one side. The alarm comes back on.

"Danger level red!" Now Danny's shouting. "Full autonomous assault." Another explosion. "Get us out of here, and kill the alarm!"

The image vibrates, but not from an explosion. Danny rocks backward. Through the window, I see the world racing away. They're going unbelievably fast, passing Outer Brewster Island, then to the Bay. Danny scrambles up to a control panel. With the wave of his hand, a floating screen is projected up and he starts 'pressing' buttons. The ship lurches again and they're out, over the Atlantic.

"Okay," he says softly to himself, "how about this?"

For the first time since the room appeared, I realize that I can walk around. I jog over to Danny's image and look at the screens (more keep appearing, flipping, floating around under his control). He flicks his fingers and a list appears: Gas. Lasers. Mechanical spiders. Napalm. Instantly solidifying gel. Poison darts. Buzz saws. Projectile buzz saws. Red hot projectile buzz saws. Force fields. Liquid nitrogen sprays. Vacuums. Magnetic waves. Microwaves. Sonic waves. Delta waves.

He highlights every one of them.

The screen shifts and a dozen cameras pop up. Well, a dozen boxes that are supposed to be cameras pop up. Half of them are dead. In one of them, an arc of electricity appears, followed by a foot. Then, nothing. A few second later, the same thing happens on the next camera. Danny just watches, his fingers tapping away at the screen. He pulls up the ship detail, a blueprint that's changing in time with the destruction Sugiyama is doing. There's a series of green lights at doors and bulkheads, the defenses Danny's activated. One by one, they're going red. Each time, Sugiyama is a little closer. Another camera goes dead, another dot goes from greed to red, and with a rumble, the ship lurches. An alarm kicks on.

"I said --" Danny shouts, but stops and stands up straight.

The alarm, it's different than before.

Calmly, he reaches out. With a flip, all the screens showing Sugiyama's juggernaut march to the cockpit slide away. Raising his hand, Danny brings a new screen up. It's all readouts and data on one side, radar on the other. There's a big blip, which I'm pretty sure is the ship. Coming closer and closer, there's a little blip.

No, not one little blip. Four tiny blips, all close together.

Danny leans in, the lenses of his goggles almost touching the projected blips. "Hello, Captain," he whispers. He moves fast, way faster than he did a second ago, but at the same time, he's moving less. His hands are flying around, bringing up screen after screen so fast that I can barely see what he's doing. A timer appears on the radar.

One minute, thirty-five seconds.

Machinery shifts and moves within the ship. A displays shows panels are being forcefully ejected from the hull. I hear guns firing. Flying sky mines are deployed, circling the ship and filling the space directly behind it. Through the huge windshield, red and orange flashes appear as rockets go flying out. There's enough firepower to decimate a damn city homing in on those four little blips.

The four little blips that just... keep... coming.

The readouts are showing some crazy numbers. From what I can see, Captain Turbo isn't actually catching up with the ship, the ship is being, like, drawn back to him. The engines are roaring, but we're slowing down, and it's exponential the closer he gets.

Wait, I know these numbers. I learned this in physics (with some tutoring from Uncle Danny). These are gravity readouts. But they're... off...

The entire room rolls around me (again, super weird because I'm totally still). Danny is thrown back and forth. Something big just happened down below. The console that he's working out of, and every other console in the room, sparks and shoot flames.

"No!" he cries as smoke fills the cabin, only to be immediately sucked out through a vent. His digital projected screens are gone. He hits a few manual buttons, but nothing works. The image of the jet is still active. It shows damage everywhere, interior and exterior.

Sugiyama is getting closer.

Danny runs to another console, but it's in no better shape. He rips off a panel and starts getting at the wires, trying to fix things.

The countdown's still working.

Forty-five seconds.

He pauses, looks at the timer, then the door, and back to the timer. He turns to the detailed ship readout. The line of green defenses is shorter than ever. The red is now more than half. His breathing slows. The franticness leaves his body. Calmly, he walks to the main console by the pilot's chair. "Show me her." A new screen comes up. The numbers are different. This isn't gravity, this is biology.

It's me, my heart rate, my temperature, everything about me in that moment. It's even reading the output from my ability.

"Incredible," he says, "Valentina..." His voice flutters. "You did great." He sighs and says in a commanding voice, "Open program, anti-Turbo protocol omega."

In the center of the room, a section of floor about the size of a table lifts up, then drops, then resets itself. I can hear a dull humming from beneath it.

"Open program emergency evac. Target, Candace."

On the console, a panel slides back and out pops -- no joke -- a big red button.

Seriously, Uncle Danny?

The screen with my stats changes. It switches over to two options: Activate or Cancel.

His hand hovers for a second over Activate. "I will keep my promise," he says. And it's weird, stupid, even. Because I'm watching a recording. All of this happened already. I'm not here. He's all alone.

But I kind of feel like he's talking to me.

He reaches.

Everything goes nuts. The entire hologram flashes in and out. Whatever hit the ship hit it hard. Even I put my arms out, which immediately causes Torture Bot 9000 to beep and honk from behind me.

"Hey," I snap, "relax."

The hologram is clear enough I can see Danny up in the air, heading

236

toward the back of the cabin, then down on the floor. A whee-oo-whee-oo-whee-oo siren starts up. While Danny struggles to get to his feet, I check the readout of the ship. The altimeter shows a drop of almost three hundred feet. On the roof, there seems to be a massive hull breach.

He's here.

Captain Turbo is here.

Danny grabs the control panel. Up above, sledgehammer fists pound. Metal screeches. The jet goes into full emergency mode and the engines throttle back. He tumbles across the floor, his back smacking into the pilot's chair. The altimeter keeps dropping as the thumps and booms and ripping of steel comes closer and closer and closer until the ceiling of the room thunders and warps and bends and, for one second, I see the shape of knuckles embedded there.

Um... what?

Part of the ceiling screams as it's pulled back like the lid of a pop-top can of tomatoes. From the hole, smoke and sparks and chunks of insulation fall. And then a massive shape, wrapped in a cape, comes down, smashing into the floor, landing in a crouch. When his head comes up and I see those eyes, when he stands... I get it. I understand why Uncle Danny was so afraid of him. He's a damn hologram, but I still back away. His body is... what the hell, man? Like, he's just, he's everywhere at once, you know? He takes up the entire room just by being there. The ship is plummeting, dropping a hundred feet every few seconds, and he's just sauntering like he's strolling down the golf course, looking to line up his next shot.

"Doctor Dendrite," his baritone rumbles across the cockpit. "Long time no see."

"Not since Japan." The reaction on Turbo's face is priceless. That whole cocky hero thing vanishes. His lips tighten, his nostrils flare.

Go Uncle Danny, don't let that bastard push you around.

"What's the game, Doc?"

Danny's gaze jumps to the console next to Turbo. I follow and see that there's only seven doors between Sugiyama and the cockpit.

Turbo puts his hands on his hips, dramatically of course. "I can't believe I actually thought you'd retired. Given up."

There's a rumble and two lights go red.

"But then you come out of the shadows --"

Down to three doors.

"-- and pull one of the craziest stunts I've ever seen."

Two.

"What's the point, Doc?"

237

The wall behind Turbo rattles. He doesn't even notice. One light to go.

"Why attack the ESOA head on? Why kill all those people?"

Danny sighs. "Would you believe me if I told you they started it?"

One door.

Turbo shakes his head and starts forward. Uncle Danny glances at the control panel. "Don't bother, Doc." Turbo growls. "The arsenal outside couldn't stop me. You're out of tricks."

"I may have a little something up my sleeve."

Turbo smirks.

God, I hate this ass-hat.

"Wouldn't be any fun if you didn't." Turbo lunges. Before I can blink, he's halfway across the room. The room erupts with a steel warping screech, and a literal typhoon of gold sparks shoot out all around the cabin door. Both guys freeze, watching as the door shakes and rumbles and turns three kinds of red before it's ripped from the floor and lifted by pillars of electricity until it vanishes.

Leaving nothing but smoke and one really, really pissed off Special Agent Sugiyama Sosuke.

"Agent, what are you doing here?" Captain Turbo says, completely oblivious to the fact that Sugiyama is clearly here to kick every ass in the room ten times over.

When he steps through what's left of the doorway, Sugiyama does it without flashiness, no flair or style. But he's not cool, either. He's ready to freaking explode. Glancing at Turbo with eyes are literally glowing hot, he says, all quiet-like, "I'm here for Dendrite. Step aside. I'll take it from here."

"Sorry, Agent." Turbo says. I realize he doesn't remember Sugiyama's name. "But I've got a score to settle here." He turns, putting Sugiyama at his back.

Dumb move.

"I said, step aside." Sugiyama's jaw is clenched. Tight.

"Don't worry kiddo," Turbo says. "When I'm done, you can haul him off to jail and get your collar. But first --"

The cockpit turns into the inside of a light bulb. I close my eyes and put my hand up, but that doesn't stop me from hearing it.

Turbo screaming.

Sugiyama is zapping him from behind, hitting him with streams of electricity that spread all over his body. Turbo squirms and jerks until the lightning stops, then drops to the floor in a smoking heap. Behind him, Sugiyama's outstretched hand is trembling.

No, his whole body is shaking. The muscles on his face all twitch around.

Something beneath his skin, something that's been trying to come out for a long, long time, is finally fighting its way to the top. And it's not justice, or righteousness, or anything like that.

It's... it's heated rage mixed with pure ecstasy, then toss in some vengeance and a splash of demented sadism just for fun. He's smiling but the kind of smile only the sickest of villains make.

"Take him to jail?" He says, practically a whisper. But then, he roars. "Jail?" He leaps forward, swinging one leg back for a massive soccer punt straight into Turbo's ribs. There's a flash of light and the smell of burning fabrics. "How --" Kick. "-- stupid --" Flash. "-- are --" Singe. "-- you!"

His foot comes down like a boulder and pins Turbo to the floor. He's so excited, he's breathing fast and heavy. "I'm not here to arrest him. I'm here to do what you never had the guts to do, what you should have done years ago." He bends down and grabs Turbo by the back of the neck. "You had so many chances, so many opportunities to just end him. But you never did it. No matter what he did, you always let him live."

"That's --" Turbo's voice is gravel under Sugiyama's heavy boot. "That's not justice."

Sugiyama snarls. Lightning pours out of his arm. Turbo howls in agony.

"He's killed millions! Because you, you chose not to stop him."

Turbo's motionless. Sugiyama's totally focused on him. And I'm totally focused on Sugiyama. I thought watching Turbo get his butt handed to him would be awesome. This dude's part of that whole group that has officially screwed up my life more than I can imagine. But there's something going on here, something I'm... I dunno. This isn't cool. This isn't Uncle Danny and my mom or even Araknis. This...

This is evil.

Out of the corner of my eye, I see Danny working his way to the screen he brought up, the one that had my stats on it and then went into, what did he call it? Emergency evacuation or something. Right next to it is the big red button.

"Heroes --" I can barely hear the word when Turbo says it. Somehow, he manages to move, to drag his arms up beneath him and, against all possible reason, he gets himself up on hands and knees.

"Heroes," he says again, "don't kill people."

Sugiyama grabs Turbo's throat and jerks his head up. "No," he says, spit flying from his lips. "But villains do!"

Electricity flies everywhere. Sugiyama lifts Turbo up into the air, slams him back to the floor, and starts pounding on him, screaming the whole time.

"They kill and they kill and they kill and you just sit back and don't do a goddamn thing!" Every punch lands. "He killed my friends!" Blood splatters. "He killed my family!" Cartilage snaps. "He killed everyone!" Bones crack. "And you could have stopped it!" Both hands come down and the flash is so intense, the entire hologram blinks out for a second. When it comes back, the cockpit is dim. Sugiyama's electricity has blown most of the lights. I can barely make out the shape of his body, straddling a motionless Turbo. But I can hear his panting. I can hear the plip-plop-plip of the blood falling from his fists.

There's a mechanical flick as Danny's mask folds back. The look on his face, I'm pretty sure it's the same one on mine.

Fear. Real, genuine fear. The kind that only comes from a total understanding of the absolute shit storm of a situation and how utterly and completely boned he is. Because right now, watching this, I get what he got in that moment.

During the press conference on TV -- holy hell, that seems like a million freaking years ago -- Sugiyama said that he and Garcia and that skinny acid-skin-guy who beat down on Araknis were chosen because they were best suited for the job and blah-blah-blah. And maybe that was true for acid-skin-guy; Araknis isn't here helping, so I have to assume he's dead. Maybe it was true for Garcia; she did her job in the end.

But not for Sugiyama. He wasn't picked because he's stronger than Danny. He wasn't picked because his power's the best to go up against Danny.

He was picked because, deep down, he's more evil than Uncle Danny ever was.

And I can tell that thought had never, ever crossed Danny's mind.

Sugiyama's voice, eerily calm, drifts around the room. "They were counting on you, they trusted you to protect them. But you were so full of yourself, so arrogant, so in love with yourself, you wouldn't even listen." Slowly, he bends down, hovers over Turbo. "You stood there, posed and pretty for the camera, while Dendrite told you, shouted how if you didn't stop, the bombs would go off. He warned you, begged you! The world's worst villain told you if you smashed his computer he couldn't stop the bombs... we saw, Captain! We all saw it! We knew, we could see he was telling the truth but you..." He sucks in a breath between clenched teeth. "You just did it anyway, you arrogant son-of-a-bitch!"

Sugiyama's hands fly out and snatch those big bracelet things on Turbo's wrists.

Off to the side, I hear Danny make a little gasping noise.

"Captain Turbo," Sugiyama says.

Danny twitches and whispers, "No..."

"This is your penance."

"No!"

Thunder shakes the cockpit as Sugiyama pours energy through the bracelet things and into Turbo's body. Sparks fly out from the metal casings like Independence Day fireworks. Alarms are going off everywhere. I can't feel the inertia, but something about those bands getting fried causes the entire ship to rock and flop in the air. Even through all the noise, I hear Uncle Danny screaming. He smacks a button on his belt and electricity pours all over his body, not as bright or as condensed as Sugiyama's but it's still there. He rushes in and slams into Sugiyama, grabbing him and pulling him to the side. Turbo drops to the floor as Danny and Sugiyama scramble around the room, their electrical fields fusing, sparking, shooting out left and right. It's too much for either of them to handle, and it's going everywhere. Fires are popping up. Screens are exploding. But they're just going at it like two angry kids on the playground.

Every readout that's still working on the walls and around the captain's chair show the ship is heading down. Not a nose dive, but things are failing fast. When I look back, Danny has Sugiyama pinned against a wall. He's throwing punches, left, right, left, right, one after another after another. It looks like Sugiyama is struggling to keep up. Then, as fast as his lightning is, Sugiyama's hand shoots out even faster. It catches Danny's jaw. Then another hits his ribs. Then two more to the face. Then three to the sides. Sugiyama adds a couple of elbows, a knee. He grabs Danny and yanks him in, driving a knee up at the same time.

Danny snarls and puts a good fist across Sugiyama's face, but two more come back and blast across his ribs. He stumbles back, and Sugiyama fills the space between them with a massive front kick. Uncle Danny goes back, but doesn't fall. Sugiyama steps in and bam-Bam-BAM, three solid punches.

But he still doesn't fall.

Sugiyama snatches the back of his neck with one hand, grabs one of the sparking consoles with his other, and smashes them together.

Clearly, the console wins.

With a bark and a spin, Sugiyama throws Danny across the room, into the captain's chair, which he bounces off of before collapsing in a gangly pile of limbs.

His chest heaving, Sugiyama tries to go after his prey, but can't find his footing. He spreads his arms and legs like someone on a particularly smooth section of ice. The hologram room around me rocks up and down, side to

241

side. I'm sure what they were experiencing was actually worse.

"Navigation's dead," Danny says. He kind of slurs -- probably from the concussions -- and kind of lisps -- probably from his lips being all swollen and a few teeth being knocked out. "We're going down."

Sugiyama wipes the spit and blood from his lips. "How long?"

Danny rolls his eyes around. "Oh," he tries to say, but a bubble comes up instead. A blood bubble. He coughs. "Two minutes. Three at the most."

Sugiyama starts working his way forward, his expression cold and hard. "That's fine," he says. "I'm going to drain every electrical pulse from your brain. When I'm done, I'll know everything you know, including where the escape pods are."

Uncle Danny laughs.

Sugiyama keeps walking. "What's so funny?"

"Sorry," he says, "no escape pods."

Sugiyama stops, right in the middle of the room, shock on his face.

"But," Danny says with a smirk. "I do have one hell of an ejector seat." Spinning, he smacks the big red button from earlier. There's a deep 'thwomp' from the rectangular section under Sugiyama's feet and, before he can even react, a massive burst of anti-gravity energy pulses upward, sending him, the inner hull, the wiring, the insulation, the steel framing, and the outer hull directly above him rocketing into the sky at three hundred miles an hour. All that's left is the wind rushing in and a thick sunbeam cutting through the smoke and haze.

I can hear the wind, see it whipping Danny's coat around, yanking on the bit of Turbo's cape that's not underneath his body. It's so loud I put my arms up, as though I'm going to feel it. I feel kinda stupid for a second, then put them down.

The hologram is really good, okay?

"Turbo," Danny says, the wind swallowing up his words. He tries to get his breathing under control. "Turbo!"

He's slid up against one of the walls, lolling back and forth with the ship, but Turbo's moving his arms a tiny bit.

Danny crawls over to him. When he's close enough, he shouts, "The bands! Show me the bands!" Turbo waves an arm in the air, which Danny grabs as though it were the last canteen in a hundred miles of dessert. But once he's got it, he realizes it's empty. He yanks off his gloves, gently caresses the burnt and blackened thing. His swollen face twitches.

I don't know why he's crying, but he is.

"Well?" Turbo's voice is barely a whisper. Danny doesn't look at him. He just lowers the arm and rests it on Turbo's chest. Then, he flops back against the nearest wall and stares up into the beam of light coming through the ceiling.

"What happens now?" Turbo asks. "With us gone."

Danny's lip twitches. "Don't worry," he says. "I've made plans."

I follow his gaze across the room. The screen on the main controls is cracked and the image behind it is warped, but I can still tell what it is.

The word Activated, blinking over and over again.

It's me, being teleported. Being saved.

Turbo makes a wet sound that may have been a sigh, but may have been a cough. "I'm sorry."

Uncle Danny looks down at him.

"I stole them."

"I know."

"And I blamed you."

"I know."

"It was... I didn't mean to, it's just... what they could do. It was amazing and I, I knew they, they would --"

"The military."

He nods. "Yeah. They would just make them into weapons. But I... " His face crunches up. "I just wanted to help people."

Danny gives him a you-don't-have-to-lie-anymore stare. Turbo sees it. He starts to repeat himself, but stops.

"You're right," Turbo says, soft. "I did it for me. To be famous."

With a grunt, Danny jerks himself up and bends over Turbo. "But how did you do it?"

"Do what?"

Eyes gleaming, voice breathy, Danny leans in. "Make them hum."

"I --"

"Did you cross-wire them?" He's excited, so excited he smiles through whatever pain he must be feeling. "Did you reverse the polarity? Increase the sine wave while decreasing the --"

"I hit them."

He pauses. "Come again?"

"You know, like when your TV goes all fuzzy. I, I just gave 'em a good whack and... bang. They started working."

"You hit them?"

"Yup."

Danny pushes out a quick breath. Then another. Then another and another and another until he's laughing. Through a throat that's raw and scratchy and past ribs that are probably broken and aching, he laughs harder

243

than I've ever heard anyone laugh before. At his knees, Turbo starts laughing too. Danny clutches at his sides and slaps a hand over Turbo's chest. Turbo grabs his arm, and they hold each other as, through the cockpit window, the blue of the sky changes to the blue of the ocean, and gets darker, and darker, and darker.

The lasers keep spinning, but the cockpit disappears. Doesn't fade out slowly, just blinks out. I'm standing on the platform in an empty room. Torture Bot 9000 finishes up and rolls away. I move my arm up and down. Nothing, no pain.

Not there anyway.

Behind me, the hologram projector keeps spinning. When I turn, the image of Uncle Danny is there, hands behind his back, waiting.

"I'm..." I sigh. "I'm sorry."

The image blinks (it's the computer pulling up the appropriate recording) and Uncle Danny says, "I don't know what you've just seen, Candace. I do know it must be confusing for you. A whole history has been kept from you, and I think it's time you were brought up to speed." He opens his arms. All over the room, lights start kicking on. "You are standing in the home base for the organization your mother, Araknis, and I built together."

"The Triad," I whisper.

There's stuff everywhere, up and down every wall.

"Here, you will find technology unlike anything you've ever seen."

Lasers. Missiles. Robots.

"You will be connected to every computer system in the world which we were able to access."

Jets. Tanks. Is that a freakin' time machine?

"Our organizations, both legal and illegal, pass through here. You can see everything that's happening with them."

Suspended animation tanks filled with pterodactyls. Some kind of miniature sun in a giant glass container.

Oh damn, that's a nice espresso machine.

"You will see how, systematically, we took some level of control for nearly every major corporation in the world." All around the room, screens slide down on the walls and begin showing displays; financial statements that have so many zeros I can't even count them without thinking hard, blueprints to machines that are far beyond anything the world has ever seen, schematics of the building I'm in with stats on every lab and every experiment. "All of this is now yours. The computer systems have already been programmed to follow your every command. As of this moment, you are the richest, most powerful person in the entire world."

244

Oh my god. Oh. My. God.

Danny crosses his arms. "I can't tell you what to do with all of this, but I want you to consider what brought you here, why you're being given all of this. Consider that for you to inherit this, it had to be taken from us. Think about what's happened to you, Candace." He leans forward. "And who made it happen."

The huge grin slapped across my face melts into a frown. "McTier..."

A computerized voice says, "Lieutenant Colonel Tamika McTier," and a floating screen with her bitch-ass face appears, along with a scrolling list of everything Danny knows about her. My eyes dance around the screen for a second, then pull into a tight squint.

"Special Agent Garcia,"

Another screen. There's a lot less data. Doesn't matter, though. All I really wanted was to see her face.

"Remember," Danny says, "who was taken from you."

I hesitate. "T --" Please, oh please. "Twist."

Her image flies up. She's wearing her mask. Behind it, more images, videos of her training, fighting, one taken with a handheld camera of her as a little kid, all loose and floppy, learning to walk. And all those things get my heart fluttering, but what sends it over the edge is the little graphic down at the bottom of the screen.

A heartbeat, slow, steady, active.

My fists clench. I'm coming for you, Annie.

"Never," I say, turning to Danny. "I'll never forget."

The image flickers. He nods and smiles. It's not a sweet and loving dad-watching-his-little-kid-do-something-adorable kind of smile. It's thin and wicked. "It's a funny thing," he says, almost sadly, "the line between good and evil is... no. It's not even a line. It's a barrier. And on each side is an opposing force, pushing, straining. What makes it interesting is how, from each side, the other seems to be in the wrong. Whatever you're feeling now, Candace, whatever is boiling up inside of you, don't let that go. Hold onto it. That is your justice, that is your drive. As hard as they push you, you must push back harder. Heroes will come and go, but villains never really die.

"They're just reborn."

The platform rumbles beneath me. I yelp and jump back as the center of it starts rotating. From the seamless floor, a circle appears and rises up, spinning. There's a mannequin inside, one that's exactly my body shape.

Damn, I need to lift more weights.

The right forearm has another control module, like the one Danny slapped on me, only it's crazy tricked out. The body is covered in a skintight outfit, made from the same stuff Danny's outfit was made from. There's built-in armor and stuff all over it. It doesn't have any color scheme or design or logo or nothing. But as it comes to a stop, I get a good look at the face.

At the mask, the mask that looks like something between my mom's and Uncle Danny's.

No.

Not my mom.

Not Uncle Danny.

Wraith and Doctor Dendrite. That's who they were. That's who I'm inheriting.

That's who I am.

But...

"I knew," I say. "My whole life, I kinda knew. She was always... she always held back. And I thought... for so long I thought it was because of me. I thought I did something or was something or... I dunno. But it was there, between us. And it made me so... mad. I just wanted to be close and she kept me away and now that I know I get it, I get it, I do, but it... shit, it just... I..." A sob runs up from my chest into my throat, but I catch it with my teeth and hold it there.

Later. She'd want me to save those tears for later.

Now's the time to fight.

"Tell me everything," I say. The hologram stares at me, waiting. "Tell me who I am." My fingers run over the war suit in front of me; and it's going to be war, let me make that perfectly freaking clear. "Tell me everything. About mom, about you. Everything."

The image flickers.

He says, "You know, I never planned on being a supervillain..."

THE BEGINNING

ABOUT THE AUTHOR

Nick DeWolf has weird dreams. At some point, he decided to start putting them down on paper. These became his books.

He's a father, a worker, a beer brewer, a defender of the Oxford Comma, and cooks a half-decent stir-fry. He waited until the age of 37 to both get a tattoo, and learn to ride a bike. He loves his five kids and incredible partner, hates prejudice, believes in science, and sometimes gets uncomfortably excited about well prepared food.

Made in the USA
Middletown, DE
03 February 2024

48514936R00139